Somewhere a Bird
is Singing

Somewhere a Bird is Singing

E. V. Thompson

LITTLE, BROWN AND COMPANY

A *Little, Brown* Book

First published in Great Britain in 1999
by Little, Brown and Company

Copyright © 1999 by E.V. Thompson

The moral right of the author has been asserted.

A CIP catalogue record for this book
is available from the British Library.

ISBN 0 316 64612 1

Typeset by Palimpsest Book Production Limited,
Polmont, Stirlingshire
Printed and bound in Great Britain by
Clays Ltd, St Ives PLC

Little, Brown and Company (UK)
Brettenham House
Lancaster Place
London WC2E 7EN

1

'If your hand comes so close as six inches from that there pie I swear I'll cut it off, you see if I don't.'

The barbaric threat was reinforced by a bloody meat cleaver, wielded by Alfie Philpott and waved menacingly at Sally Harrup. The perspiring pie-maker was wearing a grubby, well-worn straw boater and an even dirtier blue-and-white striped butcher's apron.

'Is that another of those urchins trying to nick one of our pies, Alfie?' The disembodied voice came from beyond a doorway draped with a palm-frond curtain, half-hidden behind a long wooden counter piled high with pies and cardboard advertisements.

'I wasn't going to pinch any of your bleedin' pies,' the young girl protested indignantly. 'I was . . . I was just seeing if they was fresh, that's all.' She sniffed derisively, 'I expect they're all stale, anyway.'

'I'll have less of your cheek, young lady, or one of these nights you'll disappear and end up *inside* my pies. Then you'll find out just how fresh they are.'

'You don't frighten me, not even with that old knife.'

Despite her display of bravado, Sally took a step backwards. It brought her closer to the door, which led to the cobblestone street outside. Strange rumours occasionally circulated about Alfie Philpott and the contents of his pies.

The palm-frond curtain was pushed aside and the head of the pie-man's wife appeared. From where she was standing, the woman could see a thin, pinched-face girl, wearing a threadbare brown coat, which was far too small, over a thin gingham dress that was quite unsuitable for early December.

'Lor', bless us, Alfie! She's all tongue and very little else. She wouldn't make more'n a couple of twopenny pies – and they'd be all gristle.'

'You think so, Grace?'

'I do. Tell you what, Alfie. Give the girl a pie. It'll help put a bit of flesh on her. Add a bit of taste, like, just in case we decide to do something with her sometime.'

'I'm not sure it's worth it . . .'

Alfie Philpott tried to keep up the pretence of being fierce, but he had seen the hungry eagerness on Sally's face in response to his wife's suggestion. 'Oh well, perhaps you're right. Here, you can have a pie – but just one, mind.'

He added the rider as Sally dived towards a number of hot pies, fresh from the oven, heaped in a pyramid on a large flat dish on the counter.

'Thanks, mister . . . missus.'

Sally grabbed a pie hurriedly, afraid the pie-shop owners might change their minds about making such an unexpected and quixotic gesture.

As she turned to leave the shop, the woman called to her, 'Just a minute, young lady.'

Clutching the hot pie, Sally stopped in the doorway. Some of the earlier belligerence returned to her voice as she asked, 'What d'you want?'

Whatever it was, she had no intention of handing back the pie.

'What's your name, girl? I like to know who we're giving our pies to.'

'Sally.'

'Sally what?'

'Just Sally, that's what everyone calls me.'

She had no intention of giving this woman her full name, no matter how generous she appeared to be.

'Are you honest, Sally?'

''Course I'm honest.' Sally said indignantly. At the same time she crossed her fingers. It was not easy while holding a hot pie. 'What sort of a question's that?'

'I'm asking because, if you're honest, we can give you work sometimes. Delivering pies.'

'How much would you pay me?' Sally asked uncertainly.

'A farthing for each delivery,' Alfie said quickly, before his wife got too carried away with her own generosity.

'And a free pie when you finish work,' said his wife, ignoring her husband's frown.

'*Two* pies,' Sally said promptly. 'One for me, and one for my sister. She's in bed, sick.'

'One fresh pie, and one leftover.'

'All right,' Sally tried hard not to allow her delight to show. 'When do you think you might have some work for me?'

'You can start tomorrow. We're always busy in the weeks leading up to Christmas – but you'll need to be here early. No rolling in at midday, or whenever it suits you. And have a wash before you come to work. We don't want you putting off customers with your dirty looks.'

'Blimey! You believe in getting your money's worth, don't you? All right, I'll be here early – and I'll have a wash at home first.'

As soon as Sally had left the shop, Alfie turned to his wife. 'I don't know what you were thinking of, Grace, offering work to an urchin like that. She'll probably run off with the takings, first chance she gets.'

'I somehow don't think so, Alfie. The girl was obviously hungry but that doesn't make her a thief. Anyway, if I'm wrong it won't be the end of the world for us, will it? We can afford to make the occasional mistake. Besides, how old would our Mary be now, had she lived?'

Carefully placing the meat cleaver on the wooden butcher's block, Alfie moved to put an arm about his wife's shoulders. Giving her an affectionate hug, he said, 'I knew that's what you were thinking about. Our Mary would have been seventeen. Much the same age as that young lady, I reckon, give or take a year or so.'

'And if things had been different, would you like to think that someone who could afford it would refuse to give a pie to her, if she was hungry?'

'Of course not. But if I didn't stop you, you'd get carried away by every young urchin who put her nose inside the door. That young lady's probably off somewhere right now, trying to sell her pie to someone else. I doubt if we'll ever see her again.'

'What's that you've got stuffed inside your jumper, girl?'

'Whatever it is has nothing to do with you, Charlie Shields.'

The exchange over, Sally dodged his outstretched hand with an ease born of practice. Charlie spent much of the day sitting on the doorstep of the house where Sally and her sister rented a small back room on the first floor.

A sufferer from chronic asthma, Charlie occupied the two rooms on the ground floor. He was all right most of the time, but Sally knew from experience it was foolish to take any chances with him. Drunk or sober, Charlie's hand had a nasty habit of wandering up a girl's leg if she were foolish enough to linger as she stepped through the doorway.

Nevertheless, he was sympathetic enough towards Sally and her sister and would occasionally send up a gift of a piece of fruit, or perhaps some fish. Such delicacies were brought to him by members of his large family, some of whom worked in the Plymouth fruit and vegetable market, and others who were fishermen.

When she reached the safety of the gloomy, narrow passageway, Sally paused at the foot of the stairs and called back, 'If you really want to know, it's a meat pie. Alfie Philpott gave it to me.'

'Alfie don't give nothing away to no one. I expect you've nicked it.' Charlie gave a short, throaty laugh, which promptly led to a brief but intense bout of coughing.

'I didn't need to pinch it,' Sally retorted indignantly. 'He gave it to me. What's more, his missus wants me to work for 'em.'

'You . . . work?' Breathing with difficulty, Charlie cuffed away the tears brought on by his coughing. 'What sort of work can you do? You ain't got enough meat on you to do any work.'

'I do more work than you've ever done, Charlie Shields. Enough to pay the rent, anyway.'

Turning her back on the asthmatic ground-floor tenant, Sally ascended the uncarpeted stairs with all the dignity a ragged seventeen-year-old could muster.

2

Upstairs, in a small, untidy and sparsely furnished rear room, an emaciated young woman lay beneath a blanket on a narrow bed, where, at night, she slept head-to-toe with her sister. Looking much older than her twenty-two years, the young woman's face was turned towards an open window.

The window, which was devoid of curtains, overlooked the back of a terrace of identical houses, now hidden by darkness. No more than the lengths of two tiny backyards away, the buildings were oppressively close.

At the sound of the door opening, the young woman turned her head, slowly and wearily. When she saw Sally, her tired smile gave a glimpse of the beauty she had possessed before she was ravaged by disease.

'Hello, love. What have you been up to today?' The voice was as feeble as the young woman's sick body.

'I've brought you something nice to eat, Ruth. It's still hot.'

Sally put an arm beneath her sister's wasted body to raise her. At the same time she took the pillow from the foot of the bed and rested it against the iron bed head.

When Sally thought Ruth was comfortable, she took a chipped plate from a shelf and placed the pie on it. 'Here, eat this while it's still nice and hot. It'll put some strength in you. It's not a stale leftover, either. It's fresh from Alfie Philpott's shop, hardly out of the oven.'

'You haven't been nicking for me, have you, Sally? If you're caught they'll put you away and that'd be the end of me, for sure.'

'What's the matter with everyone?' Sally's indignation was unfeigned. 'I come in with something nice for my sister and everyone thinks I must have pinched it! Well, I haven't. It was given to me by Alfie Philpott and his wife. What's more, they've given me a job too – so there!'

'What d'you mean, a job? I thought you had one at the cardboard-box factory, over by the station.'

Sally shrugged and averted her gaze from her sister. 'I got the sack.'

'Again? What was the reason this time?'

'The foreman wanted me to work overtime – and it wasn't to make no boxes, neither. Now, eat your supper before it gets cold. You'd better enjoy it, I'll be bringing a couple of 'em home every day from now on.'

'Tell me about this new job of yours.' As she spoke, Ruth broke the pie in half and put a piece to her mouth. She ate very little these days, but the hot pie smelled delicious.

'I'll be delivering for the Philpotts. They're going to give me a farthing for each delivery and two pies to bring home at the end of each day. I'll make enough money to pay the rent and be bringing home food too. There'll probably be enough money left over at the end of the week to buy something special for you, Ruth.'

Ruth took no more than three or four bites from the piece of pie she had in her hand before putting the remainder back on the plate. Pushing it across the bed towards Sally she said, 'Here, I've not touched the one half. You eat it.'

'Are you sure . . . ?' Sally's mouth had been watering as the aroma of freshly cooked beef and gravy wafted towards her. Nevertheless, she waited until her sister nodded before reaching out for the plate.

Watching her sister eat, Ruth said wearily, 'You're a good girl, Sally. You deserve a better life than spending all your time looking after a sister who's never going to get better.'

Ruth looked sadly at Sally and the younger girl reached out with her free hand. Gripping her sister's fingers, she squeezed them hard.

'I've told you before, you mustn't talk like that. I *want* to look after you, the same as you've done for me all my life.'

It was true. Their mother had died when Sally was a small girl of seven and Ruth only twelve. The girls had never known their father.

It was not until Sally was much older that she realised *how* Ruth had earned the money to keep them both. Even so, it had not come as too much of a shock. Prostitution was a fact of life for a great many young girls in the cities of England – and Plymouth was a sailor's town.

'You sure you don't want any more of this?' Sally had eaten the untouched portion from the plate and was eyeing the remainder hungrily.

'Quite sure. You have it.'

As Sally gulped down the rest of the pie, Ruth asked, 'What are you doing tonight?'

'Nothing. I'll stay home and keep you company.'

'No you won't. You ought to be out with girls your own age. Having a bit of fun.'

'I seem to remember you've always warned me against going out and having "a bit of fun".'

'You know very well what it is I've always warned you against – and hiring out your body to anyone with the money to pay for it ain't fun, I can tell you. They're paying you to give 'em what they want, whether you feel like it or not – and most times I didn't. No, Sally, it was never my idea of "fun".'

'Yet you did it – for me.'

'I did it because it was the only way I knew to earn a living. For both of us.'

Ruth smiled weakly at Sally. 'Go on, get out and enjoy yourself for a couple of hours. I'm not really in the mood for talking tonight. Besides, I'll be fast asleep in half an hour. Off you go.'

'Well . . . only if you're quite sure.'

'Of course I am . . . Listen! What's that?'

'It sounds like a band, although I've never heard one around the Barbican before.'

'Go and find it, then you can tell me about it tomorrow – but you'd better hurry, it's already dark out there. Before you go, open that window a bit more. I can listen to the band while I'm getting off to sleep.'

Crossing the bare-board floor, Sally heaved the window up on protesting pulley wheels. She could hear the band more clearly now. It sounded as though it was in the next street, beyond the houses visible from their window.

This was the Barbican, a crowded slum of run-down houses, adjacent to a small harbour that extended almost to the heart of late-nineteenth-century Plymouth.

Sally decided she would go and find the band. Afterwards, she might take a walk to the music hall. A young man who worked there claimed to be a distant relative. He had once been keen on Ruth and would sometimes allow Sally in without paying.

The music hall occasionally had a night when members of the audience were invited on stage to sing or tell jokes. If the audience liked the act they would throw coins on the stage.

Sally possessed a good voice and had once ventured on to the stage. The audience had liked her so much she had come away with more than three shillings clutched in her hand.

She should have had six, but the stage manager had insisted that half the takings were his 'by tradition'. He had also invited her back to sing whenever there was a similar evening, but had not suggested she would be allowed in free of charge.

Yes, she would go there. Today had been a lucky day. She had landed a promising job at the pie shop, and now she might make some extra money at the theatre – if it was the right night. Then she would be able to buy something *really* nice for Ruth. Something attractive to look at and bring pleasure to the girl who was confined to a small dark room in Plymouth's overcrowded Barbican.

A room she was unlikely to ever leave alive.

3

Outside the house, in the narrow confines of Pin's Lane, Sally paused. Charlie Shields, still seated in front of the doorway, said, 'Off to listen to the band, are you?'

'I might be,' replied Sally, determined to be non-committal. 'Then again, I might not.'

'You don't want to waste your time chasing after *them*. It's a Salvation Army band. You won't find any fun there. You'd get more laughs watching the fishermen unloading their catch on the quay and teasing the Scots herring women. Why don't you come and sit here a while and chat with me?'

'No thanks. I'd rather go and watch the fishermen on the quay.'

'You've got far too much backchat,' declared Charlie. 'One day you'll end up the same as your sister, you mark my words. It's as well your poor mother never lived to see the way the pair of you have turned out. It would have broken her poor heart.'

Sally had a retort ready but it remained unspoken as tears filled her eyes and she turned away. She would not allow Charlie to see that his words had found their mark. It would have revealed a vulnerability he would not be slow to take advantage of in the future.

In the years following her mother's death there had been many occasions when Sally had cried herself to sleep, longing for her mother. It had proved especially bad on the many occasions when life was treating the young sisters particularly harshly.

Sometimes, especially now Ruth was bed-ridden, the sisters would talk far into the night about the mother Sally had hardly known. With the passing of time their mother had assumed a piety she had never achieved during her lifetime.

Occasionally, too, during the quiet of the night, when only Ruth's laboured breathing broke the silence, Sally would wonder about the identity of her unknown father. It was a subject Ruth would never discuss.

She knew her mother had been 'in service' – a house servant – working for a rich family when she became pregnant with Ruth. Although she had never returned to work for the family afterwards, she had always maintained that both girls had the same father. It was all she had ever said on the subject.

As a result, Sally would occasionally allow her imagination to run riot. She wondered whether he had been a son of the rich family. Or a friend, perhaps. He might even be a titled gentleman . . . !

Rounding the corner, away from Pin's Lane, the sound of the band became much louder. It seemed the musicians were now playing on the quayside, not far from where the fishing boats landed their catches.

But she could hear another sound too. That of a crowd. A noisy crowd. Sally walked faster. This might not be the colourless entertainment Alfie had predicted after all.

There were many who did not share Alfie's view that the Salvation Army was harmless and boring. Among those most violently opposed to the teetotal Christian organisation were the breweries and the landlords of the country's inns and taverns. Disturbed that the popularity of the Salvation Army was growing, they had organised their own band of supporters. It was known as the 'Skeleton Army' – a name adopted from its skull and crossbones logo – and it attracted the hooligan element from the beer-houses and dockside taverns. Recently there had been a series of violent clashes between the Skeleton Army and the fervent but pacifist evangelists.

When the large, gas-lit cobblestone space beside the quay came into view, Sally could see the uniformed Salvation Army band formed up by the water's edge. There were about twenty of them, carrying a variety of instruments.

A number of spectators had gathered to listen, but, as was invariably the case when the band played, the Salvation Army's opponents were here too.

Sally had lived in the waterside Barbican district of Plymouth all her life and she knew its bullies and thugs by sight. She now spotted many in the crowd. Jeering the bandsmen and -women, they attempted to rival them with their discordant rendition of bawdy songs, while banners boasting the skull and crossbones logo were waved enthusiastically.

When word went around the town that the Salvation Army band was playing in the Barbican, landlords of the area's public houses urged their customers to swell the ranks of the Skeleton Army. As an incentive the drinkers were promised that their mugs would be refilled, free of charge, upon their return.

Already, the rowdy crowd of opponents was more numerous than the Salvation Army band and its numbers were increasing with every passing minute.

It was clear to Sally that there would soon be trouble. She wondered why the bandsmen did not cease playing and make their escape while it was still possible.

But the Salvation Army, created by William Booth, had not been formed only to desert its sacred duty when faced by such opposition. Booth and his followers were pledged to join battle against the devil in an all-out war aimed at winning the souls of men and women. No sacrifice was too great if it resulted in salvation for even a single sinner.

As the band played on, a young woman, wearing a simple black uniform and straw bonnet, began exhorting those in the crowd to give up their wicked ways and turn to Jesus.

By now, the Salvation Army's opponents outnumbered them by more than two to one. Those at the front of the noisy ranks of the Skeleton Army, many of them innocent bystanders who had brought their young children along to listen to the music and singing, were being forced ever closer to the band by new arrivals exerting pressure from the rear of the gathering.

One young mother had a year-old child in her arms and a pretty four-year-old daughter, who was performing a happy dance in time to the music, beside her. Not until too late did the woman realise that she and her small family were standing between the Salvation Army and their ill-intentioned opponents. Clutching the baby to her, she reached out to take her daughter's hand and lead her away.

But the young girl, who was thoroughly enjoying the music, was not yet ready to leave. Evading her mother's hand, she moved away, closer to the band – and also nearer to the quay-side.

At the same moment, one of a small group of well-wishers also realised the danger posed by the Skeleton Army. Before scurrying to safety, the man took some coins from his pocket and threw them in the direction of one of the Salvation Army women. But the coins fell short, and a raggedly dressed boy from the ranks of the opposition was quick to seize the opportunity unexpectedly afforded him. Darting forward, he picked up the silver coins before dashing back to the safety of the cheering rowdies.

However, in his haste he collided with the small girl who was escaping from her mother. Knocked off balance, the child staggered backwards, arms flailing in a vain attempt to regain her footing. Then, to the horror of the suddenly hushed onlookers, she disappeared over the edge of the quay and fell into the dark waters below.

The tide was on the ebb and there was a considerable drop to the water. The splash her small body made was lost in the cries of the onlookers – but her mother's scream was not. Rushing to the edge of the quay, the woman cried, 'Mary . . . ! MARY . . . !'

For a few moments there was utter pandemonium among the horrified crowd as the mother hysterically begged for someone – *anyone* – to rescue her little girl.

To add to the confusion, the band played on uncertainly for a few more minutes, before the sound died away discordantly.

A fisherman on the fringe of the crowd ran to some stone steps a short distance away, which led down to the water. A small boat was moored here. One of the uniformed Salvation Army bandsmen abandoned band and instrument and clattered down the steps to join the fisherman. Scrambling into the boat, they cast off the mooring rope and headed out on the dark waters of the harbour.

Meanwhile, another more enterprising young Salvation Army bandsman – and certainly more courageous than any of the other watchers – flung off his hat and jacket, pulled off his shoes and plunged head first into the harbour.

By now the followers of the Salvation Army and the Skeleton Army, their differences momentarily put to one side, crowded along the edge of the harbour, blocking off what little light was available to those attempting a rescue.

The mother of the unfortunate little girl continued to wail, joined now by her thoroughly frightened young son.

Suddenly, a man's voice called from somewhere out on the waters of the harbour. 'Hello, ashore! This is the customs cutter. What's going on?'

Twenty or more men shouted explanations. Once the customs men had caught the gist of what was happening one of them called back, 'We'll come closer and see if we can help.'

Before the cheers of the crowd had fully died away, the voice of the young bandsman who had so courageously dived into the water called from the darkness, 'I've found her. I've got her here. Can someone get a boat and take her from me?'

The cheering redoubled and now many voices were calling from the harbour itself. It appeared that the small dinghy manned by the fishermen and the customs cutter had come together in the darkness.

Then one of the two men in the dinghy shouted, 'We've got her on board – and she's still breathing.'

Now Salvationists and Skeleton Army followers united in a cheer that startled all the gulls night-roosting on the roofs of buildings around the harbour. It was followed by a movement of the crowd towards the steps to which the dinghy would return.

By the time the boat bumped against the steps the small girl had recovered sufficiently to be tearfully calling for her mother. Lifted from the boat she was passed from hand to hand above the heads of the crowd until she was reunited with her sobbing parent.

Only now did one of the Salvation Army women ask, 'Where's John? Wasn't he in the boat too?' When no one replied, she explained anxiously, 'He's the one who dived in and saved the girl. Where is he now?'

'He's probably been taken on board the customs cutter,' said the Salvation Army musician who had helped to man the dinghy.

There was a confused silence before he called into the darkness, 'Ahoy there! Customs cutter. Do you have the man who rescued the girl on board?'

'No. We thought he must have been picked up by the dinghy,' the voice from the darkness called back the chilling news.

The fisherman and the Salvation Army bandsman ran back down the steps to the dinghy. A couple of minutes later the customs cutter also returned to the area.

Soon the two boats were joined by others, but although the search continued for more than an hour, nothing was found of the missing bandsman

While the search was being carried out, one of the Salvation Army girls hurried to the bandsman's home, in the forlorn hope that he might have slipped ashore unnoticed and gone home to change.

She returned with the grim news that he had not gone home and no one there had seen him.

There was no more music from the Salvation Army band that evening. Gradually, as hope faded and the search for the missing man was abandoned, they and the members of the Skeleton Army left the scene, their differences temporarily forgotten.

Abandoning all thoughts of going to the music hall, Sally ran home to tell Ruth about the exciting happenings of the evening.

4

The next morning, Sally told Grace and Alfie Philpott about the events of the previous evening. Grace made suitably sympathetic noises, adding, 'Perhaps the young man climbed out of the water unnoticed and went home to change out of his wet clothes.'

Sally shook her head. 'No, someone checked. Besides, on my way here this morning I spoke to one of the fisherwomen. She said a body was pulled from the harbour at first light this morning. It was probably the Salvation Army bandsman. The men who found him said it looked as though he'd been hit by a boat. He was hit by the customs boat, I expect.'

Alfie was not in a very good mood this morning and was less sympathetic, 'If this so-called "Salvation Army" hadn't been there in the first place there would have been no accident. That lot have a lot to answer for, the way they go around, stirring folk up.'

Giving Sally a warning glance, Grace said to her husband, 'I'm sure you're right, dear. I must admit though, they don't seem to do anyone any harm. But then, I don't know very much about 'em, myself.'

'You're none the worse off for that,' declared Alfie. 'There's enough trouble in the world without having hallelujah hooligans making more. Now, can we get some of these deliveries on their way? I've taken orders for ten from the brewery, another twenty-five are wanted over at Stonehouse first thing this morning and we've got a whole batch of orders for midday . . . You'd better get moving, girl. If you're going to work for us you'll need to learn you don't keep customers waiting. Without them there'd be no wages for any of us.'

By the end of the day, Sally had earned one shilling and threepence three farthings. In order to achieve this she had delivered hundreds of meat pies and estimated she must have walked at least twenty miles. Her legs were tired, she was footsore and the muscles of her arms ached from carrying the heavy basket.

Nevertheless, the coins jangling in her pocket and two hot pies clutched in her hand were sufficient compensation for her aches and pains.

She had worked hard and earned an honest day's wages.

On the way home she stopped at a corner shop close to Pin's Lane. From here, the Italian owner sold ice-cream during the day and fried chips from early evening until well into the night. She bought a pennyworth of chips for Ruth to eat with her pie.

However, when Sally reached the small back room, she saw immediately that Ruth would be eating very little.

'I'm sorry, Sally,' the sick young woman said, in response to her sister's enthusiasm. 'I've had one of my bad days. I don't think I can eat a thing. It would be wasted on me. You have both of 'em.'

Doing her best to hide her disappointment, Sally said, 'I couldn't eat *two*, not with all these chips as well. But it would be a pity to waste them. I'll take a pie and some chips down to Charlie. He wasn't sitting on the step as usual. Perhaps he's not feeling too well today, either. I'll do it now, while everything's still hot. Then I'll come back and make you comfortable.'

'I'm sorry, Sally, especially as this is your first day at your new job. I know you've bought the chips for me 'specially, but I really couldn't eat them.' Ruth managed a wan smile for her sister. 'When you come back you can tell me all about your day.'

Carrying a plate of pie and chips, Sally knocked at Charlie's door. She walked into his untidy, gloomy room, without waiting for a reply. The elderly man was not ill. In fact he was seated at the table quaffing ale from a pewter mug.

He was not alone. Sitting across the table from him was a young man whose face seemed vaguely familiar to Sally.

'I'm sorry, Charlie, I didn't know you had company. I just called in to see if you'd like this.' She put the plate of food on the table. 'I brought it home for Ruth, but she doesn't feel like eating tonight. It'd be a pity to waste it.'

'Bless you, girl. It's one of Alfie Philpott's pies, too! My mouth would water every time I walked past his shop, when I got about a bit more, but he was a bit pricey for the likes of me.'

Giving her a wink, he said, 'I know you'd prefer it if it was just me here, but come and join us anyway. This is Ethan, my youngest brother's boy. He's just come visiting and has brought me some ale. No doubt we can find a drop for you.'

'I'm not stopping, Charlie. I must go back upstairs and see what I can do for Ruth. It worries me, her not being hungry. She doesn't eat enough these days to keep a kitten alive.'

She nodded at Charlie's companion, and had reached the door when she turned suddenly and said excitedly, 'I recognise you now! You're the bandsman who brought the young girl ashore last night, after she'd fallen in the harbour.'

The young man looked embarrassed. 'I didn't do very well, did I? I let poor John Albon drown – and he was the real hero of the night.'

'That wasn't your fault. I was speaking to someone this morning who said he'd probably been run down by the customs cutter.'

'I've heard the same – but it doesn't make me feel any better.'

Ethan had a quiet, self-deprecating manner and Sally realised he was incredibly shy.

'What's all this about?' While the others had been talking, Charlie had been tucking into the pie and chips. He spoke now with his mouth full of food.

'Ethan will tell you all about it,' said Sally. 'I must go back upstairs now and see to Ruth. It was nice meeting you, Ethan. Enjoy your grub, Charlie.'

Shutting the door behind her, Sally returned upstairs to her sister. Ruth listened dutifully as Sally told of her day's work, her meeting with Ethan and his part in the events of the previous night.

As she talked, Sally ate her pie and portion of chips. When they were gone, she made Ruth comfortable and began tidying up the room.

She was still working when there was a tentative knock on the door. Exchanging a glance with Ruth, Sally went to the door and opened it. Ethan was standing outside.

'I hope I haven't disturbed you,' he said with the same shy manner Sally had observed when she met him earlier. 'I came to the house with some fresh fish for Charlie. As you very kindly gave him some supper, he doesn't really need them all – and they won't keep. I thought your sister might fancy them. They'll be easier for her to eat than a meat pie.'

'Who is it?' Ruth called from her bed.

'It's Ethan, Charlie's nephew. He's brought some fish for you. He thought you might fancy them.'

'Well, don't leave him standing out there on the landing. Bring him in so I can see what he looks like.' As she spoke, Ruth struggled to sit up in bed and Sally hurried to her assistance.

As Sally lifted her sister, she called to Ethan, 'It's very kind of you. Won't you come in and say hello to Ruth? She doesn't have many visitors.'

Hesitantly, Ethan came inside the room, nodding a greeting to Ruth as he said, 'I thought you might find these fish tasty. They're easier eating than a pie.'

'Yes . . . yes, I think I might. Do you know, Sally, I really do fancy a mouthful or two of fish. Why don't you fry them up for me while I chat with Ethan. I can't remember the last time I had a conversation with a young man – especially one who's a hero. Come here and sit by the bed, Ethan. Tell me about what happened last night. Sally came home absolutely full of it . . .'

5

'How long has your sister been ill?'

Ethan asked the question as he and Sally walked together through the streets that led away from Plymouth's Barbican district. They were close to Union Street now, the busy thorough-fare that linked the main town with the naval dockyard areas of Stonehouse and Devonport.

Ruth had kept Ethan talking while Sally cooked the fish. She had then eaten a meal that delighted the younger girl. When it was gone, Ruth declared she wanted to sleep. She suggested that Sally should walk at least part of the way home with Ethan, to give her an opportunity to fall asleep without being disturbed.

After leaving the house with Sally, Ethan had explained that he was not going home immediately but was calling on his brother and his wife. They lived in Stonehouse, some little distance away.

At first, as they walked together, Ethan's shyness made con-versation difficult, but as his tongue gradually loosened Sally learned a little of his background. He was the son and grandson of fishermen and it was a life he claimed to enjoy.

Suddenly, he blurted out, 'You . . . you don't have to walk along with me, if you'd rather not.'

'Why would I "rather not"?' Sally asked, puzzled.

'Well . . . your sister didn't ask what you wanted to do. She just told you to come and keep me company.'

Sally shrugged. 'It doesn't matter to me. I've got nothing better to do.' Aware of the condition and quality of her clothes, she added, 'Of course, if you'd rather not be seen with *me* . . .'

'That isn't what I meant,' Ethan replied quickly. 'I *like* being with you, but . . .' He made an apologetic gesture. 'I can't really talk about much except music and fishing.'

'That's all right. I don't know anything about either of them things, so whatever you say, I won't have heard it before.'

She had presented him with a chance to tell her about himself and his occupation. But when he failed to take advantage of the opportunity they walked together in silence for a while.

The knowledge that Ethan was shy intrigued Sally. She could think of no other young man of her acquaintance who had the same problem. Most were quite the opposite and would seek any opportunity to attempt far more liberties than Sally was prepared to allow them.

'Do you have any sisters?' she asked.

Ethan shook his head. 'No . . . but I've got five brothers, all older than me.'

'Five!' Sally's expression was one of undisguised envy. 'I've always wished I had brothers – as well as Ruth, of course,' she added hurriedly. 'Are they all fishermen?'

'Every one. We've got our own boat too,' he added proudly.

Sally looked at him as though he'd claimed kinship with Queen Victoria. 'Charlie's always bragging about all the people he knows, but he's never said anything about having rich relatives!'

Ethan smiled. 'We're certainly not rich. My pa needed to borrow money to buy the boat. We're still paying off the loan. I sometimes feel we'd all be better off if we were working for somebody else.'

Sally was unable to comprehend that someone who actually *owned* something did not consider himself rich. Only rich people owned things like houses or boats.

Suddenly, for no reason she could think of, she asked, 'Why are you in the Salvation Army? It's not the sort of thing rich people do.'

In truth, the only thing that Sally knew about the Salvation Army was that it claimed to be concerned for the spiritual and physical well-being of the poor. Therefore it could not possibly enjoy the support of *rich* people.

Those who had money either ignored the poor or took advantage of them at every opportunity. At least that was what she had heard Ruth and her friends say on many occasions. Nothing had occurred in Sally's life to cast doubt on such an observation.

Ethan appeared somewhat embarrassed. 'I feel a bit of a fraud, really. Years ago one of my aunts gave me a flute and I taught myself to play it. I joined the Salvation Army because I wanted to be in their band.' Even more embarrassed, he added, 'I haven't told that to anyone before.'

After they had walked in silence for a few more paces, he continued, 'Everyone else seems to have joined the Salvation Army because of a burning passion to take religion to those they feel need it most. Men and women who are the greatest sinners.'

Sally frowned. 'But they only work among the poor. Does that mean rich people don't sin as much as we do?'

'I wouldn't say that.' Ethan smiled again. 'Mind you, rich folk probably don't *need* to sin quite as much. They don't have to steal in order to survive, or don't need to drink to forget the sort of life they lead or the place in which they live.'

Sally looked at Ethan quizzically. 'You sure you just joined the Salvation to play in their band? You sound just like one of them.'

'Do I? Perhaps that's because I've just been to visit Uncle Charlie. He doesn't have very much, and . . . and then I came up to your room and saw how little you have – and you've a sick sister to look after too. Before that I called in to see the family of that little girl who fell in the harbour last night . . . one of the band knew where they lived,' he explained. 'I thought I'd take them some fish too and make sure the little girl was all right.' He hesitated, before adding, 'The bandsman also told me that the little girl's father had once joined the Salvation Army. He didn't stay for very long though. He's a drunkard and spends almost every penny he earns on drink.'

Ethan paused. When he spoke once more he chose his words very carefully in an attempt to hide the depth of his feelings. 'The house was as clean as a new pin, even though there was hardly any furniture in the room. They didn't have a fire either, and it seems the little girl has only one dress – the one she was wearing when she fell in the harbour. Today hadn't been a good drying day, so she had nothing to wear. I only gave the woman a few fish, yet you'd think I'd handed her a fortune . . .'

He stopped speaking and Sally realised that Ethan was both kind and sensitive. He claimed to have joined the Salvation Army for purely selfish reasons, but she felt he was not out of place in its ranks.

During their conversation they had turned off Union Street. Now they heard the sound of raised voices and a small knot of brawling men spilled from a house into the road in front of them.

Ethan immediately took Sally's arm and led her to the opposite pavement. 'I think we'd better give them a wide berth.'

'Why? They've got no quarrel with us.'

'It sounds as though a couple of them are foreign sailors,' said Ethan, quickening his pace. 'They've probably been drinking so won't know who's on their side and who's against them. Besides, that's Mother Darling's house.'

'Who's Mother Darling?'

'She's someone young women shouldn't know anything about.'

'You mean . . . she runs a whore house?'

Ethan flushed scarlet and was glad the dim gas-lamps hid his hot cheeks. 'That's right, and there are some queer goings-on there, I can tell you.'

'What sort of goings-on?'

'Oh . . . all sort of things.'

'Well, tell me *what*, exactly,' persisted Sally. She was aware that Ethan was embarrassed but, without knowing why, she was taking a perverse pleasure in continuing to question him.

They turned the corner from the street, leaving Mother Darling's house and the fighting group behind them.

Slowing his pace a little, Ethan said, 'It's said that young country girls answer adverts in the newspapers and come to Plymouth thinking they're coming to work as servants. Many of them end up in Mother Darling's house. Then they're shipped off to France, Belgium – or even Arab countries – and are never seen again.'

Resisting an urge to look over her shoulder to ensure they were not being followed, Sally said scornfully, 'That's just talk. I don't suppose anything like that happens at all.'

'Yes it does,' Ethan persisted. 'One of my brothers saw half a dozen girls being put on board a Belgian boat not long ago. He said they all looked dopey; they needed to be helped on board, as though they'd been given something. My brother said he recognised Mother Darling's son as one of the men helping the sailors take them on board.'

'I wonder how he came to know Mother Darling's son,' Sally said provocatively.

Aware that Sally was trying to embarrass him, Ethan replied, 'I wouldn't know that, but I do know that Mary Street is no place for a young woman.'

Sally realised that Charlie could not have explained to his nephew how Ruth had earned her living before she became ill. She decided not to enlighten him, even though she told herself that what Ethan thought of her really did not matter. They would probably never meet again.

'We're almost at my brother's house now,' said Ethan. 'Will you come in with me and meet him and his wife, Sophie? You'd like her.'

'No. I don't want to be too late back or I'll disturb Ruth. Besides, I need to be up early tomorrow, for work.'

Hesitantly, Ethan asked, 'Would you mind if I called in to see you the next time I pay a visit to Uncle Charlie?'

'Of course not. It'll be nice for Ruth to have someone different to talk to.' Sally tried to sound nonchalant. She did not want him to realise he was the first man to express an interest in her. A *real* interest. She did not count Charlie or the other men like him. Their interest was not in her as a *person*.

They stopped at a door that opened directly on to the narrow pavement. 'This is where Albert and Sophie live. You're quite sure you won't come in? They'd make you very welcome.'

'No, I'll see you again. 'Bye.'

Sally walked away carrying a warm glow inside her. She

decided she liked Ethan. She had taken notice of all he had told her too. When she reached the street where Mother Darling lived, she hurried past and took another road that would take her to Union Street and so back to the Barbican.

6

The next few days were busy for Sally. At times, it seemed that most of the residents of Plymouth must have taken a sudden fancy to Alfie Philpott's pies. She was hard-put to keep up with deliveries.

It was taken for granted by the Philpotts that Sally was happy to work full-time for them. Indeed, with Christmas not far away, the pie-shop owners even discussed the possibility of employing another youngster to help with the ever-increasing need for deliveries.

Sally had not seen Ethan since his visit to the Pin's Lane house, but it was hardly surprising. From discreet enquiries she made when delivering pies to the fish quay, she knew that local fishermen were taking advantage of the current good weather. They were spending all available time at sea in order to meet the huge demands of the London market.

Late one afternoon, she returned to the shop in happy anticipation of finishing work for the day and returning home to Ruth. To her surprise, she found both Alfie and Grace still busily cooking.

'Ah! There you are, Sally.' Grace looked hot and flustered. 'We were beginning to fear you wouldn't get back in time. We've got an order for you to take out right away.'

Sally's heart sank. She had been looking forward to going

home. The weather had deteriorated during the previous night, with a gale sweeping in from the east, and although it had improved somewhat now, it was still too rough for fishing. All the Plymouth fishing boats would have remained in harbour today, and she had been hoping Ethan might take the opportunity to call and see her.

However, she could not refuse to make the delivery. The Philpotts were generous employers. Only the previous night they had given her more than a pound of beef, left over at the end of the day from their pie-making, to take home to Pin's Lane.

'Where are they to go to?' she asked.

'To Mary Street, just off Union Street,' replied Grace. 'I expect you know it.'

Sally's heart sank. It would take her almost forty minutes to make the return errand, but Grace said, 'I realise it's getting late in the day, but there'll be an extra threepence in it for you and you can go straight home when you've made the delivery and take the basket with you. The woman who came in and placed the order would have taken the pies with her, but we were nearly out. I said I'd make some fresh and have 'em delivered.'

As Grace was speaking, Sally had been trying to place the street in question. When realisation came, she asked in sudden concern, 'Who have I got to deliver them to?'

'Number fourteen. To a Mrs Darling.'

Sally's jaw dropped and Alfie said swiftly, 'What's the matter, girl, do you know the woman?'

'No . . . I mean . . . yes.'

'No – yes? What's that supposed to mean?'

Hesitantly, Sally gave the Philpotts a summarised version of what Ethan had told her and of the fight he and she had witnessed when they passed along Mary Street.

Grace was concerned, but Alfie said scornfully, 'There are fights right outside this shop most nights – and you don't want to believe every rumour you hear, girl. If you listened to some folk talking about what we're supposed to put in our pies you'd never dare deliver 'em, let alone eat 'em. Anyway, you're going to Mary Street to take the lady some pies, not in response to any newspaper advertisement. But I'll tell you what I'll do. If you don't turn up for work in the morning I'll go along to the police station and have them search this woman's house for you.' With that Alfie went off, shaking his head in disbelief.

But Grace was less sceptical of Sally's fears. 'I'm sure Alfie's right, dear, but you mind yourself when you get there. If there's the least sign of anything funny going on, you just cut and run. Fortunately they've paid us in advance, so you don't need to worry yourself about that.'

On the way to Mary Street with a laden basket over her arm, Sally almost convinced herself that Alfie was probably right. Barbican rumours were quite often grossly exaggerated – although this one had come, almost first-hand, from Ethan. She doubted very much whether he would have embellished such a story.

Her apprehension increased when she turned into Mary Street. Finally arriving at number fourteen, she hesitated fearfully for a moment or two. Then, telling herself the house was no different to any other in the street, she knocked resolutely on the door.

Much to her relief, the woman who opened the door was the antithesis of all she had been anticipating.

Small, plump and motherly, the woman beamed benevolently at Sally 'Hello, my dear, and what can I do for you?'

'I'm from Alfie Philpott. Delivering the pies you ordered.'

'Why, of course! Come in, come in. I wasn't expecting you quite so soon – but that's Alfie Philpott for you. Not only does he make the best pies in Plymouth, he's reliable, too. That's right, bring them through to the kitchen and put them down on the table. You won't mind if I count them? Not that I think for a moment Alfie would try to cheat me, but he's human, same as everyone else and we all make mistakes, don't we?'

'You'll find they're all there,' said Sally, wondering why she had feared meeting such a homely and ordinary woman. 'In fact, Grace Philpott has put in an extra pie, to make up for them not being ready when you called.'

'Well, that was kind of her. Very kind indeed.'

Despite her words, Mother Darling continued to count, until she was able to confirm she had indeed received the full order – plus one.

Before she had quite finished counting, Sally said, 'It's a whole lot of pies for one household, are you having a party?'

'A party? Why, yes dear, that's exactly it. We're having a party . . .'

At that moment a man entered the room. Big and burly, he had a couple of days' growth of stubble on his face and a long thin scratch extending from the corner of his left eye down his cheek, almost to his chin.

Giving Sally a look that brought back all her earlier fears, he said, 'Well, here's a pretty little thing, and no mistake. Has she come to work for us, Mother?'

'No, Sidney, she's a local girl who's just delivered the pies I ordered from Alfie Philpott . . . for the party.'

'The party . . . ? Oh yes, the party!' Sidney chuckled. 'Perhaps she'd like to stay for it, eh?'

'She'll be kept busy enough by Alfie Philpott . . . but you're right about one thing. She *is* a pretty little thing.'

Turning to Sally, she gave her a disarming smile. 'You know, a girl like you could be earning a lot more money than you'll ever make delivering pies.'

Uncomfortably aware there was a hidden meaning in Mother Darling's words, Sally said hurriedly, 'I'm quite happy working for Alfie and Grace Philpott, thank you.'

'Well, if you ever change your mind, you come here and see me—'

At that moment there came a scream, followed by a bump on an upstairs floor.

As Sally heard someone running down the stairs, Sidney Darling darted from the kitchen, moving impressively fast for a man of his bulk.

Another scream was immediately stifled, then a muffled voice shouted, 'I want to go home. Let me go!'

Alarmed, Sally moved towards the kitchen door, intent on discovering what was happening. She found Mother Darling blocking her way.

'I should stay here for a moment or two, dear.' Although her words were no more than a suggestion, Mother Darling made it quite clear that Sally would not be allowed past her.

Raising her voice, she called, 'Who is it, Sidney?'

From somewhere on the stairs, her son responded, 'It's that young Rachel causing trouble again.'

'Oh dear, poor girl,' Mother Darling replied with apparent sympathy. 'Put her in the front bedroom – but don't forget to turn the key. I'll come up and tend to the poor dear in a few moments.'

Shaking her head sadly, she explained to Sally, 'It's my niece, poor dear soul. She recently lost her mother – my sister – and it's quite turned her mind. We've had to call the doctor to her more than once. He's said the only thing to be done is to keep her under lock and key, in the hope she'll get her senses back one day. If she doesn't, he says she'll need to be shut away in an asylum. I can't see that happen, can I? Not to my own flesh and blood.'

Sally fervently hoped her expression of sympathy was convincing.

She breathed a big sigh of relief when, a few minutes later, she stood on the pavement in Mary Street and the door was closed behind her by the woman she was now certain was a brothel keeper.

If she needed any further proof, it came only moments later. She was still standing in the street, wondering what she could do to help the girl she was convinced was trying to escape from the house, when she heard breaking glass, the sound coming from somewhere above the spot where she stood. At the same time pieces of glass showered down about her from an upstairs window.

The same voice cried out, 'HELP! Help me . . . PLEASE! I'm being kidnapped. They've been doing things to me. Help—'

The heartfelt pleas came to an abrupt end, but they left Sally badly shaken. Not least because she had just left the house in which the girl was imprisoned.

As she stood there, undecided what she should do, Sally heard voices from inside the room. It sounded like Mother Darling and her son, cursing the girl who had shouted.

Sally did not wait to hear any more. Taking to her heels she ran from the street and did not stop until she reached the lights of Union Street.

*   *   *

In the house in Mary Street, Sid Darling threw open the door of the room in which the young girl was imprisoned. She was about to use her shoe to break another pane of glass when he caught hold of her upraised arm and threw her back against the wall.

Not attempting to rise to her feet, the girl scrambled for the door on all fours, but Mother Darling was standing, squat and solid, in the doorway, blocking her path.

The next moment, Sid Darling lifted the girl from the ground, an arm about her waist.

'Let . . . me . . . go!' Her arms and legs were flailing wildly but it made no impression on the big man.

'We've got a lively one here and no mistake,' said Sid. 'I think me and Wallace need to give her something else to think about, don't you?'

'I was hoping to get a higher price for this one as "untried goods", Sid, but you're right. She does need to be taught a lesson and she's young enough to fetch a decent price anyway. Take her up to the back room in the loft – and don't let her scream too much. We've disturbed the neighbours enough for one night. If we're not careful we'll be getting complaints, won't we?'

The evil old procuress went away chuckling. The residents of Mary Street knew better than to complain about anything that went on in Mother Darling's house.

The young girl's screams and sobs would go unheeded.

7

In the back room on the first floor of the Pin's Lane house, Ruth was having one of her better days and she listened in silence to the story blurted out by her excited sister.

'What do you think I should do, Ruth?' Sally asked the question anxiously when she had finished.

'Nothing,' Ruth replied firmly.

'What do you mean "nothing"? This girl's in trouble, Ruth. *Real* trouble. I can't just shrug it off as though nothing happened.'

'You will if you have any sense. You don't know for certain that what you were told by Mother Darling was a lie. Besides, you're not just dealing with her. Sid Darling's her son – and he's a man to keep well clear of, believe me. Many girls have rued the day they crossed him. You mustn't get involved in this, Sal. Life's picked up for you lately. Try to keep it that way.'

'Supposing it was *me* who was in trouble? Wouldn't you want someone to help me, if they could?'

'It's *not* you in trouble, and you can't go through life taking everyone's troubles on your shoulders. You've got enough to put up with as it is, looking after me. Now, make me a nice cup of tea and forget you've seen or heard anything. Then you can go downstairs to Charlie's room. Your young man's down there. He came looking for you and was disappointed when he found only me here. Rather than stay and tire me with his chatter, he said he'd wait downstairs for you.'

Sally and Ethan met on the stairs. His obvious delight at seeing her again would have thrilled her on any other occasion, but she still had the fate of the girl at Mother Darling's on her mind. Choosing to disregard Ruth's advice she blurted out the story to Ethan.

Much to Sally's chagrin, Ethan's immediate response was no different to Ruth's.

'You don't want to involve yourself with any of the happenings at Mother Darling's. She and her son are a bad lot.'

'I know they're a bad lot,' said Sally, her exasperation showing. 'That's exactly why someone *has* to get involved. They've got a young girl locked up in their house. God knows what they'll do to her . . .'

Recalling the girl's last desperate words, she added, 'In fact I can't bear to think about what they've *already* done to her. All right, if you won't help then I'll go to the police.'

'You'll get no help from them,' Ethan said bitterly. 'Make a complaint to the police and you'll most likely end up being the one they arrest. The Salvation Army knows of at least eight brothels in Plymouth. They've reported them time and time again. Most of those who've made the complaints have found themselves arrested and charged with "obstruction" the very next time they've gone out on a parade. Meanwhile, the brothels carry on their business as usual.'

Sally was aware that Ethan's statement would have come as no surprise to Ruth. She had frequently complained that although the police carried out periodic purges against the prostitutes who worked on the streets or frequented the public houses, the brothels were allowed to carry on their business unhindered. Nevertheless, she was not prepared to ignore what she had witnessed that evening.

Remembering the pitiful cries of the unseen girl, she pleaded, 'There must be *something* that can be done, Ethan? I can't stop thinking about the poor girl in that house . . . !'

Ethan remained silent for some moments, then he said, 'I know someone we can talk to. Whether she can help is another matter, but it's worth a try.'

'A woman! What can a woman do?'

'As I said, I don't know. She's a Salvation Army captain who hasn't been in Plymouth very long. She was sent from London to set up a house for women who want to give up that sort of life. She'll be at the meeting in Central Hall right now. Do you want to go and speak to her?'

Sally shrugged resignedly. 'I can't see that she'll be able to do anything, but it's better than doing nothing at all.'

Captain Eva Cassington was a small, dark-haired, lively woman, but Sally was dismayed to find she was hardly older than Ruth. She had been expecting a mature, formidable woman. Someone capable of brow-beating Mother Darling and her burly son.

Nevertheless, coaxed by the Salvation Army captain, Sally told her what she had seen and the other woman listened in attentive silence.

When Sally ended her story, Eva Cassington said, 'What makes you think prostitution is involved? That the circumstances are not exactly what this woman says they are?'

Sally looked to Ethan and he repeated what his brother had told him, adding that the house in Mary Street was a notorious brothel.

'You are of the opinion the police will do nothing if we go to them?'

'Certainly not at the request of anyone in the Salvation Army,' confirmed Ethan.

'I see. Then we'll need to do something about it ourselves, won't we? How long ago is it since you were at this house, Sally?'

'It's more than two hours now.' Sally was impressed by the decisiveness of the Salvation Army captain. 'But what can we do without the police? Mother Darling's son is a big man. From all I've heard about him, he actually enjoys fighting.'

'Then we'll need to take someone with us who's even larger and enjoys fighting more than he does. I know just the man. He's on his knees in the hall right now, giving thanks to the Lord for his salvation. Wait here while I go and fetch him.'

When Captain Eva had passed from view, Sally asked Ethan anxiously, 'Do you think she knows what she's doing? Mother Darling's not going to admit what's been going on – and her son's hardly likely to let us search the house to find the girl.'

'I'm more worried about what might happen if they recognise *you*,' said Ethan, his concern showing. 'It will be obvious you're the one who's reported them. They know you work for Alfie Philpott, so it wouldn't be hard for them to find you.'

Sally was still pondering this problem when Captain Eva returned. A giant of a man lumbered along behind her. His skin was as black as the Salvation Army captain's bonnet and he had a grin that displayed even, white teeth.

There was a gasp from Ethan and he said quickly, with awe in his voice, 'It's Zulu Joe!'

Wasting no time on introductions, Captain Eva said briskly, 'There's a girl out there in need of help. Let's go and set about the Lord's work.'

On the way to Mary Street, Ethan told the young Salvation Army captain of his fears for Sally's future safety if she were to be recognised by either of the Darlings.

'It's something that can't be ignored,' she agreed. 'Sally, tell me the story of this girl once again and explain exactly where she was when she last attracted your attention.'

When Sally had repeated her story, Eva said, 'If this Mother Darling and her son are all you say they are, then it will be better if both you and Ethan stay out of sight. I'll take Joe to the house with me and say a passer-by heard the commotion and repeated it to me.'

Mary Street was not very far and they were soon there. As agreed, Ethan and Sally remained behind in Union Street, while Eva and her large bodyguard went on to tackle the two Darlings.

Many of the shops in the busy Union Street thoroughfare were closing as the notorious area prepared to give itself over to less-savoury activities. An unwritten law existed whereby respectable women passing along the street kept to the pavement on the north side. This left the south side to the women, now putting in their nightly appearance, who earned a living selling themselves to the sailors of different nationalities who frequented the public houses.

There were still enough respectable people using the street to ensure that the young couple would not be troubled.

The chill easterly wind that had been blowing all day had eased off considerably, yet it was still cold enough to make would-be revellers hurry to seek the warmth and companionship they hoped to find inside one of the street's public houses.

'That Zulu Joe doesn't say very much, does he?' commented Sally, as they gazed in the window of a pawnbroker's shop, which would remain open for business until late in the evening.

'He can't,' replied Ethan. 'It's said that when he was a small boy, he and his mother were captured by Arab slavers. He kicked up so much fuss when the slavers attacked his mother that they cut out his tongue to shut him up.'

'That's a *horrible* story!' Sally shuddered. 'But how does anyone know what happened if he can't tell them?'

'He can write in English,' replied Ethan. 'He was taught by a missionary who brought him to England some years ago. The missionary became very friendly with William Booth, the Salvation Army's general. When the missionary died, the Army looked after Zulu Joe. He came to Plymouth from London with Captain Wardle, the officer in charge of the Plymouth corps.'

Warming to his subject, he continued, 'Bits and pieces have been added to his story recently. A soldier who came to Central Hall claimed that Zulu Joe isn't really a Zulu at all, but got his name by scouting against them for the British when he and the missionary were in Africa. I don't know how true it is, but he's no stranger to a fight. When Captain Wardle first came to Plymouth he gave a talk and described how Zulu Joe would see off gangs of roughs in the East End of London. Since Captain Eva came here, Zulu Joe seems to have taken to her.'

'Well, I hope he's tough enough to rescue that girl and give Sid Darling what he deserves,' Sally said fervently.

8

When twenty minutes had passed and Captain Eva and Zulu Joe had not returned, Sally and Ethan began to grow concerned. They were greatly relieved when the pair turned the corner into Union Street – but the girl who had called to Sally for help was not with them.

In answer to Sally's question, Eva said, 'She wasn't anywhere in the house. In fact there were only two other people there, two prostitutes who seem to be sharing a back room. I know this is so because Mother Darling proved surprisingly accommodating. She allowed us to see all over the house.'

'But . . . I was telling you the truth, honest I was. The girl *was* there. I heard her. She was terrified and begging for help.'

'I don't doubt you, Sally. Mother Darling's son wasn't in the house and she made everything far too easy for me. Had she been entirely innocent she would have been filled with indignation at having me prying into her business. She certainly wouldn't have thrown the house open to me. Besides, there *had* been people in the house – a large number of them, I'd say. How many pies did you deliver?'

Puzzled, Sally said, 'Two dozen. Mother Darling said they were having a party.'

'There was no sign of a party, but I estimate there had probably been as many as twenty people in the house recently. Whether or not they were willing guests, I wouldn't like to say, but I did notice one thing that struck me as very strange and which tends to confirm your story. There were keys in the locks of every upstairs room, where I believe the girls to have been, *and all were on the outside of the doors!'*

'Where can the girls have gone?' asked Sally. 'And what's happened to the one who was so desperate for help?'

'Again, I don't know – although I did see the broken window pane in the upstairs front room. Perhaps Ethan can help us. You told me your brother once saw this Sidney Darling putting girls on board a boat. Was it a passenger vessel?'

Ethan shook his head. 'No, it was a big deep-sea Belgian fishing boat. . .' Suddenly realising what was behind her questioning, he added excitedly, 'One just like it came into the harbour yesterday – it might even be the same one. We all noticed it especially because it didn't come alongside the fish quay, as the foreign fishing boats usually do. It berthed on the other side of the harbour, at Shepherd's Wharf, which is practically deserted right now. I can even tell you the boat's name. It's the *Astique.'*

'You don't know if the boat's still there? Might it have sailed this evening?'

'There's no chance of that. Nothing has left harbour during today's gale. The wind's been strong enough to blow a boat straight back in if it tried to put to sea. Nothing will move until morning now. The tide will be against it for the next hour or so. A stranger to Plymouth would need to be desperate to try to take his boat out in the dark.'

'Then we'll go to where it's moored and try to find out whether they've taken a cargo of English girls on board. How many men are there likely to be in the crew of this Belgian fishing boat?'

'I don't know too much about the foreign fishing boats – especially one as large as this, but they usually carry more men than we do. Judging by its size, I wouldn't be surprised if there were twelve or possibly eighteen men on board. I'd say that's too many for one man to take on – even for Zulu Joe.'

'Then we'll need to find others to help us. Yet we don't want to start something that might lead to a lot of people getting injured, especially as we're not entirely certain these girls are on board. General Booth's army fights for souls, not bodies.' Deep in thought, Eva frowned. Then she added, 'However, not everyone who comes to the meetings in Central Hall has declared for the Lord. Even if they intend doing it, I don't doubt He will be content to wait a while longer for them, in a cause such as this. But before I do anything drastic, I *would* like to confirm there are English girls on board this Belgian boat . . .'

'Why don't I take our dinghy, row across the harbour to the Belgian boat and see if I can hear or see anything?' Ethan said eagerly. 'They won't see me in the dark.'

'How long will it take you?'

'Once I reach the dinghy it'll be no more than fifteen minutes. Twenty at the most.'

'And how long will it take me to reach Shepherd's Wharf by road from Central Hall?'

'That depends how fast you walk,' Ethan declared cautiously, 'but it should be no longer than half an hour.'

Eva bit her lip thoughtfully. 'That will make it a bit late for what I have in mind, but it's better than doing something without adequate investigation. We could be made to look very foolish. All right, Ethan, off you go and do what needs to be done. In the meantime, Zulu Joe and I will hurry along to Central Hall and hope the meeting hasn't already broken up.'

'I'll go with Ethan,' declared Sally.

When it seemed Captain Eva might raise an objection, she added hurriedly, 'If we do find out something, Ethan can put me ashore. Then I'll run to Central Hall to tell you what we've found while he's taking his boat back.'

To Sally's relief, Captain Eva said, 'That makes sense. I'll be on my way to Shepherd's Wharf with as many men as I can gather from Central Hall, but I'm sure you'll find us. If you tell me there are no girls on the boat we'll sing the Belgian fishermen a few hymns anyway. It will be good for their souls.'

9

Sally had difficulty keeping up with Ethan as they hurried towards the Barbican. He had long legs and every half-dozen paces she needed to break into a trot in order to catch up with him.

'Do we need to go quite so fast?' she asked breathlessly.

'Yes,' he replied unsympathetically. 'And if these girls are on board and we're to rescue them, we need to have a plan. Perhaps Captain Eva can create some sort of disturbance on the wharf so we can get close to the Belgian boat from the harbour – we might even get on board, if there's no one about. But we need to hurry. The tide will soon be high enough for the crew to set sail if they take fright. That would be dangerous for everyone involved.'

Too breathless to reply, Sally thought about what Ethan had said until they reached the gas-lit Barbican.

A strong smell of fish hung on the air and dozens of fishing boats were moored in tightly packed lines, bows on to the quayside. Many displayed lanterns and there seemed to be a surprising amount of activity.

When Sally commented, breathlessly, on this, Ethan said, 'The wind has moved around in the last couple of hours. There are signs that the weather will be much better tomorrow, so the boats are being made ready to go to sea. At this time of year we can't afford to lose any opportunity to catch fish.'

The boat owned by Ethan's family was named *Mermaid*. He pointed out the vessel to Sally and, as they clambered over other boats to reach it, explained in haste that the dinghy they needed was secured to the fishing boat's stern.

On board *Mermaid*, two men were working by the yellow light of a lantern. The light was sufficient for Sally to recognise that both bore a strong resemblance to Ethan. One of the men was perhaps thirty years older than Ethan, the other less than ten.

As she scrambled on board the boat behind Ethan, the older man looked from his son to Sally, scrutinising her thoroughly. The younger man did not immediately see her and spoke in a jocular manner to his brother.

'Hello, young Ethan. Have you come to give us a hand to get the boat ready for tomorrow?'

'No, we've come to borrow the dinghy.'

'We . . . ?' Ethan's brother suddenly saw Sally but it was his father who spoke to her first.

'Hello, young lady. I don't think we've met before.'

'This is Sally. Sally, this is my pa – and Paul, my oldest brother.'

Sally nodded to each of the men in turn. Although she said nothing she was aware they were taking a keen interest in her.

'You'll be the maid my brother Charlie was telling me about. You live upstairs in the same house as him.'

Before Sally could reply, Henry Shields turned his attention to Ethan. 'Did you say you wanted to borrow the dinghy? What do you want with it at this time of night?'

Ethan hesitated for only a few moments. His was not a family that kept secrets from one another.

His father and brother listened in silence as he told them of Sally's visit to the home of Mother Darling and of all that had transpired since.

When Ethan ended his story, Henry Shields frowned. 'What makes you think this girl might be on the Belgian boat?'

'Our Danny saw a whole lot of girls being taken on to a Belgian trawler a while ago. He said it looked as though they'd been doped. Sid Darling was with them. It's likely there's more than one girl involved. Possibly as many as a couple of dozen.'

'If Sid Darling's mixed up in this business you're probably right about what's going on. I've known him since we were both boys. He hasn't improved with the years. But what can the pair of you do about it?'

'We're going to Shepherd's Wharf in the hope we might see or hear something suspicious on the Belgian boat.'

'And if you do?'

'I'll land Sally and she'll run to tell Captain Eva Callington, one of the Salvation Army women. She's bringing some of the worshippers from Central Hall to the wharf. Hopefully they'll be able to board the boat and rescue the girls.'

Sally realised Ethan's explanation over-simplified the whole situation. So too did his father.

'You're expecting some rag, tag and bobtail from a Salvation Army meeting to risk life and limb by taking on a boatload of Belgian fisherman? All to save some girls they don't know – and who might not even *want* to be saved? At the very best, they'll succeed in convincing the Belgians they should set sail as soon as the tide's in their favour – and that will be in less than an hour if they're desperate enough to try it. Remember too, if they run into trouble on their way out to sea they won't be at all concerned about what happens to these girls.'

Waiting a few moments for his words to sink in, Henry Shields shook his head. 'No, it's not a good idea at all, young Ethan.'

'But we can't let them get away with the girls from Mother Darling's house,' Sally said passionately. 'You should have heard the cries of the girl who was trying to escape. They were pitiful.'

'I didn't say we should let them escape with the girls. Only that we need to think things out carefully before we do anything. Where is this Captain Eva right now?'

'Gathering up the men and women from Central Hall,' Ethan replied. 'We've just left her. Once she's got enough to go with her she'll start marching them off to Shepherd's Wharf.'

'It'll take her a while to get there,' Henry Shields said thoughtfully. 'All the same, we'll need to get moving. All right, Ethan, you can take the dinghy. Go to Shepherd's Wharf and see what you can find out – but don't let yourselves be seen. If you're convinced they have girls on board, drop Sally off farther along the wharf to meet up with this Captain Eva, then come back here as quickly as you can. While you're gone I'll speak to some of the fishermen. There are enough of 'em around tonight to see off the Belgians. They'll be only too happy to do it if they believe they're trying to make off with English girls.'

Turning his attention to Sally, Henry said, 'You, girl. When you find this Salvation Army captain, tell her that when she reaches Shepherd's Wharf she's to get her crowd to make as much noise as they can, alongside the boat. Create a really good diversion. We'll do the rest.'

10

Although she lived so close to the harbour, Sally had rarely been for a trip in a boat, and never after dark. It was a cold enough night to make her shiver, yet she hardly noticed. She was both excited and fearful about the mission she and Ethan were undertaking.

The harbour was quite small but it seemed that she and Ethan, in their tiny boat, were completely cut off from the people who could be seen walking about the narrow, gas-lit streets around the water's edge.

Ethan had been rowing for no more than ten minutes when Sally whispered hoarsely, 'How long will it take us to get there?'

'Shh!' he stopped rowing and whispered the admonishment. 'That's Shepherd's Wharf, just ahead.'

Peering past him, Sally was just able to make out the inadequately lit wharf, no more than ten or fifteen boat lengths in front of them.

At first she was unable to see the Belgian fishing boat. Then she made out a tall mast silhouetted against a shadowy warehouse. The tide was still low enough for the boat to be settled well below the level of the timber-faced wharf.

Now she had located the vessel she was also able to make out a faint curtain of pale light. In all probability it was escaping from a partly closed hatchway on the deck of the fishing vessel. She gained the impression that *Astique* was a large vessel. Far larger than the fishing boat belonging to the Shields family.

Ethan was using the oars with utmost caution now, slowly easing the small dinghy closer to the Belgian boat. Suddenly, Sally heard an outburst of raucous laughter from the other vessel. There was another sound, too. The cry of a young girl!

Before the sound had fully died away, it was echoed by the shrill scream of a second girl.

'There's certainly more than one girl on board,' Ethan whispered. '*And* they're in trouble. I think we've heard enough, don't you?'

'Yes,' Sally replied fiercely. 'Land me so I can go and find Captain Eva – and quickly.'

'Tell her to hurry – and remember what my pa said. She's to create as much of a diversion as she can but nothing else. We want to get as many men as possible off that boat before Pa and the others try to board it.'

'What will you do once you've told your pa what's going on?'

'I'll stay with them . . .' Ethan had been rowing hard as they talked, and abruptly they bumped against some stone steps, some distance from the Belgian fishing boat. 'Off you go – and hurry.'

'I will . . . Take care, Ethan.'

Put ashore at the steps, Sally ran between tall, dark warehouse buildings before she reached the streets of the town. No more than five minutes later, she met up with the uniformed Salvation Army officer.

Captain Eva was accompanied by half a dozen similarly clad girls. The women, playing flutes and tambourines, marched at the head of a motley group of perhaps fifty men and women, many from the town's vagrant community.

The silent Zulu Joe was with them and the unusual group was attracting considerable attention from those it passed in the street, although no one attempted to molest it.

Sally passed on her information, telling Captain Eva what Ethan's father had said. The Salvation Army captain immediately ordered her party to increase their pace, ignoring the protests of those who were unaware of the reason for their foray on to the streets of Plymouth.

The music of the small 'band' was silenced when it reached the conglomeration of stone and ramshackle wooden buildings that formed Shepherd's Wharf.

Captain Eva brought the group to a halt at the edge of the wharf, and looked out across the dark waters of the harbour. She was unable to see anything.

'Do you think Ethan and the other fishermen will be in position yet?' she asked Sally.

'I don't know,' Sally replied anxiously. 'But I think we should do as Mr Shields asked, in case they are out there waiting.'

'You're quite right. Let's make a start.'

Captain Eva led her motley party to where the tall mast of the *Astique* rose above the edge of the wharf. She gathered her bandswomen around her, then lined up the rest of the group in front of her.

'We'll begin by singing "Storm the Forts of Darkness",' she called. 'If you don't know the words I'm quite sure you'll be familiar with the tune, so just "la-la" your way through it. Ready? One, two three . . .'

With the Salvation Army girls beating time on their jangling tambourines, and the thin notes of the flutes carrying the tune, the impromptu choir began to sing. It was immediately apparent that they possessed far more enthusiasm than musical ability.

Much to Sally's amazement the tune of the Salvationists' song was one she knew, but it was more usually sung to the words of 'Here's to Good Old Whisky'.

They had not being singing for many minutes when a head appeared above the ladder leading from the wharf to the fishing boat. For a few moments a Belgian fisherman looked at the party on the wharf, his face registering incredulity. Then, calling down to those on the boat below him, he climbed up to the wharf, closely followed by some of his fellow crew members.

When there were nine bemused Belgian fishermen standing on the wharf, Captain Eva called out gaily to them, 'Come closer. Come and join us.'

Some of the men were about to obey her, when one of their number spoke sharply to them and they stopped.

Sally felt an overwhelming urge to move closer to the edge of the wharf and see if she could detect any movement on the water, but she did not dare run the risk of alerting the Belgians. They were already beginning to show signs of boredom with the admittedly unmusical singing of the majority of those taking part in the Salvation Army's impromptu concert party.

'We must do something to keep them interested for a while longer,' Sally said desperately. 'We don't want them returning to their boat just yet.'

'I think I know what might keep them interested.' Captain Eva beckoned to one of the two flautists and spoke to her. As the singing died away, the flautist began playing a Scottish reel.

Hitching her skirt up to a height that would have incurred the stern disapproval of the Salvation Army founder, Captain Eva began dancing, one hand holding up her skirt, the other held high in the air.

As she skipped and twirled, the tambourines took up the beat and the worshippers from Central Hall began clapping in time to the music. After hesitating uncertainly for a minute or two more, the fishermen from the Belgian boat drew nearer and joined in the clapping.

Because of the noise they were creating it was some minutes before those standing on the wharf became aware of another sound.

It came from the *Astique* – the sound of men shouting, in both English and Flemish.

The first reaction of the fishermen was to return to their vessel, belatedly aware they had been tricked. Captain Eva immediately brought her dance to an end and shouted to her followers, 'Stop them! Don't let them get back to their boat.'

There was room for no more than one man at a time to swing himself onto the narrow ladder. Only one of the fishermen succeeded in gaining it before the men who had marched with Captain Eva ran to obey her command. Zulu Joe was the first to reach the ladder and he made his presence felt immediately – but it was not only men who took part in the mêlée.

Sally saw three of the black-bonneted Salvation Army girls belabouring a Belgian fishermen with their tambourines, as he fought with one of the men from Central Hall.

Suddenly, the head of Ethan's oldest brother appeared above the ladder from the boat. Scrambling to the wharf, he was closely followed by a dishevelled young girl, who seemed terrified by what was going on about her. Then a second girl appeared – and a third.

Now another Plymouth fisherman appeared and dived among the brawling, shouting throng. During the course of the next few minutes, still more fishermen and girls climbed the ladder to the wharf.

By the time the last of the girls had reached safety, the odds had turned heavily in favour of the Englishmen. The Belgians were beating a desperate retreat towards the edge of the wharf. One or two were fortunate enough to find their way back on board via the ladder. Others swung themselves over the edge of the wharf and dropped to the deck of their boat. One, in an attempt to escape the wrath of Plymouth fishermen, took a flying leap into the darkness, hoping he would not land on anything that would cause him serious injury.

An unknown number of Belgian fishermen were thrown into the water of the harbour by the Plymouth men, enthusiastically assisted by Zulu Joe.

Meanwhile, Sally was busy searching the crowd for Ethan.

Ethan's father and brother had been prominent in the fighting, but Sally had seen no sign of the youngest member of the Shields family. She had become increasingly concerned, until she saw his head appear above the edge of the wharf, as he shinned up the ladder from the Belgian fishing boat.

Greatly relieved, Sally hurried towards him, but she was almost bowled over by one of the last of the Belgian fishermen trying to make good his escape. As the big man reached the ladder, he spotted Ethan and drew back his heavily booted foot with the intention of kicking the younger man clear.

Scarcely more than an arm's length away, Sally screamed a warning to Ethan. At the same time she flew at the Belgian fisherman, who was now balanced on one leg, in readiness for a kick to Ethan's head. Sally hit the fisherman with all her might, just as Ethan jerked his head to one side. The kick struck him only a glancing blow to the side of his head and he was able to maintain his grip on the ladder with little difficulty.

The Belgian fisherman was less fortunate. Shouting in terror and with arms flailing, he lost his balance and disappeared from view, to land with a sickening thud on the deck of the fishing boat.

Sally hardly noticed. As she helped Ethan to the safety of the wharf, she demanded anxiously, 'Are you all right? Your head . . . ?'

'His foot hardly touched me,' Ethan reassured her. 'But it would have been a very different story if you hadn't been near.'

At that moment Henry Shields hurried across to them. Putting an arm across Sally's shoulders, he said, 'I saw what you did, girl. I don't know if Ethan realises it, but you've probably saved his life. If the kick hadn't finished him, the fall certainly would have.'

Sally had known very few genuine and spontaneous gestures of affection during her lifetime, and she experienced a strange mixture of pleasure and embarrassment.

In a bid to cover her confusion, she said, 'Should we go and find out whether the Belgian was badly hurt?'

'Not unless you want to go to Belgium in their place. He and the others deserve everything that's happened to them. Look over there.'

He pointed to where Captain Eva had gathered together the rescued girls in the shadows of a nearby warehouse. Sally counted seventeen in total. The Salvation Army women were comforting the bewildered and frightened girls, two of whom were in a state of near-hysteria.

Sally, Ethan and some of the Plymouth fishermen made their way to where Eva knelt beside a noisily sobbing young girl. When Sally asked hesitantly whether the girl was going to be all right, Eva glanced up at her and answered, fiercely, 'No, she's never going to be "all right". Not for as long as she lives.' The anger leaving her momentarily, she added more gently, 'But, thanks to you, that's likely to be a whole lot longer than it would otherwise have been.'

Shifting her glance from Sally to Henry Shields and the Plymouth fishermen standing silently behind him, she said, 'You performed a wonderful service tonight, on the side of the Lord.' Pointing to the still weeping girl, she asked, 'Do you know how old she is?' Without waiting for a reply the vehemence returned to her voice as she said, 'She's eleven years old and has already suffered more violence than most women will experience in a lifetime.'

Her words provoked an angry murmur from the fishermen who had heard her words. But Eva had more to say, 'Oh, don't think this is anything unusual in this great country of ours. She's the youngest of them here tonight – but only just. Two of the girls are twelve and five are thirteen years of age. Not one is older than fifteen. We've dealt with the Belgian fishermen in the way they deserve, but there are many others involved in this disgusting trade. It should really be a task for the courts to deal with. The men who have brutalised this young girl deserve to be put away in a prison for a very long time – and they're still here, in Plymouth.'

'You're already too late for that,' declared Henry Shields, looking over her shoulder. 'The Belgian crew have slipped their boat's moorings. They're on their way home. Without them you'd never get a conviction.'

'We'll see about that,' Eva said fiercely. 'Far too many young girls are suffering at the hands of these people. I'll not rest until I've put an end to this vile trade, once and for all.'

11

When Captain Eva was satisfied all the rescued girls had recovered sufficiently, she set off with them to the Salvation Army headquarters, which was close to Central Hall.

They were escorted by many of the men and women who had taken part in the battle for their freedom. The fishermen now felt a proprietorial interest in the welfare of the girls they had rescued.

The men had actually discovered twenty-one girls on board, but surprisingly four had chosen to remain on the boat. It seemed they were not entirely averse to the way of life they knew would be their lot in Belgium. One actually told her would-be rescuers that she considered it preferable to a lifetime working as a household drudge in England.

'What will happen to these girls now?' Sally asked Eva, indicating the girls who straggled along the road in comparative silence. The excitement of their dramatic rescue had given way to an appreciation of their present uncertain situation.

'They'll stay with Captain Wardle and his wife for tonight. He's the officer in charge of the Plymouth corps of the Salvation Army. He lives at the headquarters – it's really no more than a large loft in Central Street that used to be the Army's meeting place. There'll be plenty of room for everyone there, although we'll need to try to find them some bedding.'

'They won't be able to stay there forever,' said Ethan, who had been listening to the conversation.

'Of course not,' agreed Captain Eva. 'No doubt many of the girls will wish to return home. Unfortunately, some have no home they can return to. I'll try to find respectable domestic posts for them.'

'What about the eleven-year-old?' asked Sally, referring to the girl whose shoulders still heaved every few steps, as she sobbed out her pain and misery.

'Poor Rachel. She poses a considerable problem. I'll take her home to stay with me until she feels able to put this ordeal behind her. It's even possible I can use what's happened to her to benefit others.'

'How?' Sally was sceptical. 'By having Mother Darling and her son locked up for what they've done? That won't put a stop to what's happened tonight, will it? There are too many others like them, you've said so yourself.'

'You're right, of course, Sally – and not only in Plymouth, either. There are men and women just like them in Portsmouth, Exeter, Bristol – and a great many more in London. Unfortunately, no action is taken by the authorities to put an end to what is going on. One of the problems is that so many of the girls have no one to whom they can turn for help. No one who cares what happens to them. And those who have are often so ashamed of what's happened they won't talk about it – to anyone. I can't say I entirely blame them. Those very, very few who do lodge a complaint despair when the police take no action to help them. All too often the sympathies of the police seem to be with the brothel keepers. At least, that was my experience in London.'

Captain Eva's chin set in an expression that Sally would come to know well. 'I intend to change that one day – and change the age of consent too. At thirteen a girl is a mere child. Far, far too young to be dragged into the vilest trade imaginable.'

The spacious loft 'home' of Salvation Army Captain James Wardle was a huge roof space, which extended the full length of a disused warehouse. It would provide ample dormitory-type accommodation for the rescued girls.

However, as Captain Eva had anticipated, there was a desperate shortage of bedding and it was a cold night.

Despite the lateness of the hour an immediate call went out to all the Salvation Army families in the area. They were asked to donate a blanket, sheet or even a cushion to serve as a pillow.

Ethan was one of those able to help. On his way home to fetch a couple of blankets, he found the fishermen around the quay still excitedly discussing the events of the night with their colleagues.

Ethan explained to them the latest problem and within minutes men and boys were hurrying to their homes to collect contributions for the unfortunate girls.

Half an hour later, Ethan was pushing a handcart laden with a variety of bedding through the streets of Plymouth, bound for the home of Captain James Wardle.

After the delivery, he and Sally were walking back to the Barbican together, through the near-deserted early morning streets of Plymouth, discussing the events of the past few hours.

'Those girls have a great deal to thank you for, Sally,' declared Ethan. 'If you hadn't been so determined to do something about what you suspected was going on at Mother Darling's, they would all be on their way to Belgium now. I doubt if they would ever have seen England again.'

When Sally made no immediate reply, he continued, 'I'm grateful to you too. If it hadn't been for you I'd have had my head kicked in by that Belgian. My pa reckons you saved my life. He was telling Ma all about it when I went home to collect the blankets. She said I must bring you home, so she can meet you.'

'She probably won't be quite so pleased with me when she learns it was me who stirred up all the trouble in the first place,' said Sally.

'What sort of a thing is that to say? You're the heroine of the Barbican tonight – and rightly so. There's not one of us fishermen who doesn't think so.'

*   *   *

Sally might have been a heroine that night to the fishermen and the girls preparing for bed in the Salvation Army loft in Central Street, but there was one man in Plymouth who thought very differently.

Sid Darling had been drinking in a public house in Union Street when a rumour began to circulate about a fracas at Shepherd's Wharf, involving Plymouth and Belgian fishermen.

Sid Darling hurried off to learn the truth of what had happened but he found Shepherd's Wharf deserted and the Belgian trawler gone.

Returning to the Barbican public house, he listened to the excited chatter around him. It did not take him long to discover what had taken place.

But although he now knew the sequence of events that had occurred, he had heard nothing to explain what had led to the disruption of an arrangement that had worked smoothly on many previous occasions. He needed to talk it over with his mother, as a matter of some urgency.

His route home took him close to Central Hall. As he drew near he saw a crowd of people approaching him, talking animatedly. Among them was a number of men and women wearing Salvation Army uniforms.

In view of the events of the night, he thought it prudent to draw back into the shadows of a deep doorway and allow the group to go on their way without noticing him.

None of the party observed him as they passed by, chatting excitedly. He was about to leave the doorway when he saw two others pushing an empty handcart along the road towards him.

Remaining in the doorway as they passed by, he recognised Sally – and the answer to the question that had been troubling him all evening became immediately clear.

He now realised who had been responsible for interfering with the girls on the boat and putting him at risk of arrest. She had also cost him a great deal of money and might have put an end to a very lucrative business that had taken him a long time to set up.

Sid Darling's formidable reputation owed a great deal to the fact that he never allowed anyone who slighted him in any way to remain unpunished.

He would not let such a reputation be put at risk by a mere slip of a girl. He would teach her a lesson she would never forget.

12

⚜

At the shop the following morning, Sally told Grace Philpott what had happened on Shepherd's Wharf, deliberately playing down her own part in the proceedings.

The kind-hearted shopkeeper immediately insisted that Sally's first errand of the day should be to take two dozen pies to the Salvation Army's loft headquarters.

'Two dozen?' Alfie had listened to Sally's account of the night's events with tight-lipped disapproval. His displeasure was not aimed at Sally, but at the fact that such a thing should have occurred in Plymouth. However, he now voiced a protest at his wife's spontaneous generosity. 'Sally said there were only seventeen girls. Why send two dozen?'

'Don't you think some of those Salvation Army people who are helping the girls would appreciate something nice to start the day with too? They've certainly done enough to earn a treat. I tell you, Alfie, I've got a lot of time for these people. They don't preach one thing, then go off and do another. Nor do they look down their noses at them poor unfortunates most other religious don't want to know about.'

Grace faced him, hands on hips, daring him to argue with her.

There were occasions when Alfie could successfully argue with Grace, and others when he could not. This was one of the latter. He retreated to the kitchen, grumbling quietly to himself.

Returning her attention to Sally, Grace said positively, 'Two dozen pies it is. When you see this Captain whatever-her-name-is, you tell her if she needs any extra blankets tonight, I've got a couple she's very welcome to.'

When Sally left the shop with a basket containing the hot pies over her arm, Alfie was still complaining that his wife's generosity would one day prove to be the ruination of their business.

Captain Eva, Captain Wardle and their helpers were delighted with Grace's gift. They and their charges tucked into them with great enthusiasm right away.

Sally remained with Captain Eva and the girls while they ate. 'They seem a lot happier this morning,' she commented, as the girls chattered noisily, many of them sitting on the floor as they ate.

'That's because half of them will be given the money to return home today.' Less cheerfully, she added, 'They're the lucky ones who have come to no harm as a result of what's happened to them. Some of the others have. Even so, by the end of the week a few of those will have decided to go home anyway, saying nothing to their friends and families about any of this. The remainder either have no homes to go back to or are too ashamed ever to face their families again.'

'What will happen to them?' Sally was genuinely concerned. Remembering what the Salvation Army captain had said the night before, she added, 'Do you think you *will* be able to find work for them?'

Captain Eva shrugged unhappily. 'That's why I've been sent to Plymouth, to take care of girls such as these. If I can only find a house for the Army to buy, or rent, I'll be able to look after them and others and put their lives back together.'

For a while, Sally said nothing. She wondered how different her own life might have been had there been someone like Captain Eva to help Ruth earn a respectable living in order to provide for them.

She was still deep in her own thoughts when Eva said, 'It's poor Rachel I'm really concerned about. She's so young. After this experience it will be a long while before she trusts anyone again. She showed a great deal of spirit when she attracted your attention, but that seems to have gone. She's been brutally treated, poor girl.'

'Where is she now?'

'She isn't here,' explained the Salvation Army captain. 'I took her home last night to the rooms I rent. I thought she needed special care. I was quite right. Twice during the night she woke screaming and her sobbing was pitiful. But she was asleep when I left her this morning. One of the Army girls who was with us last night is staying there with her.'

'Does she have a family to go back to?'

'No one close enough to care about her.' Eva was unable to keep the bitterness she felt from her voice. 'Her father was killed soldiering. When her mother died a year later, she was put in a workhouse, in Oxford. It was the workhouse master who saw the advertisement in a newspaper, asking for young girls to go into domestic service. He promptly packed her off without making any enquiries about those who had placed the advertisement.'

She had finished eating now. Standing up, she brushed a crumb from her plain black uniform dress and added, 'Not that it would have made very much difference if he had. I doubt if the advertisement can be traced to Mother Darling. Rachel and the others were taken to Mary Street from a house just outside Plymouth. It sounds to me as though the house was rented on a temporary basis and used for the sole purpose of deceiving young girls into believing they were being offered legitimate employment.'

'So there are more people than Sid and Mother Darling involved in this?'

'Oh yes, Sally. Very many more – and not only in Plymouth. The sale of young girls to brothels, especially foreign brothels, is a well-organised and highly profitable business. There is so much money involved it's proving very, very difficult to stamp out this vile trade.'

Sally would like to have learned more from the Salvation Army captain but she remembered, somewhat belatedly, that she was employed by Grace and Alfie Philpott to deliver their pies.

Standing up, she said, 'I must get back to work. Can I call and speak to Rachel after I've finished this evening?'

'Of course. There's an important meeting being held at Central Hall this evening. I'll bring Rachel with me.'

As Sally left and was clattering down the rather rickety outside wooden staircase that led from the loft, Captain Eva called after her, 'Please thank the pie-shop owners for us. Tell them they will be in our prayers today. They are truly Christian people.'

13

That evening, Sally hurried to complete her chores as Ruth picked unenthusiastically at her supper.

'You're in a great hurry tonight, our Sal. Are you meeting that young man of yours?'

'I doubt it. It's been a fine day, he'll have been out fishing. No, I'm meeting up with the girl I was telling you about. The one who caused all the fuss at Mother Darling's and started everything off last night.'

Ruth had still been awake when Sally had returned home in the early hours of the morning, and she had listened to her sister's excited account of all that had happened.

Ruth's light-hearted mood vanished and she frowned. 'You did what needed doing, Sal, but I wish to heaven you hadn't got mixed up in it in the first place. If Sid Darling ever finds out it was you who had them girls rescued, you'll be in more trouble than you've ever known before. There's no such thing as "forgive and forget" where he's concerned. No one who's crossed him has ever got away with it. All the girls on the streets are scared stiff of him – and with just cause.'

'Then we'll just have to hope he never finds out,' replied Sally, with more bravado than she felt. 'Now, is there anything else I can get you before I go?'

'No, I've got everything I want. Everything except my health.

Try not to be too late tonight. I'll be lying here worrying about you.'

Although Sally had not expected to meet Ethan that evening, she was delighted to see him coming towards her as she turned out of Pin's Lane. With Ruth's warning on her mind, she was relieved too.

When she expressed surprise that he was not out fishing, he grinned happily. 'We put out early this morning and had hardly left harbour when we ran into a huge shoal of pilchards. Within a couple of hours we'd taken so many fish the *Mermaid* was in danger of sinking under the weight. We were the first boat back to the fish quay and so got a really good price for our catch. Not only that, Pa reckons we might be lucky enough to find the same shoal tomorrow if this weather holds. He says this could well be the best Christmas ever for the family.'

Realising he had not stopped talking since they had met up, he asked, 'Where are you off to now? Anywhere that I can come too?'

'Central Hall. Captain Eva is bringing Rachel there to meet me. I can't see any reason why you shouldn't come. You did as much as anyone to help her last night.'

It was a fine evening and Ethan's happy chatter made the distance from Pin's Lane to Central Hall seem far shorter than it actually was. Sally had never known Ethan to talk quite so much before. His shyness with her seemed to have completely disappeared.

Although he made frequent references to the drama of the previous night, much of his talk was of Christmas, which was now only ten days away.

Sally listened to him without saying anything. Christmas was not a time of the year she particularly enjoyed. It always served to bring home to Ruth and Sally that they had no family with whom to share the festivities. It also tended to disrupt the routine of life about them.

'What are you doing for Christmas?'

Ethan put the unexpected question to Sally as they neared Central Hall.

'Me? I'll no doubt be working until late on Christmas Eve, but with the money I earn I should be able to buy something nice for Ruth to eat. Then I'll spend most of Christmas Day looking after her.'

Some of Ethan's effervescence seeped away. 'Oh! I'd forgotten that you have Ruth to look after.'

When Sally looked at him questioningly, he said, 'My ma said I should ask you if you'd like to come and eat with us on Christmas Day.'

The invitation took Sally by surprise. Ethan had mentioned the previous night that his mother had expressed a wish to meet her – but to go to a strange house and sit down to a meal with Mr and Mrs Shields and their six sons . . . ! The thought of it terrified her.

'I . . . I just can't, Ethan. I couldn't leave Ruth. She always looks forward to having me at home with her. Especially on a day like that.'

It wasn't quite the truth, but it was the best excuse she could think of on the spur of the moment.

'Of course. I should have realised you would have to take care of Ruth. It won't be much of a Christmas for you, though, will it?'

Sally shrugged. 'It doesn't make much difference, we never do anything special at Christmas, anyway – although this one will be better than most, now I'm earning good money.'

'Don't you ever have a Christmas tree . . . or decorations, things like that?'

'No.'

Sally had vague memories of a room festooned with decorations, but that had been when she was very small and her mother was still alive.

'Sally . . .' Ethan spoke hesitantly, 'I know you need to be at home for most of the day with Ruth, but . . . will you come to my house to meet Ma some time during the day? Even if it's only to say "Hello" and "Goodbye"? She really would like to meet you – and I'd like you to meet her, too.'

Sally thought about it for a few moments. She was aware

that Ethan was deeply disappointed she would not be having a meal with his family – and she did not like hurting him.

'All right.'

Once her acceptance was out, it surprised her almost as much as it did Ethan, but there was no doubting his delight.

'You will? When? I mean . . . what time shall I tell Ma you'll be there?'

'I can't tell you that just yet. It depends on how Ruth is, really.'

'Of course, but the time doesn't matter. Ma will understand – and you needn't worry about being the only girl there. My second-oldest brother, Albert, is married. He and his wife will be at the house for most of the day. Joe's girlfriend will probably be there as well. Joe's the next youngest to me,' he explained, still hardly able to contain his delight.

Sally was not at all certain she wanted to meet other young women in the presence of his family. She was fully aware the clothes she owned would not stand comparison with those worn by most girls of her age, but she said nothing. A few minutes later they reached Central Hall.

14

'But Captain Eva asked me to come here tonight to meet her.'

Sally spoke with growing frustration. A burly, uniformed Salvation Army 'soldier' was on duty at the inner entrance to Central Hall. He refused to allow Sally and Ethan to enter.

'I'm sorry but I've already told you, Captain Cassington isn't here and you can't just walk in the hall in the middle of the talk. It's being given by a senior officer from London. He's a *very* important man. A commissioner – and a personal friend of General Booth!'

The Salvation Army man was adamant. Captain Eva was not in the hall; he did not know where she was – and he was not going to allow Sally and Ethan to enter while the important speaker was addressing his audience.

Suddenly, a young uniformed woman hurried from the hall looking flustered. She was one of the women who had been playing a tambourine on Shepherd's Wharf the previous evening. When she saw Sally, her expression showed great relief.

'I'm glad you're here. I thought I might have missed you. I was so excited at being introduced to Commissioner Hubble, I quite forgot I had a message for you from Captain Eva. I really am sorry.'

'Why isn't she here? Has something happened? Is it to do with the girls we rescued?'

'It is, but it's nothing bad. In fact, it's very, very exciting. She's been given a house to use as a refuge for them. She's spent the whole of the day moving them in. That's why she isn't here tonight, even though it's a special meeting. She felt getting the girls settled in was more important. She wants you to go there to see her.'

Handing over a scrap of paper, the Salvation Army girl said, 'Here's the address. It's on the Barbican, in Palace Lane.'

Sally knew the small street well. It was on the very edge of the Barbican. The houses there were old – very old – but also extremely large.

'Shall I come with you?' Ethan asked hopefully.

'I don't see why not,' Sally replied. 'Captain Eva was happy enough to have you around last night. I'm sure she'll be pleased to see you again.'

The house was very large indeed and, to Sally's mind, frighteningly impressive inside. When she and Ethan entered, they were immediately aware of an aroma of carbolic soap and furniture polish.

Eva looked very pleased to see them. As she held the door wide for them to enter, she said happily, 'Come in. Come in, both of you. Isn't this absolutely marvellous? Have you ever seen such a splendid house?'

'You said nothing about it last night. I thought you were still looking for a place.'

'So I was – then. But Commissioner Hubble came to see me this morning, at our headquarters. He's the man who's talking at Central Hall tonight. He arrived from London yesterday and stayed the night with a great friend of his, a member of a wealthy Methodist family. They'd heard what had happened at Shepherd's Wharf and wanted to meet the girls. When they asked what would happen to them now, I told them the reason I'd been sent here by General Booth. I said that if only I could find a suitable house I could take care of the girls, and others like them. I sincerely believe God must have been listening to my prayers and sent Commissioner Hubble's friend here to me. He owns several houses in Plymouth and this one just happened to be empty! He was so moved by the plight of the girls, he said I could have the house, rent free, for as long as I need it and we were all able to move in right away!'

Eva clapped her hands together in an expression of sheer joy. 'Isn't it absolutely wonderful? The house is only partly furnished right now, but it's a veritable palace. Of course, we're going to need one or two extra things. There aren't enough beds or chairs at the moment, but God will provide them. I just know he will. Honestly, Sally, I could sing for sheer joy.'

Sally knew very little of God, and religion had never seriously encroached upon her life. As a result, she felt vaguely uncomfortable with Captain Eva's fervour, but there was more to come.

'Of course, I realise it's not only God I have to thank for everything – but you too, Sally. If you hadn't responded to poor Rachel's cries for help, the girls wouldn't have been rescued and this magnificent house wouldn't be ours.'

'Ethan helped too,' said Sally, embarrassed at being singled out for such praise.

'He most certainly did,' agreed Eva. 'As he's here, he can help again. The owner of the house said there are more bits and pieces of furniture in the loft. Ethan can climb up there for us and see exactly what there is—'

'Where's Rachel? Is she here too?'

Sally put the questions before Captain Eva had the chance to begin eulogising about her once more.

'Yes.' Some of Eva's happiness ebbed away. 'I'd like to say she was grateful enough to want to thank you, but right now she's blaming the whole world for what's happened to her. She'll get over it, of course, but she *is* being rather difficult, poor girl.'

They were at the foot of a stout staircase, which led to the first floor of the house, and Eva called up, 'Rachel! Come on down. Sally's here to meet you.'

A few minutes later a slight but very pretty girl appeared at the top of the stairs. Her pale, drawn face was bruised, her lip was swollen and she had a particularly nasty graze on one cheekbone.

She came down the stairs slowly and uncertainly, her dark eyes never leaving Sally's face.

As soon as she reached the foot of the stairs, she blurted out, fiercely, 'Why didn't you do something to help me when you first came to Mother Darling's? Why did you leave me there so . . . so they could do things to me?'

Her eyes filled with tears and she turned away. Then, abruptly, she rushed back up the stairs, stumbling once or twice on the way so great was her hurry to escape the small crowd gathered in the hallway.

Sally was distressed by the other girl's words, but Eva put an arm about her shoulders and hugged her. 'You mustn't take any notice, Sally. Rachel really did suffer greatly, both at the house and on the boat. She is full of anger and wants someone to blame. It will take a long time before she can get things into perspective and is able to face the world again.'

'Poor girl,' Sally was moved to tears. 'She did so much, too. She's the one everyone should be thanking for the rescue. She was determined the Darlings weren't going to get away with what they were up to and she put herself in danger by kicking up such a fuss.'

'You both played a very important part,' said Eva. 'So too did Ethan. I'll go up and speak to Rachel in a few minutes, but after all that's happened I think we deserve at least a *little* celebration.'

Calling to one of the girls who was standing nearby, she said, 'Ethel, put the kettle on, we're going to have a cup of tea. It's time to cut into that cake Mrs Wardle sent for us, too. Afterwards we'll give thanks to the Lord for the part He has played in helping us.'

15

Rachel Green did not come down from her room again that evening. After a brief prayer session with the girls and Ethan, Eva took tea and cake to Rachel in her room, and remained there with her.

Meanwhile, Sally stood chatting to some of the girls on the top-floor landing, while Ethan handed down furniture from the loft. Gradually, as the girls talked, Sally was able to build up a picture of how they had been trapped by the Darlings.

Most of the young girls were either members of large families whose parents were finding it hard to make ends meet or had lost one of their parents. The prospect of having a daughter placed in domestic service – no longer a drain on the family resources and able at some time in the near future to contribute something, however small, to the family income – was a very desirable state of affairs.

Many of the girls had been overjoyed to leave poor, over-crowded homes to make the exciting journey to Plymouth and take up new employment, hopefully in a large town.

All agreed they had been surprised when they arrived at their destination to find an isolated house in the country, neglected to the point of dereliction. Another cause for concern was the couple who were waiting to greet them. Coarse-mannered and dressed in cheap clothes, they were hardly the type of employers they had been expecting.

The couple explained this away by telling the girls that they were running an agency, supplying servants to wealthy households in the Plymouth area. They added spice to their story by declaring that some of the girls might very soon find themselves working for titled employers.

By late afternoon there were twenty-one girls in the house, and they were given a meal and some wine to drink.

Rachel did not like wine, but did not like to say so. When the couple were not looking, she gave her drink to one of the other girls.

It was soon apparent that there was something wrong with the wine. All the girls except Rachel were falling around in a state resembling a drunken stupor, unable to control their limbs or marshal their thoughts.

The woman explained their condition away to Rachel by saying the wine was from France. As well as being some of the finest that money could buy, it was also far more potent than folk in England were used to.

Rachel had not been entirely satisfied with the explanation, but she was a very young and inexperienced country girl. She could think of no reason why the woman should lie to her, or want to harm the girls.

Late that evening, an enclosed van arrived at the house to convey the girls to Mary Street, in Plymouth, where they arrived very late at night.

They remained here in the dubious care of the Darlings until the following evening. During this time they were locked in upstairs rooms and given food and drink that kept them in a state that one of the girls described as 'dopey'.

From what they overheard later, it seemed that the plan had not involved the girls going to Mary Street at all. They should have boarded the Belgian fishing boat direct from the house outside Plymouth but, unfortunately for their kidnappers, the boat had been delayed by adverse winds in the Channel.

Rather than risk the long return journey to the large house outside Plymouth, it was decided to take the girls to Mary Street.

Locked in a room at the home of the Darlings, Rachel had belatedly realised this was unlikely to be the beginning of a career in domestic service. It was now that she made the dramatic attempt to escape, which had been witnessed by Sally.

The escape attempt had cost her dearly. Carried to an upstairs room, she had been viciously beaten, then raped, by Sid Darling. A further horrific assault had been carried out by one of Sid Darling's accomplices, who was helping him to guard the girls.

But Rachel's nightmare was not over. Her ordeal had been repeated yet again when she had been taken on board the Belgian fishing boat. Some of the other girls were also raped by the Belgian sailors, most of whom had been drinking heavily since reaching Plymouth.

Their torment did not come to an end until the dramatic arrival of the Plymouth fishermen.

Walking home with Ethan later that evening, Sally repeated what the girls had told her, adding that she could not blame Rachel for her bitter outburst when they had been introduced.

'It's understandable,' agreed Ethan. 'But I'm sure that when she's recovered from all this, she'll realise there was nothing more you could have done. You certainly couldn't have done anything any quicker.'

'I don't know,' Sally said unhappily. 'Perhaps I should have made a fuss when I was in Mary Street. Got the neighbours to help, or something.'

'If they'd wanted to do something to help they'd have done it long ago,' Ethan declared firmly. 'They must have known what's been going on in the house. They're not blind, or stupid. The trouble is, everyone is scared of Sid Darling. So scared that he could murder someone in the middle of the street and nobody would "see" anything he could be put away for. If you'd made any sort of fuss at the time you'd have found yourself on the boat with them. Then there'd have been no rescue.'

'You're probably right,' Sally agreed reluctantly. 'But it doesn't make me feel a whole lot better. I'll go back to the house tomorrow night. Perhaps Rachel will speak to me then. I'd like to be able to help her, if I can. She's got no one else.'

'She's got Captain Eva now,' Ethan pointed out, 'and she won't give up until Rachel is all right again. Happily, all the girls are safe now. Let's talk about something happier. You *will* come to our house some time on Christmas Day? I can tell my ma tonight . . . ?'

16

Grace Philpott listened with increasing horror as Sally repeated the stories told to her by the girls the previous evening.

'It . . . it's *unbelievable*!' She almost exploded with fury when Sally had ended the tale.

Turning to her husband, her distress clear on her face, she asked, 'Can you believe such things could go on in Plymouth without there being some sort of outcry, Alfie?'

'There are a whole lot of things going on in the world you know nothing about, Grace – and you're none the worse off for that.' Alfie shrugged. 'It would be different if there was something you could do about it, but there's not.'

Grace looked at her husband for so long he began to feel uncomfortable. However, her next words indicated that he had not been the subject of her thoughts.

'That's just where you're wrong, Alfie Philpott. There *is* something I can do, and I'm going to do it. Are you forgetting that Percy Mallett is my uncle?'

Alfie's startled expression was an indication that he *had* forgotten. 'You haven't had anything to do with your uncle Percy for years!'

'All the more reason why he should take notice when I go to see him now. After all, he's an alderman and chairman of the Police Authority. It's his *duty* to do something about such goings-on.'

Alfie realised his wife was about to embark on a course of action that would most probably incur the enmity of a man as dangerous as Sid Darling.

'Now, Grace, this isn't anything you should get involved in. We're running a pie shop. The goodwill of our customers is important to us.'

'Not if the customers are like the Darlings, it's not. We can do without their sort. There are plenty of the other kind who will approve of anything that can be done to stamp out this sort of thing.'

Addressing Sally, she said, 'I want you to introduce me to this Captain Eva – and I'd like to meet the poor young girl who has suffered so much because of the Darlings, too. You and I will go along to their house this evening. I'll cook something special for the girls this afternoon. We can take it along with us. I might not be able to do anything about what's happened to the poor souls, but I'll make sure they don't go hungry.'

A few minutes later Sally left the Philpotts' shop with a laden basket, doing her best to ignore the glare directed at her by Alfie.

That evening, Grace and Sally were let in to the Barbican Refuge by one of the girls. She told them Captain Eva and the others were at prayer in the large lounge.

While Grace was being shown to the lounge, Sally took the food they had brought to the kitchen to be reheated. Then she laid out plates in readiness for the evening meal. Had Grace not been so generous the girls would have eaten bread and cheese. They would welcome the improved menu.

As Sally made her own way to the prayer meeting, the occupants broke into a rousing hymn. When she entered the room she was astonished to see Grace singing with a gusto that rivalled Captain Eva's.

She took her place on a seat beside her employer. When the hymn came to an end, Grace whispered enthusiastically, 'That was a Wesleyan hymn. I used to sing it in chapel when I was a young girl. I'd forgotten how much I enjoyed those services.'

Captain Eva led her small congregation in a couple of simple prayers and the service came to an end. Sally introduced the two women and, while the girls rushed off to the kitchen to enjoy their unexpected treat, Grace explained to the Salvation Army officer her reasons for coming to the house.

'When Sally told me of all that had happened I found it difficult to believe such things could go on in our city. Those poor girls – especially that young Rachel! Which one is she?'

'Rachel didn't come down to the meeting,' explained Eva. 'She suffered a great deal more than any of the others. It's going to take her quite some time to get over all that's happened to her. She's in a small room of her own. I let her stay there.'

'Poor child!' Grace said, with genuine sympathy. 'I would like to meet her before I leave. But my main reason for coming here is to see if we can't make certain we have the two Darlings arrested and discuss what might be done to prevent anything like this happening again.'

'If we could have the Darlings arrested and convicted for what they've done it would be a very important step along the road to doing away with the trade in young girls,' said Eva. 'But there is an inexplicable reluctance on the part of the police to bring it to an end. We've tried on many occasions in London. I'm told things are no different here.'

'Then we must *make* them different,' Grace said positively. She told the Salvation Army captain about her uncle.

Grace's enthusiasm for the crusade she intended taking up matched that of Captain Eva. Soon the two women were in animated conversation.

Sally was on her way to join the other girls in the kitchen when Eva called after her.

'Sally, would you like to take something to eat up to Rachel in her room?'

Remembering the last occasion the two girls had met, Sally asked, 'Wouldn't it be better if one of the other girls took it up? Seeing me seems to upset her.'

Eva shook her head. 'Rachel and I have talked about that. She realises her outburst was quite out of order. In fact, I think she might like to see you and thank you for what you did, instead of blaming you for what couldn't be done.'

17

Sally tapped on the door of Rachel's room with trepidation. She needed to knock three times before receiving a reply.

'Who is it?'

'It's Sally Harrup. I've brought something for you to eat.'

After a few moments of silence, the reply came back through the closed door, 'I don't want anything.'

'You wouldn't say that if you knew what it is. Grace Philpott has cooked it 'specially with you in mind.'

It was doubtful Rachel had any idea who 'Grace Philpott' was, but Sally was correct in thinking the mention of the name would tantalise the other girl enough for her to open the door.

When Rachel stood in the doorway, the room behind her was in darkness, but there was enough light from the low-burning gaslight on the landing for Sally to see that the young girl had been crying.

'Who's this Grace Philpott – and how does she know about me?'

'Grace is the woman I work for. She knows about you because I've told her. Grace is downstairs with Captain Eva right now. They're talking about having Sid Darling arrested for what he did to you and so put a stop to what he and his friends are doing with other girls.'

'I know what I'd like to do to *him*,' Rachel said fiercely.

'No one would blame you, whatever you did,' Sally agreed, relieved that Rachel was talking to her. 'I feel the same about him, and he's only ever *looked* at me.'

Sally was standing outside the room carrying a meal that would not have disgraced the finest restaurants in the city. There were fruit tarts, too, which Grace had cooked as a special treat for the girls.

'Can I come in . . . ?'

Rachel stood to one side and Sally entered the room.

'Do you have a light in here?'

'There are some matches somewhere.'

A few moments later Sally could hear matches being rattled in a box; one was scraped into life and the gaslight fixed to a bracket on the wall burst into life with a pop. Looking around the small room, the crumpled bedclothes indicated to Sally that Rachel had been lying on the bed fully clothed.

As Rachel straightened the bedclothes, Sally said, 'Here, eat this before it gets too cold.'

Rachel dutifully sat down and began picking at the food on the plate. Almost reluctantly, she said, 'This is nice.'

'I told you you'd enjoy it. You must tell Grace. She'll be delighted. She's a softie, really, and she can't wait to meet you. She once had a little girl of her own, but she died when she was only three. I don't think Grace has ever got over it. She can't look at any girl who's anywhere near my age – or yours, come to that – without thinking of how her own little girl would have been, had she lived. It's very sad.'

Rachel carried on eating in silence for a few minutes until, without looking up at Sally, she said, 'I'm sorry I said you hadn't been quick enough to help me. Captain Eva has told me how much you did to help. If you hadn't gone to her I don't know where I'd be . . . Probably in Belgium, I suppose, having men do to me what Sid Darling and the others did . . .'

Rachel's lower lip began to tremble and Sally said hurriedly, 'It's all right, Rachel. Please don't get upset, or you'll upset me too. You don't know how many times I've asked myself what else I might have done to stop all those things happening to you. But . . . I just couldn't have done any more. Honest.'

'I know . . .'

Suddenly Rachel began to cry. Sally took the fork from her hand and put her arms about her, feeling desperately sorry for the distressed and abused young girl.

After Sally had been holding her for some minutes, Rachel pulled away. 'I'm sorry. That wasn't fair on you.'

'You don't have to be sorry . . . for anything. Look, eat up what you can, then we'll go and find Grace. You'll like her, I know you will.'

'All right. I . . . I'll try to finish it, but I doubt if I'll be able to swallow anything right now.'

Despite this statement, Rachel finished much of the meal. Between mouthfuls she questioned Sally about her own life.

When she heard that Sally's mother was dead and she had never known her father, she stared at Sally with an expression of deep sympathy. 'So you're on your own too! How do you manage?'

'I'm not entirely on my own,' admitted Sally. 'I have an older sister who's looked after me since I was seven. But she's very ill and now I need to look after her.'

'Where do you live?'

'We have a room in Pin's Lane.' Remembering that Rachel did not know Plymouth, she explained, 'It's not far from here, close to Sutton harbour – that's where you were when we rescued you.'

'Could I come to see you there some time?'

'Of course you can. I'll take you there myself. Ruth will be pleased to see you – she's my sister. She doesn't have many visitors. I've told her all about you and the others.'

'I'd like that. I'd like us to be friends, too,' she added hesitantly.

Standing up, Rachel crossed the room to look at herself in a small mirror hanging on the wall in a corner of the room. She ran a brush through her hair a couple of times before turning back to Sally, her head held high. 'I'm ready to go and meet this lady now.'

18

Rachel entered the room uncertainly, coaxed by Sally. Looking up, Grace Philpott saw a small and particularly vulnerable young girl, and the shop owner's heart went out to her immediately.

Tears sprung to her eyes as she said, 'My dear soul! You hardly seem old enough to be sent off to domestic service, let alone have all this happen to you. It's too dreadful for words.' She stopped, momentarily, too overcome to say more.

'This is Mrs Philpott,' Captain Eva explained. 'She's been extremely generous in helping to feed you and the other girls. Now she wants to see this Sidney Darling brought before the courts – particularly for what he did to you. If we go ahead it might prove to be a very unpleasant ordeal for you. Because of this, I feel you should be given time to think about it—'

'I don't need any time to think about anything,' Rachel declared vehemently. 'Nothing that's said or done to me now can be as bad as what he's already done. Even hanging would be too good for him.'

'You're quite right,' Grace said emphatically. 'We may not see him hanged, but I'll not rest until he's been sent to prison for a very long time.' Turning to Captain Eva, she asked, 'What's the first thing we need to do?'

'I'll go to the police station in the morning and report what's happened. If we're lucky they'll send someone here to interview Rachel and the others. If they don't show any signs of doing anything, perhaps you'll involve your uncle?'

'I can't wait in the hope that they *might* do something,' retorted Grace. 'I want to *know* they're taking action right now.'

This was the assertiveness Sally had occasionally glimpsed in the shop when Grace was determined to gain her own way with her husband.

Grace continued, 'You go along to the police station this evening and I'll call on Uncle Percy right away. You come with me, Sally. You know as much of what went on as anyone else. You can fill in any gaps about what's happened.' Giving Rachel a sympathetic smile, she said, 'I'll not sleep tonight unless I know something's going to be done. I feel ashamed to know that such things are happening in a respectable town like ours.'

Her expression softened even more as Rachel stood wide-eyed, listening to her. 'Don't you worry, my dear. Nobody's going to harm you again. Not while you've got Captain Eva and me to look after you.'

Returning her attention to Eva, she said, 'I'll be on my way now, but we'll meet again soon. I'd like to say how much I enjoyed what little piece of your service I was able to take part in tonight. It took me back to my childhood chapel days. They were very happy days. Thinking of what these poor young girls have been through has made me realise just how lucky I've been.'

'You're very welcome to come to any of our meetings, either here or in Central Hall,' replied Eva. 'I hope that one day we'll both be able to give thanks together for our achievement in bringing these men to justice.'

The reception given to Captain Eva at the Plymouth police station was all that members of the Salvation Army had come to expect from the police.

Two policemen were behind the desk in the Charge Office. One, a sergeant, was leaning on the counter, writing laboriously in a large, leather-bound ledger, while at the rear of the office a balding constable was busily sorting paper clips, pins and short pencils into separate compartments of a wooden drawer, which had been placed upon a narrow table.

When Eva pushed her way through the double swing doors, the sergeant looked up to see who was entering. He immediately returned his attention to the ledger, ponderously writing, the pen noisily scratching its way across the broad page.

Eva was wearing her Salvation Army uniform, as she always did, no matter where she went, and she was fully aware that this was the reason for the officers' off-handed manner, which verged on rudeness.

She waited patiently for almost five minutes, during which time she was patently ignored by the two policeman. Deciding she had been tolerant for long enough, she said politely, 'I would like to be attended to, if you don't mind.'

Neither policemen replied, although the constable seemed to find something amusing in the situation.

'Will I receive attention here, or shall I make my way along the corridor and find someone more senior to speak to?'

Without looking up, the sergeant said, 'Constable Waller, see what it is this young woman wants.'

'What this "young woman" wants is to see the officer in charge of your police station,' Eva said, more sharply than before. 'I have a serious complaint to make.'

'If it's anything to do with the violence that occurred during the last Salvation Army march through town, you're wasting your time,' said the sergeant. 'All the reports have already gone to the superintendent. Every one of them says the fault lay with the Salvation Army. If you hadn't chosen to march past a building site when the men were enjoying their midday break there would have been no trouble. No doubt the superintendent will ban any future marches. It's not before time, if you ask me.'

'I'm not asking you,' Eva retorted. 'And my coming here has nothing to do with a march. It concerns a far more serious matter – too serious for you to deal with, I should imagine. I wish to report a very serious attack on a young girl – on more than one young girl, in fact. I also have evidence of a trade in procuring young girls and shipping them off to the countries of Europe.'

The pen ceased its abrasive progress across the page and the constable forsook his time-wasting task. Both men were now giving her their full attention, but it was the sergeant who spoke.

'Are you the mother of the child you say was assaulted?'

'She has no mother – or father. She came to me for help.'

'She should have come straight to the police, not to you. Where is she now?'

'She's staying with me,' Eva said warily. She was not sure what action the police sergeant might decide to take.

'I can do nothing unless this girl comes here and makes a complaint personally. It's no good you coming in and giving me a second-hand story about something that might, or might not, have happened.'

'No one is reporting anything to *you*, Sergeant. I'll tell the full story to the officer in charge.'

'Well, seeing as there's no inspector here right now, that makes me the officer in charge – and I say there's nothing to be done until the alleged victim comes and makes a formal complaint, in person.'

'Very well, I'll return in the morning and speak to someone more senior then.'

Eva turned to go.

She had reached the door when the sergeant called to her. 'I suggest you take note of what I said to you about your marches – and about the band too. It's inciting trouble. We don't allow that sort of thing here in Plymouth. You and the others in this so-called "army" of yours can expect to be arrested the next time you take to the streets.'

19

When Eva returned to the Salvation Army house in the Barbican, she was still quietly fuming about the police sergeant's attitude and his refusal to accept the seriousness of her complaint.

Not that it surprised her. All over the country the police adopted a stance towards the Salvation Army that she found entirely incomprehensible. In London she had been present on various occasions when policemen stood doing nothing while a peaceful march of Salvation Army members was viciously broken up by hooligans and paid members of the Skeleton Army.

When faced with such attacks, Salvation Army members were under strict orders not to retaliate. While a few found such a policy impossible to sustain, most succeeded in 'turning the other cheek', even when they suffered severe injuries as a result.

Despite this, when the police finally moved in to break up disturbances, it was usually only Salvation Army members who were arrested and brought before the courts.

The charge against them was, in the main, 'obstruction', or some other trivial offence, but it did not prevent many being given prison sentences.

On the other hand, she could recall no occasion when the ruffians of the Skeleton Army and their supporters had been arrested.

Once inside the Barbican Refuge, Eva was surprised to find Grace had already returned. She was accompanied by Sally and a tall, distinguished-looking man, who was talking earnestly to Rachel.

Grace introduced the man to Eva as her uncle, Percy Mallet.

Taking Eva's hand, the man gave her a brief but friendly smile. 'I, too, briefly held the rank of captain, Miss Cassington. It was during the relief of Lucknow, when real officers were in desperately short supply. Your rank, I believe, was won in the equally unsavoury but far less publicised battlefields of the London streets?'

Releasing her hand, Percy Mallet became more solemn. 'I have just been listening to this unfortunate child's horrific story. I find it difficult to believe that such things can happen in our city.'

'It's happening in a great many cities throughout the land,' Eva replied grimly. 'While we continue to leave law and order in the hands of policemen lacking in vision and compassion I fear it will always be so.'

She told the story of her visit to Plymouth police station and the alderman frowned angrily.

'That sounds very like Sergeant Garrett. He should have been retired years ago. I think he's probably been in the force since it was founded. Plymouth has changed a great deal since then. Unfortunately, Sergeant Garrett hasn't changed with it.' Suddenly brisk, he asked, 'Would you be available to come to police headquarters with me tomorrow morning, say . . . ten o'clock?'

Eva nodded. 'Any time to suit you, if you think it will achieve any purpose.'

'I'll bring a carriage and we'll go and speak to the superintendent who is in charge in the temporary absence of the chief constable. We won't take Rachel, or Sally. When it becomes necessary to interview them, someone can come here.'

Inclining his head at his niece, he said, 'I am most grateful to you for bringing this to my attention, Grace. We really should see more of each other. Why don't you and Alfie come to the house one Sunday evening . . . ?'

Still talking, Percy Mallett walked with Grace from the room.

As he left, Eva turned to the two girls. 'Well! Mrs Philpott has accomplished far more than I have this evening. But it doesn't matter *how* it comes about as long as something is done about Sidney Darling and his friends – and I have a feeling it will now.'

'What's going to happen to me when it's all over?' Rachel asked plaintively. 'Will I have to go away somewhere?'

'Of course not,' Eva replied positively. 'You can stay here for as long as you wish. In fact, I'll be very glad of your help. I have an idea that once word of this affair gets around, we will be very busy here in Plymouth.'

20

Having someone wearing the uniform of an officer of the Salvation Army – especially when that someone was a woman – seated in his office was anathema to Police Superintendent Jeremiah Spindler.

However, he was careful not to allow his feelings to show. As well as being an alderman and chairman of the Police Authority, Percy Mallett was well respected in the Plymouth community and wielded considerable authority.

The senior policeman listened attentively to what the city elder had to say and maintained his silence until Captain Eva had told her story.

'There would appear to be a great many witnesses to the release of these girls from the Belgian fishing boat,' he said. 'Unfortunately, those on board are no longer within our jurisdiction. I presume there are no witnesses to the alleged defilement of this young girl?'

'I hardly think such attacks are carried out in public,' Eva retorted sarcastically. 'I can certainly testify to the girl's acute distress when we rescued her.'

'I have spoken to her too,' said Percy Mallett. 'I am in no doubt whatsoever that she is telling the truth.'

'No doubt you are right, Mr Mallett,' the policeman said. Observing the alderman's expression, he added hurriedly, 'Indeed,

I am certain you are. However, it is essential in such matters to present a case to the court that will leave no doubt in the minds of judge or jury. Where is the girl now?'

'At a house in the Barbican that has been turned over to the Salvation Army. Some of the other girls are with her.'

'When can you bring her to the police station?'

Eva looked quickly at Percy Mallett. Correctly interpreting the message contained in the glance, he said, 'I think it would be better if you were to go along to the house and speak to her there, Superintendent. You will also have the other girls readily available to corroborate her story.'

Superintendent Spindler successfully hid his indignation at the other man's words. He was not in the habit of carrying out such duties personally.

'I'll send along my best inspector to interview these girls and to carry out an investigation of this man Darling. When we're quite certain of our facts I'll have a warrant sworn out for this man's arrest. You can rest assured I will take a personal interest in this matter and it will be pursued vigorously. Very vigorously indeed.'

'Good! We can't have such things going on in our town, can we? I'll leave it in your hands for now, Superintendent. You can be quite certain I too will be taking a keen interest in the progress you make in this disgraceful matter. I sincerely hope we might keep it from becoming public knowledge until you have made the necessary arrests.'

When Percy Mallett set Eva down at the house in Palace Lane, he said, 'I think you might find things will begin to happen now, Miss Cassington.'

'I don't doubt it, Mr Mallett – and I thank you on behalf of the girls. We shall certainly include you in our prayers tonight.'

'Your prayers will always be welcome, but the knowledge that these poor girls are in safe hands is thanks enough. Goodnight, Captain.'

Eva entered the house happy in the belief that she was beginning to succeed in the task for which she had been sent to Plymouth. She also entertained hopes that it might ultimately lead to a greater understanding between the police and the Salvation Army.

Only forty-eight hours after her meeting with Superintendent Spindler, all the hopes Eva had entertained of a change in her fortunes were effectively dashed.

A very efficient police inspector called at the Barbican Refuge and took statements from Rachel and the other girls. He expressed genuine sympathy and promised Captain Eva that Sid Darling would be arrested swiftly and brought to justice for all he had done.

A warrant was duly sworn out for Darling's arrest. However, when the police raided the house in Mary Street he was not there and Mother Darling informed them she had no knowledge of his whereabouts.

She was questioned closely about her part in the offences for which her son was wanted, but she was adamant that he was solely responsible for letting out the upstairs rooms. She claimed she suffered from arthritis in her knees, which prevented her from climbing the stairs, and she had no knowledge of anything that went on there.

Unfortunately, there was nothing in the statements the inspector had taken that would incriminate her, so Mother Darling remained free – at least, for the foreseeable future.

But worse was to come for Captain Eva and the Plymouth corps of the Salvation Army.

That Sunday, she and Captain Wardle were to lead their followers through the streets of Plymouth in what would be the biggest parade they had ever staged in the town. The event had been organised to celebrate the second anniversary of the establishment of the Plymouth movement and had been publicised well in advance.

The local Salvation band, to which Ethan belonged, would be augmented by musicians from the nearby seaside resort of Torquay. They would head a procession of Salvationists gathered from many Devon and Cornwall towns.

However, in view of the publicity the parade had received, it was doubtful it would be allowed to pass off without incident.

The Skeleton Army had become more effectively organised of late. It was even producing its own newspaper, rather unimaginatively called *The Skeleton*, which was distributed throughout the country.

The newspaper had published details of the forthcoming Plymouth march and called upon its own 'soldiers' to come to the town. They were asked to 'help clear the streets of these fanatics and blasphemers who are bringing the Christian religion into ridicule'.

Such an article was a blatant incitement to riot. As such, it was inconceivable that the police were not aware of it. Yet the only action they took was aimed at the Salvation Army. Superintendent Spindler sent a strongly worded letter to Captain Wardle, instructing that the route taken for their march must not include any major thoroughfares. The superintendent warned that any riotous or provocative behviour would not be tolerated.

By now there were only five girls, including Rachel, remaining at the Barbican Refuge. All asked if they might take part in the march. However, Eva refused, insisting they must remain in the house.

When one of the girls questioned her decision, Eva pointed out that they were not soldiers of the Salvation Army. Indeed they had not even asked to be considered as recruits. Furthermore, all were strangers to Plymouth, and if violence erupted – as it undoubtedly would – the parade would be forced to scatter, and not knowing the city, the girls would not know where to run and be at the mercy of the crowd. Eva felt they had suffered enough already.

Consequently, when the day arrived and the soldiers of the Salvation Army were making their way to the gathering point outside Central Hall, none of the girls was with them. For this, at least, Eva would later be grateful.

21

Some indication of what the parading members of the Salvation Army could expect came even before they formed up outside their headquarters in readiness to commence the march.

As uniformed men and women arrived at the entrance to Central Street they were heckled and jostled by a growing number of ruffians. Singing, jeering and shouting obscenities at the Salvationists, the hooligans singled out the young, uniformed girls as particular targets.

The two Salvation Army captains leading the march went among their members, doing their best to bolster morale by reminding the 'soldiers' that they were fighting the Lord's battle, on His behalf.

Meanwhile, inside Central Hall, more experienced Army colleagues were laying out bandages, salve, soap and towels, knowing all would be needed before the day was over.

Eventually, some three hundred uniformed Salvationists had gathered. They were standing about in nervous but determined groups when Captain Wardle called for them to form ranks. When this order was carried out to his satisfaction, the band struck up a suitably stirring martial tune and the celebration march got under way.

The jeering crowd at the end of the street was more than a hundred strong now. Although it was noisy, it made no attempt to prevent the procession, bound for Plymouth's famous Hoe, from leaving Central Street. Indeed, it parted to allow the Salvationist through, falling in behind them.

The Salvation Army carried banners of blue, red and gold. Held on high, the colours represented the purity of Heaven, the blood of Christ; and the fire of the Holy Ghost.

The opposition had banners too. Made from black cloth, each carried a crude painting of a skeleton.

'What are they playing at?' Eva spoke in an aside to Captain Wardle as the Skeleton Army fell in behind the marching Salvationists. The two officers were marching side by side, between the band and the uniformed marchers. 'Why did they let us through and not attack us there and then?'

'We are too close to home.' The senior captain had taken part in marches in many of Britain's towns and cities. He was no stranger to violence and the tactics of those who used it.

'Too many of us could have escaped back to the loft or the hall. They'll wait until we're too far away to scuttle back. They've planned this very carefully, Eva. They'll hit us hard when they feel they have the greatest advantage. My feeling is that they'll wait until we reach the Hoe. There's nowhere to hide there. We'll need to trust in the shelter of the Lord.'

But Captain Wardle was wrong in his surmise of where the attack from the Skeleton Army would take place.

Sally was anxious to watch and listen to Ethan and his fellow bandsmen, and she had settled Ruth down before hurrying off to follow the parade. As she watched Ethan set off from Central Hall with the others, leading the parade, she felt a proprietorial pride.

However, as the procession approached a main junction in the centre of town, Sally sensed increasing tension among the Skeleton Army.

The letter from the Plymouth police chief had warned against taking the parade along any of the town's main roads but Captain Wardle had little choice but to cross some of the main thoroughfares. It was now, as the cavalcade reached one of the town's busiest junctions, that the Skeleton Army and its followers struck.

It was a spot where four roads met, and on a weekday it would have been crowded with town traffic. Although today was Sunday, it was still busy, but not everyone on the streets was going about their lawful business. A number of heavy farm carts, pulled by patient draw-horses, were waiting close to the junction in each of the four streets, and the pavements were crowded with pedestrians. One look at them was enough for Sally to know that this was where the Skeleton Army was going to mount its attack. Among the crowd she recognised many of the rag, tag and bobtail who frequented the public houses in the Barbican.

Concerned for Ethan and the others, Sally pushed her way through the men about her in a bid to warn Captain Eva. She was already too late.

Together with those already waiting at the junction, the members of the Skeleton Army who had followed the parade from Central Street now surged forward to surround the men and women of the Salvation Army.

At the same time, the horses hitched to the waiting wagons were whipped up. The heavy wagons trundled forward in a simple but carefully planned manoeuvre. Three wagons on each road effectively sealed off the exits from the wide junction. The Salvation Army cavalcade was trapped inside, together with a large number of the Skeleton Army and its supporters.

Fighting broke out immediately as the Skeleton Army struck out indiscriminately at uniformed men and women – and children.

At the same time, other Skeleton Army members climbed upon the wagons from outside the hastily formed arena, revealing another facet of the careful planning that had gone into ambushing the Salvation Army procession.

The wagons were loaded with a wide variety of missiles. The more innocuous were rotten eggs and vegetables; far more lethal were cobblestones and chunks of wood, some of the latter having nails hammered through them.

As the missiles flew through the air towards the trapped 'soldiers of Christ', Sally crawled on hands and knees beneath one of the wagons, heading for the spot where she had last glimpsed Ethan.

She emerged in a noisy, struggling mass of humanity, where the screams of the younger Salvation Army girls mingled with jubilant shouts from followers of the Skeleton Army.

Although members of the Salvation Army were expected to 'turn the other cheek' when faced with violence, a number were fighting back and giving a very good account of themselves.

One of these was Ethan.

Looking furious, he was actually taking the fight to the opposition. When Sally glimpsed him amidst the mêlée, he was throwing punches at a Skeleton Army supporter, who was desperately trying to protect himself as he retreated from the angry young fisherman. But Ethan was lost to view again almost immediately as a number of Skeleton Army supporters swarmed around him.

Sally fought her way towards him, clawing, kicking and making full use of her elbows and knees.

Along the way she tripped over the broken pole of a Salvation Army banner. She picked it up and wielded it to considerable effect and eventually reached Ethan.

He was still on his feet and fighting furiously, but his face was bloody and he was hopelessly outnumbered.

Sally laid about her with renewed vigour and for a moment or two the pair held their own against their opponents. However, it was unlikely they would have been able to hold the Skeleton Army supporters at bay for much longer, but succour was at hand.

It arrived from a totally unexpected quarter and in a bizarre manner. A circus, which had been touring France, had landed at Plymouth's Millbay docks that morning, but no trains were available to take it on until the following day. The owner had decided to take his circus to the open fields to the north-east of the town.

The circus owner was fully aware that he would require permission from the chief constable before parading his animals through the town. However, he thought the police could hardly object if he was merely *leading* his animals through the town to the fields, where they would remain until the train was available.

It was an opportunity to give the townsfolk a preview of what they could expect when the circus returned to give a performance in the summer. It would thus provide the circus with useful free publicity.

Unaware of what was happening at the junction in the heart of the town, the circus hands were leading horses, camels and elephants, together with caged lions and tigers, in the direction of the fracas.

Along the pavements, clowns, fully painted, kept pace with the circus procession, handing out sweets from gaily painted and be-ribboned buckets, together with notices of the next year's performances, to all the children they met. Also striding along were men dressed in bright top hats and jackets, atop incredibly high stilts hidden beneath long, striped trousers.

It was the elephants that proved to be the undoing of the Skeleton Army. As the procession ambled towards the wagons fencing in the fighting mob, one of the horses spotted them – and promptly bolted. As a second startled horse followed the first, bystanders and brawlers fled from the affray and ran for safety.

When one of the elephants trumpeted in fright, causing the tigers to roar, there was no controlling the horses. Soon everyone, Salvation Army and Skeleton Army followers alike, was fleeing from the scene, all thoughts of battle at an end. On their way they took the stilt legs from beneath the balancing circus hands, engendering more mayhem.

It was now, belatedly, that the police appeared on the scene. Many men and women were too badly hurt to run away; some were sheltering in shop doorways, others simply sitting on the kerbside, nursing their injuries.

The junction was strewn with litter and missiles of all types. Salvation Army bonnets, banners, broken band instruments and every imaginable variety of rotten vegetable.

The newly arrived police made six arrests that day.

All were members of the Salvation Army and among their number were Captains Wardle and Cassington.

22

Sally witnessed the arrest of Captain Eva, but it was done with so little fuss that she did not immediately realise what was happening.

She was walking back to Central Hall with Ethan. His face was bruised and grazed and he wanted to clean up before returning home.

Along the way Sally discovered the reason for Ethan's extreme anger. One of the Skeleton Army had snatched his precious flute, flung it to the ground and stamped on it. Ethan admitted the incident had made him go berserk for a while.

Aware of what the instrument and his music meant to him, Sally was truly sympathetic.

They were walking along the pavement, part of a long, straggling procession of bedraggled and battered Salvation Army members and their sympathisers. All were making for the sanctuary of their headquarters in Central Street.

In sharp contrast to the scene immediately prior to the attack, there were many policemen in evidence now. Walking in pairs, they kept pace with the Salvationists.

Most of the policemen maintained a disapproving silence, but a few directed jocular, albeit mocking comments at the retreating 'soldiers'.

Because of this, nobody took very much notice at first when

a sergeant and two colleagues began talking to Eva. It was not until she left her companions and turned back, accompanied by the policemen, that they realised she was being arrested.

There was an immediate protest from the Salvationists but other policemen moved in to prevent Captain Eva and her escort from being followed.

A few of the uniformed Salvation Army members, frustrated by the events of the day, protested vigorously. A series of scuffles broke out and more arrests were made.

Ethan wanted to go to Eva's aid, but Sally dissuaded him. She managed to convince him that it was not what Eva would want.

When Eva passed her by, Sally called, 'What are they arresting you for?'

Tight-lipped, Eva replied, 'I don't know. You'll need to ask the sergeant.'

'That's enough of that,' the sergeant said sternly to Sally. 'Miss Cassington is under arrest. I'll have no talking to her.'

Sally was still standing looking after the departing quartet when Eva turned around. Shaking off the restraining hand of one of the policemen, she called, 'Sally, tell them at headquarters what's happened. They must send someone along to the Refuge to take care of the girls . . .'

Two policemen now took hold of her and propelled her along the road, but she had been reassured by Sally's wave of acknowledgement and put up no resistance.

'What do you think will happen to Captain Eva?' asked Ethan.

Sally had speeded up her pace and he put the question to her as they began to overtake other Salvationists talking excitedly about this latest incident in an eventful day.

'Who knows?' Sally replied. 'It depends on the reason they've arrested her. As far as I know she's done nothing at all to break the law. The trouble back there was caused by the Skeleton Army – but I didn't see any of *them* arrested.'

'Can't we do something to try to get her released?' Ethan queried.

'I'm going to do my best,' replied Sally, 'once I've seen you treated and cleaned up and have found someone to go and take charge of the Refuge. I shall go and speak to Grace Philpott. Her uncle is chairman of the police authority and he's met Captain Eva. Perhaps he can do something to get her released.'

Grace Philpott dashed any idea of asking her uncle to help Captain Eva on this occasion.

'I know he won't be able to do anything, dear,' she said. 'It's not even worth asking him.'

Sally had called on Grace in the flat that she and Alfie occupied above the pie shop.

'He made it quite plain to me when we were discussing the problems of the Salvation Army,' Grace explained. 'He's able to take up matters that the police should be dealing with, but he can't interfere when someone's been arrested and will be appearing before a magistrate. Even so, I'll go to see him the first opportunity I get tomorrow, to let him know what's been going on.'

Standing up, she began pacing the room. 'The important thing right now is to see that the girls at the Refuge don't fly into a panic when they hear Captain Eva has been arrested. I'm especially worried about Rachel. She was just beginning to regain some confidence. I'll go and see if there's anything I can do.'

Alfie had been listening in silence to the conversation between his wife and Sally. Now he spoke for the first time. 'You don't want to go getting yourself involved in such goings on, Grace,' he cautioned. 'Leave it to the Salvation Army. They know what they're doing.'

'We're already involved,' retorted Grace. 'We have been since I took Uncle Percy around there and we met that poor little girl.' Suddenly conciliatory, she rested a hand on her husband's arm. 'I've got to go and see what I can do to help them, Alfie. You know that. If you're perfectly honest with yourself, you wouldn't want me to be any other way – and the reason I love you so much is because you *do* understand such things.'

Secretly pleased at her show of affection, Alfie said gruffly, 'Well . . . all right then, but don't forget we have a business to run. If we don't put that first you won't be able to help anyone.'

'Of course, but don't worry if I'm not home tonight. If Captain Eva isn't set free, someone will need to stay with those girls. I think I'm the best one to do it. Just get everything ready for the morning and I'll be in the shop at the usual time to begin work.'

Sally expected Alfie to be angry with Grace's decision, but he had been married to her for many years. He knew there were occasions when he might argue and win the day – and others when he needed to bow to the inevitable.

This was one of the latter occasions. He gave in graciously.

23

When Percy Mallett called at the house on the Barbican, Grace had the girls in the kitchen, trying their hand at cooking. They appeared to be enjoying themselves immensely.

He explained his presence by saying he happened to be passing. Having heard earlier in the day of the clash between the Salvation Army and its opponents, he thought he would call in to check Captain Eva was all right.

'But what are *you* doing here?' he asked his niece.

'I'm here because Captain Eva has been arrested. She's being held in the police cells. I was going to come to tell you about it later today.'

'Arrested? On what charge?' Percy Mallett was horrified.

'You'd better ask Sally. She was there.'

Sally had made her way to the Refuge after returning home and boiling a couple of eggs for Ruth's Sunday lunch. She now told the Police Authority chairman of the attack upon the Salvation Army parade by the Skeleton Army; of its succour from an unexpected quarter – and of Captain Eva's subsequent arrest.

'I've since heard that Captain Wardle was arrested too, and some of the others. I hope there's a good doctor down at the police station. A few of the Salvation Army were quite badly hurt.'

'Where were the police while all this was going on?' Percy Mallet asked, tight-faced.

Sally said bitterly, 'I never saw one of 'em until it was all over. When they did come they arrested the wrong people. Those they should have taken in are them who belonged to the Skeleton Army. The men who were paid by the landlords of the pubs to cause trouble. But I didn't see one of *them* arrested.'

'I'm afraid I can do nothing to help Captain Eva immediately, but I'll call for a full report on the whole incident,' said Percy Mallett. 'I can assure you of that.'

Turning to his niece, he said, 'In the meantime, is there anything I can do to help you, Grace?'

'Yes.' Pointing to Sally, she said, 'You can give this young lady a ride to her home in your carriage. She has a sick sister to take care of – and she needs to be in work on time in the morning if we're not to upset Alfie. He's been very patient so far, but he won't be if we start losing business.'

It was the first time Sally had ever ridden in a carriage. It was only for a short distance, but she enjoyed the experience. On the way to Pin's Lane, Percy questioned her, establishing that she was an orphan.

'That's most sad,' he said with genuine sympathy. 'Is that how you became involved with the Salvation Army?'

'No.' Sally told him about meeting with Ethan and of his part in helping to save the small girl who had fallen in Sutton harbour. 'Ethan enjoys playing in the band,' she boasted proudly. 'At least, he *did*.'

Explaining the destruction of Ethan's flute by the Skeleton Army supporter, she added, 'I don't know what he'll do now. He really only joined the Salvation Army so he could play his flute. He loves music. I doubt if he'll stay with them if he can't be in their band.'

Warming to her subject, Sally went on to tell how Ethan and his family had played a leading part in rescuing Rachel and the other girls.

'This Ethan sounds quite an exceptional young man,' commented Percy Mallett.

'He is,' agreed Sally.

In that moment she realised she really meant it. She had grown very fond of Ethan without ever intending to allow it to happen – or even being aware that it had.

In the pie shop the next morning, Alfie was having a grumble because Grace had stayed at the Refuge overnight.

'Do you realise it's the first time we've spent a night away from each other in all the years we've been married, Grace? I rue the day you got mixed up with this Salvation Army lot – and I put the blame for that firmly on you, young lady.' Alfie glared at Sally. 'I took pity on you and gave you a job, and this is the thanks I get for it?'

'*You* gave her a job? I seem to remember that was *my* idea. At the time you were threatening to take her head off with that meat cleaver of yours. Anyway, I'm glad I've been able to help those poor young girls. You are too, Alfie Philpott, so just stop your grumbling and pass me some more of that meat when you've finished cutting it up. You'll be even more pleased this afternoon. I've asked one of the Salvation Army women to bring Rachel here. You'll like her, Alfie, *really* like her, but I don't want you grumbling at her, even if you don't mean it. She's been through a lot, that poor girl, and has no one she can turn to. No mother, or father. You just be nice to her, you hear?'

Sally felt a twinge of jealousy as she listened to Grace talk about Rachel. She too was an orphan. She wondered whether Grace had forgotten.

She felt guilty almost immediately for her feelings. Grace – and Alfie – were fully aware of her situation and they had both been very good to her because of it. They were kind and caring people. Sally told herself she was glad Rachel had found someone like the hard-working couple to take an interest in her.

After all, she had Ruth to talk to when things went wrong. Even when Ruth was having one of her bad days, she still had someone to care for and someone who cared for her.

Setting off on her first errand of the day, Sally told herself she would not be selfish and unreasonable about Rachel. Instead, she would do all she could to make the younger girl realise there were many people who cared for her.

24

With the exception of Captains Wardle and Cassington, the Salvationists arrested after the aborted parade were dealt with quickly and relatively leniently.

Found guilty of a variety of charges, which included 'obstruction' and committing a 'breach of the peace', they were either given a nominal fine or bound over to keep the peace.

However, when the two captains were placed in the dock they were jointly charged with the more serious offence of being engaged in an 'unlawful assembly'. Both Salvationists were aware they faced the prospect of imprisonment.

They pleaded 'Not Guilty' but when the time came for them to present their defence, Captain Wardle refused to say anything.

When the magistrates' clerk demanded a reason, Wardle claimed that entering a defence would be a waste of his own and everybody else's time. He pointed out that the magistrate dealing with the case was a member of a prominent family of local brewers. He would therefore be biased against a defendant belonging to an organisation dedicated to promoting teetotalism.

Angrily, the magistrate told Captain Wardle that his duty was to administer the laws of the land. The Salvationist was in court for breaking those laws. He would be dealt with accordingly, without fear or favour.

Still red-faced from what he considered to be Captain Wardle's impertinence, the magistrate asked Eva whether she had anything to say in her own defence.

'Yes, your worship. We were none of us involved in any form of unlawful assembly. Captain Wardle and I were leading a parade to the Hoe, in order to hold an open-air service.'

'I go to a church service every Sunday, Miss Cassington, but I don't take a band along with me. Why did you consider that to be necessary?'

'Music is a God-given blessing, sir. One we wish to share with everyone.'

'Nonsense! You must have known it would attract curious and idle persons who had nothing better to do than cause mischief and disturb the peace of the town.'

'They are the very people we try to attract. It gives us the opportunity to bring them to God and show them the right path to his divine grace.'

'Nevertheless, you are a minority religious group, Miss Cassington. In this world, the minority must bow to the wishes of the majority, would you not agree?'

'Most certainly not, sir! The vast majority of people in this world of ours are sinners. Should I become a sinner too? Or should I try to show them the error of their ways and bring them to God? You surely must agree my way is better, sir?'

Her words brought an outbreak of laughter from the public gallery and a spontaneous burst of applause, which died abruptly when the magistrate turned a stern gaze upon those responsible.

'I will not have music-hall behaviour in my court. Another such outburst and I will have you all removed. Now, does either defendant have anything of relevance to add to what has already been said?'

'Only the hope that God's wisdom may guide your judgement,' said Eva. 'And to tell you that whatever your decision, I will pray for you.'

The magistrate leaned over his bench and held a low-voiced conversation with his clerk, which lasted for some minutes. There appeared to be some disagreement between the two men.

Eventually, the magistrate silenced his clerk with a dismissive wave of his hand. The clerk sat back in his chair, shaking his head in silent disapproval.

Returning his attention to the two Salvation Army officers standing in the dock, the magistrate said, 'I regret I am unable to inform you that there has been any divine intercession on your behalf. Neither did I feel it necessary to seek the Lord's guidance in this matter. The law of the land is quite clear.'

Clasping his hands together and placing his elbows on the bench in front of him, the magistrate looked sternly at the two defendants. 'You are both senior members of the organisation to which you belong. The chief constable made it perfectly clear to you in writing, through one of his senior officers, that you were to keep your parade off the main roads of this city. You flagrantly disregarded that directive. The result was that law-abiding citizens were obliged to witness the disgraceful scenes of violence that took place yesterday. Such a blatant disregard for law and order will not be tolerated by this court. You will both go to prison for a month. I trust . . .'

The remainder of the magistrate's words were lost in a roar of protest from the public gallery.

The uniformed members of the Salvation Army who packed the public seats stood up, stamping their feet angrily and shouting their disapproval at the imposition of a prison sentence on the two popular officers.

For some minutes the magistrate and his clerk tried in vain to restore order.

The spectators continued their racket long after Captain Eva and the officer commanding the Plymouth corps of the Salvation Army had been taken off to the cells beneath the courtroom. Eventually, the angry magistrate was forced to adjourn all further proceedings for the day.

Rising to his feet and closely followed by his clerk, he retired from the courtroom via a door behind the magistrate's chair, pursued by the booing of those in the public gallery.

When the magistrate had gone, the ushers and a number of policemen began clearing the court of the angry, shocked and temporarily leaderless Salvationists.

25

Sally heard the news of Captain Eva's imprisonment as she was returning from one of her deliveries. She met a group of Salvation Army women who had just left the magistrates' court. They were now heading for the Army headquarters to break the news to Captain Wardle's wife and to arrange for someone to take over the duties of the two jailed officers.

Sally was utterly dismayed. Not because someone she knew had been sent to prison – such an occurrence was by no means unusual in the Barbican. Indeed many of her neighbours in Pin's Lane had served sentences in Plymouth's gaol. Most were criminals and it was an accepted hazard of their way of life.

Captain Eva most certainly was *not* a criminal.

Her sole aim in life was to improve the lot of those no one else would help. She did not deserve to be thrown into prison.

The very thought of Captain Eva having to spend a month in a prison cell thoroughly upset Sally. She was still fighting back tears when she reached the pie shop.

'Ah! There you are, Sally. I've got a nice order for you to deliver to Customs House. It's not very far from where you live, so, if you like, you can pop in to see that poor sister of yours. Take her one of my fruit specials. It might tempt her to eat.' Grace had learned much more about the home circumstances of her young employee, and she would occasionally give Sally small treats to take to Ruth.

She was busily kneading dough as she talked and had hardly looked up when Sally came in. Rachel was happily helping her, but she was not as preoccupied as Grace. She realised that Sally was very close to tears.

'What's the matter, Sally? Has something happened to upset you?'

Grace looked up now and immediately stopped pounding the soft mountain of dough on the table in front of her.

'What is it, girl?'

Behind her, Alfie stopped raking out ashes from the fire beneath the large oven, in order that he too might hear Sally's reply.

'It's Captain Eva. She's been sent to prison.'

The disbelieving silence that followed her words was broken by Grace. 'What are you talking about, Sally? What nonsense is this?'

Grace rested flour-whitened hands on hips and Rachel stared in ashen-faced disbelief as Sally repeated what the Salvation Army girls had told her.

'I don't believe it. People aren't sent to prison just for parading in the streets.' Grace was having great difficulty accepting what Sally had told her.

'They kept her in the police station all last night,' Rachel pointed out.

'That was different,' said Grace. 'That was just the police being spiteful. But prison . . . ! She's done nothing to be sent there. Are you certain you've got it right, Sally?'

'That's what the Salvation Army women said and they should know. They were in court when the magistrate sent Captain Eva down. Captain Wardle was sent to jail as well.'

Brushing flour and dough from her hands, Grace picked up a towel to complete the job. Unfastening her apron, she said, 'Alfie, hurry up with that fire. When you've done you can set to work on this dough and take over the baking for the rest of the day. No . . . don't argue, you can do it every bit as good as me, when you want to.'

'Where are you going, Grace?'

'To the Refuge, to see what's happening there. Those girls need someone sensible to take care of them, Alfie. Captain Eva's not there to do it, so someone else must. If they can't find anyone else, I'll take the job on myself.'

'What about me?' asked Rachel. 'What will happen to me now?'

'You'll stay here while the shop's open. If you haven't heard anything from me by this evening, Sally will bring you to the Refuge. Is that all right with you, Sally? You can leave work early, so it needn't make you late getting home.'

Sally nodded.

'Right, I'll be off then. Alfie, before you do anything else you'd better take out the pies that are already in the oven, otherwise they'll be overdone.'

After issuing this directive, Grace hurried from the kitchen. She left Alfie, his hands black with ash and coal, looking after her, thoroughly bewildered.

'It's all right, Alfie. I'll take out the pies,' said Sally. 'You be cleaning yourself up so you can get on with the cooking. Rachel will serve in the shop when I go out. I'll help her when I'm not delivering – and she can always call out to you if there's something she doesn't understand.'

'There are far too many chiefs and only one indian around here,' Alfie grumbled peevishly. 'You sure you wouldn't like me to put on a song-and-dance act while I'm doing everything else?'

Despite his sarcastic comments, Alfie hurriedly cleaned himself up and changed into a clean striped apron before taking on the task abandoned so hurriedly by Grace.

Outside in the shop, Sally helped a nervous Rachel to serve a woman customer. When she had left the shop, Sally spoke quietly to the younger girl, so that Alfie would not hear.

'You mustn't take too much notice of Alfie when he grumbles about something. Grace never does. He's as soft as butter, really – and just as generous as Grace. He doesn't want everyone to realise it, that's all.'

26

Grace returned to the shop just before it closed for the day. She had helped to draw up an 'arrangement' for the Refuge and the girls who lived there with Captain Wardle's wife.

It was agreed that for as long as Captain Eva was in prison, two or three Salvation Army girls would remain at the Refuge during daylight hours. Grace would take over from them each evening, cook an evening meal for the girls and sleep in the house overnight.

When Alfie protested that he needed feeding too, Grace retorted that he could 'feed his face' during the day. Anyway, she added, he would benefit from losing a few pounds from around his waistline.

In a kindlier vein, she added, 'It will only be for a month, Alfie. You wouldn't want to leave young Rachel and the others all night without having anyone responsible looking after them, would you now?'

Alfie's muttered reply was unintelligible, but Grace soothed his hurt feelings by giving him a warm hug. 'You won't be neglected, Alfie, I promise, but it's nice to know you'll miss me. Some husbands would be only too pleased to get rid of their wives for a few hours.'

Embarrassed but pleased by his wife's show of affection, Alfie broke free and made an unnecessary show of tidying cooking implements in the already neat kitchen.

'You can come to the Refuge with me when I go,' Grace said to Rachel. 'It will save Sally a walk.'

'Can I come back here with you tomorrow?' Rachel asked eagerly.

'You're welcome to come here as often as you like,' said Grace, beaming at the young girl. 'You can go out with Sally sometimes when she's delivering, too. That way you'll get to know a bit of the town. It hasn't been a happy place for you so far, but you'll like Plymouth when you get to know it, I know you will.'

That evening, in the room at Pin's Lane, Sally was busily ironing the clothes she had washed the day before. She and Ruth were talking about the prison sentence imposed upon Captain Eva. Ruth agreed with her sister that it was totally unjustified.

Suddenly, there was a knock at the door, startling both girls. When Sally opened the door she was both surprised and pleased to see Ethan outside. She invited him in and they all discussed the events of the day for some time before Ethan declared he did not wish to tire Ruth by remaining talking for too long. He suggested Sally should walk with him as far as the harbour. He explained that he and his brothers had been painting their fishing boat and he would like to know what Sally thought of the new colour.

'That's a novel excuse for getting a girl to go out for a walk with you, if ever I heard one!' Ruth gave Ethan a tired but understanding smile. 'Go along, Sally.'

'I've still got some ironing to do,' Sally said. 'And I need to be in the shop early tomorrow morning. I doubt if Grace will be back from the Refuge at the crack of dawn and I can't expect poor old Alfie to do everything by himself.'

'Don't make feeble excuses just because you feel you shouldn't be leaving me,' said Ruth. 'You want to go out with Ethan, really, and the ironing isn't going to run away. You can do it another day. Anyway, you'll only keep me awake with your chatter and I'm feeling tired. Off you go now.'

'Well . . . if you're *really* tired, I'll go.'

Sally tried to sound reluctant to leave her sister, but she had already placed the flat-iron on the hob and was stuffing the unironed clothes away in a drawer.

Two minutes later she was walking on the damp cobblestones of the sloping Pin's Lane, heading towards the harbour.

'What colour have you painted your boat?' Sally asked, as they turned the corner into Southside Street, heading for the Barbican.

'Bright blue. We've only just begun to paint it today and haven't got very far,' admitted Ethan. 'But I wanted to speak to you about something and I didn't want to mention it in front of Ruth.'

Intrigued, Sally asked what it was that was such a secret.

'I called in to see Uncle Charlie before I came up to your room,' exclaimed Ethan. 'He told me someone had been to the house earlier today, asking questions about you.'

'Why should anyone want to know about *me*?' Sally was puzzled. 'Who was it?'

'It was a woman,' Charlie said. 'She didn't give him a name – and she didn't know yours, until Charlie told her. She wanted to know if "the girl who worked at Alfie Philpott's pie shop lived in the house". When Charlie asked if she meant you – Sally – she didn't seem too sure. He said you lived there, but weren't in.'

There was a lull in the conversation as they drew back in the narrow street to allow a cart laden with fish from the harbour to rumble past.

'Charlie said she asked questions about which room you lived in, and whether your ma and pa lived there with you. By this time he was getting a bit suspicious. He told her you didn't have any parents, but he didn't mention Ruth.'

'Who'd want to know about me – and why?'

'Well, that's the reason I didn't want to say anything that might worry Ruth. Charlie said that when he was talking to the woman, he felt he'd seen her before, somewhere. It wasn't until she'd gone off that he remembered where it had been. He saw her once at the Albion, just along the road from here. She was there with Sid Darling. She's one of his women. Charlie believes she has one of the rooms in Mother Darling's house, in Mary Street.'

Sally felt her stomach contract in sudden fear. 'You mean . . . Sid Darling has found out I was the one who told on him and he sent her to find out about me?'

'Can you think of any other reason why this particular woman should come to Pin's Lane asking so many questions about you?'

Sally shook her head. 'What do you think I ought to do?'

'I don't know, but it worries me, Sally. Couldn't you go off and stay with someone for a while? To the house run by Captain Eva, perhaps – or with the Philpotts?'

'I couldn't leave Ruth. Anyway, Grace is staying at the Refuge until Captain Eva comes out of prison. I can't go anywhere.'

'Then you'll just have to be careful when you're not working. I'll ask Uncle Charlie to keep an eye on you. He wouldn't be much good if Sid Darling came to the house, but he could shout loud enough to attract attention. That might be enough to frighten him off. He wouldn't want the police to catch up with him.'

'Do you think he's likely to come to the house?' Sally was genuinely frightened.

'I don't think anyone knows what Sid Darling is likely to do,' replied Ethan. 'What I *will* do is speak to my pa and brothers about it. Between us we should be able to call around to your place now and then, when you're home, to make sure you're all right.'

'Thank you . . . but I'd feel a lot better if the police arrested him.'

'Of course you would – and they will.' In a rare gesture of affection, Ethan reached for her hand and held it. 'In the meantime, I'll spend all the time I can with you. I'd like that, anyway.'

Retaining a hold on his hand, Sally realised that she would like that too. Life for her would be taking an upward turn if only the shadow of Sid Darling was not lurking in the background . . .

27

In the few days before Christmas, Alfie and Grace Philpott did more business than at any time the pair could remember. It seemed their pies had earned a reputation as the finest in Plymouth.

On one occasion a huge order came in for pies with which to feed the passengers of a large steamship. The vessel had put in to Plymouth Sound to shelter from a brief but fierce easterly gale.

On days such as this, Sally and Rachel helped in the shop and kitchen, while the delivery of the pies was made by Ethan and his youngest brother, Joe. Prevented from fishing by the inclement weather, they were happy to earn money in any way they could.

Grace was working very hard, her time divided between the shop and the Refuge. Then, two days before Christmas, Captain Wardle and Eva were released from prison on the orders of the Home Secretary.

Their release had been prompted by a public outcry against the harsh and frequently illogical sentences handed out to members of the Salvation Army. The Plymouth courts were not the only ones in the land seen to be victimising them.

In an increasing number of cases, the convictions were contrary to the evidence presented to the courts.

Particular disquiet had been voiced in London about the punishment meted out to Salvation Army members in the courts of Devon towns, Plymouth being just one of them.

Percy Mallett had himself written to the Home Secretary. He protested that such blatant miscarriages of justice were bringing the law itself into disrepute. He pointed out that the law-abiding citizens of his town were losing all respect for those whose duty it was to maintain law and order.

His letter was just one of many received by the Home Secretary from persons of authority throughout the land.

Many more had aired their misgivings through the columns of national and provincial newspapers. There were a few dissenting letter writers, but a huge majority expressed support for the aims of the Salvation Army, even when they did not always approve of the methods used in achieving them.

Alfie was delighted and not a little relieved to have Grace home with him once more, day *and* night. However, she still maintained a considerable interest in the well-being of the girls in the Refuge.

She and Alfie were both very taken with young Rachel. The young orphan, in her turn, had become increasingly reliant upon Grace.

Captain Eva had been aware since their first meeting of Rachel's workhouse-induced dislike of anything that even remotely resembled an institution. Therefore, when it was suggested to Rachel by Eva and Grace that she should move in with Grace and Alfie 'on an experimental basis' she was happy to agree.

The recently released Salvation Army captain insisted, however, that Rachel must spend at least part of Christmas Day with the other girls at the Refuge. She also wanted her to accompany them to one of the Army's meetings in Central Hall on that day.

Rachel was quite happy with this arrangement. She was also delighted when Grace insisted that the girls and Captain Eva should come to the flat above the shop. Here, albeit in grossly overcrowded conditions, they would enjoy a Christmas dinner that she would prepare and cook for them.

Sally was invited too. She and Rachel had become firm friends and Rachel implored her to accept the invitation, but Sally had already agreed to visit Ethan's home. Besides, she did not want to leave Ruth alone for too long on this special day.

Ruth did not agree. She told Sally she should accept both invitations and not be tied by her.

'I'll be fine at home by myself, Sal,' she said for the third time that evening. 'I'm quite happy being at home by myself every other day. Besides, I'll spend most of the day sleeping, you know that. It will be miserable at home here, having to tiptoe around so as not to wake me. Especially when all your friends are somewhere else, enjoying themselves.'

Sally was aware of the truth of Ruth's statement. Her sister slept for much of the time now. Nevertheless, Sally had no intention of leaving her alone for too long on Christmas Day.

Ruth had grown progressively weaker in recent weeks. Although Sally was reluctant to face the truth, she realised that this might well be the last Christmas she would have with Ruth.

'I *like* being with you, Ruth,' she insisted. 'Besides, I'll be out for quite a while when I go to meet Ethan's family. That's going to be nerve-racking enough. I don't think I could face going out twice.'

'What are you going to wear, Sal?'

It was a question Sally had spent much time pondering over in recent days. In an effort to find something suitable she had been looking in the various shops she passed whilst out delivering pies.

'I've seen a dress in a pawnshop in the high street that might do. It looks as though it should be a good fit and it isn't too expensive.'

'What's it made of?'

Sally frowned. 'I don't know. Cotton, I suppose.'

'You should have something better than cotton if you want to impress Ethan's ma. You could wear my silk dress – but it would be too small for you.'

Ruth struggled to move higher up in the bed, but when Sally

tried to help her, she said, 'No, leave me. Just pass me my purse from the shelf.'

The request puzzled Sally. As far as she was aware, the purse contained no money. All the cash possessed by Ruth had been spent long ago, during their many lean times. Nevertheless, she crossed the room, took down the worn leather purse from a shelf, and handed it to her sister.

Clumsily, Ruth opened one of the many compartments of the purse and took out a key.

'That's the key to your trunk.'

Living in the one room, the girls had no possessions that were not familiar to the other – with a single exception.

In a corner of the room stood a small trunk that belonged to Ruth. It was always kept locked. What was more, it had never been opened in Sally's presence.

Holding out the key in a weak and shaking hand, Ruth said, 'Here, open it.'

'Are you sure?' Sally took the key uncertainly. It felt wrong. Almost as though Ruth was relinquishing an important part of herself.

'Of course I'm sure. Go on, open it.'

Crossing the creaking floor to the corner of the room, Sally kneeled beside the old bow-topped leather trunk. After a quick, confirmatory glance at Ruth, she inserted the key in the lock and turned it.

The lock was stiff, as she had expected it would be, but when the key eventually turned, the lid sprang up slightly and she lifted it open.

There was a pile of clothing in the trunk. Ruth had never been a particularly tidy person, but everything here was meticulously folded.

Turning back to her sister, Sally asked, 'What am I looking for?'

'Anything that takes your fancy. Much of it is far too old-fashioned, but I know there's a nice petticoat in there. I wore it myself once, for a special occasion. Just have a look through and see what you can find.'

Sally found the petticoat. Made of layered silk, it was far

more expensive than anything she had ever seen before. Then she unfolded a beautiful, rich maroon velvet cloak with tiered lilac silk fringing. When she unfolded it she discovered it was also decorated with two heraldic crests, one on either side of the fastening at the neck.

'This is *beautiful*, Ruth. Where did you get it?'

'It belonged to our ma. Don't ask me how she got it. Probably from the big house where she worked. Take it if you like it. The slip as well.'

'Do you mean it, Ruth? You don't mind? The cloak would go beautifully with the dress I saw.'

'Of course I don't mind. She was your ma just as much as mine. She'd love you to wear it. I should have given it to you long before this.'

'No. This is just the right occasion. Oh, thank you, Ruth! I couldn't have wished for anything better.'

Hurrying to the bed, Sally gave her sister an affectionate hug, trying not to notice how thin Ruth had become.

'Go on with you,' said Ruth. 'Now, shut the chest and give me back the key.'

Sally was about to close the chest when she saw a bundle of letters, tied with ribbon. Lifting them out, she held them up for Ruth to see. 'What are these?'

'Put them back! Go on. I said you could have any of the clothes. Nothing else.'

Ruth spoke so sharply it took Sally aback. It also set Ruth coughing alarmingly.

Hurriedly dropping the letters in the chest, Sally turned the key to lock it. Then she went to the bed to lift her sister. She had to rub Ruth's back for a long time before she stopped coughing and could be laid back once more, still gasping for breath.

That night, as Sally lay in the darkness, listening to Ruth's weak and shallow breathing, she wondered what could have been in the letters to make her sister so upset. She thought they must be from a man who had once been a part of Ruth's life, although she had never spoken of anyone in particular.

As she lay there thinking her own, night-time thoughts, Sally's hand strayed beneath her pillow. She had placed the cloak there and she touched the velvet with its silk fringes lovingly.

It had once belonged to her mother. Had been worn by her. She suddenly felt warm inside.

The cloak was the best present Ruth could have given to her. The best present *anyone* could have given her.

28

❧

Christmas Eve dawned crisp and clear. Sally walked to work filled with a sense of excitement, which she contained with great difficulty.

The excitement had been building up inside her for some days now and was not entirely due to the cloak she had been given by Ruth. It had much to do with Christmas itself.

Walking around the streets of Plymouth making her deliveries, she had seen Christmas decorations appear in many of the shops and houses of the town.

The grocers in the main shopping streets had an awesome variety of goods on display in their windows: Fancy cakes, biscuits, dried fruits; goods of every description. The list was endless.

Butchers too, not usually known for their decorative skills, offered chickens, ducks, geese, turkeys and colourful pheasants, hanging row upon feathered row outside their shops, while on white trays in the window, long strings of sausages spelled out the message 'Happy Christmas'.

In the residential streets, wreaths of holly and ivy were affixed to many doors. As she passed by, Sally could see chains of coloured paper and sprigs of holly brightening even the most drab rooms.

Today was special for another reason. With Ethan and his

brother still helping with deliveries, and the demand for pies finally falling away, Grace had said Sally could take a couple of hours off, in order to buy Christmas presents. She would be spending the money she had been able to save from her pay. With the occasional tips she received, it amounted to more money than she had ever possessed before.

Rachel would be coming with her, to spend money given to her by the extremely generous Grace and Alfie.

Sally had already decided upon most of the presents she would be buying. She had chosen them from the shop windows she passed as her deliveries took her through the shopping areas.

'What are you going to buy for that young man of yours, Sally?' The question came from Grace as they worked to prepare the shop for the day and it sent a small cloud scudding across the horizon of Sally's happiness.

'I don't know yet.'

'You don't know?' echoed Grace. 'Here we are, the day before Christmas, and you don't know what you're going to buy for your young man? You've left things a bit late, girl!'

'I know,' Sally said unhappily. 'You see, I know what Ethan *wants*. He'd love to have another flute, to replace the one that was broken by the Skeleton Army.'

'That's a very expensive present to buy for any young man,' commented Grace.

'I know,' admitted Sally. 'But he's been very good to me and Ruth and I've seen a flute I know he'd love. It's in the pawnshop where I bought the dress I'm wearing to go to his house. It's beautiful – but that's just the trouble. It's *too* beautiful. The pawnbroker wants a lot of money for it. I've been in his shop five times to try to get him to sell it to me for less than he's asking, but he won't drop the price quite enough.'

'How much are you short of the asking price?' queried Grace.

'Twenty-five shillings, Sally admitted gloomily. 'It was *thirty*-five. He's dropped the price by ten shillings, but he won't come down any more.'

Grace was fully aware that Alfie was giving her a stern

warning stare. She chose not to look directly at him, and without a word, she walked from the kitchen to the shop.

Returning only a few minutes later, she took Sally's hand, put two banknotes in it and closed her fingers about them.

Opening her hand, Sally looked down and saw a pound note and a ten shilling note.

'Thirty shillings! What's this for?'

'Alfie and I have enjoyed the best year we've ever had in the shop. Far better than we expected. You've worked hard while you've been here, girl, contributing in no small measure to our success. We decided it should be a good year for you too.'

Grace used the 'we' freely, but she did not look at Alfie. He, in his turn, was trying unsuccessfully to appear as though he had been consulted on the generous gift.

'Now, off you go and buy that flute before someone else takes a liking to it,' said Grace. 'Take Rachel with you. I know she has one or two things she wants to buy.'

Hardly able to contain her delight, Sally flung her arms about Grace and gave her a warm hug. Then she repeated it with Alfie.

When the two happy girls had departed from the shop, chattering excitedly together, Alfie said huskily, 'You know, Grace, the last young girl to give me a hug like that was our Mary.'

'Then it was money well spent, Alfie. She's a fine young girl, that one. So too is Rachel. I'm glad they've become such firm friends. They're good for each other. They're good for us, too. I only hope young Ethan realises what a treasure he has in Sally. I'd hate for him to break her heart.'

Sally and Rachel's shopping expedition began on a high note. The two girls spent a long time in a haberdashery shop as Rachel chose ribbons for the other girls at the Refuge. Then she bought embroidered handkerchiefs for Grace and Captain Eva.

Sally purchased a couple of presents here too, including one of the embroidered handkerchiefs. She thought it would make a nice present for Ethan's mother.

In a nearby shop she bought a kaleidoscope. It formed a

variety of colourful patterns when shaken and held to the eye. It would keep Ruth amused for many of her waking hours and bring a welcome splash of colour into her drab and pain-filled life.

But although Sally was enjoying this part of her shopping, she was anxious to get to the pawnbroker's and secure the flute she was buying for Ethan.

She breathed a sigh of relief when they reached the shop and she saw it still displayed in the window. It was surrounded by a wide selection of unclaimed pledges, set out haphazardly.

Shoes and satin slippers were piled upon silver-tipped walking-canes. A couple of cheap watches were half-hidden by a variety of baubles – and a quantity of assorted wedding rings were threaded on a piece of string stretched between two shelves. The mark of respectability they had once represented had, in most cases, been sacrificed to satisfy a family's hunger.

The knowledge that she possessed enough money to pay the pawnbroker's asking price for the flute made Sally feel so confident she decided she would make one more attempt to drive the price down still further.

When it became evident to Rachel that the negotiations were likely to be protracted, she said, 'I'm going to have a look in the window of the jewellers we just passed. I'll see you there when you've done here.'

Sally's haggling eventually paid off. The pawnbroker knew he was unlikely to have any more customers before Christmas. He was also aware that those who would come to his shop after the holiday would be pawning goods, not buying them.

When Sally produced money from her purse as proof she was seriously contemplating buying the flute, the pawnbroker agreed to reduce the price by a further two shillings.

Delighted with her purchase and the price she had paid for it, Sally waited for the pawnbroker to fit the musical instrument into a velvet-lined carrying case. The task had just been completed when Rachel ran in the shop and clutched Sally, her face drained of colour and her eyes wide with terror.

'What's the matter, Rachel? What's happened?' Sally put the

concerned questions to the younger girl as she clung to her arm, momentarily struck dumb.

'I . . . I've just seen him,' gasped Rachel, finding her voice at last, but shaking in fear. 'He's out there – and I think he saw me!'

'Who's out there? What are you talking about?'

'*Him* . . . ! Sid Darling. He was standing on the pavement, just across the road. I'm sure he saw me . . .'

The pawnbroker had been as startled as Sally by the dramatic return of Rachel. He listened with growing concern to the conversation between the two girls.

Now he said, 'You've made an enemy of Sid Darling? How?'

'How doesn't matter,' said Sally. 'What *does* matter is that he'll kill both of us if he can lay his hands on us.'

In addition to his lawful business as a pawnbroker, the owner of the shop had a very lucrative sideline as a 'fence': a receiver and distributor of stolen goods. He was familiar with the town's criminals. Among them, Sid Darling's name was frequently to the fore; he was one of the most feared and disliked men in the criminal fraternity.

'Did he see you come in here?' he asked Rachel.

'No. A furniture van passed between us. That's when I ran in here.'

The pawnbroker peered over the board that separated the window display from the shop.

Sid Darling, appearing agitated, was still standing on the opposite pavement. He was unable to cross the road because of heavy traffic, and was trying to see into a shop farther along the street, away from the pawnbroker's.

'Quick, through here.'

The pawnbroker led the way through a door at the rear of the shop. It led into his living quarters, from where a door opened into a side alleyway.

'Go that way,' he said to the two girls, pointing along the alleyway, away from Union Street. 'It will bring you out in East Street. If Sid Darling comes in here I'll deny having had any young girls in my shop today. But if ever he catches up with you, remember – you've never been here.'

A few minutes later, after fleeing in a state close to panic through the narrow alleyway, the two girls emerged in East Street. Here they stopped running, but did not dawdle, their shopping expedition at a premature end.

Neither girl felt safe until they tumbled inside Alfie and Grace Philpott's pie shop and blurted out the story of their narrow escape.

Despite the fright she had received, Sally felt the shopping expedition had been a success. She had bought Ethan the Christmas present he most wanted.

29

❧

'Of course you're going, Sal. Ethan and his family are expecting you. Besides, you've been in all day, looking after me. That's no way to spend Christmas.'

Ruth spoke from the bed, propped up by both of the pillows belonging to the sisters. Her Christmas present from Sally lay on the quilt beside her.

The quilt itself had been donated to Ruth by the ever-generous Grace, as a result of a visit to the room in the Pin's Lane house by Rachel, a few days before. Rachel had returned to the shop and mentioned to Grace that the bed in the room was covered only by a rough blanket. The following day Grace had appeared in the shop with the quilt and asked Sally if she could make use of it. She had bought a new one, she said. If Sally did not want it she would throw it out as she had no room to store it.

'I like being at home with you,' Sally protested. 'We never seem to be able to spend enough time together now I'm working.'

'I like having you here with me,' said Ruth. 'But you know how talking tires me. I shall go to sleep very happily, thinking of you enjoying a lovely time with Ethan and his family.'

Lifting the kaleidoscope, she added, 'If you leave the lamp turned up a little higher than usual I'll be able to look through this for a while. It's a truly lovely present, Sal. The best

I've ever had. The colours in the patterns are just unbelievable.'

Ruth had spent most of her waking hours that day gazing into the kaleidoscope. It had proved to be a very successful gift.

In fact, the whole day had so far been a happy one. Nevertheless, Sally was viewing her visit to Ethan's home with very mixed feelings. Indeed, she could not remember ever feeling more nervous.

'Do you *really* think this dress is all right?' It was a question she had asked many times that evening.

'It's lovely, Sal – and so are you. Ethan's a very lucky young man. I hope he realises just *how* lucky.'

In truth, the dress was a trifle small for Sally. Accentuating the maturity of her body, it would not serve her for very long, but Ruth said nothing of this. She knew Sally was delighted with her purchase, despite the misgivings she was voicing now.

'That cloak will go beautifully with it too,' she added, as Sally placed it around her shoulders and fastened it at her neck.

Suddenly and without any warning, the happiness Sally had managed to hold inside her all day welled up and broke free.

'Oh, I'm *so* lucky to have a sister like you!' Sally flung herself at the frail, bed-ridden girl and gave her a fierce hug.

'Steady, Sal!' Ruth returned the hug with a warm but weak embrace. 'I love you too. Now, before we both get all silly, off you go and let the Shields family see what a lucky young man Ethan is.'

To Sally's great surprise, Ethan was waiting for her downstairs in the passageway of the Pin's Lane house, talking to his uncle.

'I thought I'd come and collect you, just in case you'd changed your mind,' explained Ethan, revealing an understanding of her that Sally found comforting, yet vaguely disturbing. 'I'm glad you haven't – and you look wonderful, Sally.'

His compliment pleased her more than he would ever know. Happily reassured, she slipped her arm through his. 'Come on then, before I *do* change my mind.'

'Are you going to be warm enough? It's a cold evening.'

'Of course I am. I've got a cloak that used to belong to my ma and we'll be at your house before I have time to get cold.'

She *would* be cold, it was a frosty evening, but her shivers were as likely to be the result of excitement as from any other cause.

Aware of Sally's nervousness, Ethan chatted happily along the way to help her feel at ease. He was curious to know what the parcels she carried contained – especially the long parcel wrapped in brightly coloured paper.

'I've just bought a couple of little things for your ma and pa, that's all,' she fibbed.

'That parcel doesn't look like a *little* thing to me,' he pointed out.

'Well, you'll find out what it is soon enough,' she said, squeezing his arm happily.

Ethan's home was only a few streets distant from Pin's Lane, and even though Sally was now beginning to feel the cold they reached it far more quickly than she would have liked. She was not really certain she was quite ready to meet the large Shields family.

But it was too late to turn back. Ethan pushed open the door of his house and they were immediately greeted by the sound of laughter and loud voices.

The sounds came from the ground-floor front room, but Ethan's mother was in the kitchen. She had been awaiting the young couple's arrival and hurried forward to greet her youngest son and his friend.

Sally liked her immediately. A plump, motherly woman, Doris Shields was instinctively aware of Sally's nervousness. Putting an arm about her shoulders, she squeezed her affectionately.

'So *you're* Sally? Well, everyone's been telling me what a plucky girl you are, but no one thought to tell me how pretty you are – and what a lovely cloak you're wearing! I don't think I've ever seen one quite like it.'

'It belonged to my ma,' Sally said proudly, speaking for the first time.

'Did it, indeed? Well, that makes it even more special. Let me take it from you and put it somewhere very safe.'

Undoing the fastening, Sally took the cloak from about her shoulders and proudly handed it to Doris Shields.

Aware of Sally's regard for the cloak, the motherly woman said, 'We'll put it safe on a hook in here.' As she spoke, she opened a door that hid a cupboard beneath the stairs and hung up the cloak with exaggerated care.

While this was being done, Ethan gave Sally a reassuring smile and whispered, 'See! I told you there was nothing to worry about.'

The cloak safely put away, Doris led the way to the room from which all the noise was emanating.

'Quiet everyone . . .' She needed to raise her voice and shout the request twice more before the noise subsided.

'That's better.' Putting a reassuring arm across Sally's shoulders, she said, 'This is Sally, Ethan's friend. She's come to spend a part of Christmas with us.'

As she was speaking, Sally glanced at the two other young women in the room. One of them, probably only a year or so older than herself was introduced as Phoebe. She was the girlfriend of Joe, with whom Sally had worked at the pie shop.

A dark, rather haughty-looking girl, she wore a dress that immediately made Sally feel uncomfortable about her own secondhand frock. It was in green, shot-silk and worn off the shoulder, displaying smooth skin that would have been the envy of any society woman.

She acknowledged the introduction in a manner that did nothing to dispel Sally's feeling that this girl had a very high opinion of herself.

The other woman was in her early twenties and was Albert's wife. In contrast to Phoebe, Sophie Shields was more plainly dressed and she gave Sally a warm and open smile.

'It's nice to meet you at last,' she said. 'I can see now why Ethan talks about you so much.'

'And so he should,' said Henry Shields. 'She saved his life over at Shepherd's Wharf, when all those girls were taken off the Belgian boat. I'm glad to see you again, Sally.'

Doris now introduced Sally to her other sons, rattling through their names so quickly Sally could not remember afterwards who was who.

The introductions over, there was a brief, uncertain silence. It was broken by Ethan. 'Now Sally's met everyone, I think she has a present for you, Ma. You too, Pa.'

'A present for me?' queried Doris. 'You shouldn't have spent your hard-earned money on such things, young lady.'

When the handkerchief was unwrapped, Doris shook it out and said, 'This is *lovely*, Sally. Just look at the embroidery! Have you ever seen such fine stitching?'

Henry Shields was equally effusive about the pipe Sally had bought for him, but Ethan's puzzled glance went to the long package Sally was still holding. He had believed it to be the present she had brought for his mother.

Holding it out to him, she said, 'This is for you.'

His surprise was genuine. 'What is it?'

'I'd say the way to find out would be to open it,' said his father, with a grin. 'You'll never know if you stand there looking as though you're afraid it's going to bite you.'

'Well, you never know,' Joe said cheekily. 'It could be a conger eel, like that one Bill Grady caught over by Eddystone. He gave it to his wife for her birthday. Not only was it still alive but when she hit him with it the conger bit half his ear off.'

While his brother was speaking, Ethan was taking off the wrapping paper. When he exposed the long, leather case, his other brothers made equally flippant suggestions about what it might contain.

Carefully opening the case, Ethan gasped, 'It's a flute!'

Everyone in the room crowded around to look as Ethan removed it from the case and held it up.

'It's beautiful, Sally! Absolutely *wonderful!*'

Ethan was quite overwhelmed to have received such a present. Looking accusingly at Sally, he said, 'You shouldn't have, Sally. It must have cost you the *earth*. I've never seen such a fine flute.'

Delighted by his reaction to the present, Sally said, 'I know how upset you were when your other one got broken. I saw this one and wanted to buy it for you. I got it for a lot less than the price that was being asked.'

'All the same . . .'

Ethan was worried, but his father broke in upon his concern.

'Instead of standing there saying the girl *shouldn't* have bought it, I think you should be saying a great big "thank you" to her – and I don't mean you should shake her hand, neither.'

'Thank you, Sally,' Ethan said awkwardly. 'It's the best present anyone's ever given me.'

'Then don't just stand there gawking,' said his mother. 'Give the girl a great big, grateful kiss. You've got me worrying about what sort of a son I've brought up.'

Ethan self-consciously kissed Sally and the cheer that rose from his brothers made both of them blush with deep embarrassment.

'Well, now that's done with, perhaps you can give us a tune,' said his father.

'All right, but first, I've got a present for Sally,' said Ethan. 'It's nowhere as grand as this,' he held up the flute, 'but I hope you like it, Sally.'

His present was an enamelled heart on a fine silver chain, which thrilled Sally. When he had fastened it about her neck, she gave him a kiss without anyone having to prompt her.

Afterwards, Ethan played his new flute while the others sang. The flute made a very pleasant sound and Ethan declared it not only looked good but sounded better than any other instrument he had ever heard.

The evening passed by very quickly and Sally enjoyed herself much more than she had believed possible. She found the Shields family very easy to get along with and she liked them much more than she had expected.

They ate, sang and drank, and when the clock on the mantelshelf struck the hour of eleven, it was with real reluctance that Sally said she would have to go home.

Her announcement was greeted with a chorus of protests, but Doris realised that Sally did not like to leave Ruth for longer than was absolutely necessary. She led Sally from the room after she had said a warm 'Goodnight' to everyone.

In the passageway, Doris handed Sally her cloak, then pressed something into her hand. When Sally looked down she saw that it was a silver brooch, set with a number of coloured stones.

'It's my Christmas present to you, Sally,' said Doris. 'It once belonged to my mother. She used to wear it on her cloak. I thought you might like to do the same.'

30

In the kitchen of the Shields' home, after Sally and Ethan had left, Phoebe and Sophie were washing up, while Doris was in the front room gathering dirty dishes.

'What do you think of the girl Ethan has found for himself?' asked Phoebe, with a sly glance at her companion.

'I think she's sweet, don't you?'

'She's all right, I suppose,' Phoebe agreed grudgingly. 'But that dress! I'm surprised it didn't burst at the seams during the evening. It's much too small for her across the shoulders and bosom, yet far too loose at the waist. It looked to me as though she'd bought it in a second-hand clothes shop.'

Carrying a pile of dirty plates, Doris returned to the kitchen in time to hear Phoebe's last remark.

'I've no doubt that's *exactly* where she bought the frock – and there's no shame on her for that. Where did the dress you're wearing come from, Phoebe?'

Phoebe had not intended that her criticism of Sally's clothes should be overheard by Doris. Naming one of the town's best-known stores, she replied, 'Dingles.'

'Did you pay for it with your own money?'

'No, my mother bought it for me.'

'Sally has no mother to buy clothes for her. No father, either. Not only does she have to work hard for every penny, but she has to take care of a bed-ridden sister, too. I think she's a little marvel – and generous too. Rather than spend money on herself, she bought Ethan the thing he wanted more than anything else in this world. I hope our Ethan realises how lucky he is and hangs on to young Sally. He's not likely to find another like her.'

'Well! Ethan's little waif certainly seems to have made an impression on his mother,' Phoebe said petulantly, when Doris had returned to the front room. 'I've never heard her praising me like that.'

Sophie smiled sweetly at her companion, who had been extremely parsimonious in her choice of a Christmas present for Ethan's brother Joe. 'Perhaps you should buy your clothes from the same shop as Sally.'

Walking through the narrow streets to Pin's Lane with Ethan, Sally felt happier than she could ever remember. Despite her earlier misgivings, she had thoroughly enjoyed her evening with the Shields. It was the first time in her life she had experienced what it was to be a member of a complete family, and Doris had told her she would be welcome at the Shields' home any time she cared to call.

She clung to Ethan's arm and it all added to the warm sense of belonging. She felt she was no longer a young girl buffeted this way and that by life. She had regular work and was bringing in a wage that, if not exactly high, was adequate. She also had a man who was kind, considerate and courageous – one who was beginning to play an increasingly important part in her life.

Sally was beginning to look to the future. *Her* future. A future that included Ethan and his family. Just thinking of it gave her a warm feeling deep inside and she squeezed his arm happily.

'Did you enjoy your evening after all?' Ethan asked her.

'It was the best time I've ever had. I think your ma is wonderful – and I like your brothers, they're fun. Sophie too. I could be very good friends with her.'

'How about Phoebe?' Ethan asked the question tongue in cheek.

'She's all right,' Sally said cautiously. 'But I think she might have been a little spoiled by her ma and pa.'

Ethan laughed merrily. 'Phoebe has been a *lot* spoiled, we all know that, but she's not all bad. She's quite kind, really. It's just that she hasn't had to face up to the realities of life. Joe's besotted with her, but I can't see her settling for being the wife of a fisherman.'

'Why not? I'd be proud to be the wife of a fisherman.'

They both realised the implications of her words and were silent for a couple of minutes. Then Sally said, 'Thank you for inviting me to your home, Ethan. I really did enjoy meeting your family.'

They turned a corner and were now in an alleyway where there were no gaslamps. Suddenly, without any warning, Ethan stopped, pulled Sally clumsily to him, and kissed her.

She made no attempt to stop him, but when he broke away, she said, shakily, 'Why did you do that?'

'Because . . . I wanted to. I'm sorry, I . . .'

'No, don't be sorry, Ethan. I wanted you to. I want you to kiss me again.'

She came to him this time and the kiss lasted much longer. They did not break away from each other until they heard footsteps and the sound of voices coming along the alleyway.

Now they walked along with an arm about each other, needing to say nothing. All too soon, it seemed, they reached Pin's Lane.

When they arrived at the house where Sally lived, they went inside and were talking softly in the downstairs passageway when the door of Charlie's room opened. He peered around the open door to see who was there.

'Hello, you two. What are you doing out here? Did you decide to go out again after you came home?'

Sally and Ethan looked at each other quizzically, and Ethan said, 'What do you mean, Uncle Charlie? Sally has been at our house with me and the family all evening. We've just left and come straight here.'

'Don't try pulling the wool over my eyes, you two. What you get up to is your business, but I heard you upstairs not much

more than an hour ago. I should know, that creaking floor in
Sally's room has been driving me mad for years. When she's
home I can tell you exactly where she's standing because of
the noise made by the loose boards. Ruth hasn't got out of bed
in weeks, so it must have been Sally.'

'Wait here, Ethan. I'll go up and make sure everything's
all right.'

Without waiting for a reply, Sally left Ethan and his uncle
and ran up the stairs to the first floor.

Ethan was repeating his explanation when there was a scream
that sent him bounding up the stairs to the room Sally shared
with Ruth.

At the bedside, Sally was trying to raise the inert figure of
her sister. When she saw Ethan enter the room, she cried, 'Help
me. Help me to sit her up, Ethan. Quickly.'

Ethan was shocked by the pallor of Ruth's skin. He touched
her and felt her coldness. 'Just a minute Sally . . .' He took
Ruth's arm and felt for a pulse.

There was nothing.

Gently, he pulled Sally away and laid the thin body of Ruth
back on the bed.

'It's no use, Sally. I'm afraid she's dead.'

'No . . . ! She can't be.'

Sally's wail of despair made him wince. 'She is. There's
nothing you can do for her now.' He tried to draw her
gently away from the bed, but she fought against him and
broke free.

As huge sobs racked her body, Sally shook with hysterical
shock. 'How? Why did it happen?'

'She's been very ill for a long time, Sally. This could have
happened at any time.'

'But why tonight, Ethan? Why did it have to happen tonight . . . ?'

He tried to draw her to him, but she pulled away once
again.

Trying desperately hard to regain a grip on her emotions,
Sally cried, 'No, Ethan! She didn't just die because of her illness.
I know she didn't. Someone has been here.'

'You don't know that, Sally. I know Uncle Charlie thought

he heard something, but you can't rely on anything he says. He probably imagined it, and he's been drinking, probably for most of the day.'

'No. No! Someone *has* been here. Look!'

Bending down, Sally picked up something from the floor. As she lifted it, tiny, brightly coloured pieces of shiny paper fell to the floor.

It was the kaleidoscope she had bought for Ruth. Split open at the sides, it had been crushed almost flat.

'This is the present I bought Ruth for Christmas. Someone's trodden on it. It couldn't be Ruth, she wasn't able to get out of bed. Someone *has* been here, Ethan. I know it. Charlie was right.'

She looked at Ethan, her face contorted in agony. 'Ruth didn't just die, Ethan. She was *killed!* Someone murdered her.'

31

After he had gently covered Ruth's face with the quilt donated by Grace Philpott, Ethan managed to persuade Sally to go downstairs with him to Charlie's room.

She was still sobbing and at times became almost hysterical. More than once Ethan had to prevent her from hurrying upstairs again, as she struggled to accept that Ruth *really* was dead.

'What shall I do, Ethan? What's going to happen to me now?'

'We'll talk about that tomorrow. You'd better come back home with me tonight. It'll be a bit crowded in the house, but Ma will find room for you. Come on, let's go right away. Ma will know what to do.' He put an arm around her but she wriggled free.

'I can't just walk away and leave Ruth lying up there on her own.'

'You must, Sally. She'll need to be examined by a doctor, but it's still Christmas Day. We won't be able to find anyone until tomorrow.'

'The police . . . ? They should be called.'

'They wouldn't do anything until a doctor has seen Ruth.'

Ethan doubted the police would wish to become involved in Ruth's death, anyway. They would be no more convinced than he was that her death was in any way suspicious. But he kept such views to himself.

'I don't want to go to your house, Ethan.' Sally spoke through her tears.

'Why not?' Her refusal took him by surprise.

'Because . . . because I had such a happy time there this evening. We all did. It wouldn't seem right. Not for me, nor for the others.' She began sobbing again and Ethan put his arms about her and held her to him.

He understood what she was saying, and gently he said, 'You can't stay here, Sally. Can you think of anywhere else you could go? To the Philpotts' home, perhaps?'

Sally shook her head and now the tears were as much for herself as for Ruth. She needed to face the stark reality that without Ruth she belonged nowhere. To no one. She had felt close to Ethan, especially today, but she could not expect him to assume responsibility for her – nor would she want him to. Not just yet.

'Look, why don't we go and speak to Captain Eva?' suggested Ethan. 'She'll have room for you there – and will know what ought to be done in the morning.'

After only a moment's hesitation, Sally nodded her head in assent. Captain Eva was just the person to turn to in an emergency.

Ethan had been concerned that Captain Eva might have already gone to bed and would be difficult to rouse, but there appeared to be lights on in most of the rooms in the Refuge. In fact, there had been a disturbance at the large house.

In recent days Captain Eva had given refuge to a number of young prostitutes who had expressed a desire to escape their way of life, which was her original purpose in coming to Plymouth. Tonight, for one of the girls the thought of all her former associates out celebrating had been too much. She had slipped out of the house, got violently drunk and then made a noisy return, waking all her fellow residents.

In fact, she had only returned to gather up her few belongings, intending to return to her former ways. However, she caused such a fuss that she was arrested by the police immediately after leaving the house, for being 'drunk and disorderly'.

Captain Eva pleaded in vain with the police for the girl to be released and allowed to return to the house. The young woman struggled violently, calling the two arresting constables every name she could think of from her considerable and colourful vocabulary, as she was dragged away to the police station.

This incident had only just been played out when Ethan and Sally appeared.

Eva immediately took charge of the distraught young girl and led her inside the house. Ethan wanted to remain with Sally, but the Salvation Army officer declared firmly she would take care of her and put her to bed when she was less upset.

In the morning Eva would contact a doctor, and the police, if necessary. Should Ethan care to return then, as she was quite sure he would, she had no doubt Sally would want to see him.

Ethan's route home took him past the end of Pin's Lane. Acting on an impulse he turned in to the lane and made his way to the house where Ruth lay dead.

He climbed the stairs and entered the room Ruth had shared with Sally. The lamp had been left burning, but turned down very low. It would burn until morning, giving a dim light that, in the circumstances, Ethan found eerie.

Trying not to look at the bed, where Ruth's body lay covered by the quilt, Ethan walked across the room and picked up the broken kaleidoscope. Examining it, he frowned. It certainly looked as though someone had stepped on it. If so, Sally could possibly be right. Ruth might not have met a natural death.

Of course, Sally might have trodden on it herself, in the panic of the moment when she found Ruth . . .

There was a sound from the hall outside the room. A moment later the door opened cautiously, and Charlie peered inside.

'Oh, it's you . . .' Breathing heavily as a result of his exertions climbing the stairs, Charlie appeared relieved. 'I couldn't sleep and heard the boards creaking up here. I was afraid that whoever had been here earlier might have come back. It makes a man uneasy when people wander about the house at all times of the night. Especially when there's a dead girl lying here.'

'So you're quite sure you *did* hear someone up here earlier?'

'Of course I'm sure. My chest might not be so good, but it doesn't affect my hearing. Whoever was here was a sight bigger than you, too. These boards have creaked for as long as I've been living in this house. I know every sound they make. I could tell if a cat walked across the floor.'

As they talked, they saw a lamp being lit in an upstairs room of a house backing on to the one they were in. A man and a woman were in the room. The woman stared from the window at Ethan and Charlie, before drawing the curtains.

The curtains were too small for the window. Even when drawn there was a gap of about the width of a man's hand. Through this Ethan could see the woman undressing. He turned his back on her quickly; Charlie did not.

'Who's that?' Ethan asked, embarrassed.

'"Devonport Lil". She's a tart – and a busy one. She must have picked up a shy man tonight. Half the time she doesn't even bother to pull the curtains. She'll undress and dress in front of the open window too, not caring who might be watching.'

'Do you think she might have seen whoever was in this room earlier tonight?'

'She might. She's been home more than usual, it being Christmas. But I wouldn't go over there alone to ask her. If word got back to your ma and pa that you'd been in that house they'd throw you out for sure.'

'Thanks for the warning, Uncle, but I don't think she'd appreciate me asking questions of her right now anyway. Come on, let's leave poor Ruth in peace.'

And with a final look at the still form lying hidden beneath the quilt, he followed Charlie from the room.

32

When Ethan arrived at the Salvation Army Refuge the following morning, the streets were quiet. Most people seemed to be taking full advantage of the holiday and sleeping off the effects of the previous day's celebrations.

But Captain Eva had been up for some hours. She was the ideal woman to handle a situation such as that now facing Sally.

Possessing an apparently limitless reserve of energy, Eva was an efficient organiser and, in addition, she felt a deep and honest compassion for all who were in need of help.

She had already called on Grace Philpott to inform her what had happened. Deeply concerned for Sally, that big-hearted woman, with Rachel in tow, had hurried to the house to express her sympathy. She was with Sally now, comforting her as best she could.

Eva had also called in a local doctor to certify Ruth's death and had spoken to an undertaker. She would later visit the room where Ruth lay.

For the majority of Pin's Lane's residents, their final resting place was destined to be an unmarked pauper's grave. However, the ever-generous Grace Philpott promised Sally that Ruth would be given 'as fine a burial as could be arranged'.

Such arrangements would need to wait. Sally's suspicions

about the circumstances of Ruth's death had been passed on to the doctor.

The emaciated state of Ruth's body made the doctor highly sceptical that her death had been due to anything other than natural causes, but he was a cautious man. He had her body removed to the mortuary so that a post-mortem might be carried out.

Eva told Ethan of all that had been happening during his absence and he informed her of his late-night visit to Pin's Lane, and the conversation he had held with his uncle Charlie.

'When you leave, I'll come with you,' she said. 'I think you and I should call on your uncle and also make a few enquiries around Pin's Lane. But before we do that I'll take you up to see Sally. I'm afraid she's still extremely upset.'

Ethan found Sally both tired and very depressed. She had been far too distraught to sleep, and this morning she was suffering from a deep sense of guilt. She felt it had been wrong to be out enjoying herself while Ruth was dying – in whatever manner her death had occurred.

'You really mustn't think like that, Sally,' said Ethan. 'If someone else was responsible for Ruth's death, they'd have probably killed you too, had you been there.'

'What do you mean . . . "If"? Someone *had* been in the room. I *know* it. I can guess who it was, too. It was Sid Darling and he was there looking for *me*. When he didn't find me, he killed Ruth instead. She was far too weak to do anything to defend herself. However you look at it, it *is* my fault she's dead.'

Sally had spoken vehemently, bringing herself close to tears once more and Grace, who was still in the room, tried to calm her.

'Now, Sally, such talk helps no one. If Sid Darling *is* involved in this then, from what I hear about him, he wouldn't have spared either of you. Or anyone else who got in his way, come to that. As it is, you're here, safe and sound. I don't doubt that's the way your poor sister would have wanted it to be.'

'Mrs Philpott is right, Sally,' said Ethan. He was deeply unhappy to have upset Sally, when all he had tried to do was comfort her. 'The thing Ruth would have wanted more than anything else would be to know you were safe.'

Sally shook her head, her face contorted in anguish. 'I should have been with her, instead of out enjoying myself. I could have saved her.' Suddenly, she began trembling violently and Grace immediately wrapped her arms about her.

'You must try not to upset yourself so, my love. None of this has been your fault, or Ethan's, either. You'll realise it yourself as soon as you've had time to get over the shock of all that's happened. Ethan will leave you now, but he'll be back to see you most days to find out how you are, I'm sure. You're not on your own, dear, just remember that. There are a whole lot of people about you who care. We all care very much.' As she held Sally close in a bid to stop her trembling, Grace made a faint movement of her head in Ethan's direction, indicating that he should leave the room.

Visibly upset, he did so, but not before murmuring a faint and unacknowledged 'Goodbye' to Sally. On a small table in the room he left behind a note from his mother, in which she expressed her deep sympathy. With the note was a bag of cakes she had made up for Sally.

Downstairs, Ethan found Eva battling to replace a high shelf, knocked down by one of the girls earlier that morning.

Taking over the task from her, he told her of Sally's reaction to his visit.

'You mustn't feel in any way to blame,' Eva said sympathetically. 'Sally doesn't really know what she's saying right now. She's hurt, shocked – yes, and frightened too. Sally's all alone in the world now, or believes she is.'

Ethan shook his head vigorously. 'She's not, and never will be if I have my way.'

Eva put out a hand and rested it gently upon his arm. 'I'm delighted to hear it, Ethan. She is going to need all the help she can get, from you in particular. My dearest wish is that you should both find your happiness within the Salvation Army but, whatever happens, I will pray that you find it together. Now, you seem to have fixed that shelf. Shall we go and see what we can learn at Pin's Lane?'

33

When Captain Eva and Ethan reached the Pin's Lane house, they first called on Charlie Shields. The Salvation Army captain questioned him closely to learn the exact time he had heard someone moving around in the upstairs room.

He admitted to having been drinking heavily to celebrate Christmas and, as Captain Eva later pointed out to Ethan, this would detract seriously from his value as a prosecution witness should Ruth's death result in a trial.

Nevertheless, by the dint of much patience – and a little bullying – it was ascertained that Charlie had heard someone in the upstairs room between nine and nine thirty the previous evening.

'Who else lives in the house?' asked Captain Eva.

'No one, except me and the Harrups, although I suppose it's just Sally, now Ruth's dead. I have both rooms downstairs. There's another room opening off the landing upstairs, but the woman who rented it was arrested about two years ago for robbing one of the men she brought home with her. She got three years, but someone's been paying the rent for her. When she gets out again she'll no doubt move back, but there's no one up there right now.'

'Well, let's go upstairs to Sally's room, shall we?'

The three of them went up the stairs. As a result of the

conversation they had just had, they were very aware of the creaking of the floorboards on the landing.

The sound was even louder when they entered the room rented out to Sally and her sister. Ethan's glance went automatically to the bed. The last time he had been in the room the body of Ruth was lying there. It had gone now, but the memory had not.

Eva picked up the broken kaleidoscope. Holding it in her hand, she stood at the window in silence for some time.

Abruptly turning to her companions, she said, 'Charlie, tell me what you know about the people who live in the houses that back on to here.'

At first, Charlie protested he knew nothing at all of them. He 'minded his own business' and hoped they did the same. However, after skilful and patient questioning, Eva established that he knew most of the occupants, together with their predominantly dubious occupations.

Among them was the prostitute Devonport Lil.

'I think we'll go and speak to her first,' declared Eva. 'From what you've already said, it's possible she might have seen something.'

Giving a meaningful glance at the clock on the mantelshelf in the room, Charlie said, 'She'll not thank you for waking her at this hour. She doesn't rise until the afternoon.'

'I'm not looking for her thanks,' retorted Eva. 'As for the hours she keeps . . . they're God-given and ought to be spent honouring His bountifulness, not in playing the Devil's game. Come, Ethan. Let's find out what this woman can tell us.'

The houses backing on to those in Pin's Lane were approached via an alleyway. Cluttered with filth that had accumulated over many months, it was being scavenged by dogs, cats and rats.

It was a scene Eva had encountered in the slums of many other towns and cities in England. However, familiarity did not make it any more palatable. She wrinkled her nose in disgust as she lifted her skirts and tried to avoid the more offensive rubbish.

The house they were seeking had a neglected look about

it. Paint was peeling from the door and window frames, and a number of glass panes in the ground-floor windows were missing and had been replaced with sacking and folded newspapers.

The door was opened to Eva's persistent knocking by Clara Flood, the landlady of the house. A stooped and untidy grey-haired little woman. She took one look at Captain Eva's uniform and attempted to close the door again immediately.

The Salvationist had considerable experience of dealing with householders who had no wish to speak with her. The landlady found a foot effectively preventing the door from closing.

After a couple of half-hearted attempts to kick the foot clear of the doorway, Clara conceded defeat. Reluctantly, she opened the door wide once more.

'What d'yer want?' she demanded.

'I want to have a few words with the woman who lives in the back room upstairs. I believe she's known as Devonport Lil.'

'She won't want to see *you*,' Clara replied positively. 'Not at this time of day, she won't. Come back about five o'clock.'

'She'll speak to me now.' Unceremoniously pushing open the door as wide as it would go, Eva said over her shoulder, 'Come along, Ethan.' She headed for the stairs, situated half-way along a narrow, dark, musty-smelling passageway.

With a half-apologetic shrug at the scowling woman who stood holding the open door, Ethan stepped inside the passage-way and followed the Salvation Army captain up the stairs.

There were two doors opening off the landing. Eva knocked heavily on the door of the room where she believed Devonport Lil to be.

After waiting for a few moments without receiving a reply, she knocked once more, at the same time trying the latch. The door appeared to be bolted on the inside.

'Who is it . . . ? What d'you want?' A sleepy and indignant voice came to them from inside the room.

'I want to talk to you.'

'Go away. Come back tonight.'

Eva knocked again. When she received no reply this time, she continued to knock, long and loud, before saying, 'I can keep this up all day if I need to. You might as well open the door and speak to me, then you can go back to sleep again.'

Ethan and Eva heard grumbling from inside the room before the door opened. A woman stood in the doorway. Sleep-filled eyes looked Captain Eva up and down from beneath heavy, puffy lids. Then she asked irritably, 'What the bloody hell do you want at this time of the day?'

'I want to talk to you . . .' Raising her voice, Eva added, 'Out of hearing of others.' Stepping inside the room, she motioned for Ethan to follow.

The room was as untidy as the woman. An aroma of cheap scent hung on the air, used in an apparent attempt to override the general odours of the house.

As Devonport Lil closed the door, frowning disapprovingly, Eva strode to the window and drew back the curtains.

Blinking against the sudden unwelcome influx of light, the prostitute demanded, 'Here! Just who do you think you are, coming in here and doing as you like?'

Instead of answering her question, Eva pointed across the two tiny, back-to-back yards to the room where Ruth had died. 'What do you know of the people who live over there?'

The woman's attitude underwent an extraordinary change and fear replaced belligerence. 'I didn't see nothing – or no one.'

'In view of the fact that you've answered the question before I've even asked it, it's quite obvious you *did* see something last night. Who did you see over there, Lil?'

'I told you, I didn't see no one.' Devonport Lil gave the impression of being thoroughly frightened.

'It was Sid Darling, wasn't it? What was he doing?'

'I couldn't see what he was doing. Like I just said, I can't tell you nothing.'

'So it *was* him who was over there! Do you know a girl died in that room last night?'

'One'll die in *this* room if he knows I've said anything about him.'

'I'm not the police, Lil, but the girl who died wasn't the one he was after. He'll come back to kill her too if we aren't able to stop him.'

'What do you think *you* can do against the likes of Sid Darling?' Devonport Lil spoke contemptuously. 'He'd eat the whole of the Salvation Army for breakfast. Me too if he learns I've been talking to you. Anyway, I only saw him over there. I didn't see him do anything.'

'This was about half-past nine last night, is that right?'

The prostitute nodded. 'Probably, although it might have been closer to nine o'clock. That's all I'm saying. If you bring the police into this I'll swear I saw nothing. Now, I'm not talking to you any more, so you might as well go.'

34

As Ethan and Captain Eva carefully picked their way once more through the rubbish-cluttered alleyway, he asked, 'What are we going to do now?'

'Somehow, we need to persuade the police to step up their efforts to have Sid Darling arrested. Until he's put out of the way Sally is never going to be safe.'

'But surely now we know what he's done to Ruth, the police will arrest him for murdering her?'

'What exactly do we *know* he's done, Ethan? We're fairly certain he was in the room yesterday evening – and we know that Ruth died. The woman we've just spoken to will never stand up in court and admit that she saw Sid Darling in Ruth's room. If the doctor who carries out the post-mortem confirms she was murdered, then we can tell the police all we know. When they eventually arrest Sid Darling they'll question him about it. However, we need to remember that he's already a wanted man – and the police haven't been very successful in arresting him, even though he's been seen by a number of people, including poor Rachel. This latest incident has terrified her. She believes he'll come after her as well as Sally – and she could well be right.'

'What can we do? We can't allow him to put Sally and Rachel in terror and get away with killing Ruth – and I'm convinced that's what he did.'

'So am I, but without proof he'll never be convicted in a court.' She added bitterly, 'Perhaps we should provide him with a Salvation Army uniform. That would ensure his arrest, at least.'

They walked in silence for a while before Eva said, 'I'll go and speak to Percy Mallett. He'll at least listen to what I say, and he may be able to use his influence to have Sid Darling arrested.'

Percy Mallett listened to Eva courteously. He expressed concern that Sid Darling was still at large. At the same time, he confirmed what she already knew. Without firm evidence against him and witnesses prepared to testify to what they had seen, Sid Darling would never be charged with murder.

'Nevertheless, I will speak to the chief constable about the failure to arrest this man on the charges concerning those young girls. Perhaps the knowledge that I am taking a personal interest in the case will succeed where the due process of the law has failed.'

As Percy Mallett was walking Eva to the door of his house, he said, 'We have a new inspector in the Force, Captain. His name is Ian Lovat. He has been brought to Plymouth to form a detective section. There are those who feel he is too young to hold such a post, but he had a remarkable record of thief-taking in the London Force. He spent much of his service there working in plain-clothes. Inspector Lovat accepted the post only when we agreed to give him a completely free hand to carry out his duties. The chief constable had grave reservations about allowing him such independence, but he was overruled by my committee. I think Inspector Lovat might be able to help in the matter of Mr Darling. I'll ask him to call upon you.'

'Thank you very much, Mr Mallett. I regret I don't have your faith in policemen – wherever they are from – but none of the girls in my care can afford to rest easy until Sid Darling has been arrested and brought to justice.'

When Inspector Ian Lovat called at the Salvation Army Refuge in the Barbican, the door was opened by one of the girls. After showing him in to the front lounge, she went to find Eva.

The Salvation Army officer was busy in the small linen room, on the second floor of the house. Entering, the girl said coyly, 'There's a man come to the house looking for you, Captain Eva. A very handsome man.'

'Oh! Did he tell you his name and his business?'

'No. I did ask him, but he said his business was "personal" – with you.'

Eva frowned. 'Did he, now? Very well, Joan, I'll come down and speak to him.'

With another of the girls, she had been checking through a stack of sheets that had been donated to the home by a well-wisher. It was necessary to sort out those that were too badly worn and would need to be torn up for dusters, or perhaps made into pillow-cases. She now asked Joan to take her place.

As she started down the stairs she could hear the two girls whispering together about the 'handsome man' who had come calling on her. She smiled to herself. She was aware the girls were concerned there was no man in her life. They were convinced that, at the age of twenty-three, she was well and truly 'on the shelf'.

All the same, she wondered who her visitor might be.

Ian Lovat was a tall, sandy-haired man, with a ready smile. When he spoke, it was with the soft accent of the west coast of Scotland.

'Good morning, Captain Cassington. I am Ian Lovat. Mr Mallett asked me to come along to see you to discuss the problems you are having with this man Sidney Darling.'

'Oh, you're *Inspector* Lovat? It's very kind of you to come and call on me so quickly.'

'Mr Mallett told me of your concern for the girls who are here with you. I've read the notices that have been put out about Darling, but perhaps you will tell me what you know of him?'

As they sat together in the lounge, Eva told the detective how girls had been lured to Plymouth by an advertisement offering posts in domestic service and what had happened to them on their arrival. The inspector made notes as she explained Sally's part in raising the alarm and told him of the fight at Shepherd's Wharf and the rescue of the girls.

Finally, she told him of the latest incident which had culminated in the death of Ruth in suspicious circumstances.

Ian Lovat was silent for a while, then he said, 'This girl, Sally Harrup, seems to be at the heart of all that's going on in this matter.'

'She's a bright girl, Inspector. She's nice too – in every sense of the word.'

He nodded. 'I'm sure she is. I look forward to meeting her in due course. I'll wait until she has made a full recovery from the sad death of her sister. It must have been a very nasty shock for her.'

Having a policeman express sympathy for someone even remotely associated with the Salvation Army was a new experience for Eva. However, she tried not to allow her surprise to show.

'Why did you not call in the police when you first had suspicions of what was going on?' He put the question to her as he was returning his notebook to a pocket.

'With all due respect to you, Inspector Lovat, my experience has been that it is a waste of everyone's time for a member of the Salvation Army to report *anything* to the police, no matter how serious. It serves only to bring that individual to their attention. As likely as not, it ultimately results in his, or her, own arrest.'

'I feel that's a rather unkind generalisation, but I can understand your attitude. There does seem to be a degree of resentment among certain policemen towards your organisation.'

'That resentment resulted in my being sentenced to prison shortly before Christmas, Inspector. My offence was nothing more serious than marching to a prayer meeting here in Plymouth. So my "attitude", as you describe it, is hardly surprising.'

'You have my sympathy, Captain. However, I assure you that I have nothing but admiration for the Salvation Army and its founder. I spent a while working among the people of Poplar, in London. I am aware of the wonderful work done by your organisation among the most unfortunate and under-privileged members of our society. I assure you of my whole-hearted support. I trust you will give me yours. Hopefully, we will then be able to bring Sidney Darling to justice and sound the death knoll to a vile trade that brings shame upon us all.'

Eva looked at Ian Lovat in silence for a few moments. Suddenly, she smiled. 'Inspector Lovat, I think you and I are going to work well together. Now, let me show you over the house. Along the way I will tell you what I intend to achieve here. Then I will introduce you to Rachel. She has suffered more than any of the girls because of Mr Darling. I am quite certain she will talk to you when I tell her you are the man who is going to arrest him.'

35

The inquest on Ruth Harrup was attended by Sally, Eva and Ethan. It was an unhappy and frustratingly perfunctory affair.

The surgeon who had carried out the post-mortem had been unable to discover any unnatural cause for her death. Indeed, he was unable to say with any degree of certainty exactly what *had* caused her to die.

However, he was able to inform the coroner that Ruth's lungs were in such an advanced stage of disease, it was really quite remarkable she had lived for so long.

Ian Lovat was also in court. During the surgeon's evidence, the coroner was startled to have a note passed to him from the inspector, via the coroner's officer.

Reading from the note, the coroner asked the surgeon, 'Is it possible the deceased woman might have died as a result of suffocation? By a pillow being placed over her face, for instance?'

The surgeon mulled over the question for a moment or two before delivering a somewhat cautious reply. 'It is not *impossible*, but in view of the advanced stage of her lung disease my opinion is that her death was brought about by natural causes.'

The coroner looked across the courtroom with a questioning glance at Inspector Lovat and the policeman nodded his head. A few minutes later the coroner delivered his verdict.

The recorded cause of the death of Ruth Harrup was 'Natural causes'.

Outside the courtroom, Sally was bewildered by the verdict. 'It just isn't true! Sid Darling killed her. We know he was in the room because someone trod on Ruth's Christmas present. That and the pillow from the bottom of the bed that I found on the floor. She wouldn't have moved that. She never had before.'

'Unfortunately, all that is no more than supposition, Sally,' said the inspector. 'It's hardly even circumstantial evidence.'

Sally was unsure of the meaning of both 'supposition' and 'circumstantial', but she *did* believe she knew how Ruth's death had occurred.

She continued her protest until Ian Lovat said, 'You believe Sid Darling did it – and so do I. Proving it is quite another matter. Nevertheless, I shall try, I can assure you of that.'

'No you won't,' Sally retorted bitterly. 'Because he's never going to be arrested.'

'Oh, he'll be arrested all right,' he assured her confidently. 'Even though I doubt it's imminent. I have reliable information that Sid Darling has left Plymouth for a while.'

'There you are then,' Sally said scornfully. 'He did it and now he's run off. He'll never be caught, you'll see.'

'He'll be back. Mother Darling is still living in Mary Street. He'll return to her one day. When he does, he'll be arrested.' Resting a hand on Sally's shoulder, he added sympathetically, 'I give you my word on that, Sally – and I always keep my word.'

With this promise, Ian Lovat left to return to the police station, leaving Sally with Eva and Ethan.

She had received a great deal of support in the coroner's court. Her two companions and the inspector had been with her for the whole of the proceedings. Grace had wanted to attend too, but Alfie successfully protested that, however much he sympathised with Sally, he simply could not run the pie shop with only Rachel to help him.

As a result, Grace had stayed to work in the shop. Sally would not be returning there until after Ruth's funeral. In the meantime, Grace, generous as ever, assured her she would be paid a wage equal to that she had been earning before the tragedy.

Sally had been living in the Salvation Army home ever since Ruth's death, but she knew she would need to think about her future now and decide whether or not to keep on the room in Pin's Lane.

Ruth's funeral took place on a day as bleak and cold as the occasion itself. The church was not crowded, but there were many more in the congregation than Sally had anticipated.

The whole of Ethan's family attended, including Sophie. Phoebe did not attend, but she sent an extravagant wreath.

Grace and Alfie were there, having closed the shop for a few hours. So too was Captain Eva, with all the girls from the home, together with Captain Wardle and a few members of the Salvation Army.

Some of the neighbours from Pin's Lane also attended. Among their number were a couple of the girls who had once solicited on the streets of Plymouth with Ruth.

The vicar, who had been expecting far fewer in the funeral congregation, mumbled a totally inaccurate eulogy, but it pleased Sally.

The interment in the churchyard took long enough to cause everyone present to shiver in the cold wind. Although Sally came very close to breaking down, the strong arm of Grace about her provided just enough strength and comfort to hold off her tears.

Afterwards, when the party moved towards the gate of the burial ground, slowed by all those who came up to offer their condolences to Sally, Grace asked her what she intended doing now and where she intended to live.

'Captain Eva has said I can stay in the house with her for as long as I wish. I'll probably stay for a while, at least.'

'Well, you need never be short of a place to live, dear,' said Grace. 'Alfie and me made room for Rachel. It would be no more trouble to take you in too. You could share with Rachel. It would be good company for her. We've already talked it over and she would like that.'

As Sally murmured her thanks, Ethan's mother said, 'I'm not able to offer you a home, Sally, much as I would like to. With five boys in the house and only three bedrooms between seven of us, it's more than a little crowded. I can't wait for some of them to get married and move to a home of their own. But there's always food in the house, so you need never go hungry. Come to us for as many meals as you like. We'll always be delighted to have you. I want you to remember that.'

'You are lucky in having so many good friends, Sally,' commented Eva. 'And you can add everyone at the home and Central headquarters to your list. But what are you going to do right now?'

'I think I'll go to Pin's Lane and tidy up Ruth's things. But I don't think I could sleep there on my own. Not yet, anyway. So I'd like to come back to the Refuge tonight. Tomorrow, I'll start work again and think seriously about the future.'

'Only come in if you feel like it, mind,' said Grace. 'Although we'll be delighted to have you back with us, won't we, Alfie?'

Alfie agreed with all honesty that he was looking forward to her return to work. Having no one reliable to deliver their wares had been adversely affecting the business. Rachel was a very willing young girl, but she did not yet know the Plymouth area and was still nervous about going out on her own.

'Thank you all. Thank you for helping me – and for what you've done for Ruth today. It was a lovely funeral. Ruth never ever believed she would have one like that . . .' Sally's voice broke, despite her determination to maintain tight control of herself. Recovering as best she could, she said abruptly, 'I'm going to Pin's Lane now.'

As she turned away and set off hurriedly, Ethan caught up with her. 'I'll come with you.' Aware that she was about to protest, he added quickly, 'I'll just see you to the house and stay with Uncle Charlie while you go up to your room. I know you'd rather be on your own up there for a while. Just remember I'm close at hand in case you feel you need me. Uncle Charlie isn't feeling too well at the moment. That's the reason he wasn't at the funeral today. I know he'd been hoping to make it to the church.'

Sally wanted a little time on her own while she did what needed to be done, but knowing Ethan was in the house too would be reassuring.

Without saying a word, she slipped her hand in his, thinking how lucky she was to have found him.

Behind them, at the gate to the burial ground, Doris Shields watched them walking off hand-in-hand. She wondered, somewhat wistfully, whether her youngest son would be the next to leave the family home.

Beside her, as he lit his pipe, Henry Shields had been watching the young couple too. Correctly interpreting his wife's expression, he took her arm and said gently, 'The lad could do a whole lot worse, Doris. That young girl has something about her. Reminds me a little of the girl I married . . .'

36

When Sally and Ethan reached the Pin's Lane house they found Charlie waiting for them at the door of his room. He had been seated at the window of his room watching out for them.

His first words showed he had been waiting for Sally. 'I hoped you might come back here,' he said. 'I wanted to be at the funeral, but this weather sets my chest off. I dared not leave the house. If I'd gone you wouldn't have heard nothing but my coughing in the church. All the same, I was thinking of Ruth.'

'I'm sure you were, Charlie. Thank you.'

'Will you be moving back here now?'

He sounded a little too eager and Sally remembered his habits before Ethan had appeared on the scene. 'Not for a while. I've just come back to sort out a few of Ruth's things.'

Shrugging off his disappointment, Charlie asked, 'What shall I tell the rent man when he comes this week? The last time he came he wanted to know whether he should find someone else to take your room.'

'You can tell him if I want to move out I'll tell him – and he'll get any rent that's owing him. I'm only a fortnight behind. There are many around here who owe him far more than that.' Sally spoke angrily, and Ethan said hurriedly, 'Would you like me to go upstairs first, Sally?'

'Would you, Ethan? I know it's silly, but I'll feel happier if you make sure there's no one there. Then I'd like to go through Ruth's things on my own.'

'Of course. I'll come back down here and wait with Uncle Charlie until you're finished.'

When Ethan had returned downstairs, Sally stood alone in the upstairs room for some minutes. It felt wrong without Ruth lying in the bed. Horribly wrong. She realised she needed to shake off such feelings.

Going to the window, she opened it wide. The cold air from outside made her shiver, but it drove out the smell of the damp and mustiness that pervaded the room.

Suddenly, she heard a bird singing from the branch of a solitary tree that grew in a backyard farther along the lane. The song was as beautiful as it was out of place amidst the squalor of the Barbican slum.

Listening to the song brought a lump to Sally's throat – but it did something else too. Something indefinable. The song of the lone, defiant bird held a message of optimism.

It was the frailest of threads on which to pin her hopes for the future, but it somehow gave her just a little of the strength she so desperately needed at this time.

Turning back into the room, she felt able to carry out the tasks for which she had come here.

There were very few of Ruth's clothes in the chest of drawers; just a few underclothes, a frock and two nightdresses. Ruth's outdoor clothes had been sold long before, when things were going badly for the two girls and it became clear that Ruth was never going to recover.

But there was still the trunk . . .

Sally reached up and located the purse, hidden at the rear of the high shelf. She took out the key and, turning it in the stiff lock, she lifted the lid of the trunk and began rummaging inside.

There were a few clothes and shoes that had mainly belonged to their mother. Taking them out one by one, she laid them on the bare floorboards.

Next came a few strands of cheap beads, a hat, two cheap gilded – and empty – jewellery boxes, and the bundle of letters she had seen once before, tied up with a pink ribbon.

Sally untied the ribbon with a sense of curiosity rather than excitement. Taking the first letter from its envelope, she began to read.

She was half-way through it before realisation of what she was reading hit her.

It was a letter from the man who was her father!

Trembling with excitement, Sally looked at the printed address at the top of the single sheet of paper. It was Lanhydrock House, in Cornwall.

She read through the remainder of the letter eagerly, only to find it tantalisingly brief and disappointingly formal. However, it revealed a great deal about the relationship between her parents.

In a bold, but untidy hand, the letter read:

Dear Molly,

I thank you for your letter. I must warn you yet again that your are not to write to me here and put my position at risk. If you do so again I will refuse to send you any more money and will leave you to fend for yourself in a manner to which you are undoubtedly familiar.

That I send you any money at all is because I have no wish to see the sins of the mother visited upon the child by reason of an immoral upbringing.

You ask if I might not plead with the family to take you back into their employ; you must realise this is not possible. You were dismissed because you became pregnant. The family is hardly likely to allow you to return now you have a bastard child. Besides, how would I explain to them that I am still in touch with you?

No, you must make a future for you and the child in Plymouth. Opportunities for gainful employment will exist there, even for a woman such as yourself.

I will continue to send small sums of money from time to time but, I repeat, do *not* write to me here again.

The letter was signed, 'Yours faithfully, Robert Sanderson'.

Sally looked once again at the top of the page. There was a date of 12 August 1858. She was disappointed. The date was before she was born. The 'child' referred to in the letter must have been Ruth.

Yet Ruth had always said their mother had been adamant that both girls shared the same father – and there were other letters.

More than an hour later, Sally was still reading. She now had a much clearer picture of her mother and the life she had led. She had learned something about her father too – and was quite convinced that the man who had written the letters *was* her father.

Despite his earlier demand that her mother cease writing to him, she had evidently ignored his wishes. It was apparent too that, over the years covered by the letters, his determination to have nothing to do with her mother had been eroded by her persistence.

Towards the end of the correspondence, he had written to say he had found work for her, helping a washerwoman in the Cornish town of Bodmin, not far from Lanhydrock House.

There was a gap in the letters then, for quite a while. It was broken by a single letter, filled with Robert Sanderson's anger.

Sally's mother was in Plymouth once again – and was expecting another baby. This final letter was sent in 1863, so the baby this time had to be Sally and Sanderson was again the father.

His anger was due to his belief that Sally's mother had become pregnant deliberately, in order that she might give up work. He also accused her of nursing a vain hope that he would keep her.

Apparently money *had* been sent to her, but it was accompanied by a warning. The writer warned her that if she tried to name him as the father, he would so blacken her character, she was likely to spend the rest of her life in prison.

His anger leapt out at Sally from the single page even after all these years. It was hardly surprising this was the last letter in the bundle.

Sally was still on her knees beside the trunk when Ethan returned to the room, concerned that she was still here.

'Are you all right, Sally? I was getting worried about you.'

'Yes, I'm all right.'

'What do you want to do now? Where do you want to go?'

Standing up, still clutching the letters, Sally said, 'I think I'll go to the pie shop. I want to tell Grace I won't be coming to work tomorrow after all. I'm going to see if my father is still at Lanhydrock House. In Cornwall.'

37

'Are you quite certain this is what you want to do, Sally?'

Eva expressed her concern as Sally boarded the train that would take her across the River Tamar to Cornwall and, hopefully, a meeting with the father she had never known.

Sally nodded a reply.

She was under no illusions about the reception she was likely to receive from the man she believed to be her father. The last letter he had sent to her mother had made his feelings perfectly clear.

However, she remembered the change in the tone of the letters over the years before that. Sally hoped that time might have mellowed him once more. That he would at least acknowledge her and perhaps show regret at Ruth's death.

She wondered whether he was aware her mother had died all those years ago. He might even have tried to find her. The address on the few envelopes that had been kept with the letters no longer existed, so he would have had great difficulty locating her.

Of course, there was a strong possibility he was no longer at Lanhydrock House. If this proved to be so, she might at least learn where he had gone.

Captain Eva, Ethan and Grace had all tried to dissuade Sally from making this journey – at least until enquiries had been made concerning Robert Sanderson. Whether he was still at Lanhydrock House and, if he was, his position there and his present family circumstances.

This latter consideration far from worrying Sally actually excited her. She might have other brothers and sisters – or *half*-brothers and -sisters. They would never be able to take the place of Ruth, of course, but it would be wonderful to discover a whole new family.

She had discussed this aspect of her quest with Ethan. He too had warned her against undue optimism. He had wanted to accompany her, even though it was good fishing weather, but she had declined his offer. She felt this was something she needed to do by herself. It was almost as though she owed it to Ruth.

Sitting on the train, Sally thought about her late sister. She wondered why Ruth had never said anything about the letters to her. Why *she* had never tried to contact their father . . . ?

Watching from the platform of Plymouth railway station as the train disappeared from view, Eva tried to tell herself there was probably no justification for the concern she felt about Sally's self-imposed mission to Lanhydrock House. Yet she felt decidedly uneasy about the whole business.

For all the worldliness Sally displayed here in Plymouth, she had never before travelled beyond the town's boundaries. Eva knew just how vulnerable she was at the moment, having so recently lost her sister.

At least the Salvation Army officer had been able to provide her with a stout pair of elastic-sided boots. They had come from the stock donated to the organisation by well-wishers, for distribution to the poor.

Had she not done so, Sally would have set off wearing entirely unsuitable light town shoes. Although satisfactorily shod, Eva felt Sally was not dressed for travelling so far. True, she was wearing the warm cloak that had once been her mother's, but beneath it she had on only the thin frock she had bought to wear to Ethan's house.

*   *   *

Sally knew nothing of Captain Eva's thoughts. She felt very grown-up and sophisticated. At least she believed this was what she was showing to the world.

Inside, she felt less so.

She was no stranger to trains. They were part of everyday life in Plymouth. There were few places in and about the town where they could not be heard or seen. Yet this was the first time she had travelled in one and it was very exciting.

The first part of the journey involved a crossing of the River Tamar on the high suspension bridge that linked Devon with Cornwall. Sally held her breath as she looked down to the waters of the River Tamar far below the train. Downriver, a great many warships were anchored in long lines extending beyond the Hamoaze and the naval dockyard of Devonport.

After skirting numerous creeks, each with a wide variety of small boats scattered about on mud, water and dry land, the railway line curved inland. Smoke from the engine now spread across hills and valleys.

After less than an hour, the train was steaming noisily along the side of a wooded slope, which rose from a valley road. Suddenly the train driver pulled the whistle cord and sent a long, raucous signal echoing across the valley, and the train began to slow as it approached Bodmin Road station. Sally had been told she would need to alight here for Lanhydrock House.

Now, for the first time, she wished she had accepted Ethan's offer to accompany her.

A few minutes later, standing alone on the platform as the train steamed westwards on its journey, she felt even more uncertain of herself.

'Can I help you, Miss?'

The question came from a young railway porter, scarcely older than herself. He had appeared, unnoticed, on the platform behind her.

'I want to go to Lanhydrock House – but I don't know the way,' she said, relieved to have found someone from whom to ask directions.

The young porter looked her up and down, deciding on the

form his reply would take. She wore an expensive cloak, but
the dress visible beneath it and the cheap bonnet reassured him
he was not addressing 'gentry'.

'It's easy enough to get there, but you'll find the paths a bit
muddy. You'll need to hoist your dress well clear of your ankles
if you don't want to get it dirty. Come outside the station and
I'll show you the way.'

Sally followed him to a carriage park and he pointed west-
ward, in the direction taken by the train.

'Go along there, following the path beside the railway until
it turns off to the right. You'll see a bridge then. Cross it, over
the river, and go through the iron gate on the left. You're then
on the drive that leads up to the big house.'

'How far is it?' she asked anxiously, seeing the railway line
disappearing into the distance.

'About a mile and a half. I walk up there quite often. My
ma is a lady's maid at the house. Are you going up there for
work?'

'No. I'm looking for someone, but . . . I don't even know if
he's still there.'

'If he is I'll know him. I know everyone up at the house.
What's his name?'

'Robert Sanderson.'

'The butler! I'll say he's there – but you'd better watch your
step with him. He's an absolute Tartar. He's got an eye for the
ladies, too. Especially young ones, like you. I wouldn't like to
tell you how many young girls I've seen weeping on this station
because of him. They'd been dismissed, all of 'em. Some because
they "wouldn't", the others because they "did" and ended up
in trouble. What d'you want him for?'

'It's personal,' said Sally, trying not to show the dismay she
felt at his words.

'Oh, personal, is it? Well, don't say I haven't warned you
about him – and don't let him lead you off somewhere so he
can "take down your particulars". Five minutes alone with him
and it'll be more than your particulars he'll have down. I can
tell you *that*!'

38

Walking from the railway station, Sally thought about the porter's words. She wondered how much of what he had said was the truth and how much mere malicious gossip.

Whatever the truth of it, she had learned two things. The man she believed to be her father was the butler at Lanhydrock House – and he was still there!

Sally was not entirely certain what a butler did, but it was evident from what the young porter had said that it was something very important.

The thought that such a man might very soon acknowledge her as his daughter excited her, but once again she wished Ethan was here with her. Sally felt certain *he* would know what a butler did.

She soon realised the porter had been accurate about one thing. The path beside the railway line *was* very muddy. She was forced to walk with the hem of her skirt held up almost to her knees until she left the path and turned in at the entrance to the Lanhydrock Estate.

Here, she spent many minutes cleaning mud from her boots with grass torn from the verge at the side of the roadway.

Passing through the gate into the drive she found herself on a long gravelled avenue, flanked by rows of tall, mature trees.

Even though it was winter and the trees were denuded of leaves, they were still impressive.

Even more impressive was her first sight of the house, which did not come into view until she had walked quite a way along the tree-lined driveway.

Built in a U-shape, with the open end facing her, the house was battlemented, with an immaculate garden to the front and sides and a detached gatehouse some distance in front of the house itself.

But it was the sheer size of the house that Sally found awesome. It was *huge*. Even the gatehouse was larger than three of the houses in Pin's Lane!

Stopping in front of the gatehouse, Sally looked through the archway at the house itself. She knew she would never be able to summon up enough courage to pass through and knock on the front door.

She also realised that house servants would not be allowed to use the main entrance, so there had to be another door. While she was looking around for it, an aged gardener put his head above the low wall surrounding the garden.

'Hello! You here looking for work?'

'No. I'm here to speak with Mr Sanderson – he's the butler.'

'I know very well who he is, missie. There's no one worked here longer than me. I'd been here nigh on half a lifetime before ever he came here. I've seen enough young girls like you come and go in that time, too, I can tell you. Full of their cheek they are when they arrive. Laughing at me and saying I ought to be put out to grass – I've heard 'em all right. But I've still been working here when they've gone off crying, with a bundle of belongings on their shoulder and a bundle of trouble under their girdle. Make certain it don't happen to you too, girl.'

Sally thought of telling him once again that she had not come to Lanhydrock House seeking work, but decided it would be a waste of time. He was probably deaf. However, she thought she would ask him if he remembered her mother.

'Molly Harrup?' he repeated. 'Can't say I do. What was she working as? Kitchen maid? Housemaid?'

Sally had to confess she did not know.

'Don't know? I knew what my mother did – yes, and my grandmother and great grandmother, too. They were all housemaids right here at the house. Didn't you ever ask her?'

'She died when I was very small.'

'Ah! Well, you can't be blamed for not knowing about her then, I suppose. But couldn't your father have told you?'

'I never knew him.'

'I see,' the old gardener said knowingly. 'Well, you're not the first who never knew her father, and you won't be the last. But I can't stand here talking to you. I've got work to do. I hope they take you on up at the house, but I wouldn't count on it, if I was you. They've not needed to take on anyone new for a while now. You'll find the servants' door around the corner, through the coachyard. That's where you want to go – but you'd better be quick about it. The family don't like to see servants standing about in front of the house.'

The servants' door at the rear of the great house was opened by a red-faced kitchen maid, who had a lock of untidy hair hanging down over one eye. She appeared harassed.

Wasting no time on pleasantries, she asked, 'What do you want? If you're selling something – we ain't buying. If you're looking for work, we don't need anyone.'

'I'm not selling anything and I don't need work. I've come to speak to Mr Sanderson.'

The kitchen maid's manner underwent a subtle change. Less aggressively, she asked, 'You want the butler?' Her gaze took in Sally from her bonnet to the elastic-sided boots, visible beneath the hem of her too-small dress. Clearly puzzled, she asked, 'What do you want him for?'

'I'll tell that to *him*, if you don't mind.'

'*I* don't mind, but *he* will if it's someone wasting his time, and I don't want him telling me off. Who shall I say is calling on him?'

'Tell him . . . Tell him it's the daughter of Molly Harrup.'

'Is that all?'

'That's all.'

More uncertain than ever, the kitchen maid said, 'I'll tell him, but don't be surprised if he won't see you. He's not a great one for unexpected visitors, especially when his Lordship has a shooting party staying in the house.'

When the maid had gone, Sally was left waiting outside the servants' door. She had a moment of sheer panic. The maid had mentioned 'his Lordship'! Sally knew nothing at all about the peerage. Had she been questioned about them she would have said that all lords and ladies were related to the Queen.

Now here she was, standing outside the house of a lord, waiting for a man whose daily life was tied up with such people.

And that man was her father.

39

When the door opened once more, Sally had her back to it. She was watching the Lanhydrock House grooms. They had rolled a light landau from the coach house and were busily engaged in preparing the two horses that were to draw it.

Hearing the door open behind her, Sally turned. She was taken aback by the man standing before her. He was more than six feet tall and stoutly built, with greying hair, and, dressed in white tie and tailcoat, he made a very impressive sight.

Even in her present, highly emotional state, Sally found it easy to see why young servant girls would fall for him in droves. However, his expression was not intended to charm her and when he spoke his voice was brusque.

'What nonsense is this, girl? You're not Molly Harrup's daughter. What's your game, eh?'

His greeting was not the one she had foolishly hoped he might give to her.

'I *am* her daughter. That's why I've come to see you—'

'Don't lie to me, girl. Her daughter came here some five or six years ago, begging money from me. If she's sent you to do the same, you're out of luck. It didn't work then and it won't work now. In fact, I've a good mind to call the police . . .'

'Nobody has sent me, and I don't want anything from you. I . . . I didn't know Ruth had already been to see you. She never said anything to me about it. It's just . . . when she died I found some letters you'd written to our ma.'

'Ruth Harrup's dead?' For a moment the butler dropped his belligerence, but only for a moment. 'What's this about letters? She never said anything about them to me.'

'She never said anything about them to *me*, either,' Sally replied. 'But when I found them, I realised . . . I realised . . .'

She found it difficult to say what she wanted to this large, aggressive and unfriendly man who overawed her. He was a stranger. A *cold* stranger. But the words had to be said.

'I realised . . . you are my father.'

'That is a load of nonsense, girl, as well you know.'

The butler spoke the words angrily. When he immediately closed the door behind him, Sally realised the words had been intended for any of the servants who might be listening in to the conversation.

'Now, what is all this about? Why have you come here? If it's money—'

'It's got nothing to do with money. I don't want *anything* from you.'

Sally found herself ridiculously close to tears – and she realised it *was* ridiculous. She had known when she decided to come to Lanhydrock House that she could not expect instant acknowledgement and affection from the man she still believed to be her father. Yet she had nursed a forlorn hope . . .

She was not even certain what it was she *had* hoped for. Perhaps, having lost Ruth, she wanted to feel she was not entirely alone in the world. That she belonged to someone.

'These letters . . . Do you have them with you? I'd like to see them.'

'No, I left them at home.'

Sally realised he was worried about the existence of the letters; far more concerned about them than he was about her.

She accepted now that she should not have come here. She should have listened to Captain Eva and to Ethan. Suddenly, Ethan was the one she wanted to be with more than anyone else she knew. Certainly more than with this man to whom she would never mean anything.

'You don't need to worry about the letters. You'll never hear about them again – or me, either.'

Turning, Sally began to walk away swiftly from the door.

'Just a minute, young lady. Come back here. There are a few more things I want to know . . .'

Instead of obeying his call, Sally took to her heels and ran. Her one thought was to get away from Lanhydrock House and Robert Sanderson as quickly as she could. To return to Plymouth and to Ethan.

As she fled from the coach-house yard, she ran headlong into a group of about seven or eight men, members of Lord Robartes' shooting party.

She would have carried on past them, but one of the younger men grabbed and held her.

'Not so fast, young lady. Where do you think you're going?'

'More to the point,' said an older man, 'where has she *been*? Do you see the coat of arms on the cloak she's wearing?'

The younger man who was holding her turned her around without releasing his grip and peered at the woven shields to which the cloak's clasp was attached.

'Good Lord! It's the Robartes coat of arms. *Our* coat of arms. I do believe we've caught ourselves a little thief, Uncle.'

'Where did you get the cloak from, young lady? Have you been inside the house?'

'No – and I haven't pinched anything, either. This cloak belonged to my ma. Let me go, I want to go back to Plymouth.'

'I've no doubt you do,' said the older man. 'But you aren't going anywhere just yet, young lady. In fact, I doubt if you'll be going anywhere for quite some time. Take her to the house and have her locked away, Donald. Then call the police and tell them to come and collect her. We won't let the little baggage interfere with our shooting . . .'

40

Held in the grip of two members of Lord Robartes' shooting party, Sally struggled and fought vigorously. Rather than run the risk of losing her on their way to the house, they decided to lock her in a harness room, inside the coach house.

The room possessed only a single, small window, at a height she could not reach, even when she tried jumping up at it – and she tried many times. She also spent a great deal of time and energy beating on the door and shouting to be released.

Sally was in a furious temper. Being wrongly accused of theft was bad enough but, before shutting her in the harness room, her captors had taken away her cloak. The loss of this precious piece of clothing upset her even more than the fact that she now had only a thin dress to protect her from the cold.

As it became increasingly apparent that raging against her arrest and imprisonment was futile, she calmed down. Only now did she begin to feel the cold. Fortunately, she spotted some horse blankets folded on a rack. Taking down two, she unfolded them and wrapped them about her.

Now for the first time she began to think about her predicament. She wondered what would happen to her when the police arrived. Sally realised she would find it difficult to prove she had *not* stolen the cloak, especially as it was embroidered with the coat of arms of the family who had arrested her. The police were hardly likely to accept her word against that of the owner of such a grand house.

Sally remained locked in the harness room for almost four hours before she heard voices in the coach house beyond the door. A bolt was withdrawn, and when the door was opened a groom entered the harness room. He was followed by two policemen, one wearing the stripes of a sergeant.

Both uniformed men looked at her sternly and the sergeant said, 'So you're the young thief, eh? You've landed yourself in a whole lot of trouble, young lady. Stealing from a house is a very serious offence.'

'I didn't steal nothing,' Sally declared hotly. 'That cloak belonged to my ma.'

'Oh? Are you saying it was her who stole it? Or perhaps you're trying to tell us she belonged to Lord Robartes' family?'

The sergeant's sarcastic suggestion brought smiles to the faces of the constable and the groom.

'Put the handcuffs on her, Constable,' the sergeant instructed. 'We'll take her to Bodmin and lock her in a cell while all this is sorted out.'

Turning his back on Sally, he asked the groom, 'What time will his Lordship be returning to the house?'

'Not until well after dark,' replied the groom. 'They're shooting in the lower woods. When they've done they're all going to Glynn House, down in the valley, for a drink or two before coming back here.'

'No matter,' said the sergeant. 'This young lady won't be going anywhere. I'll leave a message for his Lordship to say I'll call on him tomorrow morning. We can sort this out then.'

'He won't have much time to spare for you then, either,' said the groom. 'It's an even busier shooting day tomorrow. The Lord Lieutenant and his guests are coming across to join the shooting party. Rumour has it among the servants that the Prince of Wales might be in the party too.'

Duly impressed, the sergeant said, 'No doubt the inspector will call on his Lordship and arrange a time that's convenient to everyone. Come along, Constable. Bring this young thief out and we'll get her back to Bodmin.'

.*   *   *

When the police inspector came to Sally's cell that evening, she repeated her story. She also explained for the first time why she had come to the house from Plymouth.

It was apparent to her that the inspector was not convinced by her story.

'Are you asking me to believe you've waited seventeen years before coming to find the man you claim is your father?' the inspector asked in disbelief.

'I had no idea who my father was until I read my mother's letters yesterday,' Sally replied bitterly. 'I wish now she'd burned them years ago.'

'No doubt you do,' the inspector said wryly. 'If the letters ever existed in the first place. I don't suppose you happen to have brought them with you?'

'No, they're in my room in Pin's Lane. In Plymouth.'

'Of course.' Once again there was scepticism in the inspector's voice. 'It might interest you to know we have already spoken to Mr Sanderson, the butler at Lanhydrock. He says you came to the back door with some cock-and-bull story that made no sense to him whatsoever. He realised afterwards it was some sort of subterfuge, so that you, or an accomplice, could somehow sneak into the house and steal whatever you could lay your hands on. It was unlucky that you chose something embroidered with Lord Robartes' coat of arms. That was a very foolish mistake. But most criminals slip up in some way or another.'

'I didn't steal the cloak,' Sally repeated. 'And I want it back again. It belonged to my mother.'

'Well, even if your story is true – and I will tell you now, I don't believe you. But, even if it *were* true, she must have stolen it from Lanhydrock House in the first place, so you are in possession of stolen property. I tell you, your situation is not a happy one, my girl.'

When the inspector had left her, Sally sat on the wooden platform that served as a bed and felt hot tears burning her eyes. She *was* telling the truth, yet no one would believe her.

She wished yet again that she had brought Ethan along with her. He would know what to do.

41

When Ethan arrived at the Refuge, he found Inspector Ian Lovat already there, although it was not yet nine o'clock in the morning.

'Has Sally arrived back from Cornwall?' Ethan asked the question anxiously.

He had been at the house ten hours before, asking the same question. The answer from Eva was the same as it had been then.

'No.' Aware that Ethan was genuinely concerned, she added, 'Perhaps she was late getting back and didn't want to disturb us. She might have gone to Pin's Lane.'

Ethan shook his head. 'I went there before coming here. I've called on Grace Philpott too. Sally's not been to either place. I'm worried about her, Captain Eva. We were supposed to meet up last night, so she could tell me all about the man she was going to see – her father.'

Trying to reassure him, Eva said, 'You never know, she and her father might have got on very well together. If that were the case he might have persuaded her to stay overnight.'

'I don't think so. If he'd felt anything at all for her, he'd have tried to find her long before this. Besides, I read a couple of the letters he'd sent to Sally's ma. They weren't the letters of a man likely to welcome Sally as his long-lost daughter.'

They were holding their conversation in the kitchen, where Ian Lovat was seated with a cup of tea in his hand. He had called at the Refuge to interview one of the girls, who was certain that, on the previous day, she had seen the second man who had been at Mother Darling's when the girls had been held captive and Rachel assaulted.

'Where exactly was Sally going?' he asked.

'To a big house near Bodmin, in Cornwall,' replied Eva. 'I don't know what it is called, but I was with her when she bought her railway ticket. She was leaving the train at Bodmin Road.'

'The house is called Lan . . . something,' Ethan said thoughtfully. 'I remember – it's called Lanhydrock. That's it, Lanhydrock House.'

Writing down the name in his notebook, Ian Lovat said, 'One of my men arrested a man during the night who is wanted by the police in Bodmin. I need to send a telegraph message to arrange for them to collect him. If you like, I'll ask the inspector in charge to make a few enquiries at this house.'

'That could prove embarrassing if this man is trying to keep his indiscretions from his employers,' Eva said doubtfully.

'I shouldn't think so,' said Ethan. 'We don't even know who he is, or what he does there – but I *am* very worried about Sally. Yes, please see if you can find out anything, Inspector. If the police at Bodmin aren't able to help, I'll go to Lanhydrock myself.'

'I'll send the telegraph as soon as I return to the station. Where will I find you if I have any information?'

'Well, I should have gone fishing today, but my pa said I could take the day off to make sure Sally is all right.'

'Then you can stay here and help me shift furniture around while you wait to hear from Inspector Lovat,' said Eva, never one to miss an opportunity. Turning to Ian Lovat, she asked, 'Can you get the information to him here, if need be?'

Smiling at her opportunism, the inspector replied, 'I'll come along myself, if nothing else needing my attention crops up in the meantime.'

'Splendid! Then it's all settled. I'll make certain we have a kettle boiling for when you arrive.'

She explained to Ethan, 'I've never known such a man for his tea. If it wasn't for the fact he gets it free wherever he goes, he would no doubt spend all his earnings on it . . .'

Ethan hardly had time to shift more than a few pieces of furniture before Ian Lovat returned to the house in the Barbican. One look at the detective inspector's face and Ethan immediately stopped what he was doing.

'You've heard something about Sally? What is it? Where is she?'

'It's not good news, I'm afraid. She's been arrested for stealing from Lanhydrock House. It's the home of Lord Robartes and it was he who caught her. There was a telegraph message at the station asking if we knew anything about her.'

Ethan was so astounded by the news that he reached behind him for the table he had been moving and sat down on the edge of it.

'Sally caught stealing . . . ? I just don't believe it. She's not a thief. There must be some mistake. What is she supposed to have stolen?'

'A cloak. I'm afraid there can be no mistake. It has Lord Robartes' coat of arms embroidered on it and she was wearing it when he caught her.'

'I know that cloak,' said Ethan. 'It had belonged to her mother and was kept in a chest in her room. She was given it by her sister. She wore it when she came to our house on Christmas Day. My ma can vouch for that. She said what a splendid cloak it was. Why, it must have been in the trunk for almost twenty years before it was given to Sally.'

'That's perfectly true,' agreed Eva. 'She was wearing the same cloak when I saw her off at the railway station. I remember the coat-of-arms embroidery too. There were two of them, one on either side of the neck where the chain and clasp were attached.'

'You're quite certain of this? Certain enough to stand up in court and give evidence on Sally's behalf?'

'Absolutely.'

'Quite certain.'

Eva and Ethan spoke in unison.

'In that case, I'll telegraph to Bodmin police station again and arrange for them to collect their wanted man at Bodmin Road railway station this afternoon. I'll take him down myself. You can both travel on the same train. After I've handed over the prisoner, we'll all pay a call on Lord Robartes at Lanhydrock House.'

42

When the train came to a steam-escaping halt at Bodmin Road station, three policemen were waiting on the platform. One was the inspector who had refused to believe Sally's story.

The inspector shook Ethan's hand amiably enough, but greeted Captain Eva with a certain reserve. The Bodmin police had not yet met up with any member of the Salvation Army, but he had read of the problems encountered by colleagues in other places.

'I thought I would come to meet you. We can go up to Lanhydrock House together, while my constable takes the prisoner to town. I didn't realise you would be bringing others with you.'

'Captain Cassington and Ethan are both witnesses to the fact that Sally Harrup was in possession of the cloak before she went to Lanhydrock House,' Ian Lovat explained. 'Not only that, Ethan saw the letters Sally believed to be from her father, who works at the house. I thought that if it could all be explained to the Robartes family, the girl might be released. It's quite clear that with these witnesses – and others who would be called – a prosecution for theft would fail.'

'If all you say is true, I must agree with you,' said the inspector. 'But there are one or two things that need to be cleared up before I can release the girl and a number of matters need clarifying.

I have a pony and trap outside the station. We can all squeeze into that to travel to the house. The constables can walk back to town with the prisoner.'

Ethan was visibly impressed with his first glimpse of the house, as the pony pulling the trap trotted up the long drive between the trees. It was even grander than Edgcumbe House, the big house he would see across Plymouth Sound whenever the family's fishing boat left Plymouth harbour. This house, with its own church nestling among the trees behind it, had a feeling of warmth and timelessness. As though it really *belonged* here.

There was a moment's debate between the two inspectors as to whether they should go to the main door or first make their presence known at the servants' door.

Ian Lovat was adamant. Their business was with the master of the house. It was he who had been responsible for arresting Sally. Therefore, they should go to the main entrance.

The door was opened by a maid, who seemed as uncertain as the Bodmin police inspector as to whether she should invite them to wait in the front hall or send them to the kitchen door. The dilemma was solved for her by the older of two ladies who came into the hall while she was making up her mind.

'Good afternoon, Inspector Rowe. We don't often see you at Lanhydrock. What can we do for you?' Rather less cordially, she added, 'And who are these people?'

'Good afternoon, Lady Robartes. I came here to see if I might have a word with his Lordship. This is Inspector Lovat, head of the Criminal Investigation Department in Plymouth. The others are Miss Cassington, of the Salvation Army, and a Mr Shields. They are here on behalf of the young lady who was apprehended by his Lordship yesterday.'

'Oh yes, the girl who managed to get into the house and steal some clothing.'

'Sally didn't steal anything,' Ethan declared, indignantly. 'She's not a thief!'

'Ahem!' The Bodmin police inspector coughed hastily before Lady Robartes could react to Ethan's outburst. 'I fear there might have been some mistake, my Lady. It would seem the young lady was telling the truth when she said she did not steal the cloak.'

'But my husband said it was embroidered with our coat of arms. It must have come from the house.'

'That is quite true, my Lady. It undoubtedly *did* come from the house – but certainly not yesterday.'

Lady Robartes looked puzzled, then she said, 'I think we had all better go to my study and sort this out.'

To her companion, she said, 'Nancy, I wonder if you would tell the others I will be with them as soon as possible.' And to the visitors she said, 'Would you all like to follow me?'

Lady Robartes led the way along a passageway, to a small, cosily furnished room, which had a welcoming log fire burning in the fireplace.

When everyone was seated, Lady Robartes said, 'Now, who is going to tell me what this is all about?'

Her visitors all looked at each other and Captain Eva said, 'I think perhaps Ethan would be the best person to tell you something about Sally, of her background and the events that led up to her coming here yesterday. Ethan?'

Hesitantly at first, but with growing assurance, Ethan told of Sally's life, of her home in Pin's Lane, the story of the cloak, and of the recent death of her sister and the discovery of the letters.

When he ended, Lady Robartes, genuinely moved, said, 'What a dreadfully tragic story!' Shifting her attention to Captain Eva, she asked, 'Do you mind telling me how you came to be acquainted with the girl?'

Captain Eva related the story of how Sally had heard Rachel's cries for help, and told of all that had happened as a result.

'No doubt this is why you are involved?' she said to Ian Lovat.

'That's right, m'Lady – and from all I have seen of young Sally, I would back up everything that has been said. I believe her to be an honest, hard-working girl. In view of her background, I would say that in itself does very great credit to her. Perhaps we could speak to your butler, to see what he has to say about all this. After all, it was in his power to have prevented Sally's arrest had he wanted to.'

'I am afraid Sanderson is not in the house. He asked if he might take the remainder of the day off after ensuring all arrangements had been made for lunch today. He said he had urgent personal business in Plymouth.'

The two police inspectors exchanged quizzical glances and the Bodmin inspector said, almost apologetically, 'Mr Sanderson called in at the police station this morning. He told the constable on duty he was trying to remember whether he might have sent letters to anyone in Plymouth that might have found their way into Miss Harrup's hands. He thought that might have prompted her – and possibly her accomplices too – to plan to rob this house. He asked where she was living in Plymouth.'

'Did the constable tell him?' Ian Lovat asked sharply.

'I'm afraid so. There was no reason why he should not. Sanderson holds an important and responsible position in Lord Robartes' household.'

'Lady Robartes, may I make use of one of your servants – a groom, perhaps? I would like him to take a message to the telegraph office in Bodmin.' The request was made by Ian Lovat.

'Of course – but you surely do not think Sanderson has gone to this girl's address in Plymouth?'

'Although he's no doubt firmly convinced that Sally will be convicted of theft, he dare not risk having his letters fall into anyone else's hands. He has a great deal to lose.'

'So you really *do* believe Sanderson is the girl's father?' Lady Robartes was aghast. 'Yet he is willing to have her sent to prison unjustly rather than acknowledge her? It is absolutely monstrous!'

'Nevertheless, that's what I believe, m'Lady.'

'Then please write your message, Inspector. I will call for a maid to fetch a groom.'

While Ian Lovat was writing, the Bodmin police inspector spoke to Lady Robartes. 'Of course, there are still one or two matters that need to be cleared up before we bring this matter to a conclusion. The mystery of the cloak the girl was wearing, for instance. If she didn't steal it, then how had it come into her mother's hands?'

'How old was this young girl's sister? 'The one who has so recently died?' Lady Robartes put the questions to Ethan.

'It's difficult to say. She was so ill . . . but she couldn't have been more than twenty-two or -three.'

'I see.' Lady Robartes looked thoughtful. 'We've had a great many changes in the domestic staff since then, but Cook has been with us for thirty or more years. I'll send for her.'

There was a tapestry bell-pull beside the fireplace. Lady Robartes gave it a vigorous tug before asking, 'Tell me again, what is the name of this unfortunate young girl?'

'Sally Harrup.' Captain Eva supplied the answer.

The maid who answered the summons was promptly sent off to fetch the cook. A few minutes later a plump, rosy-cheeked woman arrived, drying newly washed hands on her white apron.

'You sent for me, m'Lady?'

'That's right, Esther. You've been with the family for a very long time. I want you to try to remember a servant who was here about twenty or more years ago. A young woman named Harrup.'

'Molly Harrup? Miss Lydia's maid? Yes, m'Lady, I remember her very well. A very pretty girl, she was. Far too pretty for her own good. That was her trouble. She had all the men hereabouts chasing after her – and she didn't run from them quite as fast as she should have. She landed herself in trouble, that's why she had to leave.'

'I see.' Glancing at the others, Lady Robartes said, 'Well, that part of the girl's story is accurate, at least.'

Returning her attention to the cook, she said, 'Now, Esther, can you recall whether suspicion for her condition fell upon any particular man? A member of the domestic staff, perhaps?'

'Nothing that came from Molly herself, m'Lady. She never breathed a word to anyone of the man responsible for her state. Mind you, I always had my suspicions, and nothing's happened since to make me change 'em. Indeed, I'm more convinced now than I was then.'

'Who do you believe was responsible, Esther?'

The cook glanced at the others in the room before saying, 'Begging your pardon, m'Lady, I'd rather not say. I have no proof, you understand. If I was to be wrong I'd be doing him an unforgivable disservice. No, after all these years it's better left unsaid.'

'Esther,' Lady Robartes spoke sharply, 'after all these years it's time a very serious and cruel wrong is put right. If the man you suspect of fathering Molly Harrup's child, or children, is not the man we have in mind, it will go no farther than this room. On the other hand, if it *is* the man we suspect it to be, you will be helping to prevent a dreadful miscarriage of justice. Now, who is this man?'

When the cook still remained silent, Lady Robartes said, 'Esther, I *demand* that you tell us THIS INSTANT!'

With exaggerated reluctance, the Lanhydrock cook broke her silence. 'Like I said, m'Lady, nobody knew for certain, but there was a couple of us was convinced it was Mr Sanderson, the butler. Him who's voice was raised loudest in saying the family ought to have her sent as far away from Lanhydrock as was possible.'

43

Once the Lanhydrock House cook had unburdened herself of her long-held suspicions about the butler, events moved swiftly.

It transpired that 'Miss Lydia', for whom Molly Harrup had once worked, had married into one of the old-established Cornish families. She was now Mrs Treffry. Her husband was a member of Lord Robartes' shooting party and they were both guests in the house that had been her home for so many years of her early life.

Called to the room where the others were gathered, she remembered Molly Harrup immediately. She was, said Lydia Treffry, a bright and happy young girl who went about her work cheerfully and efficiently. She had been very sorry to lose her services when Molly disclosed her pregnancy and was ordered to leave the house.

Lydia Treffry was intrigued by the events of the day and, as the party drank tea, she was able to solve the mystery of the cloak bearing the Robartes coat of arms.

'Yes I remember it well,' she mused. 'I had it for some years. Molly thought it was one of the most beautiful articles of clothing she had ever seen. She was so fond of it that, when she left, I gave it to her as a present.'

When told of the trouble it had caused Sally, Lydia Treffry was extremely upset. 'The poor child!' she repeated for the third time. 'You must have her released *immediately*, Inspector.'

The Bodmin policeman said he would return to the police station right away and arrange for her to be set free.

'Would it not be quicker to send a groom with a message to have her freed?' asked Lady Robartes.

The inspector explained that, as the senior officer for the area, he would need to sign the papers necessary to authorise her release.

Lydia Treffry was a lady who was used to having things done when she asked for them. 'The moment you've completed all your official nonsense, send the girl to me here. I want to see what she looks like and tell her something of her mother. Molly was a lovely girl. Why she ever became involved with that scoundrel Sanderson, I'll never know. He was always far too ingratiating for my liking. No doubt he used his position to take advantage of impressionable young servant girls.'

'I feel we must try to make amends to the girl too,' said Lady Robartes. 'I know my husband would say the same, were he here. Had he not acted so hastily she would have been spared a great deal of grief. As for that scoundrel Sanderson . . . His attitude towards her would have been sufficient to upset the most insensitive of girls, and I am given the impression she is certainly not that!'

Inspector Rowe said, 'I will leave now, m'lady, but I should be back within the hour with Miss Harrup. She will no doubt be greatly relieved to put all this behind her.'

'I believe she is more likely to be very upset by the actions of the man who is her father,' declared Captain Eva. 'The loss of her sister has left her feeling very much alone in the world. No number of friends can take the place of a family.'

'Can I come with you to bring Sally back?' Ethan asked the Bodmin police inspector.

'If you wish.' Inspector Rowe was secretly relieved. Having Ethan present when the girl was released, to explain what was happening, would obviate a need to explain the mistakes that had led to her arrest at Lanhydrock House.

'I'll come with you too,' Ian Lovat stood up to leave with them, but Lady Robartes had other ideas.

'No you won't,' she said firmly. 'You and the Salvation Army captain can remain here and tell me more about this girl, before she is brought to the house.'

Returning her attention to the Bodmin inspector, she said, 'You can send one of your men here from Bodmin, too, in case that rogue Sanderson returns. I will have his personal belongings packed and taken to the gatehouse. He shall collect them from there, together with any salary that may be owing to him. I have no wish to see him again and he will not be allowed back in the house.'

'If my guess of what he is doing right now is correct, I think it highly probable that he'll be having a spell in prison,' said Ian Lovat. 'I doubt whether it will be as long as he deserves, but it will give him a salutary lesson.'

'It is no more than he deserves,' Lydia Treffry said angrily. 'When I think of the life poor Molly was forced to lead because of him . . .'

44

When she was first arrested, Sally's initial reaction was one of indignation. It was not entirely because her freedom had been taken from her, or because she had been accused of a crime she had not committed. She was angry most of all because her cloak had been taken away from her. The cloak that had once been worn by her mother.

Conveyed to Bodmin police station and left alone in a cell for many hours, she gradually began to calm down. As she did so, realisation of the seriousness of her predicament dawned on her. All due, in no small measure, to the attitude of the Lanhydrock butler towards her.

He *was* her father. After seeing him she had no doubts at all. He possessed many facial features that reminded her strongly of Ruth. She must resemble him, too. People had always commented upon how alike she and Ruth were.

Thinking about her father now made her even more unhappy.

She had realised when she set out from Plymouth that it would be foolish to set her hopes too high. Yet there had been a forlorn hope, buried deep inside her, that if only she could have an opportunity to speak to him, everything would miraculously become all right. The empty years would fall away, he would be sorry for the way he had treated her mother and would suddenly become the father she had always secretly craved.

She now realised just how stupid she had been. It had been no more than a desperate bid to have someone to whom she belonged.

The man she had spoken too had been a stranger. An indifferent and selfish stranger. He cared for the children he had fathered no more than a stray dog would for a litter of pups it had sired.

She wondered what was going to happen to her now. Would Ethan come looking for her when she failed to return to Plymouth? She was fairly certain he would – but when?

Once she had been taken before a magistrate it would be too late. She never doubted she would be found guilty, despite her innocence. If Lord Robartes, or a member of his household, came to court and told the magistrates she had stolen the cloak, they were hardly likely to take her word against his!

Sally had plenty of time to ponder her situation. Except for a policeman who spoke no more than a few grumpy words when he brought her a meal that evening, no one came to see her.

By nightfall, she was feeling despondent and found it difficult to sleep. When she did doze off for a while she was awakened by the sound of a noisy man, apparently the worse for drink, being placed in a nearby cell.

A short while after this there was mayhem in the police station. Sally could hear the voices of a great many men – and women too – raised in excited protest. It was difficult to know what it was all about. Only an occasional word was in English.

Soon, she heard cell doors along the corridor in which her own cell was situated being opened and slammed shut. Then her own cell door was opened. Two women were roughly pushed inside and the door slammed behind them.

Now Sally understood why she had not been able to understand what was going on. The two women were gypsies. It was probable the men who had been making so much noise were gypsies too.

The women looked as though they had been involved in a

fight; one had a badly scratched face and the clothes of both were torn.

One of them spoke to her, but when she failed to understand what was being said, the women said something contemptuously to her companion. The only word Sally was able to make out was '*Gorgio!*'

Soon the two women were shouting to attract the attention of those in the cells about them. When others began replying, Sally realised there would be no more sleep for her that night.

The morning after her arrest was just as busy in the police station. All available policemen based in the market town had been called in to help convey the gypsies to the courtroom.

Many of the arrested men and women had been drunk the night before. Sally had thought this was the reason they had made so much fuss. But when most of them had sobered up in the morning, they were, if anything, even louder.

By the time the gypsies had been removed from the cells, Sally's head was aching. She also realised she was hungry, but she needed to wait for another hour before breakfast was brought to her.

The meal had been cooked by the wife of a constable who lived in a house adjacent to the police station. As a result, it was of a much higher standard than she might otherwise have received.

The woman brought it herself. A middle-aged, stoutly built woman, hers was the first sympathetic voice Sally had heard since her arrest. The woman was also more informative than a constable might have been.

'Here you are, love. I'm sorry it's so late, but you must have heard all the noise going on. A whole lot of gypsies set up a camp just outside town last night. After they'd been drinking for a few hours they decided they'd come in and take back one of their girls who was planning to marry a *didekei*. As far as I could make out that's someone who travels around like they do but who isn't a true gypsy. They're very particular about that sort of thing, or so I'm told. From what I hear, they began fighting among themselves even before they found the girl.'

As Sally sat on the edge of the wooden bed and tucked in

to her breakfast, the woman showed no inclination to leave the cell.

'Those of 'em who haven't ended up in hospital are being taken before the magistrate this morning and I hope he puts the whole rowdy lot of 'em away for a very long time.'

'Will I be going to court when the gypsies have been dealt with?'

'Well, my husband thought that's what was going to happen to you, but Inspector Rowe has had a message from someone in Plymouth. Another inspector. I don't know what it was all about, but it seems you won't be going to court before he gets here.'

Puzzled, and with her mouth half-full of fried bread, Sally asked, 'What's the name of this inspector in Plymouth – and what's he got to do with me?' She could think of no Plymouth policeman who would be sufficiently interested in her to travel to Bodmin in order to speak to her.

'Are you sure it's a policeman? It couldn't have been a Salvation Army captain, perhaps?'

'I don't think anyone would have confused a Salvation Army captain with a police inspector. No, it was an inspector all right. It's got everyone wondering just what's going on. Have you been up to anything in Plymouth that might make the police there interested in you?'

Sally could not think of anything. However, Ruth had always said that once the police had you in their clutches they were likely to accuse you of all sorts of things you knew nothing about.

Later that morning a constable brought a mop and bucket of water and ordered her to clean out the cell. He could throw no light upon what was happening.

'Your guess is as good as mine,' he said. 'One thing's certain though, you won't be going to court today, so you'd better make a good job of cleaning up this cell. You're likely to be here for another twenty-four hours, at least.'

Sally ate an indifferent midday meal. It was brought to her by a constable, who seemed determined to say as little as possible. She then decided to stretch out on the uncomfortable plank bed, in the hope of catching up on some of the sleep she had lost the night before.

She was just dozing off when she was awakened by the sound of metal grating against metal as a key was turned in the lock of the cell door.

She sat up on the bed as the cell door was swung open. The uncommunicative constable who had brought her midday meal was standing there.

With him was a tall, uniformed policeman wearing the insignia of an inspector.

Behind them was – Ethan!

45

When Sally saw Ethan, she experienced a feeling she had never known before. In that moment all her despondency lifted and she knew all was going to be well. Ignoring the others, she ran to him and flung her arms about him.

'I knew you'd come looking for me. I *knew* it.'

When her arms dropped away from him, she took hold of his hand, reluctant to release her hold on him. When the door of the cell was slammed shut behind her, she looked around in surprise.

'What's happening?'

'You're free to leave the police station,' the Bodmin inspector explained. 'All the charges against you have been dropped.'

'You mean . . . you've found out I really have been telling you the truth?'

'That's right, Sally,' said Ethan. 'Lady Robartes found the person who gave the cloak to your mother. She's a niece of Lord Robartes and once lived at Lanhydrock. She's actually staying at the house right now. It seems your mother was her maid before becoming pregnant.'

'She really knew my ma?! Where's the cloak now? I want it back.'

'You'll be given it when you get to Lanhydrock House,'

Inspector Rowe replied. 'Lady Robartes wants to meet you. One of my constables will drive you there now.'

'Will I be able to meet the lady my ma worked for too?'

The inspector nodded. 'The last thing she said when we left was that we were to be sure to take you back there. She wants to meet you.'

Sally smiled happily at Ethan, but her mood changed abruptly and she turned back to Inspector Rowe. 'What's happening about my . . . about the butler at the house?'

'He's been arrested in Plymouth. A message has just arrived. He was caught after breaking into your room. It seems he was looking for the letters he sent to your mother.'

'Oh!' Sally's expression showed her unhappiness. 'What will happen to him now?'

'You'll need to ask Inspector Lovat that question. He's at Lanhydrock House too, with Miss Cassington, of the Salvation Army. Now, there are a few formalities to complete, then you can be on your way . . .'

Ten minutes later Sally left the Bodmin police station. She was holding Ethan's hand once more, as though afraid he might disappear at any moment.

Inspector Rowe did not return to Lanhydrock House with Sally and Ethan. They were conveyed by pony and trap, driven by a constable. Although he seemed in a great hurry, he was more cheerful and talkative than any of the policemen Sally had met during her time in the Bodmin police station cell.

He told them that the gypsies had refused to testify against one another, even though some had sustained painful in- juries during the fighting between the two gypsy factions. As a consequence, they were all warned about their future con- duct and fined the maximum amount possible for disturbing the peace, with the alternative of a month's imprisonment in default.

The fines were totted up and paid in gold sovereigns by a gypsy who appeared to be their leader, but who had not been involved in the fracas.

It was quite evident that the constable did not like gypsies.

Thus it came as no surprise to Sally when he explained why he was in such a hurry to get them to Lanhydrock House. It was planned to move the gypsies from their encampment that afternoon – and he did not want to miss the 'fun'.

When they reached the big house, the constable was uncertain to which entrance he should take them. The problem was solved by Lydia Treffry, who, passing by a window in the main hall, had witnessed their arrival. Opening the door, she beckoned for them to come in.

Lydia Treffry was a tall, distinguished-looking woman who possessed an elegant beauty. Sally felt tongue-tied in her presence and it was left to the other woman to speak first.

'So you are Sally! You know, I really believe I would have recognised you had we met elsewhere. You are so like your mother. My poor dear, what we have put you through – and all because I made a present of a cloak to your mother so many years ago. We are so dreadfully sorry – but come along and meet Lady Robartes. We have been having a most interesting chat to Miss Cassington – or *Captain* Cassington, as I believe she prefers to be known.'

Walking in front of them down the hall, she continued, 'That handsome young police inspector is with her too. You have made some very good friends, Sally. They have been telling Lady Robartes and myself how your keen sense of duty saved those poor unfortunate girls who would otherwise have been taken to Belgium. Your mother would have been very proud of you, Sally. She too was a girl with high principles. At least, she was before she fell under the influence of that scoundrel Sanderson.'

Opening a door, Lydia Treffry preceded them into the room where the others were seated.

Eva immediately sprang to her feet to greet Sally. Holding out her arms, she embraced Sally warmly, exclaiming, 'You poor girl! Thank the Lord we were able to get here before you were committed to prison. I shudder every time I think that had we not arrived when we did you might have been sent to that awful place.'

Before Sally could be formally introduced to Lady Robartes,

the older woman said, 'I am terribly sorry that we were responsible for your arrest, child. What can we possibly do to make amends for such a ghastly mistake?'

Sally replied by asking a question that took everyone by surprise. 'What is going to happen to Mr Sanderson?'

Ian Lovat had been reading the telegram received by Inspector Rowe at Bodmin police station and it was he who replied. 'Sanderson's been arrested and has been taken to Plymouth police station and lodged in the cells there. He'll be charged with breaking into your room with intent to steal. He will no doubt be sent to prison.'

'I don't want that to happen,' Sally said unexpectedly. 'I don't think he's a very nice person and he treated my ma badly, but she never made trouble for him and I don't want to, neither.'

'He would have let *you* go to prison without raising a finger to help,' Lydia Treffry spoke gently and sympathetically.

'That doesn't matter now,' Sally replied stubbornly. 'I don't want him to be put away.'

Lydia Treffry looked at Ian Lovat questioningly. He shrugged. 'We can't proceed against him without Sally's co-operation.'

'I think I can understand Sally's feelings,' said Lydia Treffry. 'But it is galling to think that Sanderson will walk away from this mess scot-free.'

'Not quite,' Lady Robartes said in a firm voice. 'He will be dismissed from Lanhydrock House and I doubt he'll ever again find gainful employment.'

'That wasn't meant to happen, either.' Sally was unhappy at the way things had turned out. 'I came here because I just wanted to see him. I hoped he might have been just a little bit happy to see me. I didn't want anything from him – nor did I want to see him punished.'

'If I'm perfectly honest, my dear, he should have been dismissed years ago,' said Lady Robartes. 'There have been a great many rumours about him. I ignored them because butlers are very hard to find these days. Unfortunately, I allowed him rather too much authority. He was allowed to dismiss any servants he felt were unsatisfactory. Looking back over the years, I realise now that some went in rather puzzling circumstances. It is quite clear to me now that he took advantage of the authority vested in him.'

Sally was still unhappy, but the subject was changed by Lydia Treffry.

'I have something here I feel you might like to have, Sally.'

She passed over an attractive silver frame, which held a photograph of a pretty young girl of about twenty years of age, dressed in a maid's uniform. She looked very much like Ruth. Sally realised immediately who it must be.

'It's my ma!'

'That's right. When I was living here a photographer was brought to Lanhydrock. Everyone in the household had their photograph taken. This was hanging in the servants' hall with the others. Lady Robartes found a frame for it and we thought you might like to take it with you, as a present.'

'It's a wonderful present . . . I've always wondered what she looked like . . . ! I only wish Ruth could have seen this.' Tears sprang to Sally's eyes and she could only manage an emotional, 'Thank you.'

Eva had told Lady Robartes and Lydia Treffry of the tragic death of Ruth on Christmas Day. The latter now said, 'My dear child, it is a very small gesture of contrition on our part. I believe my aunt wishes to give you a small sum of money, by way of compensation for your suffering and I have an offer I would beg you to consider. I have an invalid daughter at my home, in Fowey. I would be most happy if you would consider entering domestic service in my house and helping to take care of her. No, you do not have to give me your answer right away. Please think about it and call to see me if you would like to take the post. It is a very happy household. I have no doubt you would enjoy it there.'

An hour later, Sally was being driven to the railway station in the Robartes' coach, accompanied by Ethan, Captain Eva and Ian Lovat.

She had Ethan by her side, was carrying the silver-framed photograph of her mother, had twenty guineas jangling dully in a pocket of her dress, and had been offered a secure post in domestic service with Lydia Treffry.

Wistfully, she wished Ruth was still alive so she might have been able to share such good fortune with her.

But Ruth was dead. The only relative Sally now had was Sanderson, Lanhydrock House's disgraced ex-butler.

46

To all who looked for the signs, the countryside in and around Plymouth was hinting that spring was not far away. Snowdrops had come and gone, primroses were in abundance, and yellow daffodils danced to the tune of a boisterous wind.

Sally was still living at the Salvation Army Refuge, but she continued to pay the rent for the room in Pin's Lane and had been returning there more often just recently.

On occasions, if she felt particularly nervous about the possibility of meeting up with the still-elusive Sid Darling and Ethan was not able to accompany her, she would take Zulu Joe along for company.

The giant African was now employed at the Refuge as a handyman-cum-night watchman – and was a friend to everybody who lived there.

Always proudly dressed in his Salvation Army uniform, Zulu Joe was perfectly happy with his simple and silent way of life.

Although unable to talk, he could often be heard humming a tune as he worked about the large house. Whenever he went out, his large uniformed figure did much to draw attention and he was an impressive advertisement for the Salvation Army.

Sally was still working for Alfie and Grace Philpott – and seeing Ethan as often as she could.

She was concerned for him at the present time. The weather

had been consistently bad for weeks and Plymouth fishermen were able to put to sea for only the occasional day. The profit made by the Shields family before Christmas was now no more than a wistful memory.

There was no work for Ethan or his brother at the pie shop either. The residents of Plymouth seemed to have been practising prolonged thrift after the excesses of Christmastide.

Not that Ethan was wasting his time. One of the Salvation Army bandsmen had been teaching him to read music. Unfortunately for Sally, this meant that he was not always able to meet her as often as both of them would have liked.

Sally was thinking of all these things as she walked along Union Street with an empty basket. She had just made a couple of deliveries to shopkeepers unable to leave their premises for a lunch break. Now she was on her way back to the pie shop to collect more orders.

As she approached one of the many public houses in the street, she saw a man lurch drunkenly from the premises to the pavement outside. Once there, he began walking as though the pavement was a flight of stairs he was having difficulty negotiating.

Sally stepped into the gutter to avoid him. As she passed by, she thought there was something familiar about him. Looking back, she stopped suddenly.

She watched him for a few moments with increasing disbelief. Not until he looked directly at her did she know for certain. It was Robert Sanderson, ex-butler to Lord and Lady Robartes of Lanhydrock House.

Her father!

But this was not the imposing, smart man feared by the other servants. A man who had set standards for the household of a peer of the realm.

He must have had almost two weeks' growth of stubble on his cheeks. His clothes were stained and creased and looked as though they had not been taken off since he last applied a razor to his face.

Obviously intoxicated, he was able to stand – but only just.

As Sally watched, he staggered to the edge of the pavement.

She held her breath in alarm as it seemed he might fall into the busy road, in the path of passing traffic.

At the last minute, he recovered and lurched in the opposite direction. Colliding with the wall of a shop, he stood with his back to it, for support.

Retracing her footsteps, Sally stood looking at him uncertainly.

Peering at her, Sanderson made a visible effort to concentrate. 'Molly . . . ?' He shook his head in confusion. 'No, it can't be.'

Suddenly, he seemed to partially sober up. 'I know you! You're the one who had me thrown out of Lanhydrock. Molly's daughter. No wonder I thought you were her. You said you were *my* daughter, too.' He shook his head again, this time so vigorously it caused him to momentarily lose his balance.

Recovering with difficulty, he said, 'No daughter of mine would have had me dismissed after thirty years of service. Thirty years . . . and they threw me out. Wouldn't even let me go to the house to collect my things. They had them heaped up in the gatehouse. Thirty years. Thirty wasted years . . .' His voice tailed away and his chin dropped on his chest.

Sally thought with alarm that he was about to cry. 'We ought to get you home. Where are you living?'

'Living? You call this *living*. No, girl, I stopped living when they threw me out of Lanhydrock House. After thirty years. Can you believe it.'

Pushing himself away from the wall, he stood swaying before her dangerously. 'Of course, *you* can believe it. You're the one who caused it to happen.'

'Where are you staying in Plymouth?' Sally persisted, 'I'll help you get there.'

'Where am I staying?' he repeated. 'This doorway. That doorway, what does it matter? I'm a vagrant, that's what the constables call me. A vagrant. After thirty years of living in one of the finest houses in the land . . .'

Sally knew she should leave him where he was. Robert Sanderson was trouble. He had been the downfall of her mother and she doubted very much whether his present adversity had done anything to change his selfish and uncaring nature.

Nevertheless, he *was* her father. Nothing could change that. She would take him to the room in Pin's Lane.

47

When Sally finished work that evening she did not return immediately to the Refuge. Instead, she went to Pin's Lane. With her, she carried one of Alfie's pies. It was to have been for her own supper, but she believed the man who was her father had far more need of it.

Much to her surprise, she found Ethan at the house. He had been on his way to see her, but called in on his uncle first, to deliver a meal his mother had cooked for him.

Charlie had not been well for a week or so. The cold and wet weather had aggravated his chest complaint, preventing him from maintaining his usual vigil on the steps in front of the house.

However, there was nothing wrong with his hearing, as his first words to Sally proved.

Spitefully, he said, 'Taking up your sister's old habits now, are we?'

Frowning, she said, 'I don't have the faintest idea what you're talking. What habits am I supposed to be taking up?'

'You know very well what I'm talking about. Does our Ethan know you've been taking men up to your room?'

As Ethan protested to his uncle, Sally said, 'You're a wicked, trouble-making old man, Charlie. I thought you'd changed for the better, but you haven't. The "men" you're talking about is one man. I took him up there this afternoon and, no, I haven't had time to tell Ethan about him yet.'

Ethan was looking bewildered and Sally explained, 'It's my father. I found him in Union Street today. He . . . he wasn't well, so I brought him here.'

'Not well?! Drunk, you mean,' Charlie said scornfully. 'I can tell the sounds of a drunken man – and anyone who's sober doesn't pee out of the window – not in daylight, anyway.'

Ethan was looking to Sally for a further explanation and she gave it to him. 'He was in danger of falling in front of a horse and cart, so I brought him here. I hardly recognised him, Ethan, he's let himself go so much – and it's me who's responsible for that.'

'You're not responsible for anything he does, Sally. He has no one to blame but himself. He deserves everything that's happened to him – and more.'

'That's all very well for you to say, Ethan Shields. You've got a father – yes, and a mother and brothers too. He's all I've got in the world.'

'You have me.'

'When I see you. You're usually off doing something else these days.'

It was a most unfair observation and Sally recognised it as such, but she felt angry with both Ethan and herself. She felt hurt too. This was the first quarrel she and Ethan had ever had.

'Anyway, I'm not standing here arguing with you. I've got his supper here. I'm taking it up to him before it gets cold.'

She swept up the stairs from the passageway outside Charlie's room. Although he had not been asked to accompany her, Ethan followed Sally up the stairs.

The lamp in the room was burning although the curtains had not been drawn, and Robert Sanderson was lying on the bed. He was not asleep.

He turned his head when Sally and Ethan entered the room. Glaring at Ethan, he demanded irritably, 'Who's this?'

'Ethan.' She did not feel it necessary to explain their relation-ship. 'He's been visiting his uncle who lives downstairs. I've brought supper for you. I thought you could probably do with something to eat.'

'You're right there, girl. I feel as though I haven't eaten for a week or more.'

Sally put the pie on a plate and passed it to him, together with a knife and fork. He began eating it immediately.

'What are you going to do with yourself now?' asked Sally. 'Do you have any plans for finding work?'

'Looking like this?' The hand holding the knife made a gesture indicating the clothes he was wearing. 'Who's going to employ a butler with no references and dressed like this?'

'There's other work you could do apart from being a butler,' Ethan said unsympathetically. 'Half the fishermen in Plymouth need to find other work in winter when the weather's the way it is now. You don't find them staggering around Union Street looking for someone to feel sorry for them.'

'Ethan! That's not fair.' Sally rounded on him.

'Isn't it? I didn't notice him running to help *you* when you were arrested at Lanhydrock for something he could have put right with just a word to someone.'

Ethan glared at Sanderson, before saying to Sally, 'I'll be downstairs with Uncle Charlie for a while. Then I'll get on off home. You know where to find me – if you want to.'

When he had left the room, Robert Sanderson said, 'What's that young man to you?'

'He's a friend. A very good friend.'

Sally was extremely upset by the manner of Ethan's leaving, but she would not allow her father to see that it mattered to her.

'I'm sorry to have come between you and your friend,' Sanderson said, with an uncharacteristic display of humility. 'If you think I should leave I can always find myself somewhere else to stay. I managed before you found me.'

'There's no need for that.'

Sally was in a dilemma. She wanted to go downstairs, find Ethan and put things right between them. But she felt she could not just walk out on her father. 'What *do* you intend to do with yourself?'

'I need to find work but I don't have experience of anything except being a butler. Anyway, I have no hope of finding work while I'm like this. Will you let me stay here for a while so I can get myself cleaned up and in a fit state to work?' He made an exaggerated gesture of helplessness. 'I know I have no right to ask any favours of you at all. I'll quite understand if you turn me out to fend for myself – but I would be extremely grateful if I could stay for a while. Who knows, we might be able to find what's been absent from both our lives all these years. You, a father, and me – a daughter.'

Sally hesitated. She did not fully trust this man – and yet . . .'

'All right, you can stay for a while – but not for ever. I have to pay rent for this room so I'll expect you to help towards it.'

'Of course. I have no money right now, but as soon as I find work I'll be able to pay a share of the rent.'

'When you find work, you'll need to get a place of your own, too,' Sally pointed out.

'I realise that. Now, my being here will pose certain problems. What do you suggest we do for the sleeping arrangements?'

'That's no problem,' declared Sally. 'I won't be sleeping here. I'm staying at a house owned by the Salvation Army. I'll call in most days, to see how you're getting on.'

Sally thought he seemed disappointed and she was pleased. If he wanted her around there was hope that he might turn out to be the father for whom she had always longed.

'I must go downstairs now and see if I can catch Ethan before he leaves.'

'Before you do, will you explain to me where everything is. The toilet, water . . . that sort of thing. And how far away are the nearest shops? I don't know Plymouth very well.'

He kept her talking for far longer than she had intended remaining with him. By the time she went downstairs Ethan had left.

Sally walked to the Refuge with very mixed feelings that night. The gap between herself and her father had been bridged to a certain extent, but she had fallen out with Ethan and this made her deeply unhappy.

48

'What's the matter with Sally? Whenever I talk to her I might as well be standing in the next room for all the response I get.'

'She's all right,' replied Rachel. 'She's got a lot to think about at the moment, that's all.'

She and Grace were talking as they worked together in the kitchen of the shop. Sally had just left with a basket of deliveries for the staff at the railway station. On two occasions Grace had spoken to her and had had to repeat her words twice because Sally did not hear her the first time.

'How do you know? Is something going on with that young man of hers that I should know about as her employer? She's not going to tell me she'll have to give up work because she's pregnant, or anything like that?'

'No. In fact, I think she and Ethan have had a little quarrel, that's all. She's not happy because she feels she's to blame.'

'Oh! What was the quarrel about?'

'I don't know.'

Rachel did not like lying to Grace, but Sally had told her in confidence about her father after the two girls met up with him when they were out making a delivery together.

Rachel had taken an immediate dislike to Sanderson, but she would not betray the confidence Sally had placed in her. Rachel was also an orphan. She knew what Sally must be feeling to have the father she had never known suddenly come into her life.

'If you learn anything more, be sure to let me know. We can't have her moping about as though she's in a different world to the rest of us. She and Ethan need to sort things out quickly. He's a nice young man. The two of them are meant for each other.'

Sally's preoccupation stemmed from two causes. The first was her father. He showed no indication of either attempting to obtain work or moving away from Pin's Lane. Indeed, he was trying to persuade her to move back there, to take care of him and in order that they might 'get to know each other a little better'.

Her other concern was the one Rachel had given to Grace. Ethan. There had been no opportunity for her to put things right between them. The morning after her father moved in to Pin's Lane, the Plymouth fishing fleet had put to sea.

Rumour around the quayside was that it had been forced to go far beyond its traditional fishing grounds in search of its quarry. Competition was particularly fierce this year. In addition to the Cornish boats, the traditional rivals of the Plymouth men, there was a huge fleet of steam-powered east coast drifters in the west countrymen's traditional fishing area. Foreign boats were also moving in.

The Plymouth boats had been at sea for three days and there was still no sign of their return, although some of the east coast boats had put in to Plymouth to sell their own harvest of the sea.

The east coast boats had been at sea for some time and their particular fishing methods had brought them good catches. As a result, the Barbican quay was a hive of industry. Fish was being brought ashore, prepared, then boxed for despatch to markets throughout the country.

Such activity meant that the publicans in the harbour area were also having a busy time. Fishermen and their many helpers drank heavily as they worked. They also needed to eat and the publicans ordered a great many of Alfie Philpott's pies.

Most sent their pot boys to collect them, but there were not always enough cooked and ready, so Sally spent a great deal of time going back and forth to the quay.

It was on one such visit that she unexpectedly met with her father. He was going towards a public house called The Jolly Waterman, in company with a man who looked as though he might well be a chimney sweep.

Marching up to him, a basket over her arm, Sally said, 'I thought you were going out to find work today?' Pointing in the direction of the public house, she added, 'You're not going to find it in there.'

Angrily, her father said, 'Don't you *dare* tell me what I should or shouldn't be doing, girl. Not unless you want to have your ears well and truly boxed. Now, clear off. I'll talk to you later.'

'No you won't!' Sally was equally angry. 'And when you get back to Pin's Lane you'll find what few belongings you've got outside, on the pavement. You'd better not be too long getting back there. They won't stay very long before someone runs off with them.'

Sally turned and walked away. Before she reached the next corner, her father caught up with her. Grasping her arm and pulling her to a halt, he said, 'I'm sorry, Sally. I shouldn't have spoken to you like that, but I'm not used to being told what I should be doing by a young girl. Any young girl. The man I'm with is . . . is a business associate. We're discussing something of importance.'

'You're discussing business with *him*,' Sally said scornfully. 'Don't tell me you're thinking of becoming a chimney sweep. I won't believe you.'

'I'm not thinking of doing it myself, but I'm hoping to be able to put something his way. Something that might prove lucrative for all of us.'

'What do you mean?' Sally eyed him uncertainly. 'Is it something dishonest?'

'I can't say any more about it right now, girl. I tell you what, though. You be waiting for me in the room later this evening and I might be able to tell you more then. Right now I've got to go back and speak to this man – and he won't wait for ever. Will you be at Pin's Lane when I get there?'

'Are you telling me the truth? You really are going to talk business with this bloke? You're not just saying it because I've threatened to throw your things out in the street?'

'Be back at the room when I get there and you'll find out.'

'All right – but don't be too late. I'm not going to wait up half the night for you.'

'Good girl! I'll see you later.'

Her father hurried away, leaving Sally wondering whether she had done the right thing. She did not entirely trust him, but it would be a great step forward in their relationship if he decided to take her into his confidence.

Moving on, she wished Ethan was not at sea with his father and brothers. He was the only one she could have talked to about what was going on.

She was missing him far more than she had believed she ever would. She determined that when he returned she would apologise for the cross words that had passed between them and they would make up.

This thought made her even happier than the belief that her father was about to confide in her.

49

When she finished work that evening, Sally went directly to Pin's Lane. She met Charlie in the passageway outside his room. He was carrying a mug of tea from his small kitchen to the room at the front of the house, where he now spent much of his time sitting at the window, as the weather was too cold for him to sit outside on the step.

'Well, well! What are you doing here? Moving back in, are we? I hope so. You're a lot quieter than him you've got staying up there – and *you* were always home before the rest of the street had gone to sleep. He isn't. It wouldn't be so bad if he came in sober. He's usually so drunk I'm surprised he hasn't fallen back down the stairs and injured himself before now.'

Charlie coughed and then cleared his throat noisily before continuing. 'He's no quieter when he gets upstairs. It sounds as though he's falling against every bit of furniture in the room, knocking over just about everything that can fall down. I'll be surprised if you've got anything left in one piece up there.'

'Well, he should be back earlier tonight. He's coming to tell me about some business he's been discussing.' Sally spoke defensively, but Charlie was not impressed.

'Him, discussing business? The only business he knows is *funny* business. You ask Devonport Lil. He was over there with her only yesterday.'

'You're lying, Charlie Shields. He wouldn't go with her – even if he knew about her.'

'Oh, he knows, all right. I was out in the backyard when she had someone up in her room – the curtains only half-drawn, as usual. He was watching her too, from the window up in your room. Oh, he realised what she was doing all right and he wasted no time getting over there. I saw him there myself. You should have listened to our Ethan and had nothing to do with him. You've got along without him for all these years. You could have managed well enough without him now.'

Leaving Charlie still grumbling, Sally made her way up the stairs. She thought Charlie was probably making up the story about her father and Devonport Lil. He had never allowed the truth to stand in the way of his imagination.

Entering the upstairs room, it was immediately evident that despite the position he had held at Lanhydrock House, Robert Sanderson was not a naturally tidy person. It was doubtful whether he had made any attempt to clean the room since he had been there. Even the bedclothes were strewn on the floor beside the bed.

The room was also cold and unwelcoming.

There was kindling wood and coal in the cupboard in a corner of the room. Lighting a fire, Sally put the kettle on.

Before it boiled, she made the bed and began tidying up. It still gave her an uneasy feeling to be in the room without Ruth being here too, lying in the bed she had occupied for so long.

It had been hard to take care of Ruth and at the same time go out to work, bringing in enough money to pay the rent and keep them both. Yet, looking back on it, Sally remembered only the loving companionship there had been between them. How she had looked forward to coming home to her sister each day, knowing that Ruth would be equally pleased to see her.

That was the way families should be. The way the Shields family felt about one another. It was how she had hoped things would be between herself and her father.

Perhaps they might still be like that one day.

However, it soon became clear that her hopes he might return early would not be realised.

When the clock on the mantelshelf chimed the quarter hour at ten forty-five, she decided to return to the Refuge. Zulu Joe occupied the room closest to the front door of the Salvation Army home – he would hear her, however lightly she knocked on the door. But if Captain Eva was still awake she would want to know where Sally had been and she was not yet ready to tell her the truth.

The tidying of the room had been completed long before and Sally now moved the slowly steaming kettle to one side of the hob. She was about to leave when she heard someone ponderously climbing the stairs.

She knew it had to be her father. From the noise he was making she realised Charlie had not been exaggerating about that, at least. Robert Sanderson had returned to Pin's Lane, but he was not a fully sober man.

Sally had turned down the wick of the lamp in the room. Now she turned it up once more and replaced the kettle on the glowing coals. It sounded as though he had need of a strong coffee. She had already checked the food cupboard. There was just enough left in a tin to make a couple of cups.

The door opened and her father entered the room. It was immediately apparent that he had drunk far more than was good for him.

Blinking in the light given out by the lamp, he seemed puzzled by the fact that it was lit. Then he saw Sally.

'Molly! What are you doing here?'

'It's not Molly,' she retorted. 'It's Sally, your daughter. I'm here because you promised that if I waited for you here you'd be home early.'

'Did I? I can't remember.'

'Well, you did. You said it just before you went inside The Jolly Waterman with someone you needed to talk business with – or so you told me. You promised to come home early and tell me about it.'

'Ah yes! I remember now. You told me off, didn't you?' He wagged a finger unsteadily in her general direction. 'You always were a spirited girl, Molly. It's one of the things I particularly liked about you – but it wasn't the only thing, mind.'

'It's *Sally*, not Molly,' she repeated. 'Anyway, what was this business you were going to tell me about?'

'Ah! You're not the only one who would like to know that, my girl. No doubt Lord and Lady Robartes would like to know, too. In fact, m'Lord and Lady would like to know more than anyone else, but they're not going to. Not just yet, anyway.'

'What do you mean? What have they got to do with any business of yours?'

'Never you mind, Molly,' her father said drunkenly. 'It's nothing you ought to know about. But they'll be sorry.'

'This is a stupid conversation,' said Sally. 'I might just as well have gone back to the Refuge when I finished work and left you in the mess I found this room in. I'm going now. I'll come back when you're sober – if you ever are. Perhaps you'll make more sense then.'

'No, don't go. You don't want to go yet, do you?'

'Yes, I do.'

Sally moved towards the door, but he lurched to one side and stood in front of it.

'Do you mind standing out of the way? It's getting late.'

'Late? We've got the whole night in front of us. It'll be just like old times, do you remember them, Molly? Yes, of course you do. Come on, show me you haven't forgotten . . .'

He reached out for her but she slipped under his arm and grabbed for the door latch. She had hold of it and pulled hard, but the door opened no more than a hand's breadth. Robert Sanderson's foot prevented it from opening any further.

He took a rough grip on her arm and yanked her hard away from the door. Caught off balance, she crashed against the bed and fell back on to it – and he fell with her.

He still had hold of her arm and she attempted to throw him off with violent movements of her body, but it seemed only to excite him.

As they struggled, he drove a knee into a muscle on the inside of one of her thighs. The sudden pain caused her to open her legs involuntarily. His body covered hers completely and he was pushing against her.

'Stop it. STOP IT! You're my father. Stop it, I say—'

'Who says I'm your father? Is that what she told you?' He did not sound quite so drunk now. Sally realised he was fully aware of who she was – and of what he was trying to do.

'Your father could have been any one of half a dozen men, but I was the one she decided had more to offer her than any of the others. Come on, now. Don't tell me you haven't done this before . . .' As he spoke, he pushed his arm between their bodies and forced his hand down between her legs. As he fumbled, clumsily, he hurt her and she screamed.

'Shut up, you stupid little bitch!'

His face was close to hers. Forcing her head up from the bed, she caught his nose between her teeth and bit him – hard.

He shouted in agony and as his grip on her relaxed, she was able to push him away and wriggle free, falling to the floor beside the bed.

Unfortunately, she fell on the side of the bed farthest from the door. By the time she reached it, he had recovered sufficiently to grab her once more.

This time, he hit her with his free hand and she was knocked back into the room. Coming after her, he struck out again – and yet again. When she fell to the floor he dragged her to her feet and struck her once more, thoroughly enraged.

'I'll make you suffer before I do it, believe me. You'll never bite me again, even if I need to knock out all your teeth to make certain of it.'

She could taste blood in her mouth now and she was terrified that he was going to kill her. His next blow knocked her back to the fireplace. As she fell against it, her flailing arm struck the kettle standing on the hob.

It was hot. Normally she would have taken a cloth with which to pick it up, but not now.

Snatching hold of the handle, she swung the kettle in an arc and threw it, striking Sanderson on the side of his neck. The lid flew off and boiling water cascaded over him.

Now it was his turn to scream. It was an agonised sound that seemed to go on for ever.

He was still screaming when Sally reached the foot of the stairs and ran past a startled Charlie.

'What's happening? What's going on up there?'

Sally did not answer. Pushing past him, she fled out to Pin's Lane and carried on running through the rain-washed streets of the Barbican.

50

Sally ran all the way to the Salvation Army Refuge but saw nothing of the streets or the people she passed along the way. Blinded by tears for much of the time, she was guided more by instinct than sight.

When she reached her destination she hesitated for a moment before knocking at the door. It was a blustery night and her hair was wet and in disarray. Her face ached so much she knew it must be badly bruised as a result of the beating she had taken from her father. Her wrist was painful, scalded by water from the kettle and her frock had been torn during the struggle.

Aware of the state she was in, she contemplated not knocking at the door – but there was nowhere else she could go tonight.

She rapped on the door quietly, hoping she might be able to slip past Zulu Joe and hurry to her room without him noticing her injuries.

Her hopes were not realised. The door was opened not by Zulu Joe but by Captain Eva.

'Ah, there you are. I knew you weren't in and had come down to see if . . . Sally! What have you been up to? What's happened to you?

She gripped Sally's arm, causing her to wince. The arm had been bruised by Sanderson when he threw her back from the door.

Eva drew Sally to the gas-light in the hall. Here she inspected her bruised face and torn frock.

Looking grim, she said, 'You'd better come with me to the bathroom . . . Joe, do you think you could go to the kitchen and brew up some tea for us?'

In the bathroom, Eva inspected Sally's bruised face and scalded hand and demanded once more that Sally tell her what had happened.

Hesitantly and still very close to tears, Sally told the Salvationist of the meeting with her father in Union Street, which resulted in her taking him to the room in Pin's Lane. Then she outlined much of what had occurred that evening.

The Salvation Army captain's first reaction was one of anger and she scolded Sally. 'You were a very silly girl for not telling anyone what was going on. Tonight might well have ended in tragedy for you . . .'

Standing back to hold Sally at arm's length, Eva gazed at her bruised face and distraught expression. Suddenly her expression softened. Wrapping Sally in her arms, she pulled her close.

'You poor girl! You've been treated abominably. Any man in his right mind would be absolutely delighted to discover he had a daughter like you. In spite of the way he behaved to you at Lanhydrock House, you took pity on him and let him stay in your room – only to end up being treated like this. He may, or may not, be your father, Sally. He certainly doesn't deserve a daughter like you.'

'I think I must have scalded him badly . . .' Sally choked on her words. 'What will happen to me if he dies?'

'He probably wasn't hurt as badly as you think.' Eva tried to allay Sally's fears. 'After I've put some opium ointment on those bruises I'll send Zulu Joe to Pin's Lane to find out how he is. We'll also wrap something about your wrist. The scald is already blistering. We don't want anything infecting it. Ah! Here's Joe with the tea now . . .'

When Zulu Joe returned to the Refuge from Pin's Lane, he wrote a single word on the piece of paper Captain Eva gave to him.

'Gone.'

'Gone where?' asked Sally.

Zulu Joe shrugged and wrote, 'Man in downstairs room said he went soon after you ran from house. Took all things with him.'

'There you are,' said Eva, much relieved in spite of her earlier proclaimed confidence. 'He couldn't have been hurt as badly as you thought.'

She smiled comfortingly at Sally. 'I know it's not what you were hoping for from him, Sally, but the best thing that could happen now would be for him to get out of your life forever. However, there's nothing to prevent you praying for him. I will do the same. Now, I think it's time you went to bed. If you wish, I'll tell Grace Philpott in the morning that you aren't well enough to go in to work.'

'No,' Sally said firmly. 'I'll be all right to work. Besides, when I was at the fish quay today they seemed to think the fishing fleet would probably return to harbour tomorrow. I've got a large delivery to take there and hope I might see Ethan. I'll tell him that he was right all along and say I'm sorry for quarrelling with him.'

'Good girl!' Eva put an arm about Sally's shoulders and hugged her once more. 'My mother always used to say that next to a good square meal, there's nothing appeals to a man quite as much as having a woman apologise to him.'

Later, lying in bed, thinking about the events of the day, Sally realised she had forgotten to tell Captain Eva what her father had said about Lord and Lady Robartes. That they would be sorry for dismissing him.

She decided she would tell her in the morning.

The boiling water from the kettle saturated Robert Sanderson's upper body and sobered him far more rapidly than any known beverage.

The agony from his burns brought previously dulled nerves to life, cutting incisively through the alcoholic fog that enveloped his brain.

When his screaming died away, it left him gasping for breath – but he was thinking now.

He realised he must get away from Pin's Lane as quickly as he could and find someone to help him.

Robert Sanderson knew very few people in Plymouth. It would not be easy to find medical aid at this time of night, especially someone who would help without asking too many questions.

The only person he could think of immediately was the woman who lived in the house backing on to Pin's Lane. Devonport Lil.

Gathering up any belongings that came immediately to hand, he stuffed them in a battered suitcase. The exertion caused him to whimper in pain. Then, slowly and painfully, he picked up the suitcase and made his way down the stairs.

From the doorway of his room, Charlie Shields watched the other man making his way cautiously down the stairs, carrying his suitcase. There was insufficient light to allow him to see the scalds on the other man's neck.

'Leaving are we?' snapped Charlie, unable to disguise his delight. 'It's not before time. I don't know what you've been up to tonight, mister, but if it's what I think it is, you'd better go a long, long way from here. Sally's young man has five brothers and they're all fishermen. Come tomorrow they'll be looking for you – and they'll find you if you're still in Plymouth. You'll have no reason to go looking for girls once they've finished with you.'

Charlie was still standing in the doorway of the house, chuckling, when Robert Sanderson left Pin's Lane behind and passed out of hearing around the corner.

51

The door to the house where Devonport Lil had her room was kept locked. Clara Flood took a fee from her lodger for every man she brought back, and by not allowing the prostitute to have her own key, the mercenary old landlady ensured she was not cheated of any of her dues.

When Clara Flood opened the door and saw only Robert Sanderson standing there, she said, 'Devonport Lil's not in. She's been spending nights on one of the ships lately. It's so as she don't have to pay me anything extra, I expect.'

Robert Sanderson was in great pain. It had been an effort to get this far. Only the thought that he might find someone here to help had kept him going.

His shoulders sagged in acknowledgement of defeat.

There was a strong smell of gin on Clara Flood's breath, but she was not drunk. Peering at the suitcase he was carrying, she said, 'Are you looking for a room? If you are, I've got one I can rent to you. It'll be a week's money in advance – no matter how long you're staying.'

Sanderson grasped at the unexpected lifeline eagerly. 'Paying in advance is no problem, but I need to see a doctor urgently. Do you know one who'll see me – now?'

Clara Flood had been opening the door to him, but now

she stopped. 'What's wrong with you?' she demanded. 'Is it catching? Something you've caught from one of the girls?'

'I've been badly scalded – in an accident. I need treatment right away.'

'You certain that's all it is?'

'Quite certain. Now . . . can I come in?'

'I'll treat it for you, if you like – but it'll cost you extra.'

'You? What do you know about medicine?'

'As much as most of your so-called "doctors". I followed the army in India with my husband for twenty years before he died in my arms. I've treated every kind of wound you could think of. Yes, and helped surgeons amputate enough limbs to serve a whole regiment. There's nothing you could have that I haven't seen before. Where are you scalded?'

'My neck's particularly bad, but the boiling water went through my shirt to my chest, back and shoulder.'

'Come on inside and I'll take a look at it. Once I've decided what needs to be done I'll want payment before I treat you.'

'Just do whatever needs to be done. You'll get your money.'

'Right, your room is upstairs, at the front of the house. Go up there and take your coat and shirt off. I'll be with you in a minute or two.'

Clara Flood worked for more than an hour cleaning and dressing Sanderson's scalds. When her ministrations were finished, she told him that although the scalds were extremely painful, all except a wound on the side of his neck would heal fairly quickly.

She then gave him something to help him to sleep and left him alone in the dingy and not-too-clean room.

The injuries inflicted by Sally upset Sanderson's plans to settle his score with Lord and Lady Robartes. He had expected that in the process he would acquire enough money to set himself up in a small business.

The man who was to help him in this ambitious and criminal venture was Harry Maggs, a chimney sweep Sanderson had met recently in a Plymouth public house. As a small boy Maggs had swept the chimneys at Lanhydrock and claimed to know the house intimately.

He was well aware of the many items of value kept in the house. He was an apprentice when his master had been caught pilfering from Lanhydrock during one of his professional visits and had been transported. It was a fate Maggs had avoided only because transportation had now been abolished. He had, however, served many terms of imprisonment.

Maggs had always nursed a grudge against the Robartes, holding the family accountable for all that had happened to him; in his view, they had been responsible for having his master imprisoned, leaving him to 'fall into bad company'.

The meeting with Sanderson allowed both men to share their grievances on the Robartes, and Maggs had eagerly agreed to the ex-butler's plan, which would make them rich and the Robartes somewhat poorer.

The planned robbery had been carefully thought through. Sanderson had kept a duplicate key to the servants' door at the side of Lanhydrock House. The door was locked and bolted from the inside at night, but Sanderson was aware that some of the house servants were in the habit of sneaking out for romantic liaisons, leaving the door unbolted.

The ex-butler had lost none of his womanising traits with the passing of the years. Before the abrupt termination of his employment, he had been carrying on an affair with one of the housemaids. He suspected that she had fallen pregnant. If so, she would be deeply concerned about her future and he could use this to his advantage. He had written to her expressing a wish to meet her one night. She was to creep out of the house when the family and servants were asleep. He would send her another letter giving details of the time and place.

It was Sanderson's intention that, when a meeting with the housemaid had been arranged, he would give his key to the sweep. While the girl was absent, the sweep would enter the house, armed with a list, drawn up by the ex-butler, directing him what to take and where he would find it.

There were some extremely valuable items in Lanhydrock and the two men would be able to sell them on for a very good price.

But stealing was not all that Sanderson had planned. Thanks to Sanderson's knowledge of the household routine, Maggs would have already spent two days inside the house sweeping chimneys and reacquainting himself with the layout. During this time he would stuff a number of paraffin-soaked sacks up the kitchen chimney in a strategic spot, using his expert knowledge.

The next time a fire was lit in the kitchen, the sacking would catch light, causing considerable damage to the ancient house. In this way, Sanderson felt, he would have gained revenge for his dismissal.

His injuries had caused an unexpected setback, but the plan had been delayed by only a few weeks. That time would be spent ensuring the sweep knew exactly what he had to do and became thoroughly conversant with the current layout of Lanhydrock House, thus ensuring the full success of their venture.

52

'Are you quite sure you're feeling well enough to make the deliveries today, dear?' Grace's concern was clear on her face as she put the question to Sally. 'You don't look too good this morning.'

'I'll be far better working than moping around feeling sorry for myself.'

Unable to hide her bruises, Sally had told Grace and Alfie about allowing her father to use her room in Pin's Lane and had relayed the events of the previous evening. Grace had been particularly incensed, uttering blood-thirsty threats of what she would do to Sanderson if ever their paths crossed.

'Well, as long as you're feeling up to it – but I'll not rest easy until that young man of yours is back to look after you.'

'He may already be back,' said Alfie. 'I spoke to one of the fishmongers from town when I was opening up the shop. He said many of the Plymouth boats came in overnight. It seems they've not had much luck and have returned with poor catches. The weather was bad and they had to shelter in the Scillies for much of the time.'

The thought of seeing Ethan again thrilled Sally. She really missed him and after the events of recent weeks she *needed* him – although she wished her face was not so badly bruised.

She was confident that once she had apologised for her

behaviour when they last met, they would be able to put their foolish quarrel behind them.

When she took a delivery to the quay later that morning she looked around eagerly for the *Mermaid*. It was nowhere to be seen and she was deeply disappointed.

When she questioned one of the fish buyers, he seemed surprised but not concerned that the Shields' boat was not in harbour.

'A dozen or so boats are still out,' he said. 'Don't worry, they'll all be in by tonight – and I hope they'll bring in more fish than the others.'

Sally made two more deliveries to the fish quay that day, and on each occasion she enquired after the *Mermaid*, but it had still not returned to harbour.

By the time Sally's working day came to an end it was dark, but she went to the quay one last time.

The fish sales had come to an end for the day now, but a number of fishermen were still working on their boats. From one of them she learned that the *Mermaid* was now the only boat belonging to the Plymouth fishing fleet that had not returned to harbour.

When she expressed her concern, the fisherman shrugged, 'Henry Shields is a man who likes to go his own way. The fish didn't seem to be running, so he probably went somewhere else to find them. I only hope he caught more than the rest of us did.'

As she walked away from the fish quay, Sally thought of what the fisherman had said. She should have been reassured by his words, but she was not.

She was walking slowly in the direction of the Salvation Army Refuge, but acting upon a sudden impulse, she turned and retraced her steps. She had decided to pay a call on Doris Shields.

When Sally arrived at the house, she discovered she was not the only person worried about the *Mermaid* and its crew. The door was opened by Sophie, and when Sally entered the kitchen she saw Phoebe seated there, drinking tea with Doris Shields.

When Doris saw Sally, she exclaimed, 'My dear child! What have you been up to? Your poor face . . . !'

Sally had been so preoccupied with thoughts of Ethan, she had temporarily forgotten the bruising on her face. Now, inhibited somewhat by the presence of Phoebe, whose attitude exuded disapproval, she gave Ethan's mother a brief version of the previous night's events.

'Ethan warned me against having anything to do with my father,' she concluded. 'I should have listened to him.'

'He wasn't happy about leaving you in the house with him,' Doris agreed. 'He spoke to me and his pa about it. He even thought of returning to Pin's Lane. I'm sorry to say it was me who talked him out of it. The hour was getting late and I knew he and the others would be making an early start next morning. I should have listened to him, he's always been a good judge of people.'

'I don't suppose I would have taken any notice of him,' Sally said unhappily. 'Not then, anyway. All I could think of was having my father with me at last. Me and Ethan came very close to quarrelling about it.'

'I don't think Ethan saw it as a quarrel,' Doris said reassuringly. 'He understood how you felt. He was reluctant to say anything against your pa – but he *was* worried for you.'

'I know – and I've come here because I'm worried about *him*. I thought the *Mermaid* would have returned with the other boats. Do you know what might be happening?'

'We're all worried about them,' said Sophie. 'We expected them back today, whatever the other boats did.'

'Tomorrow is my birthday,' Doris explained. 'My fiftieth birthday. For weeks all the family have been making a big thing about it. Ethan's pa has always brought me flowers for my birthday. He wouldn't want to miss this one. Besides, the boys were planning to give me a party – that's another thing Ethan was going to talk to you about on the night before they sailed. He wanted to invite you and ask your opinion about one or two things.'

'You . . . you don't think anything could have happened to them?' Sally put the question hesitantly.

Doris shook her head emphatically. 'There's not a finer fisher-man along the whole of this coast than my husband. In all probability he's found the fish the others were looking for and is staying out until he's taken as many as he can. There's no doubting we can do with the money. They'll be back tomorrow absolutely full of themselves, just you wait and see.'

53

Inspector Ian Lovat had become a regular visitor to the Salvation Army Refuge. Although his visits did not always have a purely professional purpose, he justified them by the fact that he occasionally picked up a snippet of useful information from one or other of the girls who were resident there.

However, today he had called at Eva's request, to discuss an advertisement placed in a provincial newspaper, which had been sent to her by a colleague. The advertisement was identical to the one that had brought Rachel and her companions to Plymouth. The only difference was that this one gave an answering address in Falmouth in nearby Cornwall. However, it was close enough to arouse suspicion.

'Of course, it might be a perfectly legitimate and respectable organisation,' Eva said now to Ian Lovat, 'but the wording is almost identical to the last advertisement. I'm also suspicious because the address is not too many miles from here. I believe the same people as before are involved.'

'We can't be certain of that,' Ian Lovat replied cautiously. 'The problem is that the address to which these girls are asked to write is a box number. I could have inquiries made, but my jurisdiction doesn't extend beyond Plymouth.'

'Does that mean you can't do anything to help?' Eva was indignant.

'No, it merely means I mustn't be seen to be doing anything that might possibly be construed as exceeding my duty. I can certainly ask the Falmouth police to make a few inquiries about the people behind this – but I've no doubt the group will have covered their tracks well.'

'Wouldn't they be likely to be scared off and move else-where, away from the West Country, if the police start making inquiries?'

'Probably,' the inspector agreed, 'but it will at least save those poor unsuspecting girls who reply to this particular advertisement.'

'That's merely a short-term solution. I want to stamp out this trade once and for all – even if it means breaking the law to do it.'

'You shouldn't be saying that to me,' Ian Lovat pointed out, but it was only the gentlest of reprimands. He knew the strength of Eva's views on this subject and respected them. He also enjoyed her company.

Eva looked forward to his visits too. She found she was able to converse with him more freely than with anyone she had ever known, male or female, in or outside the Salva-tion Army.

Nevertheless, she was passionate in her opposition to this particular aspect of vice. 'I am prepared to go to any lengths to bring this vile trade to an end. No price would be too high to pay. If I were younger and could enlist the aid of a reputable newspaper to publish my findings, I'd answer one of these advertisements myself and expose these people for what they are.'

'Finding a newspaper would pose no problem,' said Ian Lovat, not really believing Eva was entirely serious. 'A friend I made during my days in London is Carl Milton, editor of the *Mayfair Gazette*. He feels almost as strongly as you do about organised vice. As a matter of fact, he has run numerous campaigns against it in his newspaper. However, for you – or any other woman, for that matter – to play such a part would be far too dangerous. The people involved in this business – and that's exactly what it is, *big* business – have far too much to lose to allow a woman to stand in their way. You would simply disappear.'

'That wouldn't happen if someone was monitoring each move as it was made,' Eva persisted. 'Besides, just think of the magnificent victory if it were to succeed!'

'And if it didn't?' countered the policeman.

'What is one life, willingly given, when weighed against the hundreds, thousands, even, who might be spared a lifetime of shame and degradation?'

'You're really serious about this!' Ian Lovat was suddenly genuinely alarmed. 'It's madness. You couldn't rely upon the police to co-operate in such an unorthodox scheme. Quite apart from any other consideration, the route taken by these people crosses far too many boundaries – both national and international. There would be no continuity in police action. You could disappear forever anywhere along the route. Even worse, you might end up as just another victim of the vice trade.'

'"Just another victim", Ian? Each of the victims is a decent, ordinary young girl, like Rachel. Every one of them possesses thoughts and feelings and standards of decency that match my own. Yet they will be degraded and brutalised in a manner that beggars description. How would I feel – how would *you* feel if we knew I was about to suffer such a fate and no one was prepared to lift a finger to help? Would you use these "boundaries" of which you speak as an excuse for doing nothing? It is because those in authority can find such excuses that this trade flourishes. Such thinking ensures that the brothels of Europe will be supplied with innocent young English girls for as long as they want them.'

'Your feelings about this are both understandable and commendable. I can assure you that, as a policeman, I'll take all possible measures to stamp out this trade in Plymouth, but I can do very little beyond the boundaries of this borough. However, if you want to ensure it's brought to the attention of those in a position to really do something about it, I'll write a letter to my editor friend. I'll suggest he gets in touch with you with a view to running the story of what happened to Rachel. It won't please my chief constable, or the members of the borough council, but, as you rightly say, there is no place for such a degrading trade in a civilised country like ours.'

'Thank you, Ian, you're a very good friend.'

Eva occasionally wondered whether it might be possible for Ian Lovat to become more than a friend, but it could not be. She had dedicated her life to the cause of the Salvation Army.

Ian Lovat was still at the Refuge when Sally returned there later that evening.

'We were beginning to worry about you,' said Eva. 'I've told Inspector Lovat what happened to you last night. He would like to speak to you about it.'

'I've already told you everything that needs telling,' Sally said guardedly. 'There's nothing more to say.'

'The bruising on your face makes explanations unnecessary,' Ian Lovat said, tight-lipped. 'It must have been a vicious attack.'

'Have you been to Pin's Lane this evening, Sally?' asked Eva.

'No.'

Almost afraid to ask the question, Sally asked Ian Lovat hesitantly, 'Have you?'

'I went there this afternoon. Your room was empty. The man on the ground floor said Sanderson left soon after you ran from the house. He was carrying a suitcase.'

'Charlie doesn't miss much that goes on around him,' Sally mused.

'Captain Eva has told me you met up with your father in Union Street. Was anyone with him?'

'No.' Sally wondered why he had asked such a question.

'You're quite certain?'

'He was on his own – and very drunk.'

The inspector seemed disappointed with her reply and Sally added, 'I didn't see anyone with him then – but I did yesterday. They were going into The Jolly Waterman together.'

'Was it a man? Can you describe him to me?'

'He was too dirty to tell what he really looked like. I think he was a chimney sweep.'

'Ah! That's the man,' Ian Lovat said enigmatically. 'You've no idea who he is?'

'None at all. Why do you ask?'

'Someone overheard Sanderson and this man talking. It sounded as though they were planning a burglary, but my informant heard no more than that. If I knew who this man was I'd have him followed.'

Sally hesitated, wondering whether she should repeat the threats her father had made against the owners of Lanhydrock House. She decided against it.

One reason was the natural suspicion all residents of the Barbican had of the police – even this man, who had done so much to help her. Another was that, despite all he had done, Robert Sanderson was still her father.

Ian Lovat was disappointed. He believed Sally knew more than she was telling him, but he did not press her on the matter.

Sensing Sally's conflict of loyalties, Eva changed the subject by asking her where she had been since leaving work. She suggested Sally should keep away from Pin's Lane unless she had Ethan with her.

'Ethan was the reason I didn't come here straight from work,' Sally explained. 'His boat hasn't returned to harbour with the others today. Nobody seems to know where it is, so I went to see his mother to see if she knew anything.'

Eva immediately put thoughts of Robert Sanderson to one side. 'The whole of the Shields family are on that boat! Is there reason to believe something might have happened to them?'

'Ethan's ma doesn't think so, and one of the fishermen said that Ethan's pa tends to go his own way, but I can tell that everyone's worried. Tomorrow is Mrs Shield's birthday – her fiftieth. Ethan's pa has never failed to spend a birthday with her. If the *Mermaid* doesn't return tomorrow I think she'll really be worried. We all will.'

Eva looked at Sally, standing before her wearing second-hand clothes and with a badly beaten face. Her heart went out to the young girl, yet again. She would pray particularly hard tonight that another tragedy was not about to strike Sally's young life.

54

The Shields' boat did not return to Plymouth on Doris's fiftieth birthday. Nor did it enter the small harbour the day after.

The absence of the small boat from its home port was now causing great concern among the Shields' fellow fishermen. Nevertheless, Doris still insisted her family would bring the *Mermaid* safely into harbour, riding low in the water with the fish they had caught.

Her faith no longer convinced anyone. Sophie confessed her deep concern to Sally late on the second day after Doris's birthday.

The two young women were together on the fish quay. They had come here because a number of east coast boats had arrived with their catches, netted off the Isles of Scilly. Both young women hoped there might news of the *Mermaid*.

Their hopes were all too quickly dashed. All the fishermen told the same story. The Plymouth fishing boat had not been seen.

'I'm becoming really worried now, Sally.' Sophie was close to tears. 'I don't know what I'll do if Albert's lost. I just don't.'

'Don't even think about it,' Sally replied, with far more optimism than she felt. 'You've heard everyone say that Henry Shields is the best fisherman along the whole of this coast. He wouldn't do anything to put his boat and all his sons at risk. Albert and the others will come back and we'll both feel silly for having worried about them.' In a bid to change the subject, she said, 'I've not seen Phoebe lately. Has she been to the house?'

'No, and I doubt if we'll see her again,' Sophie said bitterly. She only came around the other day because she sensed a drama. She wanted to be at the centre of it and have everyone feel sorry for her. It's been dragging on too long for her now. There's no drama in a *missing* boat. Besides, I believe she's seeing someone else and has been for quite some time. It will please her parents. They would never have accepted a fisherman in the family.'

The two girls parted temporarily, to pass either side of baskets of fish being unloaded on to the quayside from the east coast boats.

'Mind you, there are others who care, even though they don't know us very well. That Salvation Army woman, Captain Eva, for one. She came around to the house today, to speak to Ma Shields and me. She said the whole of the Plymouth corps of the Salvation Army are praying for Ethan and the others.'

'We should all take heart from that,' Sally said in a bid to cheer up the other woman. 'Captain Eva doesn't do things by halves. You can bet that when she prays, God listens. Ethan, Albert and the others couldn't wish for anyone better on their side and praying for them.'

Sophie gave Sally a weak smile. It disappeared again very quickly as she asked, 'What do you *really* think, Sally? Do you honestly believe they'll return safely?'

It was a question Sally had tried not to ask herself. She had avoided facing up to the probable reason behind the *Mermaid*'s failure to return to Plymouth.

Nevertheless, she knew what Sophie wanted to hear and phrased her reply accordingly. 'I'm certainly not willing to believe that Ethan and the others *aren't* coming back. Neither are you – and Ma Shields certainly isn't.'

Unseen by Sophie, she crossed her fingers firmly as she added, 'They'll come back safely, you'll see . . .'

Sally's confidence was desperately shaken two days later when another steam-trawler from Lowestoft put in to Plymouth. It had been working fishing grounds to the south of the Scilly Isles, and pieces of splintered wood, painted bright blue, had been hauled on board in the trawler's nets.

The crew had made enquiries from fishermen on a boat they met up with just off Plymouth and learned of the missing boat.

The broken wood was taken to the Shields' house and when Sally arrived at the house that evening, she saw it piled in the passageway, just inside the door. Immediately she remembered Ethan telling her that the boat was being painted. He had even told her the colour . . . it was bright blue!

Suddenly, she felt unable to stay and face Doris and Sophie Shields. Sally turned around and ran blindly through the streets of the Barbican.

Unwilling to share her emotions with anyone, she could not return to the Refuge. She did not want to speak to anyone, anywhere. All she wanted was to be alone with her sorrow.

The only place she could think of was the room in Pin's Lane. Blundering through the front door, she ran upstairs.

It was dark here, but she did not want a light. She felt a need to hide from the whole world. Everything in her life was going wrong. Desperately wrong.

Giving way to an uncharacteristic bout of self-pity, she believed she must be the unluckiest person in the whole world.

Like a small, hurt animal, she crouched in a corner of the room, her head against the wall.

55

Captain Eva was visiting Rachel at the flat above the pie shop when Alfie came in. He brought news of the Lowestoft trawler that had come into Sutton harbour with wreckage, almost certainly from the *Mermaid*.

The Salvationist felt the pain of the news as acutely as though someone had dealt her a physical blow.

'I must go to the Shields' house and speak to Ethan's mother,' she said, rising to her feet immediately. 'Doris Shields has six sons and a husband on that boat. This is enough to derange her.'

'See if Sally is there too,' said Grace. 'That poor girl has had more to contend with than should come into any young girl's life.'

'I'll come with you,' Rachel said to Eva. 'I'd like to help Sally if I can, just as she helped me when I needed it.'

'You really shouldn't be going out at all, dear,' said Grace. 'You haven't been very well these last few days. You're still looking very pale.'

'I'll be all right. I'll just go and get my coat.'

When Rachel had left the room, Grace spoke to Eva in an exaggerated whisper. 'She's not been her usual cheerful self just lately. Tired and moping around the house. She's as likely as not to burst into tears at the slightest provocation.' Nodding conspiratorially, she added, 'I think it must be her age.'

As Eva and Rachel made their way to the home of the Shields family, Eva broached the subject of Grace's anxiety.

'Grace is very concerned about you, Rachel. I know she's not used to having a young girl about the house, but is there anything wrong that I can help with?'

Rachel looked up at her companion. 'I'm all right. Grace worries too much about me – but she's very kind.' It was too dark for Eva to be able to read the girl's expression.

'You're lucky to have found her, Rachel. She thinks the world of you.'

'I know, but she sometimes speaks to me as if I was the little girl she lost all those years ago. I'm not, though. It's a great responsibility.'

Eva smiled. Rachel was growing up. She had no doubt that Grace was right in her assessment of what was wrong with her.

Eva and Rachel did not stay very long at Doris Shields' house. The wreckage was still piled in the passageway and Sophie was obviously very close to tears. But not Doris Shields.

She was refusing to accept that her family and their boat had been lost. Despite the evidence of the splintered timbers, she was adamant that her husband and sons would soon return safely to Plymouth.

Faced with such unshakeable faith, Eva realised that sympathy would be out of place. She expressed her thoughts aloud to Sophie as Albert's young wife escorted the two visitors from the kitchen to the street.

The expression on Sophie's face told Eva that she did not share the convictions of her mother-in-law. The strain of maintaining the pretence was beginning to show.

'I'm afraid of what she'll do when all hope has finally disappeared and she realises just how great her loss is,' she said. Close to tears, she added, 'I'm not sure I'll be able to cope with it, either.'

'I'll come visiting as often as I can,' Eva offered. 'In the meantime, if you need anything, don't hesitate to call for my help. You know where you can find me.'

She was about to walk away when she remembered the other reason she and Rachel had come to the house. 'By the way, do you know where we might find Sally?'

'She was here earlier this evening. She came inside the house, took one look at the wreckage in the passage, then turned and fled. I never had a chance to say a word to her. Like me, she doesn't share Mrs Shields' optimism. I didn't worry too much about her when she left because I thought she would go straight back to you, at the Refuge. Are you certain she isn't there?'

'She might be there now,' replied Eva. 'We'll look in at Pin's Lane on the way back, just in case she decided to go there so she could be on her own.'

She hoped her reply would satisfy Sophie. She had no wish to add to her worries. If Doris Shields had indeed lost her entire family in one cruel stroke, Albert's wife would be taking on a great burden.

When Eva and Rachel reached Pin's Lane and entered the house, Charlie came to the door of his room.

'What's going on tonight? I've never known so many people to be coming in and out.'

'Why, who else has been here?' Eva asked sharply, suddenly fearful that Sid Darling might have been one of the 'many' visitors to the house.

It immediately became apparent that Charlie had been exaggerating.

'Well, apart from you two, someone came running through the passageway and up the stairs about an hour ago. It sounded like young Sally, but I wasn't going upstairs on my own, in case it was someone else.' Sniffing noisily, Charlie added, 'Whoever it is, they're very quiet up there now. They haven't made a single sound since they came in, but I know they haven't come back down again. What's going on?'

'Haven't you heard about Henry Shields' boat? I felt certain the family would have told you . . .'

'Told me *what*?' Charlie demanded impatiently. 'Whatever it is, I'm obviously the last to know. That's the trouble with not being well enough to get out and about. You have to rely on others to let you know what's going on in the world.'

'Go back in your room and sit down and I'll come in and tell you.' Eva was aware she was dealing with a sick man who might take the news badly.

At the same time she gave an uncertain glance up the unlighted stairs. Aware of her concern, Rachel said, 'It's all right, while you're speaking to Charlie, I'll go upstairs and see if Sally is there.' Hesitating for a moment, she added, 'But I would like a candle to light the way. It looks dark.'

'Take that one,' said Charlie, pointing to the stub of a candle burning in a chipped enamel candleholder. 'But don't forget to bring it back down again. I keep it burning there to show me the way to my kitchen.'

56

Holding the candle at head height in front of her, Rachel made her way cautiously up the creaking stairs. In truth, she was not as brave as she had tried to appear to Captain Eva. Charlie had been fairly certain the footsteps he had heard going upstairs were Sally's, but the knowledge that he had heard nothing since was unnerving.

What if someone had been waiting in the room for her? What if . . . ?

When the candle and holder began shaking in her hand, Rachel made a determined effort to pull herself together. She told herself she was being foolish. Had anyone been waiting for Sally in the upstairs room there would have been *more* noise, not less.

Despite her determination to be brave, her heart was beating faster than normal as she gently pushed open the door to Sally's room.

She held the candle high in front of her, as she peered into the room, so as to shed its light as far as possible. Unable to see anything at first, she grew puzzled. Taking a first step inside the room, she held the candle even higher.

A slight movement in a corner of the room was so unexpected and sudden that Rachel almost dropped the candle in fright.

'Is that you, Sally?'

'Yes.' Her voice sounded thick and slurred, as though she had been drinking. 'What are you doing here?'

'Captain Eva and me went looking for you at Ethan's house. The wife of one of his brothers said you'd been there but had run off again. Captain Eva thought you might have come here. She's downstairs now, talking to Charlie.'

When Sally made no immediate reply, Rachel asked, 'Do you want me to light the lamp for you?'

'No! And I didn't need anyone to come looking for me. All I wanted was to be on my own for a while, in the dark.'

'That's the way I felt for a few days after I'd been taken off the boat. I was glad afterwards that you, Captain Eva and Grace were there to help me though.'

When Sally remained silent once more, Rachel asked uncertainly, 'Do you want me to go?'

Sally shook her head. 'It's all right.' She still sat in the corner of the room, her arms locked around her drawn-up knees.

Rachel set the candle down on the table, then walked across the room to stand by the bed.

'I . . . I'm sorry about Ethan.'

'Nobody knows for sure yet what's happened to him and the others,' Sally snapped fiercely.

'No, of course not,' Rachel agreed hastily.

There was silence between the two for a while, before Rachel said hesitantly, 'Sally, I know this isn't the right time to talk about such things, but . . . could you tell me something? Something important?'

'What?'

'How can you tell if you're having a baby?'

Sally was startled out of her deep unhappiness. 'How do you . . . ? Why, there are a whole lot of ways, I suppose. Your body changes. You—' Belatedly, the import of the question penetrated Sally's dulled brain. 'Rachel! You don't think . . . ? Oh no, it couldn't happen to you.' Her own deep misery momentarily pushed to one side, she looked aghast at her companion. 'But . . . you *can't*. You're too young!'

'I was twelve a few weeks ago,' Rachel replied wretchedly, '. . . and I think I *am*. What can I do, Sally?'

'There's nothing you can do. At least, nothing that's really safe.'

'I don't care about *safe*. I'll kill myself before I have Sid Darling's baby – or the baby of any of the others who did this to me. But I think it must be his.'

'Have you spoken to anyone else about this? Captain Eva . . . ?'

'I don't want anyone else to know – ever! I've only told you because I trust you – and because I need your help. You must promise never to tell Grace, Sally. If you do I'll run off and kill myself. I promise you I will.'

'You mustn't talk like that, Rachel. Whatever happens, no one will even blame *you*. This certainly isn't your fault.'

The loss of the *Mermaid* was still a heavy, black load that weighed Sally down, but Rachel's revelation had made it lose its immediacy.

'I don't care about any of that. I'm just *not* going to have it . . .'

At that moment, both girls heard the stairs creaking loudly as someone made their way up them. A few seconds later Captain Eva entered the room.

'Hello, Sally,' she said sympathetically. 'I'm desperately sorry to hear the tragic news about Ethan's fishing boat.'

The hurt returned, but Sally said defiantly, 'They've only found a bit of old wreckage. It doesn't mean Ethan and the others have been lost.'

'That's quite true,' admitted Eva. 'And you're absolutely right. We must cling to hope for as long as is reasonable.'

Although she was convinced there *was* no hope, Eva believed the impact of the loss of Ethan would lessen for Sally with the passing of time. She was not as certain the same would apply to Doris Shields, faced with her far greater tragedy.

'Do you want to stay here tonight, Sally, or will you return to the Refuge with me?'

'I'll come to the Refuge a little later. Perhaps Rachel will stay with me for a while?'

'I'm sure she will.'

Unaware of the true reason for Sally's suggestion, Eva was delighted the two girls had become such firm friends that each could be a comfort to the other at a time of such deep trouble.

'I'll go downstairs and make certain Charlie is all right before I go. He knew nothing about his brother's boat being lost. It's hit him very hard. Afterwards, I'll go and tell Grace what Rachel is doing. I'll see you later at the Refuge. May I say I'm very impressed with your courage and fortitude, Sally – but I'm not really surprised.'

When Eva had gone, Sally said, 'Now, what are we going to do about you, Rachel? I still think it would be best to tell Captain Eva, or Grace.'

Rachel shook her head vigorously. 'If I can get rid of the baby there's no reason why anyone apart from you should ever know.'

'I don't think getting rid of it is quite that easy,' said Sally. She was standing up, close to the window now. As both girls looked out a lamp was lit in the kitchen beneath the room occupied by Devonport Lil.

A few moments later, Clara Flood could be seen moving about, busying herself in the kitchen.

Pointing to her, Sally said, 'If you're not sensible, you could end up in the hands of someone like her. Ruth used to say she's got rid of more babies than King Herod, but I wouldn't want to have her doing anything to me. She's a horrible old woman.'

Turning away from the window, she continued. 'I believe there are one or two things you can take to try to get rid of a baby, but they don't always work. I'll ask some of the girls who are staying at the Refuge if they know of anything. I don't doubt some of them will have had to deal with a similar problem.'

'Beg them to help, Sally. I'm sorry to have troubled you at a time like this, but I've been worrying myself sick about it. I couldn't think of anyone else I could turn to.'

As the girls left the house in Pin's Lane a little later, Sally realised that having Rachel's very real problem to think about had somehow made her own sorrow easier to cope with.

57

Questioning the girls in the Refuge about getting rid of an unwanted baby was much easier than Sally had anticipated – but it also proved embarrassing.

Without exception they thought she must be pregnant by Ethan, who had now been lost at sea and so could not marry her.

Each of the girls had her own recipe for procuring a miscarriage. Most involved mixing a potion, the main ingredient of which was alcohol.

Sally explained this to Rachel as they walked around the streets of Plymouth together the next day, making deliveries for Grace and Alfie.

'Do you think I'll be able to take it without Grace knowing?' asked Rachel.

'Are you used to strong drink?' Sally countered.

'No, I don't like it.'

'Then you'll never be able to keep it from her. You'll be drunk long before you've taken enough for it to do what you want it to.'

'What can I do then?'

Sally shrugged. She felt dreadfully tired. She had not slept the previous night. Every time she dozed off, Ethan's face haunted her dreams and she woke herself, and Rachel once, by calling his name aloud. 'I don't know. Have the baby and decide what you're going to do about it then, I suppose.'

'I'm *not* going to have it, Sally. I'm *not*!'

Rachel spoke so vehemently that a woman passing by looked at her disapprovingly and stepped from the pavement to avoid her.

The girls walked on in silence for a while before Rachel said, 'Would I be able to take this stuff in the Refuge without anyone knowing?'

Sally was about to give her a negative reply. Then she remembered that only a few nights before she had been invited to join some of the girls at the Refuge, who had consumed the contents of a bottle of gin before going to bed.

'You might,' she admitted.

'Then that's what I'll do. I'll stay there with you for a while. Until I've got rid of it.'

'What will you tell Grace? She'll be very unhappy if you move out from her place.'

'She'll be even more unhappy if I inflict an unwanted baby on her. I'll tell her I'm staying there to be near you while you're so upset about Ethan.'

'Thank you very much!' Sally spoke indignantly. 'Don't you think I've got enough to worry about as it is?'

'Yes, you have,' admitted Rachel. 'But I'm desperate for help, Sally. Any help I can get.'

'All right,' Sally relented. She had grown very fond of Rachel and did not like to see her so unhappy. 'You make your excuses to Grace and I'll arrange with Captain Eva for a bed to be put in my room for you. I don't like lying to her, and she certainly wouldn't approve of what we're doing, but I feel she'd at least understand.'

Both Grace and Captain Eva agreed to the temporary arrangement so readily that it made Sally feel even more guilty. However, she told herself she was doing the right thing for Rachel.

It also gave her something to think about other than Ethan . . . yet she managed to feel deeply guilty about this too.

That evening, Sally heated gin in a saucepan balancing on the fire in her room. On the table, folded in a small paper bag, was a brown, spicy-smelling powder that had been purchased for Sally by one of the recently 'saved' prostitutes. It was to be poured in the gin when it was sufficiently heated.

'Is it going to work?' Rachel asked anxiously.

'I don't know,' Sally replied honestly. 'Annie gave me the stuff to put in the gin. She said sometimes it works, sometimes it doesn't.'

'How much of it do I have to drink?'

'As much as you can. All of it, if possible.'

Rachel looked aghast. 'But . . . won't it make me ill?'

'Probably – but I think that's the idea. If you make yourself really ill you might lose the baby.'

As she was speaking, Sally moved the saucepan from the fire, using a cloth to hold the handle. She half filled a mug with hot gin, then spooned a quantity of powder from the paper bag into it.

After she had stirred it vigorously, Sally passed the mug to Rachel without comment.

Taking a sip, the younger girl recoiled in disgust.

'Ugh! It's *horrible!*'

Despite the seriousness of what they were doing, Sally gave her friend a weak smile. 'You're not drinking to enjoy it, Rachel. If it does what you want it to do it'll be the best drink you've ever had, won't it? Now, get it down, there's lots more left.'

Rachel downed the concoction in a series of great gulps. Occasionally gagging, she did her best to control the urge to be sick. When the mug was empty, she stood in the middle of the room fighting for breath, her cheeks flushed and red.

Expressionless, Sally took the mug from Rachel's hands, mixed more powder and hot gin and held the mug out to the younger girl once more.

'I'm not sure I can take any more, Sally. I feel funny. All light-headed.'

'You'll need to take a whole lot more than you have if it's to do anything. Annie told me she's known some girls who've had to drink two whole bottles of gin before it's had any effect.

You've had no more than half a mugful. Look . . .' She held up the half-full bottle. 'There's a lot to go yet.'

Rachel groaned. Feeling increasingly light-headed, she took the mug from Sally and lifted it to her lips.

58

That night, Rachel was so violently ill that Sally feared Eva would hear her and come upstairs to find out what was happening.

Fortunately, the Salvation Army officer was at a meeting and did not return to the Refuge until late. She did call out a soft 'Good night' outside the door but, receiving no reply, took herself off to bed, believing the two girls to be asleep.

Sally wondered what Eva's reaction would have been had she known Sally was inside the room, holding a towel to Rachel's mouth as a gag to prevent her groans from being heard.

The following morning, Rachel felt twice as ill as Sally told her she looked. Although she was convinced she was dying, Rachel had not aborted the baby she was carrying.

As the two girls walked to work at the shop, Rachel asked, 'Will I have to go through all that again, Sally?'

'You tell me. You're the one who wants to get rid of a baby.'

'Then I'll do it . . . but isn't there something else I can take? Something that doesn't taste quite so horrible.'

'All the girls have different ideas on what should be taken. We'll try another one tonight – but I doubt if you'll enjoy it any more. It involves hot gin again – they all do. It's only the stuff that goes in it that's different.'

Rachel groaned. 'People who drink for pleasure must be mad!

Once this is over I'll never touch another drop for as long as I live – but I *am* going to get rid of this baby.'

When they arrived at the shop, Grace threw up her hands in horror when she saw the state Rachel was in.

'My dear soul, look at you! Anyone would think you hadn't slept for a week! You're not much better, Sally. I'd better not give either of you very much to do today.'

'Why don't you give them each a pie and put 'em to bed?' Alfie asked sarcastically. 'I sometimes wonder how we manage to make any money at all, Grace. It wouldn't surprise me if you were to tell me one day you wanted to turn the whole business over to the Salvation Army!'

'We could do a whole lot worse than that, Alfie Philpott, and it would stand us in good stead when we are brought before our maker.'

Alfie realised his attempt at sarcasm had gone seriously wrong. Alarmed that he might have put a radical idea into the mind of his unpredictable wife, he said hurriedly, 'I've no intention of going to meet my maker just yet. When I do, I doubt if he'll frown on the fact that I've worked hard and made a success of the life he gave to me.'

'He'll look more kindly upon you if you can show you've been generous to those less fortunate than yourself during your lifetime,' Grace retorted. 'Anyway, we won't lose any customers today. I'll make the deliveries myself, if I have to.'

'You won't need to do that,' Sally assured her. 'Rachel and me are tired, but we're not invalids. We can make all the deliveries.'

'Well . . . all right, if you're quite sure,' said an unconvinced Grace. 'But you make certain you both come back here for a proper meal when the midday deliveries have been made.'

The last thing Rachel wanted to think about right now was food, but she said nothing. She sincerely hoped Sally had been telling the truth when she said she would feel better as the day went along.

That evening's attempt to bring about a miscarriage was no more successful than the previous evening's. If anything, Rachel was more ill than she had been the night before and was once more quite convinced she was going to die.

But Sally soon had something more to worry about. The next afternoon, as she was making her deliveries, she called in to see Doris Shields and found Sophie deeply concerned about the mental state of her mother-in-law.

'She refuses to face the facts,' Sophie said unhappily. 'I'm quite certain she lies awake for most of the night grieving for Henry and the boys, but she won't discuss it with me, or with anyone else. My fear is that if she carries on like this she'll go out of her mind. I'm finding it very hard to cope with, Sally.' Hesitantly, she asked, 'Do you think you could move in and stay with me for a night or two? I'd really appreciate having your company.'

Sally thought of Rachel and her problem. The younger girl had already hinted that she doubted if she could take any more of the alcoholic treatment. Besides, it did not seem to be succeeding in its aim.

'Let me go back to the Refuge to collect a few things, then I'll return.'

'Thanks, Sally,' Sophie said gratefully. 'It will help just having you here to talk to, even if neither of us are able to do anything to help Mrs Shields.'

At the Refuge, Rachel seemed as relieved as Sally had hoped she might be. She admitted she did not feel she could cope with deliberately making herself violently ill for a third night.

'But what else can I try, Sally?' she pleaded. 'I *must* get rid of it, somehow.'

'Let me think about it.'

In fact, Sally had already given the matter some thought. She would be staying in the Shields' home with Sophie. Albert's wife had worked on the quay with the Scots fisherwomen who came down to help their men-folk when they were fishing the Channel waters at certain times of the year.

The Scots women had a vocabulary that was the equal of Cornish fishermen. They also brought with them a reputation for immorality that had grown to near-legendary proportions over the years.

Sophie might have heard them discussing the best means of procuring a miscarriage. However, Sally did not want her jumping to the same conclusions as the girls in the Refuge. She decided she would let Sophie into Rachel's secret. She had absolute trust in the wife of Ethan's brother, and felt certain she would prove to be a useful ally.

59

Sophie was utterly appalled to hear of Rachel's condition. She believed, as did Sally, that the unfortunate young girl had already suffered quite enough.

'She's so *young*, Sally. To have gone through all that's happened to her – and now to have to face this . . . It seems all wrong. Yet the man who is the cause of all this is still out there somewhere. Why haven't the police caught up with him?'

'No one can find him. He's certainly gone from Plymouth. Inspector Lovat believes he's probably left England. Wanted notices have been sent to every police force in the country. If he was around he would have been caught by now.'

'Where does this inspector believe he's gone?'

'Most probably to Belgium. That's where the girls were being sent. He knows people there.'

'It's appalling to think there are such men in the world.' Although Sophie had her own problems with which to come to terms, she asked, 'Is there anything I can do to help?'

'Not unless you know of a foolproof means of getting rid of the baby she's carrying.'

Sophie shook her head sadly. 'There's no such thing, Sally. I've listened to the Scots women down the quay talking about it – other women too. If you're lucky – very lucky – something you try *might* work. Most times it doesn't. She'll have to get used to the idea of having the baby. Once it's been born she might be able to have it adopted, or something. Mind you, that won't be easy, either. It seems there are far more babies being born than there are women who want 'em.'

'I've already told her she should wait until the baby's born, but she's determined to get rid of it now.'

'It seems everyone has more than their share of problems. Right now, Albert's ma is mine. I keep hoping she'll break down and cry, or become hysterical, or something. I'd find it a lot easier to take than this quiet, unshakeable faith that the *Mermaid* is going to come riding in on the next tide.'

Sophie's statement sounded harsh, but even as she spoke tears began rolling unchecked down her cheeks.

Putting an arm about her, Sally said, 'I'll do what I can to help, Sophie. I know these last few days can't have been easy for you.'

Seated at the kitchen table, sharing a meal with Sophie and Doris Shields, Sally soon realised what Albert's wife was finding so difficult.

Doris Shields' self-control was unnerving. There were no tears and she showed little emotion. She seemed to have complete control of herself.

Half-way through the meal, Doris looked at the clock and said, 'I wonder if Henry and the boys will bring the *Mermaid* in on tonight's tide? They'd better not leave it too late if they are. The tide will be turning in another half an hour or so. When they do arrive they'll no doubt be hungry. Is there plenty of food in the house, Sophie?'

Sophie had been gazing down at her plate while Doris was talking.

When she looked up, she said, 'There'll be more than enough for everyone.'

'Good. There's nothing like fishing to give a man an appetite.' Shifting her attention to Sally, she said, 'They'll certainly eat more than you, young lady. You've been prodding and picking at that food as though you might have lost something in it.'

'I'm sorry, Mrs Shields. I don't seem to be very hungry this evening.'

'That's the result of working in a pie shop, with the smell of cooking in your nostrils all day. It's bound to take the edge off your appetite. Why don't you two girls finish your meal and go on down to the harbour? See if there's any sign of Henry and the boys. I'll clear the table and wash up while you're gone.'

'I'll stay and give you a hand,' said Sophie. 'It's a bit cold out there for me.' Humouring her mother-in-law, she added, 'Albert doesn't always walk home the same way from the harbour. It depends where they're able to berth the boat. It won't be easy today, with so many east coast boats in. I wouldn't want to miss him if he came home one way and I went to the harbour the other.'

Aware that Sally was worried about Rachel, Sophie gave her an understanding smile. 'There's no need for you to stay in. I'll be all right.'

'Thanks. I'll just pop out and have a few words with Rachel, then I'll come back and keep you company for the remainder of the evening.'

Sally expected to find Rachel at the Refuge. She had said she intended staying on there for a few more days. But there were only three girls in the house and Rachel was not one of them. The others had gone to a meeting at Central Hall with Captain Eva, and Sally thought Rachel must have gone with them.

In two minds about whether to return to the Shields' house immediately or to go to Central Hall first, Sally chose the latter option.

The prayer meeting was already in progress in the hall and was well attended – but there was an opposition meeting taking place outside.

About forty men, some of them holding aloft Skeleton Army banners, were singing bawdy, music-hall songs at the top of their voices in an attempt to drown the sound of those inside, but Sally had no difficulty slipping past them and into the hall.

Inside, the worshippers were doing their best to ignore the

competition from the street outside. Standing at the back of the hall, Sally tried to locate Rachel in the crowd.

Opposition to the Salvation Army had escalated in recent weeks. The large number of broken windows in the hall bore testimony to the violence of the Skeleton Army.

It made the hall colder than it might have been, particularly for those of the congregation who were inadequately clothed.

Sally thought it would probably not have displeased the founder of the Salvation Army. Captain Eva had once told her that General William Booth had decreed his 'soldiers' should take a cold bath daily. He believed it to be both hygienic and strengthening for the forces of the Lord.

He would no doubt have been well pleased with the congregation too. What it lacked in physical comfort was more than compensated by its spiritual enthusiasm and religious fervour.

Captain Wardle was conducting the meeting, with Captain Eva on the platform beside him. A tall, distinguished man, his oratory was attracting men and women to the front of the hall to pledge themselves to the Lord's cause.

Sally was not seeking salvation, but Rachel, and this was not easy. Then, to her surprise, she picked out Grace Philpott in the crowd, close to the front of the hall.

The congregation was standing and Sally was unable to see whether Rachel was with her, but she felt she probably was. If so, she would be unable to discuss Rachel's problems with her this evening.

There was little point in staying. Sally turned to leave when there was a sudden commotion at one of the broken windows.

The next moment, a great many pigeons flew into the hall, released from a large basket held up to one of the windows.

The sudden influx of the confused and frightened birds should have provided a sufficient diversion in itself, but someone had hit upon the idea of attaching loose paper packets of fine-ground red pepper to each of the birds.

As the panic-stricken pigeons flew around the hall, the packets broke open and clouds of choking red pepper floated down upon the congregation.

Coughing and sneezing and with their eyes smarting, members of the congregation stampeded for the door. Those who
made it to the street first were greeted by the jeers and blows
of the Skeleton Army.

Evading most of the waiting rowdies, Sally did not wait to
see how the others fared. She ran for the Shields' home, leaving
the mayhem of Central Hall behind her.

She hoped Rachel and Grace would escape safely, but was
not unduly concerned for them. Salvation Army officers were
used to such happenings at their meetings. Once the pepper
had settled they would keep the majority of their congregation
in the hall. Their opponents would soon tire of their 'fun' and
return to the public houses from which most had set out earlier
in the evening.

60

Doris Shields was quite rational the following morning. After expressing surprise that Sally had spent the night in her house, she cooked breakfast for herself and the two younger women.

While she cooked, Doris speculated on whether the *Mermaid* was likely to return to harbour that day.

When she added that she was beginning to feel anxious about her menfolk, Sophie and Sally looked at each other but said nothing. Both believed that the situation had passed way beyond the stage when she should be feeling anxious; Doris Shields should by now have been sharing the grief her daughter-in-law and Sally were experiencing.

Before setting off for the pie shop, Sally promised Sophie that she would return to the house that evening.

Her route to work took her past the fish quay, where boats were setting out for the day's fishing. Although the wreckage in the Shields' passageway should have provided irrefutable evidence of the fate of the men of the family, and despite her concern that Doris was not facing up to the facts, a part of Sally still held out hope for a miracle, and her eyes scoured the harbour.

As Sally made her way along the quayside, she was greeted sympathetically by those few fishermen who were aware of her association with the Shields family.

At the shop, Sally found Alfie already swabbing the floor. It was a task she usually performed.

'You're late, girl,' Alfie scowled at her.

'I'm sorry, Alfie. Mrs Shields put me all behind this morning.'

As they spoke she took off her coat. Tying an apron about her waist, she said, 'Give me the mop. I'll finish cleaning the floor.'

Instead of handing the mop to her, Alfie demanded, 'What do you mean, Mrs Shields put you all behind? Have you been to her house this morning? Was Rachel with you, or did you leave her at the Refuge?'

Sally looked at him in bewilderment. 'Isn't she here? I thought . . .'

Her thoughts were never voiced. Grace put her head out of the kitchen and said cheerfully, 'Hello, Sally. Is Rachel with you?'

Sally was confused. 'No. I thought she was with you. I . . . I didn't stay at the Refuge last night, I slept at Ethan's house. I was keeping Sophie company because she was so worried about Doris Shields.'

As she spoke, she was thinking of the true reason Rachel had stayed at the Refuge the previous couple of nights. Sally thought Rachel must have decided to spend a third night there after leaving Central Hall. She might have tried yet again to bring on a miscarriage, helped in her efforts this time by the reformed prostitutes at the Refuge. But she could not explain this to Grace or Alfie.

Thinking quickly, she said, 'No one at the Refuge must have thought to wake her up. Knowing I wasn't there, they must have forgotten her.'

Grace's expression was one of puzzlement. 'But . . . if you weren't staying there, why didn't she come back here for the night?'

'Perhaps I didn't make it clear to her that I would be spending the night at the Shields' house.' Stripping off her apron, Sally added hurriedly, 'I'll go and wake her. I won't be long. I'll run all the way.'

Before Grace could question her further, she ran from the shop, pretending not to hear Alfie's protests.

She did not stop running until she reached the Refuge, fearful that this time Rachel might have made herself seriously ill. And with no one on hand to help her, anything might have happened . . .'

The front door of the Refuge was standing open. Zulu Joe was inside the entrance, cleaning panes of coloured glass set into an inner door.

He gave Sally a broad smile, but her response was to ask him if he had seen Rachel that morning.

When Zulu Joe shook his head, Sally pushed past him. 'I'd better go to my room and see if she's still asleep there.'

Zulu Joe followed Sally and was close behind her when she opened the door and discovered the room to be empty. 'Oh! She must have already gone out. We probably passed each other somewhere between here and the pie shop.'

There was a tap on her shoulder. Sally turned to see her companion writing in the small notebook he always carried in his pocket.

When he handed the notebook to her, she read, 'Not here last night.'

Sally's expression showed her concern. 'Are you quite sure, Joe? Isn't there a chance she came to the Refuge without you noticing?'

He shook his head and wrote on the pad, 'Trouble last night at Central Hall. Captain Eva checked all rooms in case anyone hurt. Looked in here before remembered you away for few nights. Expect Rachel with lady you both working for.'

'No, I've just come from there. Could I have a page from your notebook, Joe. I'd like to leave a message in the room for her, just in case she comes back here. I want to tell her to come straight to the shop. We're all worried about her.'

Sally had a sudden thought: Zulu Joe would have been at the meeting at Central Hall the previous night, for a time, at least.

'Was Rachel at the meeting last night?'

He shook his head.

Sally should have been relieved to know that Rachel's disappearance was not connected with the violence at the meeting, but she was not. She was fully aware of how determined Rachel was not to have the baby she was carrying and how upset she had been when everything the two girls had tried so far had failed. Sally tried to ignore the nagging suspicion that in her desperation the younger girl might have contemplated committing suicide.

She shuddered and tried to shake off such thoughts. She needed to keep calm and think sensibly. It was going to be difficult enough breaking the news that Rachel had disappeared to Grace and Alfie.

61

'Why would Rachel just disappear like this without telling anyone? Without telling *me*? It just isn't like the girl.'

Explaining to Grace that she had been unable to discover the whereabouts of Rachel had been quite as difficult as Sally had anticipated.

The pie-shop owners were not only hurt but also concerned for Rachel. They had become extremely fond of the young orphan girl, and had even discussed adopting her.

It was Alfie who replied to his wife's questions now. 'Perhaps she's met up with a young man and gone off with him somewhere.'

'Nonsense!' replied Grace. 'She's much too young for that. Besides, Sally would have known about it if she had, wouldn't you?'

Sally nodded silently. She felt extremely unhappy about keeping the secret of Rachel's pregnancy from the couple who had been so good to them both. However, there might be a simple explanation for Rachel's disappearance. If there was and Rachel returned to find Sally had told the couple about her condition, relations between the two girls would be very difficult.

On the other hand, if Rachel had tried to do away with herself . . .

'Do you have any idea why she might have wanted to go away,

Sally? She's had no messages from members of her family that she never told Alfie and me about?'

'Nothing I know of,' Sally replied miserably. 'While I'm delivering today, I'll ask around, just in case anyone's seen her. I've left a note for her at the Refuge – and Zulu Joe will let Captain Eva know that she's gone missing. Try not to worry, I'm sure she'll be found.'

'That's a whole lot easier to say than do, Sally. To tell you the truth, I'm worried sick. I really don't know how I'm going to get through the day. I'd report her missing to the police if I thought it would do any good . . .'

'We'll make the effort to carry on here as normal,' said her more practical husband. 'It will help no one if our business suffers. All our regulars know Rachel. We'll tell them she's gone missing. You never know, one of them might have seen her, or know where she is.'

'Well, you're going to have to manage without me for half an hour,' said Grace. 'I'm off to the railway station to ask if anyone there has seen her. Then I'll pop along to the Refuge just in case Captain Eva's learned anything.'

Grace's enquiries at both places drew a blank. When she returned, the pie shop was not a happy place to be. Sally was glad to escape and begin her deliveries. Nevertheless, she too was very concerned about the missing girl.

One of Sally's last deliveries that afternoon was to customs officers in a bonded warehouse close to the harbour.

The customs officer in charge insisted upon examining the half-dozen pies before he would pay for them. He pointed out that one had a broken crust. The damage was hardly worthy of note but the officer refused to pay for it. He suggested Sally might care to donate it free, as a sign of goodwill.

Sally retorted that she would take the pie away with her. She was not particularly perturbed that the customs officer had expressed dissatisfaction with her wares. It had happened before with customers and no doubt would again.

When she left the warehouse she decided to take the rejected pie to Pin's Lane for Charlie Shields; she knew Grace would not mind.

Charlie was depressed because of the absence of any news about the *Mermaid*, but he did his best to sound optimistic. 'The Lowestoft boat only brought in *pieces* of their boat. She could be badly damaged but still afloat. I've heard Henry say more than once that she was the best boat he ever sailed in – and he's sailed in a few.'

Taking the pie from her, he said, 'I'll just put this in a dish on the hob to keep hot while I set the table. It's a sight better than the chunk of cheese I was going to have with the bread left over from the weekend.'

As Charlie busied himself heating the pie, he continued talking. 'I'm pleased to see you looking so well too. I was a bit worried about you when I found the blood after you'd left. Where was it you cut yourself? I can't see no bandage.'

Sally looked at him as though he had taken leave of his senses. 'What are you talking about? I haven't cut myself. Even if I had, how could you possibly know?'

Now it was Charlie's turn to appear puzzled. 'I'm talking about last night, when you came to the house. After you'd gone I found heavy spots of blood in the passage. On the stairs too. I thought you must have cut yourself and come here to bind it up before having it properly seen to – and don't try to tell me it wasn't you who came into the house. I know different.'

'Are you saying you thought you saw me come to my room yesterday?'

'I didn't exactly *see* you, but I recognised your footsteps on the stairs – and I know I wasn't mistaken. Them floorboards was creaking under the weight of a young girl. If it wasn't you, who else would it have been, eh? Tell me that.'

Sally thought she probably knew the answer to Charlie's question, but she asked, 'What time was this – and are you quite certain that you heard whoever it was go out again?'

Less positive now, Charlie replied, 'I couldn't be certain, but it must have been about an hour or so before I went to bed – I'm going earlier these nights. A sign of growing old, I suppose, but it saves burning oil. As for the time you, or whoever else it was, left, it couldn't have been more than ten or fifteen minutes later. I was in the kitchen when the front door slammed shut—' Suddenly breaking off, Charlie looked thoughtful before adding, 'Come to think of it, the door might have blown shut when I opened the back door to the yard. It's done it before and there was quite a strong wind blowing.' He looked at Sally, still not entirely convinced. 'But if it wasn't you, then who could it have been?'

'I've got a very good idea.' Thinking about the blood Charlie had found on the stairs and in the passageway, Sally added, 'But I hope I'm wrong.'

She hurried up the stairs, leaving Charlie looking after her, uncertainly.

At the entrance to her room, Sally paused, suddenly reluctant to confirm what she suspected.

Bracing herself, she pushed open the door – and her worst fears were realised immediately.

Lying on the bed, eyes closed, was Rachel. The lower half of her dress and the bedclothes about her were stained with blood and Sally knew immediately what must have happened.

Rachel had found someone to abort her baby – and it would seem it had gone hideously wrong.

62

Soon after Sally had told Rachel she would be spending the night at the Shields' and had left the Refuge, Rachel left the house too, telling no one where she was going, or how long she would be out.

She headed for the Barbican but was careful not to pass within sight of the pie shop belonging to Alfie and Grace Philpott.

In the maze of narrow streets, Rachel headed for Pin's Lane in order to get a sense of direction. Skirting the lane itself, she turned into an alleyway that ran parallel with it.

She had been here earlier in the day, to make certain she would be able to identify the house for which she was now making – should the need arise. But when Sally told her she would not be spending the night at the Refuge, it seemed to Rachel an opportunity that was not to be wasted, and now was the time to act.

Arriving at the door of the house she had pin-pointed earlier, she hesitated, remembering the warnings Sally had given her about the course she was about to take.

Then Rachel's resolution hardened. She was determined not to have Sid Darling's baby, whatever the cost to her might be.

The door was opened in response to her knock by Clara Flood, landlady of Devonport Lil and one-time Indian mutiny 'nurse'.

'What do you want?' Clara Flood demanded surlily. 'If it's a room you're looking for, they're all taken – unless you can do what you want in less than an hour.'

'I'm not looking for a room. If you're Clara Flood, I came looking for *you*. I . . . I'm in trouble. I was told you'd be able to help me.'

'*You*, in trouble? Why, you're hardly old enough to know what trouble is.'

'I know, right enough, and I was told you could help me.'

'I'm always ready to help any poor soul that's in need, but there's a limit to what a body can do. Especially a poor widow-woman with no one to support her.'

'I can pay for any help you give me.'

'Pay? How much?'

'I've got five pounds here,' Rachel said eagerly. She had saved most of the money given to her by Grace and Alfie over Christmas. This, together with the generous wage paid to her for helping around the shop, plus two pounds she had 'borrowed' from the money drawer behind the counter amounted to more than five pounds. But she was wise enough not to disclose to Clara Flood the full amount she possessed.

'Five pounds? Are you asking me to risk spending the rest of my life in gaol for a mere five pounds? I'm sorry, dearie, but you'll have to find someone else to do it for you.'

As Rachel turned away, disconsolately, Clara Flood added hurriedly, 'Mind you, if you was to offer me *ten* pounds, I might just do it as a special favour, seeing as how you're so young.'

'I haven't got ten pounds. I could give you six.'

'Make it eight and you can go off and start life afresh,' said Clara Flood. 'No one will ever know you did anything wrong.'

Rachel took out a tapestry purse that had been a present from Sally at Christmas. Carefully counting the coins, she said plaintively, 'All I have is six pounds, four and sevenpence.'

'If that's all you have, then I wouldn't see a young girl's life ruined for the sake of a few shillings. Give me the money and come on in.'

'Now?' Rachel was taken by surprise.

'You were expecting to make an appointment?' Clara Flood

asked sarcastically. 'No, you come on in, dearie. The sooner it's done the better. How many months gone are you . . . ?'

As she followed the woman to a back upstairs room a man came down the stairs past them – and Rachel's heart missed a beat. It was Robert Sanderson. Sally's father!

She put her head down and hurried past him, hoping he had not recognised her on the dark staircase.

Had she looked back, she would have seen him standing at the foot of the stairs, looking up at her, his expression a mixture of dismay and disbelief. But Clara Flood was already ushering her into a small room, in which the only piece of furniture was a narrow bed. In place of bedclothes, the bed was covered with a red, india-rubber sheet.

'Take your underclothes off, dearie, then get up on the bed and pull all your clothes up above your waist.'

When Rachel hesitated, Clara Flood snapped irritably, 'Come on, it's too late to be shy now. The time for that was when you let your young man get you in this condition.'

'I didn't *let* anyone do anything to me,' Rachel retorted bitterly. 'I just couldn't do anything to stop them.'

Clara Flood rounded on her immediately. 'You were raped? Are the police involved in this? I'm not doing anything to help you if the police have got anything to do with you.'

'No one knows about it – and they won't,' Rachel lied. 'Anyway, the man who did it isn't around now.'

'Well, as long as you're quite certain. I've got too much to lose if anyone learns I go around doing favours for girls like you. If no one knows then it's all right – and we'll keep it that way. It'll be better for you and it's better for me. Now, are you ready?'

Lying back on the bed, Rachel pulled her clothes up about her waist, trying not to be embarrassed. The rubber sheet was cold on her bottom and she made an involuntary movement.

'Now, whatever I do, you must keep absolutely still, do you understand? This is an operation. A delicate operation.'

'Will it hurt?' Rachel asked fearfully, staring at the other woman, who was now holding a long knitting needle in her hand.

'Not half as much as having a baby would. Now just you look

away. Better still, close your eyes. But, whatever I do, try not to move. Just leave me to get on with it.'

Rachel tried to do as the abortionist told her, but she did not find it easy. First of all she could feel the woman's broken nails digging into her flesh. It hurt, and she whimpered. Then, without warning, Rachel felt something sliding inside her and she realised with horror that it must be the knitting needle.

Suddenly, the woman pressed hard and Rachel felt a horrific pain, which seemed to fill her stomach and her groin before travelling down to her thighs.

Despite the instructions she had been given, Rachel cried out and writhed in agony.

'That's enough! Please stop – it hurts!'

'Damn you, girl! Keep still. I'm not finished yet. Keep still, do you hear?'

There was another wave of excruciating pain – then Clara Flood had finished. She stood holding the bloody knitting needle and Rachel saw perspiration running down the side of her face, from her temples.

'That's it. Now, off with you. Go back to wherever it is you live and lie down. You'll feel awful for a day or two, but then it will all be over. Come on, up you get and go.'

Rachel still felt pain, but it was not as bad now. She told herself that if it didn't get any worse and she really had lost the baby, she would be able to cope with it.

She had left the house and was walking along the alleyway towards Pin's Lane when the pain came flooding back. She realised too that she was bleeding quite severely.

The pain was like a severe cramp that became steadily worse until she found walking almost impossible. If it did not let up she realised there would be no way she would make it back to the Refuge – or even to the home of Grace and Alfie.

Holding her lower stomach, she was doubled up in agony, when she left the alleyway and found herself in Pin's Lane.

Further along the lane she could see the open door of Sally's house and she headed for it in a crouching run. Passing through the doorway she made her way along the passageway. As she climbed the stairs, it seemed to her she was tackling a mountain and she found herself praying that Sally's room would be unlocked.

It was. Moments later, moaning in agony, she was in the room. Not even bothering to kick off her shoes, she climbed on the bed and must have passed into unconsciousness within minutes.

She regained consciousness more than once during the next twenty-four hours, although by now time meant nothing to her. The pain had grown until it felt as though it was consuming the whole of the inside of her stomach.

She was delirious too, on occasions, seeing strange creatures lurking in the corners of the room. Once she felt quite certain her mother was beside her, holding her hand.

But nothing was quite real until she opened her eyes and saw Sally standing beside the bed looking down at her, an expression of horror on her face.

63

Sally's first thought was that Rachel was dead – and there was no doubt in her mind what had killed her.

When Rachel opened her eyes, Sally felt overwhelming relief. Taking the younger girl's hand, she said, 'Rachel! What have you been up to? Why didn't you come and find someone to help you?'

'I'm sorry, Sally. It . . . came on so sudden. I've made a mess of your bed . . .'

'That doesn't matter. What *does* is that I find someone to help you, as quickly as I can.'

'Don't tell Grace!' Rachel pleaded.

'This can't be kept a secret now, Rachel. I'm going to have to call on Grace to get you to a hospital. I don't know what you've done to yourself, but you need a doctor to see to you.'

Rachel closed her eyes and her face screwed up in agony. Sally was not certain whether it was physical pain or the knowledge that her condition could no longer remain a secret.

'I'll be as quick as I can. In the meantime I'll ask Charlie to listen out for you. He can't climb the stairs, but if he hears you call out he'll go and fetch one of the neighbours.'

'Sally . . . fetch me a drink of water before you go. My mouth feels so dry.'

'I'll go and get some from Charlie's kitchen.'

Downstairs, as she took water from a bucket in the kitchen, Sally gave the bewildered man brief details of what was happening.

He agreed to listen for any sound from upstairs, but asked, 'How did she get herself in such a state?'

'I don't know and she's too sick to ask right now – but it's one more thing Sid Darling will have to answer for one day.'

It became apparent to Sally when she raised Rachel in the bed in order to drink that the young girl was in great pain. She was deeply concerned.

After making her as comfortable as she could, she hurried off to tell Grace.

The two pie-shop owners listened in growing dismay and disbelief as Sally told them how she had found Rachel and of the condition she was in.

'You mean . . . she's been carrying a baby all this time and never told me about it?'

'She never told me until a couple of days ago and made me swear not to tell anyone else.'

'It's not the sort of secret you should have kept to yourself,' Grace said with stern disapproval. 'She's far too young to have this hanging over her. Do you have any idea how she brought this miscarriage about?'

Sally shook her head. 'I think it might be more serious than a miscarriage.'

'You mean . . . you think she might have had an *abortion*?' Grace looked at Sally in disbelief. 'She wouldn't have known how to go about such a thing . . .' Looking at Sally suspiciously, she added, 'Would she?'

'I certainly never told her,' said Sally.

She had forgotten pointing out the house where Clara Flood lived and warning Rachel that if she was not careful she might end up in the hands of someone like the elderly abortionist.

'Right now she needs to get to a hospital urgently. She's lost a lot of blood and seems to be very weak.'

'Go and stay with her, Grace,' said Alfie. 'I'll fetch a doctor and a carriage to take her to the hospital. Meanwhile, you stay here and look after the shop, Sally. I won't be long.'

Left in the shop on her own, Sally did not have very many customers to serve. She had time to think of the new disaster the day had brought but hoped Rachel's condition would prove to be less serious than it appeared.

Somehow, after Rachel had been taken to hospital, Alfie and Sally got through the remainder of the day until it was time to shut up the shop. Grace had still not returned and Alfie said he would go to the hospital to learn what was happening.

Sally felt she could not face Grace again immediately. She told Alfie she would go to the Refuge and tell Captain Eva what had happened. Then she intended going to see how Ethan's mother was.

She would visit the hospital later that night to enquire after Rachel. She secretly hoped Grace might have gone home by then. Sally did not want to have to submit to more awkward questioning.

Nevertheless, she felt very guilty about not telling Grace about Rachel's pregnancy. It would also have passed responsibility to someone who might have been able to deal with the problem differently.

64

When Sally arrived at the Salvation Army Refuge, she found Eva drinking tea in the kitchen. Inspector Ian Lovat was with her.

One look at Sally's face was sufficient to bring Eva to her feet. 'What's the matter, Sally – is it something to do with Rachel?'

Zulu Joe had told her of Sally's visit and of the search being carried out for the young girl.

The guilt Sally had been feeling since finding Rachel suddenly overwhelmed her. She could only nod, numbly, wishing she had found Captain Eva alone.

'Here, come and sit down. I'll pour you a cup of sweet tea while you talk to Captain Eva.' Ian Lovat rose from his chair and pushed it towards Sally.

Sally sat on the chair with Eva's arm about her shoulders, as the policeman crossed the room to where the teapot sat on the gas stove.

'Can you tell me about it, Sally,' the Salvationist coaxed her.

After taking a few moments to compose herself, Sally said, 'Rachel was expecting a baby. I think she's done something silly to get rid of it.'

'A baby? Surely not? Why, she's hardly old enough.' Eva's reaction echoed that of Grace Philpott.

'Rachel is quite sure she is . . . or *was*. I don't think she is any more.'

'Who is the father . . . ?' Even as Eva put the question, the answer came to her. She spoke his name out loud, 'Sid Darling!'

Sally nodded once more. 'Rachel thinks so. Him, or one of the Belgian fishermen. Whichever one it was, she's determined not to have the baby.'

'You must have known about this before today, Sally. When did she tell you?'

'A couple of days ago. She made me promise not to tell anyone.'

'That's one promise you shouldn't have kept. But it's too late for recriminations now. What has poor Rachel done – taken something?'

'It's worse than that. I believe she's found someone to do something to her. Either that, or she's done something to herself. I found her lying on the bed in my room at Pin's Lane. She'd been there since yesterday. There was blood everywhere.'

'Dear God!' exclaimed Eva. 'What an utterly stupid thing to do. Where is she now?'

'I ran to tell Grace. She and Alfie have got her to hospital. Grace has been there with her ever since. Alfie went there as soon as we closed the shop.' Scarcely able to hold her emotions in check, she added, 'I think she's very, very ill.'

'I'll go to the hospital right away. First I must tell Zulu Joe and the girls what I'm doing.'

Half-way to the door, Eva stopped and turned to ask Sally, 'Do you think any of the girls here had anything to do with the condition Rachel's in?'

'I don't know. I don't think so.'

'Good. All the same, I'll have a word with them later tonight.'

When Eva had left the kitchen, Sally sipped the tea Ian Lovat had placed on the table beside her, her hand shaking. Now the detective said, 'You do realise that abortion is a serious criminal offence, Sally?'

'So is what Sid Darling did to Rachel, but you haven't caught him yet, have you?'

'No,' he admitted. 'But I can assure you it's not for the want of trying and we'll continue to search for him until we find him.

Right now we're talking about Rachel's abortion – if that's what it turns out to be. The law regards it as a very serious offence. If you know more than you've said, you had better tell someone everything you know. It would be far better for you if that someone were me. Do you have any idea who else might be involved?'

'No.' Remembering the two nights she had spent with Rachel trying to induce a miscarriage, Sally hoped she sounded more convincing than she felt. She added, 'I didn't think she'd do anything as stupid as this. I told her the best thing she could do was to have the baby, then see about having it adopted if she still didn't want it.'

Ian Lovat nodded his approval. 'I'll need to speak to you again sometime. Unfortunately, now I know about it I am going to have to make an official report. How ill do you think she is?'

'Very ill. I've never seen so much blood anywhere as there was on the bed.'

'I sincerely hope she's not as serious as it sounds, Sally. The trouble is that people who do this sort of thing usually end up killing someone. It's an operation that even a skilful surgeon is reluctant to perform.'

Sally was still trembling as a result of his words when Eva returned to the kitchen to say she was leaving for the hospital.

Ian Lovat said he would go with her. Before they left the house, Captain Eva asked Sally if she would like to accompany them.

'I don't think it would be wise to see Grace again just yet. She's angry with me for not telling her that Rachel was expecting a baby. She said I should have told her, but I couldn't say anything to her – or to you. Not after promising Rachel I wouldn't.'

'Don't worry, Sally. Grace is a very understanding woman. When she's had time to think about things she'll realise what a difficult situation you were in. She'll be very worried about Rachel right now, as we all are. I'll speak to her if the opportunity arises.'

In truth, there was another reason Sally did not want to

accompany Captain Eva to the hospital. She needed to think about what Ian Lovat had said. She wondered whether she could get into trouble for what she had done in the earlier attempts to bring about a miscarriage for Rachel.

65

When Harry Maggs stopped outside the house of Clara Flood, force of habit caused him to look furtively around before knocking at the door.

It was opened by Clara Flood and Maggs was taken by surprise – he had not been expecting a woman.

Looking him up and down with increasing distaste, Clara Flood said, 'I don't need a chimney sweep. When I do I'll send for someone I know, not a sweep who's going to bring more soot into the house on his clothes than he takes from my chimney.'

Maggs was not a prepossessing man. Small and slightly built, his shoulders hunched forward unhealthily and every line of his gnarled face was heavily ingrained with soot. From the age of six he had spent his life cleaning chimneys and had deeply held convictions that bathing and sweeping chimneys were mutually exclusive.

'I'm not here to sweep chimneys. I came to see if Mr Sanderson was home?'

'And what would he be wanting with the likes of you?'

Harry Maggs decided that Clara Flood had dominated the conversation for long enough. 'Is Mr Sanderson here? It's him I want to be talking to, not you.'

'Is it now? Well, you just wait there and I'll see if he wants to speak to *you*.'

The door was slammed shut in Maggs' face and he was left standing uneasily in the narrow street.

Inside the house, Clara Flood wheezed her way up the stairs and banged on the door of her lodger. When it was opened by Robert Sanderson, she said, 'There's some chimney sweep outside. He says he wants to talk to you.'

'Maggs? What's he doing here?'

'You'll need to ask *him* that, not me, but if you have him inside the house make sure he does all his talking standing up. I'm not having a man wearing such clothes sitting on my furniture.

When Sanderson opened the door to Harry Maggs, he repeated the question he had asked Clara Flood, 'What are you doing here? How did you know where to find me?' Before Maggs could answer, the ex-Lanhydrock butler said, 'We can't talk out here. Come in.'

He led the way to his room, the two men standing to one side on the narrow stairway to allow Clara Flood to pass on her disapproving way back to her room on the ground floor.

When they were inside Sanderson's sparsely furnished room and the door firmly closed, Maggs said, 'I hadn't seen or heard anything of you for a few days. I went to the house in Pin's Lane where you'd been staying and a bloke by the name of Charlie said you'd gone. He said I should try here. That you used to spend as much time here with Devonport Lil as over in Pin's Lane when you were living there. I thought I'd better come and see if you were here, to find out what's going on.'

Robert Sanderson looked with distaste at the man standing before him. Had he not needed him for the plans he had made, he would have scorned even to speak to him.

'You're a fool! If anyone sees us together we'll never be able to do as we've planned.'

'You've nothing to worry about,' Maggs said sulkily. 'There's nobody in Plymouth who knows who you are, or where you once worked.'

'That's where you're wrong,' retorted Sanderson. 'There's this Charlie – and there was a girl in this very house only yesterday who knew me. Now, if you've nothing else to say, I suggest you go.'

'You still haven't told me when we're going to do the job,' protested Maggs. 'I'm losing business waiting for you to make up your mind.'

'When we do what we've planned, you'll never need to worry yourself about going to work again. I can't tell you when it's going to be until I get a reply to the letter I've sent to the housemaid at Lanhydrock House. It should be any day now. When it arrives, I'll come and find you at The Jolly Watchman, so just be patient for a while longer. Now, it's time you went, before Clara Flood comes up here to make sure you're not sitting down on any of her furniture.'

When he had let Harry Maggs out of the house, Robert Sanderson turned around to find his landlady standing in the passageway.

'Who's that man you've just let out?'

'No one in particular. I met him in a public house a while ago and took pity on him. It was a mistake. He called today trying to borrow money from me.'

'You can tell him I don't want to see him here again. He lowers the tone of the house. If you've got many friends like him I'll be asking you to leave, too.'

'He won't be coming here again, I promise you that. Talking of visitors, who was that charming young girl who was with you when we passed on the stairs yesterday? I suppose she's not a friend of Devonport Lil? If she is I'd like to be introduced to her.'

Clara Flood rounded on him so suddenly he took a pace backwards in surprise. 'You saw no girl here yesterday – you understand? Any more than I saw the man who was just visiting you. People in this house either mind their own business – or they go.'

'Of course. I understand. We neither of us saw anyone at all.'

Despite his assurance to Clara Flood, Robert Sanderson questioned Devonport Lil that evening about the girl he had seen with the landlady.

They were sharing a bottle of gin in the prostitute's room.

Lil was having a lean time at the moment; a great many Plymouth-based naval vessels had been sent to South Africa because of troubles being experienced there with both the Zulu nation and the Boers.

Lil reiterated what Clara Flood had told him. 'Forget you've ever seen the girl. That way you can plead you know nothing of what goes on in this house. It'll be better for you in the long run.'

'But why? She was just a young girl. What harm could she possibly be up to?'

She looked at him pityingly. 'Where have you been all your life? Don't you know why the girl was here? Clara's been carrying out abortions for years. She's not the best, by any means, but she's certainly well known by the girls who work Union Street.'

'You mean . . . that girl was here to have an abortion? But she was so young!'

'So what? If you're going on the game you've got to make a start while you're young enough to make good money. Some of us started earlier than others. Now, have you come here to do business with me, or just to drink all my gin . . . ?'

66

The subject of the conversation between Robert Sanderson and Devonport Lil died the following day. The cause of her death was septicaemia. According to the doctor who had been treating her since her admission to the hospital, it had been caused by the instrument used to bring about the abortion; it had been neither clean nor accurately wielded.

Sally learned of Rachel's death that evening from Eva. Afterwards, she spent many hours in her room, weeping for the death of the young girl who had known such unhappiness and brutality in her short lifetime.

The manner of Rachel's death meant that the Plymouth police now became actively involved. But Ian Lovat was not the investigating officer. Instead, a rather dour police inspector came to the Refuge to interview the girls living there.

Although Sally had been Rachel's close friend and had been the one to find her at Pin's Lane, she was interrogated at no greater length or in any more detail than the others.

Once the policeman had established a possible reason for Rachel taking refuge in Sally's room in the first place, he seemed to lose all interest in anything Sally might have been able to tell him.

His manner and apparent lack of enthusiasm angered Sally, who was already distressed by the death of her friend.

After the inspector had left the Refuge, Sally asked Eva why Ian Lovat had not been put in charge of the investigation.

'He isn't able to make a decision on what cases he will or will not take on,' she replied. 'Anyway, he's away for a few days. Before he left he hinted he might be leaving Plymouth altogether in the near future.'

'Why?' Sally voiced her dismay. 'He's not been in Plymouth for very long.'

Eva shrugged. 'No doubt he has his reasons. We may be friends, but he doesn't tell me everything.'

She sounded unhappy and Sally suddenly felt very sorry for her. It had been apparent to the occupants of the Refuge for some time now that Captain Eva was growing very fond of Ian Lovat. It was generally assumed that he felt the same way about her, and the girls had been waiting with some interest to see whether a romance would develop between the couple.

Later that evening, Sally attended a highly emotional prayer meeting in the Refuge to pray for the dead girl. Eva took the meeting, which was attended by all the other women and girls who lived in the house, and who had known Rachel.

An additional problem in Sally's life, one she found particularly upsetting, was the unforgiving and unbending attitude Grace now adopted towards her.

Grace had spent many hours in the hospital with Rachel and was with her when she died. Not unnaturally, she was deeply affected by all that had happened.

The morning after Rachel's death, although still distraught, Sally decided she should go into work. To her dismay, when she arrived at the shop Alfie told her it might be better if she did not show herself there for a while.

When Sally wanted to know why, he told her that Grace was particularly bitter that Sally had not told her of the young girl's condition. Had she done so, Grace was convinced they might have been able to prevent her tragic death.

'But Rachel made me promise,' said Sally, reduced to tears by Alfie's words. 'She felt so ashamed because she was expecting. Grace was the last person she wanted to know about it.'

'I realise that,' Alfie said sympathetically. 'Grace will too, in time. But if she sees you now she'll probably say things that won't be easily mended, even though she might regret them later. Stay away for a few days, Sally. I'll get word to you when I feel the time is right for you to come back to work again.'

Going to the cash drawer in the shop, he took out a couple of pounds and handed them to her. 'All that's happened is not your fault, I realise that. Take this to tide you over until you're back working with us once more.'

Sally was grateful for the money, but she left the pie shop with a very heavy heart, uncertain of what the future held for her now. She had become fond of Grace. Both she and Alfie had been very kind to her.

She realised she would probably never return to their employ again. Grace had really loved Rachel and would be reminded of what had happened every time she saw Sally. Working together would simply not be possible.

It seemed to Sally that her whole world was collapsing about her. She felt lower than at any time since Ruth's death.

She spent the remainder of that day sharing Sophie Shields' problems. Doris Shields had seemingly lost touch with reality, and was making life very difficult for her daughter-in-law.

Each and every day, she spoke as though she was expecting her husband and sons to walk through the door at any moment. Sally did not know how Sophie managed to cope with her. She was glad when it was evening and she could find an excuse to return to the Refuge to speak to Captain Eva.

Eva was sympathetic to Sally about her problems, but she said, 'I wish I could feel that Rachel was likely to be the last victim of the evil men who raped her, but the trade in girls is still going on. Look . . .' From her desk, she took a piece of paper torn from a newspaper and handed it to Sally.

It was a repeat of the advertisement she had been sent by her colleague, seeking girls for domestic service. It now suggested that suitable applicants might soon find themselves working for titled families. They were promised lucrative posts with some of the most important families in the land, together with the opportunity to travel with them on their European journeys.

It concluded with the suggestion that the posts advertised were ideally suited for young girls contemplating a full-time career in domestic service. Preference would be given to girls with no home ties, who could devote themselves to their career and be free to travel wherever their employers wished to take them.

'This sounds too good to be true,' commented Sally. 'It's just the kind of thing that brought Rachel to Plymouth. Where does it come from?'

'This one is from a Dorset newspaper,' replied Eva. 'One of my friends sent it to me, but I've seen others, right here in Devon.'

'Do you think Sid Darling is involved this time?'

Eva shook her head. 'I don't think so. Inspector Lovat says Darling is out of the country, and I believe him – but I do think this is a very suspect advertisement. The address to write to is in Falmouth. It's hardly a central base from which to place servants all over the country. My friend sent it to me because, if it *is* genuine, she has a girl she would like to send there.'

The Salvationist threw the cutting down upon her desk in a gesture of frustration. 'I *know* it isn't genuine. The trouble is proving it. Dear God! I would dearly love to be able to put a stop to this trade once and for all. I tell you, Sally, if I was younger I'd reply to the advertisement myself and show these people up for what they are.'

As Eva shook her head angrily, Sally was thinking hard. Now she said, 'Why not let me do it instead?'

'*You*? No, Sally, I couldn't ask you to do anything like this.'

'You're not asking, I'm suggesting it to you.'

'But . . . why? You of all people should realise just how dangerous it would be to get yourself involved in something like this.'

'I don't know. I feel I owe it to Rachel, somehow. Besides, I can't think of anyone better, can you? I know all the dangers involved and I'd be going into it with my eyes open. The only thing is . . . what would you be able to do to make certain I *wouldn't* end up in Belgium, or somewhere like that?'

'I could organise all that, Sally – and I'd let you know exactly what we are doing, every step of the way. If you're really serious about this I'll contact the editor of a London paper with whom I have already been in correspondence. That would ensure maximum publicity. With the Salvation Army behind you, we would ensure, first and foremost, that you would never be in danger. That would be my prime consideration, I assure you.'

Eva was quivering with excitement at the thought of what they might achieve. Yet she wanted to be quite certain that Sally knew what she was letting herself in for.

'Would you really do this, Sally? I don't want to bring any sort of pressure on you, but putting a stop to this has been my life's ambition. Ever since this despicable trade was first brought to my notice. Are you absolutely certain?'

In truth, although she had volunteered herself, Sally had very real doubts about the venture, but she nodded. 'Yes, I'll do it.'

67

A few days later Eva took a train to London to seek the backing of the authorities at Salvation Army headquarters for her scheme to expose those who were luring girls into prostitution. Meanwhile, Ian Lovat returned to Plymouth.

Within hours, he paid a visit to the Refuge.

He was disappointed when Sally informed him that the Salvation Army officer was not there, but he accepted her offer of a cup of tea.

When they were both seated in the kitchen, Sally asked, 'Have you come to speak to Captain Eva about Rachel?'

'No, another officer is still dealing with that,' replied Ian Lovat. 'I can't interfere with his investigation right now, although I might well take over from him in the very near future. It's a very sad business. I hope this abortionist is soon caught and put away. I doubt very much whether Rachel was her first victim.'

'Poor Rachel didn't deserve to have something like that happen to her.'

Aware of her distress, Ian Lovat changed the subject. 'Do you know why Captain Eva has gone to London? I hope the Salvation Army is not considering moving her on.'

'You'll need to ask her about that, when she comes back.'

Ian Lovat smiled wryly. 'If it's something she feels I ought not to know, I doubt if she'll tell me.'

'Then you can't expect me to tell you anything that she wouldn't,' declared Sally.

'Oh! So there *is* something going on that I would like to know about?'

'I didn't say that,' retorted Sally. 'Besides, do you always tell her what *you're* doing? Where you've been for the last couple of days, for instance?'

'No,' confessed the policeman. 'But I will, in due course.'

'Good! I think Captain Eva was quite hurt that you went away without saying where you were going.'

'Did she tell you that?' There was eagerness in Ian Lovat's voice as he asked the question.

'She didn't have to.' Encouraged by his interest in Captain Eva's reaction to his absence, Sally asked, 'Are you in love with her?'

The detective inspector remained silent for so long that Sally thought she might have overstepped the bounds of familiarity with him. Then he said, quietly, 'Yes, Sally, I am.'

'Do you intend asking her to marry you?'

'You're asking some very personal questions, young lady. The answer is . . . I don't know. We are each of us very committed to the work we do. We're both doing something that's important, to us and to others, but it sometimes clashes. That poses a major problem. If I'm not prepared to give up my work, I could hardly ask Captain Eva to give up hers.'

Disappointed that there seemed to be no hope of the two getting married in the near future, Sally asked, 'Couldn't you tell her what you've just told me and see what she has to say about it?'

Putting his cup down on the table, Ian Lovat shook his head as he stood up to take his leave.

'No, Sally. If I were to mention marriage to her and she turned me down, nothing would ever be quite the same between us. I enjoy her company too much to want to risk losing it. We'll leave things as they are. For the time being, at least.'

'But . . . you could go on like that until you are both old!'

He smiled. 'That's very true, but I'd rather do that than risk losing her altogether. Now, if there's nothing else you feel I ought to know, I'll leave and come visiting again when Captain Eva has returned from London.'

When he had gone, Sally wondered how anyone in love could look at their relationship in such a calculated and matter-of-fact manner.

She knew that if there was any hope of Ethan returning to her, there would be no sacrifice too great to make in order to ensure nothing ever came between them again.

Thoughts of Ethan made her deeply despondent. It seemed that since he had gone missing, nothing in her life had gone right. She had lost her work; the girl who was possibly her closest friend; her father – and, of course, Ethan himself.

Now she was about to embark on a venture that was both dangerous and fraught with difficulty. She consoled herself with the thought that if it was successful, it could prove to be a turning-point in her life – and it *had* to be successful.

It was a chance to achieve something positive, something that would help bring to an end the kidnapping of young girls for the brothels of Europe, saving thousands of girls from a life of brutality and degradation.

If she never did anything worthwhile in her life again, Sally felt she could always look back upon this one thing with great pride.

She hoped Captain Eva would receive the support she was seeking in London. Sally wanted things to begin moving as quickly as possible.

Until she took up her role in Captain Eva's crusade, her life would be in limbo. She could not seek work, neither could she discuss with anyone else what was being planned.

Sally decided she would spend the day at the Shields' house. There might be something she could do to help the hard-pressed Sophie to cope with the problem of her disturbed mother-in-law.

68

Robert Sanderson and Harry Maggs each journeyed in his own fashion from Plymouth to their common destination in Cornwall.

The ex-Lanhydrock House butler travelled in comparative comfort, by coach, taking a somewhat circuitous route. He had decided against using the train; he was well known at Bodmin Road railway station and did not wish to draw attention to himself and his changed circumstances.

Harry Maggs enjoyed none of the comforts enjoyed by Sanderson. He crossed the River Tamar on the ferry to Saltash and walked through the narrow lanes of Cornwall. He pushed before him a wheelbarrow on which were a quantity of sacks, a large flagon containing paraffin and the brushes that constituted the tools of his trade.

Heading for Lanhydrock House, he had been fully briefed by the ex-butler. If he carried out his crucial part of the plan, their foray into Cornwall would make them both rich and satisfy Sanderson's determination to make the owners of the great house suffer for his humiliation.

It was a simple but clever plan.

The itinerant chimney sweep who visited Lanhydrock House annually to carry out his work always arrived during the first week in May. It was now very early April.

Maggs would say he had been sent by the regular sweep,

who had been forced into retirement by ill-health. Sanderson had given him sufficient details of the other sweep to ensure his story would sound genuine.

The timing of the plan was crucial and Maggs would state that the two days of this week was the only period available for him to carry out the work involved.

Fortunately, due to the passage of years no one in the household would possibly be able to identify Maggs as the boy who was apprenticed to the sweep transported for stealing from the house: he had changed a great deal since then.

Another factor in Maggs' favour was the appointment of a new butler only the week before. When Maggs put in his appearance at the servants' door, the butler referred the question of chimney sweeping to the Robartes' steward. That important official considered it to be so far beneath him to discuss such a matter that Harry Maggs was told to get on with whatever needed to be done.

This he proceeded to do, informing the steward that the previous sweep had described the layout of the chimneys in such detail that Maggs felt he was, 'as familiar with them as I am with the back of me own 'and'.

Repeating the conversation to the new butler, the steward remarked that he doubted if the ingrained soot to be found on Maggs had allowed him to view the back of it for more years than he was able to count.

Once in the house, Maggs set about carrying out the plan formulated by Robert Sanderson. Going from room to room, ostensibly checking out the various fireplaces, he pinpointed all the items the ex-butler had declared to be worth stealing.

Maggs then began work on the chimneys. He made an excellent job of them, and had cleaned more than half by the end of the first day.

As a result of this day's work he was not watched quite so closely when he returned the following morning. The kitchen fire was dowsed after lunch, enabling him to climb up inside the huge chimney.

It was here the chimney sweep would set in motion the plan that was designed to destroy all evidence of the proposed burglary. At the very least, it would ensure that the loss of items would not be discovered for some time to come.

His instructions were to leave in place the majority of the soot in the kitchen chimney. Before claiming to have completed his work, he would place four paraffin-soaked sacks on a chimney ledge, at the rear of which was an exposed wooden beam that had been thoroughly dried out by more than two hundred years of proximity to the heat drawn up the chimney from the kitchen fire. The fire that was bound to ensue would cause great confusion among family and staff. No one would go around checking whether valuable items remained in their proper places – or whether they were there at all.

The robbery was planned for that night, after Maggs had completed his second day's sweeping. Entry to the house would be made by means of the key retained by Sanderson.

At the time of the robbery, the ex-butler would be 'entertaining' the enamoured housemaid in one of the outbuildings beside the house. The maid would have drawn the bolts on the inside of the servants' door in order to slip out, and, having locked the door behind her with a key kept in a cupboard in the servants' hall, in case of fire, she would feel the house was adequately secured.

During her absence, Maggs would slip inside the house, fill two sacks with silver and other valuables, and lower them out of the window of the dairy scullery. They would then be collected by himself and the ex-butler when the latter had parted company with the housemaid.

The whole operation was planned to last no longer than two hours, commencing at midnight.

Afterwards, the two men would load the stolen goods into the sweep's barrow and make their escape under cover of darkness.

Robert Sanderson's plan relied very heavily on the chimney-sweep carrying out his instructions to the letter.

However, as the ex-butler was fully aware, his accomplice was not the most reliable man to successfully carry off such a daring burglary.

69

Robert Sanderson's carefully thought-out plan began to go wrong long before the housemaid quietly drew back the bolts to the servants' door, opened it with the key from the hall cupboard and slipped into the night to meet her discredited lover.

When Harry Maggs completed his second day's work at Lanhydrock House, he did what he had been doing for very many years at the end of his working day with money in his pocket.

He went in search of a drink.

Sanderson had told him to keep clear of the well-policed town of Bodmin and Maggs kept to this part of the plan at least. After making enquiries of the servants, Maggs made his way to the hamlet of Sweetshouse, about a mile from Lanhydrock. The landlord of the small country public house earned only a meagre living from a small number of regular local drinkers, and so the thirsty chimney sweep was given a warm welcome.

Maggs had promised Sanderson he would enter Lanhydrock House soon after midnight, but at that time he was still in the Sweetshouse public house. It was more than an hour later before he turned the key in the lock of the servants' door and, somewhat unsteadily, entered the house.

He carried with him a small bull's-eye lantern, lit by a piece of candle. It was a lamp that he found useful when he was working inside some of the darker chimneys.

Leaving the servants' hall behind he carried the lantern beneath his coat, using it only occasionally. His drunken clumsiness would have left Sanderson aghast, but it seemed the household was not alert tonight.

All the finest household silver was kept locked in a safe in the butler's ground-floor pantry, with the bed of a young male servant beside it. Fortunately for Maggs, the young man was a very heavy sleeper and would hear nothing beyond the walls of his cell-like 'bedroom'.

The chimney sweep made his way from room to room, taking the pieces listed by Robert Sanderson. He also added a considerable number of additional items of lesser value, which had earlier taken his fancy.

He was still filling the first sack when the housemaid returned from her nocturnal liaison. By this time he was well behind schedule.

The plan had been that he should be well clear of the house by the time she returned and bolted the door once again.

Harry Maggs shrugged off the certain knowledge that Sanderson was going to be very angry with him. The ex-butler might be very clever at making plans and telling others how they should do things, but he was not the one who had to carry them out.

That had been left to Maggs. Now he would do it *his* way.

When the second sack had been filled, it was heavier than the first, but it followed its fellow out of the dairy scullery window.

With the window open, Maggs listened, expecting to hear some sound from Sanderson. All was silent.

He was not to know that the angry ex-butler was at that very moment carrying the first laden sack to the chimney-sweep's barrow, hidden in the woods behind the house.

The burglary should have been completed by now and the two men heading away from the house with two sacks bulging with stolen valuables. However, Maggs had still not collected all the items listed by his accomplice – or all the additional items he planned to steal.

He would not leave until he had filled a third sack – but his greed proved his undoing.

Finally collecting all the items he intended taking, he put them through the window, as before. Then he made his way to the side door, drew the bolts and felt in his pocket for Sanderson's key.

It was not there.

Searching feverishly through all his pockets, he found many holes, but no key.

Had Maggs only known, he was standing within an arm's length of his means of escape – the same key used by the housemaid. But he did not know.

Nevertheless, he considered that losing the key was more a nuisance than a disaster. He would return to the dairy scullery and exit the house by squeezing through the narrow window.

No sooner had he reached this decision than he was alarmed by the sound of voices at the top of the stairs that led to the women servants' quarters.

Hurrying along the passageway, he passed by the foot of the stairs before the women reached the ground floor. Farther along the passageway, he had almost reached the men's staircase when he heard someone coming down these too, and a light was casting a flickering shadow on the wall.

Caught between the two groups of servants, Maggs panicked. Opening the nearest door, he found himself in the kitchen. He realised the danger this posed only when the two groups met and began talking outside the door.

The handle turned but the door opened no more than a couple of inches before it stopped. The woman opening it paused to make a crude remark to one of the men approaching from the other staircase.

There was only one escape route left open now – and Maggs took it. His feet had just disappeared out of sight up the chimney when the first of the servants entered the kitchen, holding a candle aloft.

'What's this then?' Maggs heard one of the men say, 'Has no one brought in any kindling? It should have been done last thing by the scullery maid. She knew we were having to start cooking early today in readiness for the party.'

'No need to fret yourself about having no kindling,' a woman's voice replied. 'The chimney's only just been swept. Put the wood and coal in. We'll pour some paraffin over it. We'll have it going in no time at all.'

'You'd better not let Cook catch you using paraffin on a kitchen fire,' said another woman. 'She says you can taste it in the food.'

'Well Cook's not here, is she?' said the man who had spoken before. 'Come on, get the fire going and put the kettle on for a cup of tea. Then we can open all the windows. There won't be the faintest whiff of paraffin time Cook comes down.'

Harry Maggs climbed the chimney much faster than he would have moved had he been working. A paraffin-fed fire would send flames far up the chimney. He wanted to be well clear before that happened.

'What's that noise?' One of the women, helping to light the fire, had heard Maggs making his escape.

'Probably a jackdaw,' replied one of the men. 'There's been a pair of them around just lately. Get that fire going and they'll be away fast enough.'

Maggs reached a junction where another chimney joined that from the kitchen. Moving into the other chimney, Maggs breathed a sigh of relief. He was safe for the time being at least.

Trapped in the house, he would not be able to make good his escape until everyone had gone to bed. That was likely to be very late if they were having a party.

However, it was not a total disaster. If Sanderson had removed the three sacks, the night's contents would be safe enough hidden in the woods. Maggs would find the ex-butler when he left his refuge that night. They would divide the spoils then.

The chimney Maggs was now in led down to a bedroom fire that had been bricked in to make it smaller. He would not be able to escape that way, but he was not unduly concerned. There was a shelf here, wide enough for him to settle down and sleep the day around. He would think about making his escape when he awoke.

70

Harry Maggs awoke suddenly. For some moments he did not know where he was. When he reached out and his hand dropped from the ledge into the emptiness inside the chimney, he remembered.

But there was something else. Something that had nothing to do with chimneys. It was a strange noise and it puzzled him. The sound seemed to fill the air all about him. A frightening, unceasing crackling. It was the sound of wood being consumed by fire.

He could smell smoke too now and, with a spasm of fear, he realised it was not the comforting aroma of a fire burning in a household grate.

It was not even a cooking fire, burning in the huge kitchen fireplace of Lanhydrock House.

This was a greedy, all-consuming fire, fanned by a wind that had been building up the previous night when he had entered the house.

The extent of the fire could be measured by the fact that smoke was being sucked up through the chimney that led from the bedroom beneath. Yet, when he looked down, he could see no domestic fire burning in the grate.

It meant the fire had to be in the room itself. The house was on fire!

Still half stupified from sleep, Maggs was belatedly galvanised into action. He scrambled to his feet on the ledge that had provided him with a sleeping space.

There was no escape for him down the chimney where he was. The alterations to the fireplace in the room below meant it was much too small to squeeze through.

He would need to make his escape through the kitchen.

He climbed towards the junction of the chimneys. Reaching it, he was alarmed at the amount of smoke pouring up from the kitchen. It was so thick he began choking.

But, despite the discomfort, he had to escape – and he needed to move quickly. Nevertheless, he began his descent cautiously, coughing all the while.

He had not gone far when he became aware of an intense heat rising from the kitchen.

The chimney also was on fire and, suddenly, Maggs remembered the paraffin-soaked sacks he had placed alongside the exposed beam in this very chimney. That must have been what had started all this.

Retching and choking, he was forced to return up the chimney, climbing blindly in the thick smoke.

He had a moment of panic when he missed a foothold. For a few terrified moments he was convinced he would tumble back down the wide chimney, into the fire below.

Then, gasping for breath, he reached the junction with the bedroom chimney once more. There was little respite for him here. The smoke from the bedroom was far more dense than before.

Maggs realised there was only one possible route to safety. He would need to climb to the top of the tall chimney and make his escape over the roof.

It would not be easy. The soot he had left inside the chimney was burning, giving off acrid, lung-searing smoke.

The heat from the kitchen fire was also increasing. He could feel it even at this great height. Most alarming of all, the very bricks of the chimney were hot to the touch. He was aware that the heat could only be coming from *outside*.

His eyes smarting and with agonisingly painful lungs, Harry

Maggs somehow managed to claw his way up the inside of
the chimney, heading for the lighter grey of the sky outside,
glimpsed intermittently through the darker grey of the smoke
from the burning house.

His lungs labouring for air, he was not yet aware of the roar
that grew louder as he neared the top of the chimney. He thought
there must be a fierce gale blowing outside the house.

Suddenly and virtually unseeing, his head emerged from the
top of the chimney. There *was* a gale-force wind blowing away
much of the smoke but, as he filled his lungs with life-giving
air, he became aware that the sound he could hear was not that
of the wind.

Rubbing his eyes in an effort to clear them, he took in the
frightening scene about him.

Much of the roof on this wing of the house had already
collapsed, the great beams burned away. The remainder might
have been a scene from Dante's *Inferno*.

Flames, fanned by the wind, were being blown sideways, but
they still climbed high into the sky, far beyond the height of the
tall chimneys.

The roar he had heard was the sound of the great house being
consumed by the voracious appetite of the conflagration that he,
Harry Maggs, had begun.

There would be no escape for him by this – or any other
– route.

Even as the realisation came to him, he was granted a merci-
fully swift release from his terror. From somewhere far below
there was an explosion. It came from within the kitchen area.

The chimney beneath him shook alarmingly – then collapsed.
Tons of masonry crashed down through the burning house, into
the very heart of the inferno.

It was the dying spasm of a once-magnificent house.

Harry Maggs died with it.

Waiting impatiently in the darkness, Robert Sanderson fumed at
the incompetent recklessness of his accomplice. He had already
taken two sacks of stolen items to the wheelbarrow hidden in
the woods, but there was still no sign of Harry Maggs.

Returning to the rear of the house, he unexpectedly came across the third sack. He guessed immediately what the chimney sweep was doing.

Castigating the absent Maggs for a greedy fool, he picked up the third bag to take it to the woods and hide it with the others.

As he did so, he saw the light from lamps come on in the kitchen and heard voices. His first thought was that Maggs had been discovered. Then he heard a woman laugh as the kitchen window was flung open.

Sanderson guessed that there was to be some kind of function in the house that day. On such occasions it was usual for certain members of the numerous kitchen staff to rise very early. They would bring the ovens up to the correct heat and have everything in readiness for the appearance of the cook.

The most serious question for Sanderson right now was the whereabouts of Harry Maggs. Was he hiding somewhere in the house – or had he already made his way outside and they had missed each other in the darkness?

Sanderson cursed his accomplice. The man was an utter fool!

Had Maggs kept to the plan they had made, they would both have been many miles from Lanhydrock by now, with property worth hundreds of pounds. Thousands, even.

Now his plans were in ruins. The only thing that was certain was that it was unsafe for him to remain in the vicinity of the house.

He would make for Bodmin. When it was light and people were moving about the town, he would find a small inn to purchase breakfast and a cheap room.

It was still far too close to Lanhydrock for comfort but, with any luck, the beard he had grown and the cheap clothes he was wearing would stand him in good stead. He would not be recognised as the once-immaculate butler of Lanhydrock House.

71

Robert Sanderson had been awake for more than twenty-four hours and his activities during the night had left him physically and mentally exhausted. As a result, in spite of his concern for the fate of Harry Maggs and the plans they had made, he slept heavily.

He did not wake until mid-afternoon, and was immediately aware of a great deal of activity in the street outside the small inn. There seemed to be far more people and vehicles than was normal in the quiet country town. Rising from his bed he opened the window, and felt an indefinable sense of excitement in the air.

After splashing some cold water over his face, he made his way downstairs to the dining room and ordered a drink and a meal. As he ate, he could see through the windows that most of the people seemed to be heading out of Bodmin along the road to the south of the town.

When he commented upon the activity to the serving girl, she said, 'It's the fire, sir. Up at Lanhydrock House. They say the whole house is burning to the ground. All the policemen in town have gone there. They've sent soldiers from the barracks, too. No one in the county has ever seen a fire like it. Everyone who isn't doing anything else has gone there to watch what's going on. Frightening, they say it is. Poor old Lady Robartes has had to be rescued from an upstairs window and one of the servant girls hurt herself when she jumped from another one. 'Tis a terrible thing to happen to such a lovely place.'

'Does anyone have any idea how the fire was started?'

'Doesn't seem like it. I heard say that it probably started in the kitchen chimney. But my sister works in the kitchen at the house, and she was telling me only last night about them having the sweep in there. Shifty-looking man she said he was. Doesn't sound as though he was very good at his job, either, not if the fire really did start in a chimney. Now, shall I pour you another cup of tea?'

Despite his changed appearance, Robert Sanderson felt it wise not to risk being seen in the vicinity of Lanhydrock House in daylight. Not with all that was going on there. He was known to have a deep grudge against the family. If he were recognised, an astute policeman might start asking him awkward questions. He decided to wait until it was dark before going to look at the burning house.

When the sun had gone down, Sanderson set off for the great house. There were many people on the road, all travelling in the same direction.

Men, women and children, their day's work over, were hurrying to witness the greatest disaster to occur in the area in living memory.

One of the county's grandest and most beautiful residences, the house had been at the heart of all that happened in this part of Cornwall for hundreds of years. It had been a focal point in times of trouble.

When a bitterly fought Civil War was raging throughout the land, Lanhydrock House had changed hands on more than one occasion. Yet its importance was appreciated by both sides and it had survived, intact.

The head of the Robartes family had fought on behalf of the Parliamentary cause, yet he managed to retain ownership of the house and lands when the war ended. Then, with Charles II on the throne, the fortunes and influence of the family increased with passing years.

Now the focal point of the family's power was being carried on the wind to the farthest corners of the extensive estate.

Standing amidst the crowd, watching firemen, policemen and soldiers fighting a losing battle against the fire, Robert Sanderson should have felt a deep and malicious joy. He had struck a devastating blow against the family for whom he bore a deep and bitter grudge. But the knowledge gave him no satisfaction whatsoever.

As he watched, flames leapt three times higher than the remaining tall chimneys of the house, fanned by a lessening, but still strong wind.

An eerie red glow illuminated the huge crowd. It showed the Herculean – but futile – efforts of the many fire-fighters.

A huge pall of smoke billowed from the conflagration, sweeping across the Cornish countryside for very many miles, contaminating the air inside cottages far removed from the Lanhydrock Estate. Meanwhile, the glow in the night sky was visible to those as far away as the north and south coasts of Cornwall.

Standing silent in the crowd, Sanderson heard many and contradictory rumours about the fate of the Robartes family, whose home this had been.

One was that Lady Robartes, heartbroken by the devastation of the house she loved, suffered a breakdown and had been escorted to the home of the local vicar.

Viewing the fire that had been planned by himself as an act of revenge, Robert Sanderson suddenly felt very frightened. All he wanted now was to put many miles between himself and the scene of his Pyrrhic victory.

On his way here from Bodmin, he had intended making his way to the woods behind the house to ensure the property stolen by Maggs was still safely hidden.

He had nursed a faint hope that the chimney sweep had made a miraculous escape from the blazing house. But he now realised it was not very likely. Having seen the extent of the fire, he was convinced the body of Harry Maggs was somewhere inside the burning house and would probably never be found.

Sanderson did not have the will to carry out his intentions

tonight. Besides, although the policemen in the area were fully occupied, there were far too many people wandering around the countryside, on their way to or from the blazing manor house.

Suddenly sick of everything about him, Robert Sanderson hurried from the scene of the fire. Throwing caution to the wind, he made his way to Bodmin Road railway station. Purchasing a ticket, he hid in the shadows until the arrival of the last train back to Plymouth.

He sat huddled in a seat in the corner of a carriage, lost in his thoughts. It was impossible not to dwell upon the enormity of all that had been brought about as a result of the plans he had made with the Plymouth chimney sweep.

72

During the two days she spent in London, Captain Eva had three
meetings with Carl Milton, the influential editor of the *Mayfair
Gazette*. Milton would provide any assistance she might need
to carry out her plan and promised that all the resources of his
newspaper would be placed at her disposal.

However, much to her dismay, the newspaper editor's enthusiasm for her crusade was not shared by senior officers of the
Salvation Army.

It was, perhaps, unfortunate that William Booth and his
second-in-command were both out of the country. Without
his decisive leadership, no one at the Salvation Army's London
headquarters was prepared to offer active support to such a
daring scheme. They were aware that it was likely to have
widespread repercussions, not only in England but in Europe
too.

Eva was advised to delay carrying out her plan until she had
been able to discuss it in detail with General Booth. The suggestion fell only marginally short of a command, but Captain Eva
knew she could not wait. If she did not take action immediately
she would be abandoning an unknown number of girls to a life
of enforced prostitution.

There was also the possibility that future advertisements of a
similar nature might not be brought to her attention.

Eva was convinced it was of the utmost importance to act *now* and she had already set the wheels of her plan in motion.

Before leaving Plymouth she had replied, on Sally's behalf, to the address in the newspaper, giving the house of a Plymouth Salvation Army supporter, living in a country area of Devon, as the return address. The response from the advertiser would be brought to Eva at the Plymouth Refuge as soon as it was received.

By the time she returned from London, Eva had decided she would ignore the advice of her superiors.

Back in the Refuge once more, she discussed with Sally the implications of the reluctance of the Salvation Army head-quarters' staff to become involved with the scheme she had planned.

'You don't have to go ahead with it if you'd rather not,' she said to Sally.

'Why should I want to back out?' Sally asked defiantly. 'Is what they say going to make any real difference to anything you want to do?'

'No, I can still count on the support of my members in the West Country, unless headquarters send out a direct order forbidding them to help me – and I don't think they will do that – but—'

Sally interrupted Eva. 'If we don't do something, there are likely to be a lot more girls who will end up like Rachel. As long as I know Zulu Joe is close enough to hear me if I scream for help, I'll be all right.'

'You're a brave girl, Sally. You have my word that I wouldn't allow you to do this if I wasn't convinced we would be able to help you if anything goes wrong.'

Despite her assurance, Captain Eva would have been much happier to have had the backing of William Booth and the staff at the Salvation Army headquarters.

The reply to Captain Eva's letter was brought to the Refuge two days later from the false address she had given at Okehampton in Devon.

The letter would have satisfied all but the most suspicious recipient. It declared that so many girls had replied to the advertisement, it had been decided to take on no more prospective domestic servants. However, Sally sounded as though she was just the type of girl they were looking for and, in view of this, they had decided to make an exception in her case.

She was to catch a train to Truro in Cornwall, where she would transfer to another train to Falmouth, arriving there at eight o'clock in the evening. Travelling with her would be all the other girls who were to enter domestic service.

They would be met at Falmouth railway station and taken to a house in the town. After a meal they would be allocated a room in order that they might have a good night's sleep before beginning their new life the following day.

It all sounded highly organised. However, reading the letter, Sally had a funny feeling in her stomach as she realised that it was no longer merely a vague plan. It was really going to happen.

The day before setting off for Falmouth, Sally attended Rachel's funeral with Captain Eva. It had been organised by Grace and Alfie and was a very moving service.

Both pie-shop owners were at the church and Alfie acknowledged Sally's presence with a nod of his head. His lips moved too, but he was too far away for Sally to hear what, if anything, he said.

Grace was standing beside him. She looked ill and strained and she never once glanced in Sally's direction.

Sally was very hurt by Grace's indifference. She wanted to go and speak to the woman who had been such a kind employer, but Eva dissuaded her. She suggested that in view of the anguish Grace was quite obviously suffering, she could not be expected to behave rationally. Eva felt quite certain that Grace would feel differently about everything when sufficient time had elapsed to allow her grief to subside.

In view of all that was going to happen in the next few days, Sally would have liked things between her and Grace settled before she went, but it was apparent it would need to await a more propitious moment.

73

Sally set off for Falmouth late on Saturday afternoon, travelling on a train from Plymouth. No uniformed Salvation Army officer was present at the station to see her off.

There was a strong possibility that other applicants were travelling on the same train, and a careless word dropped in the hearing of those who met them might well arouse suspicion.

Captain Eva was not in Plymouth. She was aware that if her plan were to succeed, it would be necessary for the officers of the Falmouth Salvation Army to become heavily involved. She had travelled there the day before, in order to make the necessary arrangements.

Nevertheless, Zulu Joe travelled on the same train as Sally. So too did a couple of the Plymouth Salvation Army 'soldiers'. More would be in the vicinity of the railway station when Sally arrived at her destination.

Eva was well aware that she was playing a very dangerous game and she was doing all within her power to ensure Sally's safety.

When Sally changed trains at Truro she was able to pick out other applicants. They all gathered somewhat self-consciously on the same platform, each carrying a pitifully small amount of worldly possessions.

Most, although not all, appeared to be younger than Sally

and she realised it had not been entirely necessary to give a false age.

Gradually, the girls drew together in a group, introducing themselves to each other.

There were fifteen altogether, including Sally. All were greatly excited at the thought of taking up a new way of life. It upset Sally to think of the disappointment in store for them.

Yet she was happy in the knowledge that she would be instrumental in saving them from a way of life that would bring them even more unhappiness than they had already known.

The girls talked of the life they thought lay ahead of them. There was laughter among the other girls when, in a moment of bravado, one of them said, 'I hope I go to a house with lots of men servants – *young* men servants.'

As the laughter died away, a young girl who reminded Sally painfully of Rachel sidled up to her. Small and quiet, Sally thought her a natural victim.

Shyly, she said, 'My name's Constance – although I'm always called Connie. What's yours?'

'Sally.' She smiled at her.

'That's a nicer name than mine. What sort of house do you hope to go to?'

Sally shrugged. Then, remembering she was acting a part, said, 'I don't really mind very much. How about you?'

'I don't care, either. Anything will be better than the work-house I've just left.'

Connie's likeness to Rachel grew in Sally's mind and she asked, 'Don't you have any parents?'

'No. They both died when I was small. I was brought up by my grandma, but she died two years ago too. Since then I've lived in the workhouse – although I'd hardly call it *living*. Everyone just exists there, one day at a time, hoping the next day's going to be better. It never is.' With a wan smile, she shook off the image she had just created and asked Sally, 'Do you have any family?'

'I lived with my sister for almost as long as I can remember. She died on Christmas Day.'

'I'm sorry,' Connie's sympathy was genuine. 'That must have been awful for you.'

A train arriving noisily on a nearby platform brought all conversation to a halt for a few minutes.

When the sound died away, Connie asked, 'Do you know anything about being "in service"?'

'Not really.'

'Or me, but I don't care. The thought of learning something, of belonging somewhere, is exciting enough. Do you think some of us will go to the same houses? It would be nice to be with someone we knew, wouldn't it?'

As they talked, Sally glimpsed Zulu Joe standing farther along the platform. He did not appear to be watching her, but Sally knew he was keeping her in view. It made her feel considerably safer.

She had been concerned that he might be conspicuous, but Falmouth was a very busy and cosmopolitan port. In fact there was a party of Lascars on the station, as well as a group of West African seamen. All were on their way to join ships.

Glancing about her Sally wondered which of her fellow passengers were also members of the Salvation Army?

The plan was that they would follow the girls to the house to which they were being taken. When the girls' destination was established, one of the Salvation Army members would inform the officer commanding the local corps. Captain Eva would be with him.

Men and women would then be despatched to maintain a vigil, night and day if necessary, until the girls were moved from the house.

It was at this point that Eva's plans became somewhat vague. When Sally had left Plymouth it had still not been decided whether the rescue should take place at the house.

Eva favoured leaving it until the girls were at the dockside, before they were taken on board a boat. She was convinced there *would* be a boat at Falmouth, somewhere, waiting for them, but the rescuers would first need to locate it.

All who knew what was happening agreed that a rescue at the house would be far safer. However, the newspaper editor felt that a last-minute rescue – perhaps just as the girls were about to be carried off to a continental brothel – would have a much more dramatic impact upon his readers.

It should also impress those in authority, who, it was hoped, would tighten up the laws to prevent a similar occurrence in the future.

Connie carried on chattering to Sally, seeming not to care whether or not she received replies from her companion. She was happy just to be free of the constraints of the workhouse, able to talk to someone close to her own age.

A few minutes later the train for Falmouth arrived and the girls all clambered on board, crowding into two compartments.

Connie made quite certain she was in the same compartment as Sally. The journey did not take very long and the younger girl grew increasingly excited as they neared their destination, especially when the crowded harbour came into view.

Indeed, the girls behaved more as though they were on a Sunday-school outing than travelling to take up menial tasks in someone else's home.

Connie remained close to Sally when they disembarked. She seemed glad to have found a companion who appeared to be both sensible and dependable.

A man and a woman were waiting for the girls. They introduced themselves as Victoria and Wallace Pearce.

As she remembered the men who had been involved in the attempt to kidnap Rachel and the other girls in Plymouth, Sally took an instant dislike to Wallace Pearce. He was not a pre-possessing character, being both surly and shifty.

It was the woman who did most of the talking. So much so that few of the girls were able to put any of their excited questions to her. Those who succeeded were told that all their queries would be answered when they reached the house where they were to spend the night.

There was a closed van waiting outside in the station yard, in which Wallace would drive the girls to their destination.

It was crowded inside the van and there were no windows, only two ventilated grilles high up on the sides of the van, but the girls were too excited to care. Seats made of wooden slats were placed along either side of the van. There was room for all the girls on them – but only just.

However, the crowding and the jostling and falling about when the van got under way only added to the general feeling of adventure. The girls continued to squeal and giggle, even when Wallace called in through one of the grilles for them to be quiet because they were passing through a 'select residential area'.

Unable to see where they were going, Sally realised they were climbing a hill from the station. At one stage they jolted over a cobbled stretch of roadway that bounced the girls about and rattled their teeth, causing them to squeal even more.

Eventually, after perhaps twenty minutes, the van came to a halt and the rear door was opened.

'Here we are,' said Victoria, as they all stepped from the van. 'Inside the house, all of you. There's a nice meal waiting for you there. When you've eaten you'll meet the woman in charge of the agency. She's the one who'll allocate you to the families who will be employing you. There are very pleasant surprises for some of you, I can tell you. We've had applications for staff from some of the most influential families in the county. At least half of them have titles. Now, gather your things and follow me inside the house.'

Walking down a steep path to a large, fairly modern house, Sally found her heart beginning to beat much faster in anticipation of what lay ahead.

It was hard to resist the urge to turn around to see if she could spot Zulu Joe or any Salvation Army men or women near. She would need to trust that they were not far away and would come to the rescue when they were needed.

Even had Sally noticed the twitching of the lace curtain at an upstairs window, she would probably not have been particularly concerned.

But had she recognised the woman who had disturbed the curtain in order to get a clearer look at the girls coming along the path, Sally in particular, she would have turned around and fled.

The woman at the window was Mother Darling.

74

Ian Lovat called at the Refuge to talk to Eva little more than an hour after Sally had left Plymouth bound for Falmouth. Due to his own pressures of work and Eva's absence in London, he had not seen her since her return. Now he learned she had gone off somewhere else.

The young Salvation Army lieutenant left in charge of the house during Eva's absence knew where her superior had gone, and why, but she had been sworn to secrecy. Newly arrived in Plymouth from London, she had learned to distrust policemen and she told Ian Lovat merely that Captain Eva was 'not here'.

'Then can you tell me when she'll be back? Better still, where she is now. I'll go and find her.'

'I don't know where she is.'

Despite the young Salvation Army officer's assertion, Ian Lovat felt she was being deliberately evasive. It served to increase the suspicions he had about Eva's whereabouts – and he was genuinely alarmed.

'Look, this is important. Very important! If you can help me at all, you must.'

'I've told you, I don't know.'

The young woman sensed the urgency in Ian Lovat's plea. For a moment she weakened and almost told him what he wanted to know. Then she remembered how adamant Captain Eva had been. She had been ordered to say nothing to *anyone*.

Ian Lovat made one last plea. 'I hope you're telling me the truth. Captain Eva might have placed herself in very great danger.'

Once again the lieutenant almost weakened. However, stories of the subterfuge used by members of the police Criminal Investigation Department in order to convict members of the Salvation Army had been rife among those with whom she worked. Determined not to be taken in, she said, 'I can't tell you what I don't know.'

Ian Lovat realised he was wasting time – and time could be of vital importance. He turned to go. Suddenly he stopped and swung around to face the young woman once more.

'I'd like to speak to Sally.'

Taken by surprise, the Salvation Army lieutenant replied, 'She's not here either.'

'Will she be back tonight?'

'I . . . I don't know. I don't think so.'

Now Ian Lovat was certain that his uneasiness was justified. The plan that Captain Eva had been wanting to put in motion for so long was taking place. He made one last desperate plea.

'I've no doubt you've been told to say nothing about what's going on, but I *do* have a very good idea what it is and I am not exaggerating when I say that Captain Eva and Sally are in grave danger. Is that something you and your conscience are going to be able to live with?'

The young lieutenant felt as though she was standing on the edge of a deep abyss. She wished she might have been able to turn to Captain Wardle for advice, but he was in London and besides he was not aware of what was happening. At this precise moment she was the senior Salvation Army officer in Plymouth.

She said doggedly, 'I have nothing more to say to you, Inspector Lovat.'

He decided he had wasted enough time. Besides, he had just thought of someone who might know exactly what was going on.

*   *   *

The telephone Ian Lovat used in order to call London was one of a very few in Plymouth. It was installed in the office of the admiral who was Flag Officer for the busy naval base.

Ian Lovat called Carl Milton, editor of the *Mayfair Gazette*.

At first, although the two men were long-standing friends, the London editor was as reluctant as the Salvation Army lieutenant had been to tell the detective inspector what was happening.

'I'm sorry, Ian. I'd like to tell you what is going on, but it would mean breaking a professional trust. I can't do that.'

'Damn your professional trust, Carl. The lives of two people, Captain Eva and, more particularly, Sally Harrup, are seriously at risk. You talk of professional trust. This matter is so serious that I'm willing to break *mine* – but if it ever gets into print I'll see that you lose your job and never again get to be so much as a teaboy on any newspaper in the land.'

Satisfied that the newspaper editor was fully aware of the seriousness of the situation, Ian Lovat continued, 'Now listen carefully. You've no doubt been told about Mother Darling's part in the business involving young girls being shipped to Belgian brothels? Well, she's disappeared. I believe she's gone to join her son. I don't know whether you're aware that he's wanted for questioning by police here in connection with the death of Sally's sister. I believe he and his mother are behind the latest advertisement offering posts in so-called "domestic service" for young and gullible girls. They both know Sally. Mother Darling has met Captain Eva too. If, as I believe, Sally has been sent to answer this advertisement then she'll be recognised. Once the Darling's realise a trap has been laid for them they'll be even more dangerous. If I can learn what's going on, I might be able to do something to save them. If I don't, this whole mad scheme that you and Captain Eva have cooked up is likely to have tragic results.'

Pausing only long enough to give the London editor time to digest what he had been told, Ian Lovat said, 'Now, are you going to tell me exactly what's going on?'

After a lengthy pause, Carl Milton said, 'Are you telling me the truth about this, Ian? You're not deliberately exaggerating the danger they're both in?'

'I've never been more serious in my life, Carl.'

The London editor took a deep breath before saying, 'Then I have no alternative, do I? You're right, Sally volunteered to help expose what's happening to the girls who apply for posts in domestic service. She answered the advertisement and is on her way to Falmouth at this very moment – a number of other girls will be doing the same. Captain Eva went there herself last night. There are a great many people keeping track of Sally and the other girls. I doubt if anything can happen to them – at least, not if the people who are behind this don't realise we are on to them. If they do . . . ? Well, you know the answer to that better than I do. We don't have an address in Falmouth for the girls, but if you need any more help, contact the senior Salvation Army officer there. He knows what's happening and should be able to tell you where the girls and Captain Eva are, and what he and his people are doing to help. I have a reporter and a photographer in Falmouth too. They'll be with Captain Eva, wherever she is.'

'Thanks, Carl. I'll get on to it right away and I'll go down to Falmouth myself, just as quickly as I can.'

'By the way, try to give me a story on this one, Ian. If it comes off we should be able to blow this filthy business sky-high.'

Grimly, Ian Lovat said, 'If everyone comes safely out of this you'll get your story. If not . . . I'd say you're likely to get ten years, instead.'

The Flag Officer's telephone had been installed in a small room off the admiral's office, accessible to no one but the senior naval officer and his private secretary. Only the urgency of the detective inspector's need had persuaded them that this was an emergency that could not be resolved by any other means.

During Ian Lovat's telephone conversation with Carl Milton, the door between the telephone room and the admiral's office had been left ajar. As a consequence, much of the conversation had been overheard by the senior naval officer.

As Ian Lovat came out of the telephone room, the admiral commented, 'You have a problem on your hands, Inspector.'

'Yes, sir. A number of young ladies are in trouble in Falmouth. I need to get there very quickly and see what I can do to help.'

'Can you tell me about it?'

Ian Lovat hesitated. It was unethical to discuss police business with outsiders – however exalted their position. Furthermore, although he was grateful for the help given to him by the admiral, he was also anxious to get on his way.

'The problem is at Falmouth, I understand?' persisted the admiral. 'Am I right in thinking you need to go there as a matter of some urgency?'

'Yes. I'll catch the first available train.'

'I don't think there is one for a couple of hours,' the admiral said knowledgeably. 'When you do catch it you'll need to wait at Truro for a connection. However, if there really *is* great urgency I can probably get you there far more quickly. Tell me about it.'

The admiral's words cut through Ian Lovat's reluctance to divulge information. The naval officer had probably already overheard enough of the conversation with Carl Milton to have formed a good idea of what was happening.

He gave the admiral the background to Captain Eva's crusade against the luring of young girls to the brothels of Europe, outlining the action he believed she was taking. He then explained the developments he felt put her and Sally in grave danger.

'Is such a trade really going on in this country of ours, Inspector?' The admiral was more outraged than shocked. 'I know it goes on in north African countries. The navy has been involved on occasions in trying to put a stop to it there. But right here on our own doorstep, with young *English* girls . . . ? It's unthinkable.'

'It's nevertheless true, sir. In fact, unless I can get to Falmouth in time we can probably add murder to what will take place there.'

'Then the navy will need to come to the rescue,' the admiral said firmly. 'A steam packet is due to leave for Falmouth this evening. I'll have the sailing brought forward. You can go with it. I'll send orders to the captain right away. You can accompany the messenger and be in Falmouth within four hours. There are marines on board too. If you need them, they are at your disposal.'

75

Inside the Falmouth house, Mother Darling stayed well out of the way of the girls, remaining in the upstairs room from which she had seen Sally.

After about half an hour, 'Victoria Pearce' made her way to the room to find out why she had not come downstairs to meet the girls. Mother Darling alarmed her by saying she had recognised one of the girls.

'She's a pretty little thing. Slim, with fair hair, wearing a green coat and with a green ribbon in her hair.'

'That sounds like Sally,' said the other woman. 'She comes from Devon. Near Honiton, I believe.'

'Sally's her right name, but she doesn't come from Honiton. She's a Plymouth girl, from the Barbican, and she's mixed up with the Salvation Army. It's her who had the fishermen raid the Belgian boat and take off the girls the last time we did this.'

The woman was frightened and it showed. 'Do you think she's going to try to do the same again? What shall we do?'

'Carry on as planned – at least we will as far as the other girls are concerned. I'll arrange something special for this little madam. There are a few old scores to be settled with her.'

'But what about the Salvation Army? You know how they feel about what we're doing. If they've taken a hand in this we could be in real trouble. I don't like it. I don't like it one little bit.'

'No one's asking you to like it. I'm not saying *I* like it, but I think we can teach this particular young lady a lesson she'll wish she never learned. I know someone who's going to be very happy to get his hands on her. She's caused my Sid more trouble than any man should have to put up with.' Rubbing her hands together in malicious glee, Mother Darling added, 'Oh yes, he'll be *very* pleased to teach her a lesson.'

'But what about her friends in the Salvation Army?' persisted the other woman. 'If this girl's up to something she won't be in this alone.'

'Of course she won't, but they're going to have to prove we've done something to break the law. Before they can do that they'll need to have her back with them. They'll find that's not going to be quite as easy as they think.'

'What if they've had her followed and are watching the house right now? They'll have seen her and the other girls arrive.'

Mother Darling looked at the other woman contemptuously. 'What if they *have* seen them arrive? We'll make quite sure they don't see them leave again. I had this house chosen with just this sort of problem in mind. There's a small gate from the back garden. It leads to a narrow footpath that comes out on a street way down the hill. Unless you'd been shown it you'd never know the gate, or the lane to it, existed. When we've dealt with this particular girl we'll get them all out that way. Her friends can watch the front of the house for as long as they like. By the time they realise they've been wasting their time, young Sally whatever-she's-calling-herself will have got her comeuppance.'

She sniffed disapprovingly. 'If we'd been using this place for the last lot we'd never have been rumbled and Sid wouldn't be a wanted man now. The trouble was, he got lazy and a bit too cocky. He thought it was easy and he wouldn't listen to me. He decided to bring everything closer to home. Look where it got him!'

Her companion was still uneasy. 'What do I do where this girl's concerned?'

'Go back downstairs and behave as though everything's perfectly normal. Treat this Sally exactly the same as you do everyone else – but watch her. See if she drinks any of the wine. She probably won't. When the others are too stupid to know what's going on send Wallace up here to fetch me. But whatever you do, don't leave the girl on her own. We don't want her getting up to any of her tricks. We'll deal with her when I come downstairs.'

The woman shook her head doubtfully. 'I still don't like it. Too many people seem to know what's going on. If something goes wrong . . .'

'Just do as you're told and leave me to do the thinking. We'll be out of here by midnight. Once the girls have gone no one will be able to prove anything, no matter what they might believe. If Sid had done that in the first place he wouldn't be in the mess he is now. Go on, off you go. Do as I've told you and think of the money you'll get when the girls are on board the boat.'

The woman went off, still shaking her head dubiously, leaving Mother Darling staring after her contemptuously.

Instead of being reassured by everything that should have marked the beginning of what she believed was going to be a new way of life, Connie was more uncertain than before. As a result, she stayed very close to Sally.

When the girls were seated around a huge kitchen table, wine was brought to them in two large jugs, as a special 'treat' to have with their meal.

Sally was tempted to suggest the younger girl leave the wine alone, but that would have meant making up an explanation for her suggestion. She decided against it.

The drugged wine – and Sally was certain it *was* drugged – would help to relax Connie. When the time came for Captain Eva and the other members of the Salvation Army to move in and rescue them, she would ensure nothing happened to the nervous young girl.

She wondered exactly when Captain Eva intended making her move. The most likely time would be as they were about to board the boat that was probably moored somewhere in Falmouth harbour. When it happened, Sally would be ready to take her part in the action . . .

'Aren't you drinking your wine, dear? Come along now, there's lots here. It was bought 'specially for you girls. We can't waste it now, can we?'

'I'm a slow drinker.' Sally smiled in what she hoped was a disarming fashion at the woman.

Some of the girls were already beginning to show signs that confirmed her suspicions. When the meal was begun there had been much excited conversation, accentuated for a while by the wine. That had now ceased altogether. Those who had drunk too freely were beginning to nod off to sleep. Others were having difficulty stringing words together in order to hold an intelligible conversation.

Sally was the only girl not affected by the wine and she realised the woman was looking at her suspiciously.

Then one of the girls slipped off her stool. The woman went to her aid and had great difficulty lifting her to a chair.

Sally took the opportunity to pour her doctored wine into the mugs of Connie and the girl seated on her other side.

She then tried to act as though she had drunk as much as the others in the room.

In another twenty minutes the room was silent. Unable to talk coherently, the girls had given up trying. It was doubtful if any of them would have been able to walk unaided.

When the woman left the room, Sally thought something must be about to happen. She felt excitement surge through her.

She was quite right. Things *were* about to happen, but they were not what she was expecting.

The door opened and the woman returned, but she was not alone. With her was the man she had introduced to the girls as her husband – and Mother Darling!

Sally was utterly dismayed. Her instinct was to flee, but she realised she would not have made it to the door. Dropping her head and resting her chin on her chest, she hoped Mother Darling would not see her face and recognise her.

Such subterfuge was a waste of time, although for a moment she felt a glimmer of hope. It seemed the man and two women might pass her by. Then a hand gripped her hair and pulled her head back viciously.

She looked up into the face of a vindictive Mother Darling.

'Hello, dearie. How nice of you to come calling on me. I've been hoping we would meet again.'

For a wild moment, Sally considered bluffing it out and pretending she was as drugged as the others. Then common-sense took over. She realised it would not work. There was no point in play-acting any more.

'Let go of my hair, you're hurting me.'

'Hurting you? You've not begun to feel pain yet, dearie – but you will when Sid gets hold of you.'

Sally went cold at the mention of the bullying procurer's name.

'Let me take her upstairs for a while,' Wallace said eagerly. 'I'll give her a taste of what she can expect when she gets to Belgium. I'd enjoy that.'

'You might' agreed Mother Darling. 'But you're not going to. That's something Sid will want to do himself. Since you're itching to get your hands on her, why don't you hold her while we pour some of this lovely wine down her throat. It would be a pity to waste it. I don't think she's even tasted it yet.'

As she was speaking, Mother Darling pulled Sally to her feet by her hair.

Sally tried to turn upon her, but 'Wallace Pearce' stepped forward and wrapped his arms about her. He held her in a grip that defied the most determined attempts to fight against him.

While Sally was held with her arms pinioned to her sides, the woman who claimed to be Wallace's wife held her nose and Mother Darling began to pour drugged wine down her throat.

Sally choked, gagged and tried to spit out the wine, but it was in vain. By the time her three captors had completed their work she had drunk more than any of the other girls.

Her head began to swim. She was still able to think, but it was in a vague, abstract way.

Eventually, she realised she was losing control of her limbs. She could feel herself sinking in the arms of the man holding her, yet she could do nothing about it.

Sally tried hard to fight against the feeling of acute lethargy, but she heard Mother Darling say, 'I think we've done a good job there, Fred. We'll not have a peep out of her until she's on the boat. I've no doubt Sid will be able to bring some feeling back to her then. In the meantime, if her friends are waiting for her to give some signal to them, they're going to be disappointed.'

Her gloating ceased and she became briskly efficient. 'Right, the van's waiting at the bottom of the path behind the house. Take her first.'

It sounded to Sally as though Mother Darling was speaking from far away and what she was saying had nothing to do with her.

She was half carried, half led from the house, but it felt as though she was observing something that was happening to someone else.

Sally was placed in a van that might or might not have been the one that had brought her and the other girls from the station.

She was hardly aware of the others being brought to the van. Then they set off and those girls who had been placed upon the wooden seats fell to the floor.

Moments later, Sally lost consciousness.

Her last thought was of Ethan and she tried to call out to him. She felt certain he would know what to do . . .

76

At the Shields' house, on the Barbican, Sophie was in the kitchen, peeling potatoes in readiness for the evening meal she would make for herself and Doris Shields.

Miserably, she thought how this used to be a happy time for her. Sophie and Albert had been married for only a year and with each homecoming came the thrills felt by a new wife very much in love with her husband. She enjoyed preparing a meal for Albert, having it ready for when he returned to their small house after a day's fishing.

Now, everything in her life had changed. Instead of welcoming home a lively and loving husband, she was merely going through the motions of producing edible food for herself and a woman who seemed to have lost all touch with normality.

It would be a dismal mealtime, as all meals had been since the men of the family had been lost at sea.

Doris would sit down and eat her meal in silence before suddenly saying, 'I wonder what Henry and the boys are doing now? They won't be eating as well as us, I'll be bound, but I hope they're taking care of themselves.'

The first few times it had been said, Sophie tried gently to convince Doris that the men and their boat had been lost. She no longer made the effort. Doris did not seem to hear a word that was said to her on the subject and firmly refused to face up to what must have happened.

It was almost as though God, or nature – Sophie's faith had been sorely tried just recently – had shut off the part of Doris's brain that was capable of accepting such facts.

In all other respects, Doris Shields behaved perfectly normally. In sharp contrast, Sophie increasingly felt her own life was taking on an air of unreality.

Doris was at this moment in the small back garden of the house, planting some flower seedlings given to her by a sympathetic neighbour.

While Sophie was working, thinking her own unhappy thoughts, she heard a knock at the door. It was a positive, imperious sound. One that *demanded* an immediate reply.

Frowning, Sophie picked up a small towel and dried her hands as she walked from the kitchen to the front door. She wondered who it could be. The only person who occasionally called in was Sally, if she was delivering in the area. But she would not knock at the door in such a fashion.

Opening the door, Sophie was surprised to see a uniformed naval petty officer standing there. In his hand he held a yellow envelope.

'Mrs Shields?'

When Sophie nodded, not considering which Mrs Shields he might be asking for, the sailor said, 'I've got a telegraph message here for you, ma'am. It arrived at the Flag Officer's headquarters this afternoon.'

Sophie went cold. It must be something to do with Albert and the others. Perhaps a naval vessel had found one of the bodies . . .

Raising a hand to his forehead, the sailor walked away, leaving Sophie with the sealed envelope.

Closing the door, Sophie walked along the passage to the kitchen, the envelope and the message it contained in her hand.

It was not until Doris Shields called from the garden to ask who had been at the door that Sophie ripped open the envelope, her hands trembling.

She read the first few lines and suddenly the room reeled around her. She reached out for the table to support herself, but the room would not stay still.

Suddenly, hot tears sprang to her eyes. She needed to brush them away before she could read on.

But these were tears of the sheerest joy.

At that moment Doris appeared at the kitchen door, her hands covered in earth.

'Who was that at the door—'

Her words were cut off as Sophie leapt forward and hugged her so tightly the older woman began to protest.

'It's Pa and the boys, Ma. THEY'RE SAFE! They're *alive!*' She continued to hug her mother-in-law, tears coursing down her face.

Suddenly, she became aware that Doris was trembling. Drawing back, she looked at the older woman in concern.

Her face bloodless and dark-eyed, Doris asked tremulously, 'Are you certain . . . ? How do you know?'

'It's true, Ma. We've just had a telegram delivered from the naval Flag Officer at Mount Wise. He's had a telegram – from Gibraltar. Listen, this is what it says:'

'"Regret fishing boat *Mermaid* was sunk by HMS *Roarer* south of Isles of Scilly. Happy to report that crew of seven, all members of Shields family from the Barbican, Plymouth, are safe, although Joseph Shields sustained broken arm. All transferred to steamship *Eastern Prince*, bound for Falmouth."

'It's signed, Flag Officer, Gibraltar.'

Tearfully jubilant, Sophie looked up from the telegram and was immediately concerned by what she saw. The older woman's face seemed to crumple before her eyes and Sophie needed to help her to a chair.

The next moment, Doris did what everyone had been waiting for her to do ever since her family had gone missing. She began to cry.

Dropping to her knees beside the chair, Sophie held her mother-in-law to her. Doris cried as Sophie had never heard anyone cry before and was inconsolable for a long, long time.

When the tears eventually ceased, Doris's body was racked

by sobs for many more minutes. Then she pushed Sophie away.

'I'm all right now. The boys are safe, Pa's safe, and, God willing, they'll be home with us soon. I never thought we were going to see them again, Sophie. Never.'

Astounded by the unexpected admission, Sophie said, 'But you're the one who always said they *would* come back! You had the faith the rest of us lacked.'

'I had to believe that, Sophie. Had I thought otherwise I would have gone mad. I couldn't have lived – because there would have been nothing to live for.'

Looking at her in open admiration, Sophie said, 'Ma Shields, you're a remarkable woman.'

'No, Sophie, I'm a very ordinary woman – and I've been a very frightened one. Now I'm very, very happy, but I feel absolutely drained of energy. I'm sure I could sleep for a week or more.'

'I feel the same, Ma. I was peeling potatoes, but I can't even think of doing anything so ordinary right now. I . . . I just don't know what to do.'

'You can go and tell Sally. In her own way that girl's felt as deeply about the loss of Ethan as any of us. She ought to be told the good news right away.'

'I'll go straightaway, Ma – but are you going to be all right?'

'How could I be anything else at such a moment, Sophie. Go on, away you go.'

Sophie pulled off her apron and hurried from the kitchen. She had reached the front door when Doris called after her.

'Sophie?'

'Yes, Ma?'

'I want you to know that I think you've been absolutely marvellous through all this. I couldn't have wished for a better daughter and I realise it hasn't been an easy time for you, either.'

'It hasn't been easy for any of us – especially you.' Running back to the kitchen, Sophie kissed and hugged Doris.

Then, bubbling over with happiness, she said, 'I'll go and

tell Sally now. I'll let the men on the fish quay know along
the way. Then I'll bring Sally back with me and buy something
so we can have a bit of a celebration. I feel so happy I
could burst.'

77

⧓

Believing that Sophie already had enough to worry about, Sally had not told her of the strained relationship between herself and Grace Philpott. For the same reason, she had not mentioned that she was no longer working at the pie shop.

As a result, when Sophie sought out Sally, it was there she went first of all.

Alfie was working behind the counter. When Sophie introduced herself and asked after Sally, he said, with some embarrassment, 'She isn't here. In fact, she doesn't work here any more. Hasn't she told you?'

The news came as a shock to Sophie and she said so. 'Why not? How long is it since she left . . . ?'

'Alfie! Are you busy out there? I could do with some help in here . . .'

Grace's head appeared through the bamboo slats of the hanging curtain between shop and kitchen and Alfie said, 'This young lady's come asking for Sally.'

'Well, she's not going to find her here.' Emerging from the kitchen, Grace added, 'What do you want with her?'

Instead of resenting Grace's nosiness, Sophie was delighted to be able to share the good news she bore.

'I'm Sophie Shields, married to Ethan's brother. I'm looking for her to tell her some wonderful news. Ethan's safe. All the boys

are safe. Their father too. The *Mermaid* was sunk by a warship
but Albert and the others were all picked up and put on board
a steamship. They'll be coming back and landed at Falmouth.'

'I'm absolutely delighted to hear the news about Ethan. He's
a very nice young man. I'm just as pleased about the others too,
of course. It's marvellous news for you – and for Ethan's mother
in particular. It was unthinkable that a woman should lose her
whole family in such a tragic fashion. But I can't pass on the
news to Sally. She doesn't work here any more.' Grace's mouth
clamped shut in an uncharacteristic expression.

'But . . . why has she left? She seemed so happy working
for you.'

'I thought I could trust her,' Grace said bitterly. 'She let me
down very badly over something involving a poor young girl
who was living here. Someone Alfie and I had grown very
fond of.'

'You're talking of Rachel,' said Sophie. 'So it must be the fact
that Sally never told you Rachel was pregnant.'

'You knew about it too?! I must have been the only one around
here who *didn't*!'

'The reason Sally kept it from you was because Rachel made
her promise not to tell you. Sally isn't a girl who would break
a promise. I'd have thought you would know how trustworthy
she is; she was working for you for quite some time.'

'If it hadn't been for her, Rachel might still be alive today.'

'That's not true,' said Sophie. 'Rachel was desperate to get rid
of the baby without you finding out. Sally didn't agree with her.
She tried to persuade her to tell you. She felt you *ought* to know.
As it was, when Rachel refused point blank, Sally tried to help
her get rid of the baby by taking something. She even asked me
to speak to the Scots fisherwomen down on the fish quay, to see
if they knew of any way it could be done. When nothing worked,
she warned Rachel that if she didn't forget all about trying to get
rid of the baby, she'd end up in the hands of someone like the old
abortionist who lives in one of the houses behind Pin's Lane.'

'An abortionist lives there? Who is she, do you know her
name?'

'No, but I do know that Sally would have done anything

to prevent what happened. She thought the world of Rachel. To punish her on top of all that happened is very unfair. She must have been very hurt. I'm going to Pin's Lane now, to see if she's there.'

When Sophie had left the shop, Alfie said to Grace, 'She's right you know, Grace. We've been very unfair to young Sally, in more ways than one. You treated her almost like a daughter before Rachel came along. Then you shifted your affection, although young Sally never changed. She never became jealous, as many other young girls might have done. In fact, she was delighted that Rachel had found someone to love and care for her. She cared and tried to protect her too, as best she could. The way we treated Sally must have been very hurtful to the girl.'

'I still think she should have told me what was going on,' Grace said defensively.

'Do you, Grace? Even though she'd given her word? I think it shows just how fond of Rachel she was. It would have been an opportunity for her to ingratiate herself with you by breaking Rachel's trust. She didn't.' Aware that his words were having an effect on her, Alfie continued, 'You were always the one to tell me Sally deserved a chance – and you were right. Now it's you who are denying her that.'

Turning away from him, Grace went back into the kitchen without saying a word in reply.

For perhaps twenty minutes the sounds of pots and pans could be heard as she cooked, washed and cleared up. Then she appeared from behind the bamboo curtain once more.

Less belligerently than before, she asked, 'Do you really believe I behaved so badly towards Sally, Alfie? I was terribly hurt that she didn't tell me about poor Rachel's condition, you know.'

'No, Grace. You were hurt because you allowed yourself to grow very fond of Rachel and you lost her, just as we did our Mary. You wanted someone to blame and you turned on Sally, even though it wasn't her fault. She did the right thing by Rachel.'

'If you thought that, why didn't you say something to me at the time?'

'You weren't ready to listen to anything anyone said to you then, Grace. Besides, I knew you would come round to seeing things right, sooner or later.'

'Losing Rachel did hurt, Alfie. I haven't felt pain like that since . . . since we lost our Mary.'

'I know.' Alfie put a comforting arm about his wife's shoulders. 'It upset me too. More than you'll ever know. But I think you ought to do the right thing by Sally now. After all, we have each other. She's had no one she could turn to, has she? Not since she believed she'd lost young Ethan too.'

'Are you telling me I should go and find her and tell her I'm sorry?'

'I'm not *telling* you anything Grace. I don't think I need to. No one could ever take the place of our Mary. I'm not at all sure either of us really wants them too – but one thing I do know. In all the time she was working for us, young Sally did many a good turn for us – and never a bad one.'

Grace was silent for some minutes, then she said, 'You're quite right, of course, Alfie. There's no one knows me better than you.' Close to tears, she asked, 'What do you think I ought to do?'

'You don't really need me to tell you that either, Grace. Go and find Sally. Tell her you're sorry. You'll never have a better opportunity than today. If she's at the Salvation Army house with that woman captain you'll be able to tell her that Ethan's safe after all. For being the bearer of such news I don't doubt she'd forgive you anything.'

Dabbing at her eyes with a corner of her apron, Grace gave him a watery smile. 'Bless you, Alfie. I don't know what I ever did to deserve a man like you, I'm sure. Whatever it was, I'll always be grateful for it. You're quite right. I'll go and find Sally, tell her the wonderful news of her young man and say I'm sorry for what I said and did to her. I'll try to put things right between us.'

She started to untie her apron. Startled, Alfie said, 'You're going right this minute?'

'You know me, Alfie. I don't waste any time once I've made up my mind to do something. Besides, as you said yourself, I ought to put things right as soon as I can – and there's no time like the present.'

For a moment it seemed Alfie might argue with her, then he shrugged his shoulders. 'All right, Grace. You do whatever you feel is best. The sooner we have her back here working for us, the better it will be for everyone. It will make the loss of a few hours of business worthwhile.'

Arriving at the Refuge, Grace asked first after Sally, then for Captain Eva.

She received the same reply in respect of each of them, as had Ian Lovat, and from the same young woman.

The young Salvation Army lieutenant added, 'I don't know why the two of them are so popular today.'

'Why, who else has been asking for them?' Grace thought that perhaps Sophie Shields had called at the Refuge.

'It was a detective inspector. He seemed very agitated to find they had both gone.'

'Ian Lovat? What did he want with them?'

More cautiously, the young lieutenant said, 'I don't know and I couldn't tell him any more than I'm telling you now.'

Sensing a mystery, Grace asked, 'Are Captain Eve and Sally off somewhere together? When are you expecting them back?'

'They didn't leave together. More than that I can't tell you, Mrs Philpott. Although I do know they won't be back tonight.'

Grace was not satisfied with the Salvation Army officer's reply, but she was aware she would learn nothing more here. She would go and find Ian Lovat.

78

Once Grace Philpott took the bit between her teeth, she was not an easy woman to be diverted from any chosen course. Like Ian Lovat, she suspected something was going on that involved both Captain Eva and young Sally.

Believing, quite rightly, that she knew what it was all about, Grace was thoroughly alarmed.

She knew how passionately Captain Eva felt about the scandalous trade in providing English girls for prostitution on the Continent. She would not be above taking unjustified risks involving herself – and others. Determined to put a stop to the trade, she would count the cost later.

Grace already knew from various conversations with Captain Eva of the most recent advertisements placed in regional newspapers. Sally's place in Captain Eva's scheme was less clear, but she looked younger than her years and it did not take an intellectual to work out the part she was best suited to play.

The knowledge that her own actions might have prompted Sally to take such an active and dangerous role did not make Grace feel any more comfortable about what she believed was going on.

Sally had gone through a thoroughly miserable time. First losing her sister, then believing Ethan had been lost at sea and finally being thrown out of work and blamed for the death of Rachel, the girl she had helped and befriended.

Grace was an explosive, emotional woman, but she was also fair-minded, and was honest enough with herself to accept she had unfairly laid the blame upon Sally for what had happened to Rachel.

She was determined that Sally would come to no harm as a result.

Detective Inspector Ian Lovat was, of course, not at the police headquarters. Despite Grace's insistence that she needed to speak to him as a matter of great urgency, she could learn nothing of his whereabouts.

Eventually, quietly fuming at the frustration of having to deal with unhelpful policemen, she left the building. Outside the main entrance, she was startled to see her uncle being escorted to his carriage by a tall, distinguished-looking man, who was wearing a uniform Grace did not immediately recognise as being that of Plymouth's Chief Constable.

'Uncle Percy!'

The chairman of the Police Authority turned to see Grace calling out his name as she hurried towards him.

'You're just the man I want to see.'

If Percy Mallett felt a momentary sinking feeling at her words, he did not allow it to show. 'Grace! You're the last person I expected to meet here. What are you doing at Police Head-quarters?' Suddenly remembering his manners, he introduced her to the man who was seeing him off the premises. 'Grace, may I introduce Chief Constable Frost? Chief Constable, this is Grace Philpott, my neice.'

The two shook hands and Grace said, 'I came here looking for Ian Lovat, but he's nowhere to be found. No one in there . . .' she jerked her head contemptuously towards the building she had just left, 'seems to know where he is.'

The chief constable smiled. 'I think I can answer your question, Mrs Philpott. Detective Inspector has gone to Falmouth. He took passage on a naval vessel this afternoon.'

'Falmouth? Why Falmouth? Is that where Captain Eva and Sally are?'

Now it was the turn of the chief constable to appear startled.

'Captain Eva Cassington, of the Salvation Army? I know nothing of what she might be doing – and I doubt if Inspector Lovat does. He has gone there in the hope of arresting a man who is wanted on warrant in this city.'

Grace was disappointed. She had felt certain Ian Lovat would have learned what Captain Eva was up to and left the city in search of her.

Suddenly, she said, 'This wanted man . . . what's his name?'

For a moment it seemed the chief constable would refuse to give her an answer, but he saw that Percy Mallett was interested too.

'His name is Sidney Darling. He's wanted for questioning about a serious assault on a young girl.'

'Sid Darling's mixed up in far more than assaults on girls, I can tell you that for nothing,' Grace said vehemently. To her uncle, she said, 'I think Captain Eva might have used Sally to answer one of those advertisements, offering young girls attractive posts in domestic service and giving them a Falmouth address to reply to. But domestic service isn't where they're going to end up. What's more, if Sid Darling's there he must be mixed up in this. Sally will be in grave danger. Sid Darling knows her – and he has a score to settle. If Captain Eva had known Sid Darling was involved she'd never have gone ahead with this.'

'Are you certain of what you're saying, Grace . . . ?'

'I'm not certain of anything, but Sally and Captain Eva aren't at the Refuge – and Ian Lovat's gone to Falmouth because he believes Sid Darling's there. It all hangs together a little too well for my liking.'

Percy Mallett was thoughtful for a few moments, then he nodded his head. 'You're probably right, Grace. This could be extremely serious.'

Successfully hiding the irritation he felt, the chief constable said, 'Would you care to tell me exactly what is going on? Or, at least, what is *believed* to be going on?'

Grace was the first to answer him. 'Sid Darling is a very dangerous man who is heavily involved in shipping unsuspecting young girls to brothels on the Continent. You remember the scandalous case we had in Plymouth at the end of last year?

It's the reason a warrant was sworn out for Sid Darling. The trade has being going on for a very long time. Captain Eva is absolutely determined to stamp it out. It's highly probable she's connived at having a young girl reply to the advertisement in order to expose the whole thing and put a stop to it.'

'If she has taken such a course of action then she is behaving in a highly irresponsible manner! Matters such as this are best left to the police to deal with.' Chief Constable Frost was indignant.

'Perhaps – but at least she's doing *something*. What are *you* doing to bring this trade to an end?' Grace issued the challenge to him.

'If someone can provide evidence that it really is going on here, in Plymouth, I will order that action be taken immediately,' replied the chief constable

'Where it's happening doesn't matter a great deal if you're one of the girls being shipped to a brothel in France or Belgium. As for the evidence . . . no doubt that's what Captain Eva is gathering right now.'

Turning to her uncle, Grace asked, 'What can we do to help? Can we get to Falmouth tonight?'

'We won't be able to travel there today, Grace. Why not telegraph a warning about Sid Darling to the Salvation Army in Falmouth? They could probably warn Captain Eva.'

'We might already be too late,' declared a very worried Grace. 'I'd be much happier if I were there myself.'

'By the time a telegram reaches Falmouth, Inspector Lovat should already be there,' said the chief constable. 'He's a very capable and resourceful man. He'll sort things out, I have no doubt at all – but I will send a telegram to the chief constable of Cornwall, requesting that he gives Lovat every possible assistance.'

'Ian Lovat doesn't even know what Sid Darling looks like,' retorted Grace. 'I do. We'll send a telegram – and hope the man in charge of the Salvation Army at Falmouth knows what's going on. But I can't leave it there. If we've heard nothing by morning I'm going too – and I know who'll help me get there. The fishermen down at Sutton Harbour were absolutely incensed at what was going on when Sally foiled Sid Darling and his gang

342 E. V. Thompson

before. One of them will take me, I'm certain of it. Uncle Percy, will you drive me to the telegraph office, then I'll go down to the harbour . . .'

'I will,' Percy Mallett was suddenly enthusiastic. 'What's more, if you make this journey tomorrow, I'll come with you.'

'I'll see that you are kept fully informed of developments, Mr Mallett. Hopefully, the matter will be fully resolved by morning and save you an unnecessary journey.'

'You'll do more than that, Chief Constable. If this matter puts an end to this vile trade, you'll add Inspector Lovat's name to the next promotion list – and I'll ensure that he is selected.'

79

It had been a confusing time for Ethan and the male members of his family. When the *Mermaid* collided with the warship events happened so speedily the fishermen had had no time for fear. No time for anything except survival.

The *Mermaid* had been fishing south of the Isles of Scilly on her own. Most of the other boats had given up all hope of a good catch. Bringing in their nets, they had set a course for Plymouth.

There was a heavy sea mist in the area. This not only prevented the lookout on HMS *Roarer* from seeing them, but also muffled the sound of the warship's engines. By the time the crew of the *Mermaid* realised a ship was bearing down on them it was too late to take action to avoid a collision.

The iron warship cut the fishing boat virtually in half and it sank within minutes. Ethan jumped over the side only moments before HMS *Roarer* ploughed into the smaller vessel. His father and two of his brothers did the same.

The other brothers made their escape from the stricken fishing boat moments later, but Joe was struck by a piece of broken mast and was floundering in the water with a broken arm.

Swimming to the aid of his brother, Ethan towed him to a piece of floating wreckage. This soon became a focal point for each member of the family.

Fortunately, the warship's lookout had spotted the fishing boat seconds before the collision. Although his shouted warning came too late to avoid disaster, it meant that HMS *Roarer* came to a halt almost immediately. A boat was quickly lowered to rescue the fishermen and take them on board.

While the ship's surgeon set Joe's arm, the others were lent dry clothing. Then they were given liberal tots of rum, which served to warm them and lessen the shock of losing their boat.

The Plymouth men were made to feel very welcome on board the warship. The commanding officer and Henry Shields were also able to agree on a joint report of the collision. It would be filed when the warship docked at Gibraltar for coaling.

Before this occurred, they met up with a passenger-carrying steamship. The *Eastern Prince* was bound for Falmouth, from the Far East. At the request of the warship's commanding officer, the other vessel's captain agreed to take the seven shipwrecked men on board.

The fishermen were transferred when both vessels were off the coast of Portugal, after the warship's captain promised that a telegraph message would be sent to Doris Shields when he reached Gibraltar.

Unfortunately, the warship was intercepted by a small naval sailing vessel when still some miles from its destination and sent to North Africa, to demand the release of a number of sailors shipwrecked and imprisoned there. As a result the telegram to Doris Shields was not sent until much later than was anticipated.

The fishermen's voyage home took quite a long time, too, the steamship making two ports of call before reaching Falmouth. As a result, Ethan and the others found themselves exploring the streets of Bilbao in Spain and, later, Brest in France, before reaching England.

They had little money in their pockets when the *Mermaid* went down, but the passengers on the ship that had taken them on board had made a collection. Enough money was donated to enable the shipwrecked fishermen to purchase a number of lace handkerchiefs in Brest as presents for Doris, Sophie and Sally.

*   *   *

It was with great excitement that the seven Plymouth men caught their first glimpse of the Cornish coast at The Lizard, on their return. They were not on the main deck with the other passengers, having been invited to the bridge.

They shared their privileged vantage point with the captain and a pilot, as the steamship nosed its way past Black Rock and turned to enter Falmouth's sheltered harbour.

Each of the men was occupied with his own thoughts. Believing that Doris had known for some time that he and the others were safe, Henry Shields was already thinking ahead to the type of fishing boat he would purchase with the money he expected to collect from the insurer of his boat.

With the additional compensation he had been told he might expect from the Royal Navy, he hoped to be able to purchase a steam-trawler. His recent experiences had convinced him that this was where the future lay for all men who earned a living from the sea.

Ethan was looking forward to being with Sally once more. He hoped she had been worried about his absence – but not *too* much. Sally would have been relieved had she known that he had completely forgotten about the 'quarrel' that had so played upon her mind.

Suddenly, as the ship edged slowly towards its berth, Ethan frowned. Pointing to a large trawler moored alongside a small jetty, away from most of the other shipping, he said to the others, 'Look! Do any of you recognise that boat?'

There was some shaking of heads before Joe said, 'It looks like that Belgian fishing boat we had in Sutton harbour. The one that had young Rachel and the others on board. What was it called, can anyone remember?'

'It was the *Astique*,' Ethan replied. 'And it certainly looks like the same boat.'

'I can't say I know the name, but it's Belgian all right,' confirmed the pilot. 'They came in late yesterday. Didn't want a pilot and asked for a quiet berth. Said they had a few problems and wanted space to spread their gear out. I reckon they must have had a day off today, though, there's not been much sign of anyone doing any work.'

'I doubt if you'll see any work being done,' Ethan said, tight-faced. 'Not if it's the boat I think it is. I doubt if it'll be there come morning, either.'

The conversation with the pilot came to an end at this point. A large sailing vessel was leaving port and the pilot of the steamship soundly cursed the man at the helm of the other vessel as he was forced to stop engines and make a series of complicated manoeuvres in order to avoid the risk of a collision.

Minutes later the seven fishermen clattered down the ladder to the main deck as the steamship prepared to come alongside the quay.

The Shields family had been lent sufficient money to make their way to Plymouth by train. All were anxious to get home. Henry and Albert Shields, in particular, being eager to be reunited with their wives.

Ethan was anxious to see Sally again, but the boat moored alongside the Falmouth quay bothered him greatly. When he set foot on dry land, he looked across to where the Belgian vessel was moored and reached a sudden decision.

'I'm not happy seeing that boat there. If I don't do something about it, I'll forever wonder what it's up to. I'm going across to have a look at it. If is the *Astique* I'm going to the police.'

'Now don't get mixed up in anything,' cautioned his father. 'We've had enough excitement to last us a lifetime these past few weeks. Besides, I want to get home to your ma. She'll know we're safe, but that won't stop her worrying.'

'I don't suppose it will take me long,' said Ethan. 'I'm as anxious to be home as you are – but I wouldn't forgive myself if it's the *Astique* and its crew were up to their usual tricks and I did nothing about it. Hopefully I'll be proven wrong and be with you in time to catch the same train.'

'I'll come with you, Ethan,' Joe said unexpectedly. 'I can't do much with this broken arm, but I can keep you company – and if they're at all suspicious they wouldn't expect trouble from someone with his arm in plaster.'

80

The fishing boat was indeed the *Astique* and a couple of men dressed as fishermen were standing talking on deck. Ethan thought they had most probably been posted as lookouts.

Fortunately, as Joe had predicted, they saw nothing sinister in two young men, one with a broken arm encased in Plaster of Paris, walking on the quayside. Once past the foreign boat, the two brothers pretended to gaze out to sea from the end of the quay, before strolling back towards the town again.

When trouble came, it was not from the men on the trawler. Ethan and Joe were clear of the jetty and out of sight of the trawler, when they were stopped by two men who emerged from a nearby building they had thought to be empty.

'What were you doing along there on the quay?' one of the men put the unexpected question to them.

Uncertain who the men were, Ethan said, 'Nothing in particular. Just taking a walk.'

'I shouldn't have thought there was much to see,' commented the second man. 'Nothing that couldn't be better seen from elsewhere – unless, of course, you have an interest in the Belgian boat?'

When neither of the Shields brothers made any reply, the first man said to his companion, 'Do you think Mr Lovat would be interested in them?'

Ethan seized upon the name immediately, 'Are you talking of Ian Lovat? Inspector Ian Lovat?'

'You know him?' The first man put the question to Ethan.

'Yes – and if he's interested in the *Astique* I'd like to get a message to him.'

Both men looked at each other and the older of the two nodded. 'All right, I'll take you to him.'

To his companion, he said, 'You stay here. I'll be back as soon as I can.'

They did not have very far to walk. Ian Lovat and a Cornwall Constabulary inspector had taken over a room in the main customs building, close to the harbour-side.

Ian Lovat was seated at a table talking when the three men entered the room and he got to his feet immediately, an expression of delight on his face.

'Ethan! What are you doing here? Everyone in Plymouth feared you and your family were lost at sea! It was even reported in the newspapers . . .'

'We were sunk by a warship and have just arrived back on a steamship – but explanations can wait. As we came in I saw a Belgian fishing boat. Joe and I have just been down to take a closer look. It's the one we took the girls off, in Sutton harbour.'

'I thought it was!' Ian Lovat glanced at the Falmouth policeman triumphantly. 'That's why we're having it watched.' Suddenly, his expression changed and he became serious. 'There was another advertisement in the newspapers, offering posts in domestic service to young girls. Captain Eva decided she would take the opportunity to show these people up for what they really are. She has the support of the editor of one of the London newspapers. We believe she's out there somewhere, probably watching a house where they've taken the girls.'

'Good for her,' declared Ethan. 'It's time someone acted to put a stop to what's going on . . . But you said she's *probably* watching a house. Don't you know for sure? Aren't you working with her?'

Ian Lovat shook his head. 'She didn't tell me of her plans because she knew I didn't approve of her getting mixed up in something like this. This is work for the police, not for an organisation like the Salvation Army.'

Ethan shrugged. 'The police don't seem to have put themselves out to do anything about it in the past. I'm with Captain Eva.'

'You might change your mind when you hear the full story – or as much of it as I know. It would appear she's sent someone along pretending to want to go into domestic service to learn what's going on. That someone is Sally.'

Ethan's mouth dropped open and his expression turned to one of horror. 'Sally? But why? Why should she want to do something like this?'

'That's a long story too, Ethan. Briefly, Sally thought she had lost you, then young Rachel discovered she was pregnant, found someone to abort her – and died as a result. Grace Philpott blamed Sally and dismissed her from the shop.'

'Oh my God! What a mess. Poor Sally.'

'I'm afraid it's not just *poor* Sally. I believe her life is in very real danger,' Ian Lovat said grimly. 'It's probable that Sid and Mother Darling are mixed up in this business – just as they were before – and, of course, they both know Sally.'

Ethan looked at Ian Lovat aghast. 'If Sid Darling gets his hands on Sally he'll kill her. What are you doing about it – and where's Sally now?'

'There's very little we can do right at this moment. We don't know where anyone is – although it's certain all the girls are somewhere in the Falmouth area. The Salvation Army officer in charge of this area is helping Captain Eva – but he seems to have disappeared too. Our only hope is the boat. I wasn't a hundred per cent certain it was the right one until you confirmed it. All we can do now is keep the boat under observation and move in when the moment is right. That means, when the girls are taken there.'

'But what about Sid Darling? He wouldn't think twice of killing Sally if he believed it might help to save him. Where is he?'

'I wish I could answer that, Ethan. I can't. We must hope he's on the boat with the fishermen.'

'But what if he isn't? What if he's ashore somewhere – in the same house as Sally? You know what he did to Rachel. He could be doing the same to Sally . . .' Ethan's voice broke as he thought of the unthinkable.

'We can do no more for now, Ethan. It won't be long until it's dark. As soon as it is we'll move off to the jetty where the Belgian boat's moored. If luck is with us we'll have this whole thing wrapped up within the next few hours and everyone will be where they ought to be. That includes Sid Darling.'

As he pulled up chairs for the two Plymouth fishermen, Ian Lovat tried not to think of what might happen if luck was *not* on their side.

81

Outside the house high on the hill above Falmouth harbour, where Sally and the other girls were being held, Captain Eva waited in hiding with the Falmouth Salvation Army officers and those who had accompanied her from Plymouth, as the sun sank over the distant horizon and gaslights illuminated the streets and houses of the town.

It was now that Eva expected the girls to be taken from the house to a waiting boat, while it was still early enough for a closed van being drawn through the streets not to excite attention.

As time passed and nothing happened, Eva began to feel uneasy. She shared her thoughts with the Falmouth commanding officer.

'I don't like this. It's too quiet. I would have expected things to be happening by now.'

'The girls must still be inside the house. Nothing has arrived to take them away.'

Eva entertained her own thoughts on the matter, but she did not want to say anything at the moment.

They continued to keep watch on the house until one of the Plymouth Salvationists said, 'Look! The lights are going out on the ground floor. It seems the girls are about to be moved.'

'I don't think so,' Eva replied grimly. 'If you ask me, I'd say that whoever is in the house is preparing for bed.'

'You mean . . . they're going to keep the girls in the house overnight?' The question came from the Falmouth commanding officer.

'No. I believe we're wasting our time here. We've been tricked. I think the girls have already gone.' Eva made the statement with a sick feeling in the pit of her stomach. If the girls *had* been taken from the house it meant that her planned exposé had gone disastrously wrong. Not only would she have failed to prevent the unsuspecting girls from being abducted, but she had been responsible for sending Sally off with them.

'There must be something we can do to find out.' The voice of the Falmouth commanding officer broke into her tortured thoughts.

'Yes. We'll call on whoever is in the house right now and try to learn what's going on.'

'But if the girls are still in there all your plans will have come to nothing.'

'If we find the girls inside the house I'll fall on my knees and thank the Lord,' said Eva. 'But I fear He'll be hearing only a *plea* from me tonight.'

By the time Captain Eva, accompanied by a number of fellow Salvationists, reached the door of the house, the light in the front hall had been extinguished. Eva's repeated knocking brought a slow response. Eventually, she could hear the grumbling of a woman as she descended the stairs, holding a lighted candle.

When the woman reached the door, she called out, 'Who is it? What do you want at this time of the night?'

'It's the Salvation Army. I want to talk to you.'

'Can't it wait until morning? I was about to go to bed.'

'No, it can't wait. If you don't open the door now I'll call on the police and have them break it down.'

There was more grumbling from inside the house. Then there was the sound of a bolt being drawn. When the door opened, an elderly woman stood in the doorway, holding a candle aloft.

'*You!* What are you doing here?' Eva's worst fears were realised as she saw Mother Darling standing before her.

'I might ask the same of you, dearie. You seem to make a habit of disturbing folk late at night.'

Mother Darling's response appeared to be that of a reasonable woman indignant at being disturbed. The commanding officer of the Falmouth Salvation Army looked at Captain Eva uncertainly.

'I think you know why we're here, Mrs Darling. Where are the girls?'

'Girls? I don't know what you're talking about, dearie. I'm here for the sake of my health. It isn't what it used to be and I need to get away from Plymouth every so often. As for girls . . . I suppose you want to search the house, same as you did in Plymouth. Well, you're quite welcome, I'm sure – but you can be quite certain that I'll be lodging a complaint with the police tomorrow. I'm not having you following me around the country, forcing yourself into my house late at night whenever you've got nothing better to do. Well, are you coming in? I'm not standing out here all night, catching me death of cold just to talk to you.'

Captain Eva knew instinctively there would be nothing to find inside the house. At that moment, a hand tugged at her sleeve. It was Zulu Joe. He motioned for her to follow him.

She turned away and hurried after the African Salvationist without another word to Mother Darling.

As the door closed behind the evil old woman, those still standing outside could hear Mother Darling chuckling to herself as she drove home the bolt on the door. She was convinced she had once more outwitted the Salvation Army officer from Plymouth.

82

When Zulu Joe showed Captain Eva the hidden gate leading from the garden of the house, a sense of panic threatened to engulf her.

Not only had she and the other Salvation Army watchers been tricked, but – far more seriously – the Darlings were part of the operation and they knew Sally's true identity.

Sally was in grave danger. It took a very real effort on Eva's part to control her fear and to think effectively.

'What shall we do?' Less directly involved than his Plymouth colleague, the Falmouth commanding officer was nevertheless concerned. If things had gone seriously wrong, Captain Eva would face the full wrath of the Salvation Army's explosive leader, but he too would suffer censure.

'You must call on every man and woman you can muster. Tell them to go out on the waterfront. Speak to anyone who might know something. We're looking for a boat that isn't what it's purported to be. Most probably it will be a foreign one. I believe it will probably be Belgian. It will be moored alongside, probably somewhere quiet. It will certainly be well away from other boats and clear of busy areas.'

'What are you going to do?'

'I'm going to the police station to speak to the officer in charge.

When I see him I'll confess to everything I've done and ask for his assistance.'

'What of all your plans – and your own future? This could put an end to everything to which you've devoted your whole life.'

'I knew what I was putting at risk when I took this action. What I foolishly didn't realise was the sacrifices others might need to make. It's become far too serious for concern about what happens to *me*. We have to try to save these girls – Sally especially. If anything has happened to her I will never be at peace with myself again.'

In the Falmouth house that served as a small police station, the constable on duty did not appear to take very seriously Captain Eva's request to see a senior police officer. There was little sense of urgency, until a man came in who introduced himself to her as the 'Superintendent of Police'.

It was now Eva realised why it had been so difficult to convince the constable that a serious crime was taking place in the town. The Superintendent told her the Falmouth police force comprised only himself and two constables. His own somewhat grandiose title meant nothing. Before being placed in charge of the borough police 'force', he had been the town's watchman!

Eva was dismayed. Sally and the other girls had probably been taken to a boat crewed by tough Belgian seamen. It would take more than three policemen and a handful of Salvation Army officers to prevent them from setting sail.

However, the 'superintendent' persuaded her to tell him what was happening. She had hardly begun the story before he interrupted her.

'Ah! We heard something about such goings-on and realised it was too much for us to handle. As soon as I learned about it, I sent a telegraph message off to Cornwall's Chief Constable. He's sent men to help and more are following.'

'Thank heaven for that!' exclaimed Eva. Then, puzzled, she asked, 'But . . . how did you come to hear about what was happening?'

'I think the best person to answer all such questions would be that Inspector Lovat, from Plymouth.'

'Ian Lovat is here, in Falmouth?' Eva's bewilderment increased with each piece of information she received from the Falmouth policeman.

'That's right, he's at Customs House, down on the quay. I'll take you there.'

Outside, Eva gave the briefest explanation to Zulu Joe as they followed the policeman through the town, heading for the dockside area.

On the way they learned that only six or seven county policemen had so far arrived in the town. Eva said nothing, but she believed it would be far too small a force to prevent the Belgians from carrying off the girls.

The party had almost reached its destination when they became aware of a great commotion, somewhere along the sea front, to the south of the customs quay.

'That sounds as though it's coming from where the Belgian fishing boat is moored,' the Falmouth policeman commented. 'Inspector Lovat was very interested in that boat. I believe he sent two of the Bodmin men to watch it.'

'If it's a Belgian boat, that'll be where the girls will have been taken,' said Eva, alarmed by the disturbing sound that could be heard. 'Let's get down there quickly and see if we can help.'

She began to run, with Zulu Joe at her side. This in itself was hazardous. The quay was ill-lit and small boats, piles of rope and other obstructions were strewn all about them.

The Falmouth policeman paused to light a bull's-eye lantern he was carrying, before hurrying after the others.

Suddenly, as they neared the spot where the *Astique* was moored, they heard the sound of a shot – then another! Eva went cold. If the Belgians were carrying arms there was no chance at all of preventing them from carrying out their intentions.

It seemed others thought so too. The shouting ceased, although excited voices could still be heard.

Just then, someone came running towards them. The policeman shone his lamp ahead and the light picked out a rough-looking man dressed as a fisherman.

'Stop! Stop right where you are!' The policeman ran to obstruct the fleeing man, but the man, desperate to get away, struck and knocked the policeman to one side. The man continued running.

The policeman's lantern had fallen to the ground, but the darkness did not deter Zulu Joe. He succeeded where the police 'superintendent' had failed. The would-be escapist was wrestled to the ground. He fought furiously and although he could not escape from his silent captor, he succeeded in regaining his feet.

Zulu Joe grappled with him and both men staggered to the edge of the quay.

'Look out!'

Eva's cry of warning came too late. Both men fell from sight and there was a loud splash as they hit the water.

By now, the Falmouth policeman had regained his feet. Locating his lantern, he relit it. Standing at the water's edge, Eva called, 'Quick. Bring the lantern here.'

The policeman joined Captain Eva and, in the yellow light of the lantern, they were able to pick out Zulu Joe, treading water.

There was no sign of the other man.

'Over here.' The policeman shone the lamp towards a metal ladder, secured to the quay wall, and Zulu Joe swam in that direction.

When Zulu Joe was safely ashore, the policeman swept the water with the beam from his lamp, but there was no sign of the other man.

'Let's get along to the boat and see what's happening there,' said Eva. 'I'm concerned for the girls. Those gun shots . . .'

'Be careful,' warned the policeman. 'If someone is shooting, it will be dangerous for you.'

'Whoever it is, it can't be the Belgians,' Eva pointed out. 'Otherwise the man who fell in the water wouldn't have been so anxious to make his escape. Let's go and find out what's going on.'

At the boat's moorings there was a number of men carrying lanterns, which were shone in the direction of the new they approached. Among those about the boat was a group of red-jacketed Royal Marines – and these were the men who were carrying arms.

Captain Eva could not imagine how British Marines had become involved in what was going on. However, it was evident they had played an important part in turning the tables in favour of the policemen.

'So you've finally put in an appearance!' Ian Lovat's words were directed at Eva from the darkness behind one of the lanterns. 'It's a good job we were here, or your little plan was likely to have gone horribly wrong.'

Captain Eva ignored the implied criticism in his words. There were a great many questions she wanted to ask him, but for now she posed the one that was uppermost in her mind. 'Do you have the girls?'

'We have. They're all a bit dozey – from some form of drug, I suspect. A few are still only semi-conscious but as far as I can make out they haven't been harmed. We won't know for certain until they are able to speak sensibly to us.'

'Is Sally with them?'

'She is.'

'Thank God!' It came out as a mere whisper, but the two words could not have been more meaningful. 'Where is she now? Can I see her?'

'Of course.'

Despite his earlier implied criticism, Ian knew exactly how Eva was feeling. In fact, he knew far more about the real person who chose to hide behind the Salvation Army uniform than she realised.

'She's being taken care of by Ethan.'

'ETHAN?!' For just a moment, Captain Eva thought the Plymouth detective had gone out of his mind. 'But . . . he's been lost at sea.'

'Well, now he's been found. You've got a whole lot of catching up to do, Eva.'

It was the first time he had used her Christian name without preceding it with her Salvation Army rank, but she hardly noticed.

'Is Sally aware that he's with her?'

'I don't think so. For some reason, she appears to be far more heavily drugged than the others.'

'That would be Mother Darling's doing. She was at the house where the girls were taken. She must have recognised Sally. The poor girl.'

'It would have been far more serious than "poor girl" had we not got on to this in time. You shouldn't have tried to do this on you own, Eva. It could have had disastrous results for everyone concerned.'

'I do realise that now,' she admitted, displaying an uncharacteristic humility. 'But how did you learn about it?'

'We've been keeping watch on Mother Darling for some time. She was seen to take a train from Plymouth, bound for Falmouth – and here we are. Unfortunately, we don't appear to have captured Sid Darling, although I'm convinced he was involved in this too. Unfortunately, one of the men from the boat managed to escape; I have an uncomfortable feeling it might have been him.'

'I doubt if he's still alive – whoever he is.' Eva pointed to Zulu Joe who was dripping water and shivering. She told Ian Lovat of the fight.

'It's a great pity we didn't get him, if only to be certain who he is. It might have been one of the Belgians for all we know. All we'll ever know, perhaps.'

Zulu Joe touched Eva's arm. When she looked at him, he shook his head. Touching his lips, he pointed first to the Salvationist, then to the policeman.

'Zulu Joe is saying the man he fought with spoke English.'

'Then it probably *was* Sid Darling. I'll have boats put out to see if we can find him – or his body. If he's drowned it will save everyone a great deal of trouble.'

'At least we've recovered Sally safely. You shouldn't have let her take part in your scheme, Captain Eva. It was only the sheerest luck that she isn't on her way to Belgium right now – with Sid Darling.'

Ethan came out of the darkness to direct his fairly gentle criticism at Eva.

When she had hugged him tightly and said how happy she was that he was safe, Eva said, 'I'm sorry about what happened to Sally, Ethan – but, as you said, she is safe, although I still don't know what's going on right now. It seems to become more confusing by the minute.'

'It's becoming clearer,' said Ethan. 'One of the policemen speaks French. He's been questioning the Belgians. It seems Sid Darling *did* come here as a member of the crew of the Belgian fishing boat. When Inspector Lovat signalled for the Marines to come in and help arrest the crew of the fishing boat, he made a bolt for it. We'll talk about the rest later. I want to get back to Sally. I don't think she'll come round for another hour or more, but I mean to be with her when she does.'

83

Sally came to her senses slowly and painfully, in a darkened room. As she had never been intoxicated, she did not recognise her symptoms as those of a hangover, exacerbated by the drug that had been added to the wine.

She groaned. Her head felt as though knuckles were being kneaded into her temples and waves of nausea threatened to overwhelm her.

She was about to groan once more, consciously this time, when memories flooded back. She remembered the Falmouth house – and Mother Darling forcing drugged wine down her throat. There were less clear memories of a bumpy and uncomfortable ride in a van.

That had been her final memory. The knowledge that she and the others were being taken somewhere. Probably to a boat that would transport them to a brothel in Europe . . . But where was she now? Surely they had not arrived at their destination? She could not believe she had been unconscious for such a length of time.

Feeling about her, she ascertained she was lying on a bed. She could also hear voices somewhere in the distance. Sally could not understand what they were saying and for a few moments imagined they were talking in a foreign language. If so, she *must* have arrived at the European destination.

Then, as Sally focused on the voices, she realised she could not understand what they were saying because they were coming from some distance away. Probably from a downstairs room. It was distance not another language that made it impossible for her to understand the conversation.

Despite the throbbing pain in her head, Sally tried hard to concentrate on the voices. They were definitely speaking English.

That at least was something in her favour. If she could make good her escape she would not be in a strange country. She might be able to call for help from someone nearby.

There was a moment of panic as she imagined the voices to be those of Sid and Mother Darling and their accomplices.

The thought brought her sitting upright much faster than was wise in her present condition. The increased pain in her temples made her flinch, but her main thought now was of escape.

Although the room was in darkness, light was showing beneath the door. She would need to be cautious when she left the room.

She was summoning the will-power to swing her feet to the floor when she heard footsteps outside the room. They were followed by the sound of a hand on the door latch.

Flinging herself back on the bed, Sally closed her eyes and lay perfectly still.

Someone crossed the room towards her. Sally was aware that a light, probably from outside the room, was shining across her face. She tried to relax and breathe as though still unconscious.

She sensed it was a man standing beside the bed. He remained in the room for so long, she began to fear it would not be possible to keep up her pretence for very much longer. Then, to her great relief, he tiptoed away.

He had reached the door when a voice called from downstairs, 'Is there any sign of her coming round yet?'

The voice sounded familiar, but she was unable to identify it immediately.

The door closed before the man who had been in her room

replied, 'She's still unconscious. I'm worried about her, Joe. I think I'll ask Captain Eva to call out the doctor again.'

The man who had called from the ground floor spoke once more. He did not think it necessary to call out the doctor, who would surely only repeat what he had said before – but Sally was not listening. She had recognised the voice of the man who had come to her room.

It was Ethan – and he was talking to his brother Joe.

For the briefest of moments, Sally wondered if she was hallucinating. Then, convinced she was not, she cried, 'Ethan! ETHAN!'

Scrambling from the bed, Sally headed towards the strip of light visible beneath the door. She was far more unsteady than she had realised. Veering seriously to one side of the door, she had great difficulty correcting her course.

'ETHAN!'

As she called to him once more, she crashed into a chair and stumbled to the floor. There was a moment of panic when she feared Ethan had not heard her and would go away from her again.

Then the door was flung open and Ethan stood in the doorway. It took a moment for him to locate her. Then he found her and was holding her close to him.

To her great distress, Sally suddenly began crying uncontrollably. As Ethan held her, she sobbed, 'I'm sorry, Ethan. Sorry we quarrelled before you went away.'

'Quarrelled? What quarrel? Anyway, it doesn't matter. Nothing matters now we're together again. Nothing at all.'

Sally clung to him, only vaguely aware people were crowding in the doorway of the bedroom. They were people she knew, but she could think of no explanation for them all being here together.

She recognised Ian Lovat, Captain Eva, the reporter from the London newspaper, whom she had met briefly in Plymouth, Joe Shields, Zulu Joe . . .

There were others too. Some in the uniform of the Salvation Army, others were policemen.

It was all too confusing. Sally clung to Ethan ever more tightly.

There would need to be lengthy explanations later. For now it was enough to have Ethan with her. Safe and well – and *real*. Explanations could wait.

In the early hours of the morning, many of those who had participated in the events of the night were crowded in the sitting room of the Falmouth Salvation Army chief, piecing together all that had happened.

Ethan's story had already been told. Ian Lovat's too. He had been aware of the pitifully small complement of the Falmouth police force, and had feared reinforcements from the County Police would not arrive in time. He had decided to take advantage of the admiral's offer to call on the services of the Royal Marines on board the vessel that had brought him to Falmouth, a decision that had decisively turned the tide of events in his favour. When the girls were seen to arrive on the jetty in the van, a signal had been flashed to the warship, moored offshore.

Minutes later, the Marines, who had been waiting in a steam launch, swarmed over the side of the Belgian steam-trawler. The fierce fight that ensued ended when the Sergeant of Marines ordered his men to fire two warning shots into the night air.

The girls, still suffering from the effects of the drugged wine, had been taken to the homes of various Salvation Army members.

Five of them, including Sally and Connie, were carried to the Salvation Army chief's home.

All had awakened frightened and bewildered. Recovering now, they sat with their rescuers and listened in wide-eyed silence to the story of how close they had come to being carried off to a life of degradation.

The girls felt great relief that the plans of Sid Darling and his colleagues had been foiled, but relief was accompanied by disappointment. They had left their homes in expectation of a new and more fulfilling life. Now their hopes had been dashed. For some, there could be no return to the life they had previously known.

One such girl was Connie.

The sharing of experiences came to an end when Eva told

of her part in setting the wheels in motion in a bid to trap the would-be abductors. It was a plan that had been foiled by Mother Darling's appearance on the scene.

'What will happen to Mother Darling now?' asked Sally. 'Will she be put in prison for the part she's played?'

'Probably not,' admitted Ian Lovat. 'The men sent to arrest her say she's offered to turn Queen's Evidence and testify against her accomplices – including her son. I'd like to see her put away, but Sid Darling is my first priority. I have a dying declaration, given to me by Rachel. It will stand up in court, but we're going to need Mother Darling's evidence if we're to convict everyone of the charges that will be brought against them.'

Standing up, Ian Lovat stretched wearily. 'I think we all ought to go off and try to snatch some sleep now. There aren't many hours left in the night and we all have a busy day ahead of us tomorrow.' Smiling at Eva, he said, 'For a while I thought things were going to go wrong, but in the end everything happened just the way it should.'

'Thanks to you,' Eva admitted ruefully. 'If you hadn't become involved it would have been a total disaster. It's taught me a very serious lesson.'

'I'm glad it's all ended well for everyone,' the reporter from the London newspaper chipped in. 'As far as I'm concerned, I have the story of a lifetime. My editor is going to be delighted. We have a story that will be the envy of all the London newspapers. I have no doubt at all it will influence the men who make the laws of our country. The trade in young English girls may not come to an end immediately, but it will soon – thanks to all of you.'

'Talking of the law . . .' An inspector of the Cornwall Constabulary, who had been one of the last to arrive in Falmouth, now spoke to Ian Lovat. 'I have a man in custody in Bodmin who is asking to speak to you. He says he has some important information about a young Plymouth girl who died after an abortion.'

Aware of the glances that were exchanged between Ian Lovat, Captain Eva and Sally, the policeman continued, 'He obviously hopes you'll put in a good word for him, of course, but you might like to see him.'

'I most certainly would,' said Ian Lovat. 'What's his name?'

'Sanderson,' replied the Bodmin policeman. 'Robert Sanderson.'

84

Sally had been shaken by the news that her father was in custody, suspected of stealing from the home of his former employers, but it did not entirely surprise her.

She felt guilty that she had no wish to see him, but now that Ethan had been returned to her, she did not want to let him out of her sight. She was even reluctant to leave him when everyone snatched a couple of hours' sleep in the house of the Falmouth Salvation Army officer.

Once morning came and the young couple were reunited, Sally never left Ethan's side. With Captain Eva, Zulu Joe, Joe Shields and the Salvation Army 'soldiers', they caught a train first to Truro, then a connection to Plymouth.

Also with them was Connie.

Meanwhile, Ian Lovat was travelling in a carriage to Bodmin with the Cornwall Constabulary police inspector. Once there, he would learn exactly how much Robert Sanderson knew about the fatal abortion performed upon Rachel.

When the large party arrived in Plymouth, Ethan and Joe were anxious to be reunited with their mother. Sally had told them of Doris's refusal to accept that she had lost her entire family, despite the evidence of the wreckage found by the Lowestoft boat. Sally accompanied the brothers to their home.

Connie wanted to go with her new-found friend, but Eva took

her instead to the Refuge. Here they encountered an anxious Grace, who was still desperately trying to learn what Sally and Captain Eva were up to, and was within an hour of making an arranged sea voyage to Falmouth in a fishing boat.

The Salvation Army captain gave Grace a résumé of the previous night's activities and introduced her to the young orphan who had accompanied her to the Refuge.

Looking sympathetically at the small and rather frail young girl who was standing forlornly in the centre of the Refuge kitchen, Grace said, 'It's lucky for you Captain Eva decided to take action when she did, young lady. If she hadn't set out to rescue you from the likes of Sid Darling, no one else would have. She's an angel in her own right, I'm telling you.'

Embarrassed by such fulsome praise, Eva said, 'Connie was befriended in the first place by Sally. It seems Sally looked after Connie as best she could, right up until the time Mother Darling recognised her and had drugged wine poured down her throat until she passed out.'

'Where's Sally now?' asked a concerned Grace. 'Why hasn't she come back here with you? Is she all right?'

When Eva told her of Ethan's return and of the part he had played in the rescue, Grace said emotionally, 'I'm so happy for her – happy for them both, of course, but especially for Sally. Perhaps life will be good to her now. For a while, at least. It's no more than she deserves, poor little soul. When you see her, tell her to come and see me. I've an apology to make.'

To Connie, she said, 'If Sally's taken you under her wing, you've found yourself a staunch friend, young lady. One who'll stand by you, come hell or high water.'

She looked at the vulnerable young girl and her heart went out to her. 'You look as though you could do with a bit of fattening up. I believe you were a workhouse girl?'

Connie nodded unhappily.

'Never mind, you'll soon put that behind you and we'll see what can be done to put a bit of meat on your bones.' Speaking to Eva, she said, 'Let her come home with me for now. I'll bring her back to the Refuge later on. Come along, young Connie. I'll introduce you to my husband. You can tell him all that Sally's been up to. Got a soft spot for her, has Alfie. Always has had, right from the first. He'll take to you too, I know he will . . .'

Watching the two go off together, Eva knew that Connie had already gone part of the way towards filling the place in Grace's heart left empty by the death of Rachel.

Thoughts of Rachel saddened Eva. She consoled herself with the thought that she – or, to be more truthful, Ian Lovat – had prevented the same thing happening to other innocent young girls. However, until the fate of Sid Darling had been established, there was always a strong possibility that such a thing would happen yet again, somewhere else in the country. This despite the countrywide publicity that would be given to recent events by editor Carl Milton and the *Mayfair Gazette*.

When Ethan and Joe walked through the door of their Barbican home, Doris Shields' happiness was complete. There were tears and excitement all round.

Eventually Henry Shields asked his sons about the Belgian fishing boat they had gone to investigate. Ethan and Joe filled their family in on all that had happened in Falmouth and of the part Sally had played.

Now it was Sally's turn to receive the attention of the whole family. The role of heroine was an embarrassing one for her, and she tried to pass it off by speaking of her happiness and disbelief when she came to her senses in the bedroom of the Falmouth house and realised Ethan was alive and in the room with her.

As she watched the looks that passed between the young couple, and their evident unwillingness to stray more than an arm's length from each other, Doris realised it would not be long before she would lose Ethan again. This time for good.

She thought he could not have found a girl she liked more.

Then Sophie insisted that Sally be shown the presents the men had bought on their way home in the *Eastern Prince*.

The remainder of the day was very happy for everyone in the house. It was a day Sally would always remember: the day when she truly felt she had been accepted as a full member of a large and close family.

85

Robert Sanderson was arrested when he returned to the woods beside Lanhydrock House. His intention had been to retrieve the stolen property hidden there on the night of the fire that had almost completely destroyed the great house.

The fire had also resulted in the death of Lady Robartes a few days afterwards. She had never recovered from the shock of seeing her precious home destroyed.

The hidden hoard had been discovered by one of the Lanhydrock Estate gamekeepers. He had promptly reported his find to the Bodmin police, who had kept watch on it, ever since.

Fortunately for Sanderson, the police believed the property to have been stolen by someone else, during the confusing aftermath of the fire.

Sanderson's, story was that when he heard news of the fire, he had returned to view the damage caused to the great house where he had been employed for so many years. Aware that he would not be welcomed by the family, he did not take the most public route. Instead, he made his way there through the woods.

As he neared Lanhydrock, he claimed to have heard someone approaching along the path towards him. Not wishing to be seen, he sought a hiding place off the path. In so doing, he stumbled across the cache of stolen property. Unsure of what to do about it, he had left it there.

It was only after giving the matter a great deal of thought that he had decided to return to the wood, collect the stolen property and take it to the police station. After all, he had worked for the family for a great many years. He still felt a certain duty towards them . . . !

The policeman interrogating Sanderson pointed out that when he was arrested he had been pushing the sweep's cart in the opposite direction to the nearest police station, which was in Bodmin.

Sanderson's response was that he was too embarrassed to take it to the county town, where the circumstances of his dismissal would be known. He was taking it instead to Lostwithiel, a small town to the south of Lanhydrock.

'Do you believe him?' Ian Lovat put the question to the Cornish inspector as they drove to Bodmin in a light carriage belonging to the Cornwall Constabulary.

'No,' the other man replied firmly. 'I believe the man to be a liar. Unfortunately, he is a plausible liar. I have no evidence against him of theft and I think he might convince a jury he is telling the truth.'

'He's certainly a very nasty piece of work,' commented Ian Lovat. 'He was seen with a chimney sweep in Plymouth some time before the fire. They were overheard planning something that might well have been a robbery at Lanhydrock – but that, of course, would have indicated prior knowledge of the fire!'

'Do you know where this chimney sweep is now?' asked the inspector.

Ian Lovat shook his head. 'He hasn't been seen for a week or two. But have a word with the Lanhydrock servants. Sanderson wasn't particularly liked by the household staff. They might be able to tell you something. Someone might have some useful information about either Sanderson or the sweep.'

'What about your own case? This young girl who died from the abortion? News of it reached us at the time. It was a very nasty business indeed. I don't want to put your inquiries in jeopardy by upsetting Sanderson at this stage.'

'We don't know yet whether he has any useful information to

give me. If he has, I'll get it in writing to make certain he doesn't try to retract at some future date.'

Robert Sanderson was desperately unhappy at being locked up in the Bodmin police station. Ironically, he was in the same cell occupied by Sally during her stay there.

His first question to Ian Lovat was whether, by giving him information about the abortion, the Plymouth inspector could arrange for him to be given bail.

'No,' Ian Lovat replied without preamble. 'If you have information about a serious crime, it is your *duty* to tell me about it. If you do, I'll make certain you are given full credit for your help when you are brought before the court.'

He looked unsmilingly at Sanderson, remembering the way this man had behaved towards Sally. 'On the other hand, if you know something about the abortion carried out on this unfortunate young girl and *don't* tell me, I will make it my business to ensure the judge is told about that too. He'll no doubt bear it in mind when he comes to sentence you.'

'That's not fair,' protested Sanderson. 'I'm not guilty of anything. All I was doing when I was stopped in the wood was trying to help the police—'

'I don't want to hear anything about the offence for which you've been arrested. That's between you and the Cornwall police. I'm here because I was told you have something to tell me. If you have, I'm ready to listen. If not, I'll go.'

Sanderson licked his lips uncertainly. 'Do I have your promise that you'll put in a good word for me if I tell you what I know?'

'I've already said so. But I don't deal in rumour or surmise. It will need to be something I can use – and I'll want it in writing. Now, what do you wish to tell me?'

Avoiding the eyes of the uncompromising detective, Sanderson said, 'The abortion was carried out by Clara Flood. She lives in Jed's Alley – that's at the back of Pin's Lane.'

'What number – and how do you know about it?'

'It's number three and it's where I'm living – or was living – before I was brought in here. I know about it because I saw the girl there with Clara. I'd seen her before with Sally – that's Sally Harrup. I know the room where the abortion was carried out, too. It's upstairs, next to mine. I had a peep inside once, when Clara was out of the house. There's not much in there except for a bed with a rubber sheet on it, a few bowls and some things that look like knitting needles.'

'I see.'

Ian Lovat had been watching the other man as he spoke. He was convinced Sanderson was telling the truth, but he still asked, 'Is there anyone else in the house who can corroborate what you've just told me?'

Sanderson hesitated, but for only a few moments. 'Yes, Devonport Lil. She has the other room upstairs, the one over-looking the backyard. She told me she'd seen the girl leaving. Doubled over in pain she was, according to her. She said she knew what had been happening to the poor kid and declared it wasn't the first girl she'd seen there, not by a long chalk. But she said that this one was the youngest she'd ever known Clara do it to.'

'All right, I'll have a word with this Devonport Lil. When we've got all this down in writing I'll tell Inspector Rowe you've been helpful. I suggest you are just as forthcoming with him. You'll find it the best policy in the long run.'

Later, when Ian Lovat had recorded Robert Sanderson's statement and left the Bodmin police station, the ex-Lanhydrock butler thought about the advice he had been given, by the Plymouth detective inspector.

He knew he could tell the Bodmin superintendent nothing. If the Cornish police knew the truth of what had happened at Lanhydrock, he would never be a free man again.

86

On his return to Plymouth, Ian Lovat reported to his chief constable the results of his foray in Cornwall. Also present in the office was Percy Mallett, the chairman of the Police Authority.

Although the man Ian Lovat had travelled to Falmouth to arrest had succeeded in avoiding arrest, the circumstances of his escape left it doubtful he was still alive. Apart from this setback, the outcome of the detective inspector's actions was considered to be highly satisfactory.

An organisation that had shipped many hundreds of young English girls to the brothels of Europe had been broken up and its latest operation foiled. Many arrests had been made and a report praising the efficiency of the Plymouth detective force was to be published in a national newspaper.

The chief constable and Percy Mallett were both extremely pleased with the results, and Ian Lovat left the office with the praises of his chief constable ringing in his ears. He was accompanied by the chairman of the Police authority.

'What will happen to those unfortunate young women now?' Percy Mallett asked, as the two men walked along a corridor in the police headquarters.

'Some will stay with the Salvation Army in Falmouth until they decide what they want to do. Others came to Plymouth. No doubt those who have homes will want to return to them.

One of them – the youngest – has no one at all. She returned to Plymouth with Captain Eva.'

'No doubt I'll hear all about her in due course, from my niece, Grace,' said Percy Mallett, smiling wryly.

'I'm quite certain you will, sir. She has a very similar background to Rachel and isn't dissimilar in appearance.'

'Oh dear! I do hope she won't bring similar sorrow with her. Grace is always seeking someone to take the place of her daughter Mary. She has never got over the tragic loss. But how about this other girl, the plucky young thing who went into the hornets' nest, purporting to be a candidate for domestic service?'

'Sally had a very lucky escape,' admitted Ian Lovat. 'One of the women involved in procuring the girls is Mother Darling – the mother of Sid Darling. She was at the house the girls were taken to in Falmouth and, unfortunately, she recognised Sally as the girl who had foiled their previous operation. Sally was forcibly plied with far more drink and drugs than the other girls and was deeply unconscious when we rescued her. I shudder to think what would have happened had we not got to her when we did. She'd have been at the mercy of Sid Darling. That's a fate I wouldn't wish upon man or beast.'

'Is there some way we can officially recognise this young girl's courage?' asked Percy Mallett. 'Perhaps award her a substantial sum of money? I understand she is an orphan and in somewhat straitened circumstances. Such an award would be a practical and popular gesture.'

Ian Lovat shook his head. 'It would indicate official approval of what was basically a most irregular adventure. I am very fond of Captain Eva and a great admirer of her dedication and determination, but I cannot officially condone a scheme that carried with it such a high degree of risk. I doubt if the Salvation Army itself will pat her on the head and tell her how well she's done once the full story is made public.'

Ian Lovat was correct in his assessment of the reaction of the Salvation Army towards Eva's actions.

When the detective inspector called at the Refuge, the day after his return to Plymouth, he learned that Eva had been summoned to the Salvation Army's London headquarters.

He had called at the Refuge to take a statement from Sally about the events leading up to Rachel's death. Once his official business was complete, Ian Lovat expressed disappointment that Eva was not at the Refuge. He had that morning received a very important letter and wanted to discuss its contents with her.

'Did she give you any indication of when she was likely to be back?' he asked Sally.

'I don't think she knew. I suppose it depends on how much of a ticking-off they decide to give her. Did you know they told her she wasn't to go ahead with her plan to catch Mother Darling and the others?'

'She didn't tell me in so many words, but I would have been very surprised had they agreed to go along with it. I think she organised it by having those she involved believe it had the sanction of their headquarters. It could be very serious for her. The Salvation Army shows a great deal of understanding towards the sinners with whom it works, but I'm afraid it doesn't extend to those within its own ranks who fail to toe the official line.'

'What do you think will happen to her?' Sally asked anxiously. 'Will they punish her in some way?'

'I'm afraid I can't give you an answer to that.'

As he gathered up the papers on the table in front of him, Ian Lovat smiled. 'However, I'm sure we'll be able to work something out for her.'

87

Eva was not having a happy time in London. She had caught the early-morning train from Plymouth, arriving at the headquarters of the Salvation Army soon after noon.

Unfortunately, Lieutenant Commissioner Bolt, the senior staff officer who would interview her, had just gone to lunch. Eva waited outside his office for more than two hours before finally being shown inside.

Seated on the far side of a large leather-topped desk, the senior officer wasted no time on niceties.

Frowning his disapproval, he pushed a newspaper across the desk towards her. 'I presume you have read this, Captain Cassington?'

Bold black headlines stared up at her. 'SALVATION ARMY LASSIE EXPOSES PROCURERS OF YOUNG GIRLS'. Beneath the banner headlines, somewhat smaller but still bold in typeface, it declared, 'Plymouth Salvation Army lass rescues young English girls, bound for the brothels of Europe'.

'I bought a paper at Paddington railway station and read it while I was waiting for you to finish your lunch,' said Eva, refusing to be browbeaten by the very senior Salvation Army officer.

Lieutenant Commissioner Bolt flushed angrily. 'Do you remember standing before me only a few days ago and being told categorically that you were not to go ahead with this foolhardy idea of yours?'

'We discussed the matter, yes.'

'Yet you went ahead, even though you were aware it would most likely bring the reputation of the Salvation Army into disrepute. Why?'

'I disagree that it has brought us into disrepute. Indeed, I believe it has shown everyone the Salvation Army not only cares about such matters, but that we are prepared to take action to put things to rights.'

'It is not a part of your duty to assess public opinion, Captain Cassington. That is for officers of far more senior rank than yourself. Can you offer any other excuse for your blatant disregard of a direct order?'

'Yes. You are talking of orders, regulations and public opinion. My concern was with the lives of a number of young girls – real people – who would have ended up in brothels had something not been done to prevent it happening.'

'Did you not consider passing your information to the police, whose duty it is to deal with such matters?'

'When did the police last act on something *you* told them, Commissioner Bolt?'

The senior Salvation Army officer flushed again. He had recently been arrested by police after he had complained to them of missile throwers at an open-air meeting.

'You prevaricate, Captain. When you were last in London you were told not to proceed with the plans you laid before me. Despite that, you went ahead with a scheme that was foolhardy, ill conceived – and in direct contravention of an order.'

Containing her anger, Eva said, 'With due respect, Commissioner Bolt, you *advised* me against the course of action I took. You did not *order* me to abandon it. Besides, had I done nothing, fifteen young girls would have been held prisoner in European brothels now. Instead, they have been given an opportunity to lead decent and useful lives – and reason to be everlastingly grateful to the Salvation Army.'

'Other means of rescuing these girls were open to you, Captain Cassington. Fifteen girls may be grateful, but many thousands, no, *tens* of thousands of decent people are shocked that the Salvation Army should ally itself with a newspaper in order to provide salacious reading for those who delight in such filth.'

'That was never my intention, Commissioner, nor that of the editor—'

Eva's protest was interrupted fiercely by the senior Salvation Army officer. 'The road to hell is paved with good intentions, Captain. I have no doubt your *intentions* were admirable. For that reason – and that reason alone – I will not dismiss you from the service. However, your blatant disregard of my order – or *advice*, call it what you will – has led to a great deal of criticism and adverse publicity for the Army. It comes at a time when it is least desirable – for reasons best known to those of us who are required to take such considerations into account when directing Army policy. It is because *we* and not *you* possess such knowledge that unquestioning obedience is required from all who serve as officers in the Salvation Army. You have fallen short of the standard expected of you, *Captain* Cassington. I regret this is the last occasion you will be addressed as such. I order that you be reduced to the rank of sergeant and transferred from Plymouth forthwith.'

Leaning back in his chair, Lieutenant Commissioner Bolt added, 'You may return to Plymouth now and settle your affairs. Details of your new appointment will reach you within a few days.'

Eva was shaken by the severity of her punishment. 'But . . . what of my work? The Refuge . . . and the girls there?'

'The work will be continued by an officer with suitable qualifications, *Sergeant* Cassington. It will perhaps provide you with another salutary lesson. Only the Lord Himself is indispensable.'

Eva left the office of the Salvation Army staff officer, her eyes burning with unshed tears. She felt she had been dealt with unfairly and with undue harshness.

The action taken to save the girls had been successful. True, it had come *close* to disaster, but that had been averted, thanks to Ian Lovat.

In the end, the Salvation Army had come out of it with

considerable credit. Besides, the trade in young girls needed to be exposed in such a manner. It would not be brought to an end by ignoring it and pretending it did not exist. That was hypocritical.

She was very upset too that she was being ordered to abandon the Refuge in Plymouth that she had worked so hard to create.

For the first time since joining the Salvation Army, she wondered whether her own ideals were shared by those who held high office.

88

The girls and women living at the Salvation Army's Plymouth Refuge were distraught at the news that Eva Cassington was to be demoted and transferred, and someone else would take over the running of the hostel.

She had called them all together the morning after her late-night return from London and broken the news to them.

'Why should they want to *punish* you for what you've done?' One of the girls saved from Falmouth expressed the bewilderment of the others. 'What would have happened to us if you hadn't rescued us? Where would we be now? If the Salvation Army doesn't care about ordinary working girls like us, then who does it care about?'

'It does care, Rose. Perhaps Lieutenant Commissioner Bolt has things wrong about this, but he isn't representative of the Army as a whole.'

'He's representative enough to send you away because you've saved us. If that's how much the Salvation Army cares then I for one don't want to know about it. I'll go back to my village and put myself "on the parish" if I can't get any work.'

'I don't think I want to stay here, either,' said one of the recently reformed prostitutes. 'It's been all right having you in charge, but I wouldn't want to stay here if they put the likes of that young lieutenant in your place – I'm talking about

the one who looked after the Refuge while you was away in
Falmouth. She behaved as though she was afraid she might
catch something if she came too close to any of us. She made
me feel really uncomfortable.'

'Please don't do anything foolish just yet. We'll talk about it
again when we've all had time to learn what is involved and
who's likely to take over from me here.'

'Whoever it is will be coming to an empty house,' commented
another of the girls. 'It's not just that they're making you leave
– although that's bad enough. It's because no one has thought
of *us*. What we might think – or even what's best for us. We
came here because we thought the Salvation Army *really* cared.
It seems it isn't them who cares, but you – and you're being sent
away because of it.'

'That isn't so. It really isn't,' Eva said desperately. 'The Salvation Army *does* care for you, because God cares. But the members
of the Salvation Army are only human. We don't always get it
right. But things will work out. I *know* they will.'

The support and loyalty of the girls in the Refuge upset and
alarmed Eva; she had no wish for all their hard work to be
undone. But worse was to come.

Later that afternoon, Captain Wardle came to the Refuge with
bad news.

Eva had called at his home the previous evening on her
return from London. He and his wife had still been up, having
conducted a late-night prayer meeting. Both had been deeply
distressed by the actions of Lieutenant Commissioner Bolt. They
and Eva had prayed together before she made her way back to
the Refuge.

While Eva had been talking to the girls that morning, Wardle
had received a visit from the owner of the house in which the
Salvation Army Refuge had been established. He had become
a frequent visitor to the Salvation Army's Plymouth headquarters and took a keen and generous interest in the work
being done there.

When he was told of Captain Eva's demotion and the reason
for it, he was incredulous. '*Demoted!* For organising the rescue of
those young girls? I've never heard of anything so preposterous!

She should have been promoted. Indeed, if the views held by this lieutenant commissioner are those of the commanders of the Salvation Army, someone should put her in charge of the whole organisation.'

The generous Methodist's anger simmered during the whole of his visit. As he was leaving, he said to Captain Wardle, 'The more I think about the treatment meted out to Captain Eva, the angrier I become. You will inform your London headquarters that, in view of their actions, I intend to repossess my house as soon as they can find alternative accommodation for the present residents. I allowed my house to be used as a refuge because I was fired with the enthusiasm of the Salvation Army. I now realise the enthusiasm came from Captain Eva and is not shared by those who shape the Army's policies. It is most regrettable.'

When the wealthy philanthropist had left the headquarters, Captain Wardle sat down and composed a telegraph message. When it was done, he sent it to Commissioner Hubble, the Salvation Army commissioner who had been visiting Plymouth when the house had been loaned to them as a refuge.

Then he went to call on his demoted colleague.

89

Ian Lovat had spent a very busy day investigating the movements of Robert Sanderson during the period leading up to his arrest. The inquiries were being made on behalf of the Cornwall Constabulary, but it gave him the opportunity to visit the house of Clara Flood without arousing her suspicions.

When the army widow left him alone upstairs in the house, so that he might search Sanderson's room, he took a look into the small room on the same floor.

All was exactly as had been described by Sanderson. The detective had no doubt at all that the room *was* used for carrying out abortions. All he needed now was a statement from Devonport Lil, confirming all that the ex-butler had disclosed.

He later discovered from one of his detectives, who had many informants working in the dock area, that he would need to wait a while before he could interview the dockyard prostitute. She was spending a couple of days and nights on board a Russian timber-carrying ship, currently unloading its cargo in the main Plymouth dock.

But for now, all Clara Flood would tell him was that her lodger was 'away from home on business'.

His day's work almost at an end, the detective returned to the police station and found Sally waiting for him.

Sally was feeling desperately sorry for her Salvation Army

friend and had gone to the Plymouth police station to tell Ian the result of Eva's visit to the Army's London headquarters.

'I think I might be able to cheer her up a little,' he said, when Sally ended her story with the statement that she had never seen Eva so unhappy.

On his way to the Barbican Refuge later that evening, Ian Lovat wondered whether the news he carried *would* be as well received as he hoped it might. He would soon know.

He was let into the house by a gloomy Zulu Joe, and was shown upstairs to the two rooms occupied by the Refuge's founder.

Eva was packing her things. She was pleased to see Ian and her expression showed it, but he thought she looked very tired and dispirited. She might even have been crying.

After listening to her account of her London interview with Lieutenant Commissioner Bolt, the sympathetic detective inspector said, 'I think the Salvation hierarchy is being very foolish. Most of the country's newspapers are carrying the story and are full of admiration for you and the Salvation Army. I even heard policemen in the station here in Plymouth praising what you did. It was indeed a superb achievement.'

Looking at the policeman to make quite certain he was not being sarcastic, Eva said, 'You know that isn't true, Ian. The whole rescue attempt came closer to disaster than anyone but you and I will ever know. Had you not taken the action you did, the girls, including Sally, would have been in Belgium now, and I would have been forced to resign.'

'Had you not been so determined to stamp out this trade, the girls would have been in Belgium anyway.' He stoutly defended her actions.

Ian suddenly seemed less certain of himself. He watched Eva packing for a while, then, nervously, he asked, 'Eva, will you stop what you're doing for a while? I want to talk to you.'

She looked up at him in surprise. 'Is it something to do with what happened in Falmouth?'

'Not entirely – although if it hadn't happened, I wouldn't be speaking to you like this at all.'

His words made very little sense to her, but she obligingly

put the rose-coloured glass vase she was wrapping down on a table and perched herself on the edge of a wooden chair.

The detective did not seem to find it easy to put the right words together. Eventually, he said, 'It's not only your life that is taking a new direction, Eva. Mine is too.'

'You don't mean that *you're* in trouble over what happened at Falmouth? That would be most unfair.'

An amused smile briefly crossed Ian's face. 'Not exactly. Do you remember that I was away from Plymouth for a few days a couple of weeks ago?'

Eva nodded. She had been hurt that Ian had not told her he would be away, or given her any explanation upon his return.

'I remember.'

'Well, I went out of the county – for an interview.'

'You mean you might be leaving Plymouth too?'

'That's right, but I didn't receive confirmation until yesterday.' Taking a deep breath, he said, 'I've been offered the post of Chief Constable of Brighton.' Ian Lovat tried to keep the pride he was feeling out of his voice, but he did not quite succeed.

'Ian! I'm delighted for you – but aren't you exceptionally young for such a responsible post?'

'Well, it's by no means the largest police force in existence, but they tell me I'll probably be the youngest chief constable in the country.' Pride crept back into his voice.

'Oh, I'm so happy for you, Ian. You are very, very clever – and you've kept it all so quiet! How could you?'

He shrugged, almost shyly. 'I couldn't say anything until it was confirmed. I thought I *might* be offered the post because the interview seemed to go so well, but I wanted to be absolutely certain before I told you.'

'And now you are! Well, we really should share such good news . . .'

She stood up, but Ian said, 'I haven't finished yet, Eva. Will you please sit down again?'

Surprised, Eva did as she was requested.

Nervously, he continued, 'If you could perhaps persuade your headquarters to send you to Brighton too, I'll ensure you have my full official backing to open a hostel for fallen women there.

I'll also be in a position to ensure the Salvation Army has the support of the police – *my* police. It would be a considerable step forward for them, Eva.'

'It would indeed,' agreed Eva. She spoke thoughtfully, then added excitedly, 'It would also mean I could continue the work I really believe in—' Suddenly her enthusiasm died away. 'But I'm in disgrace at the moment and have been demoted. They wouldn't agree. Lieutenant Commissioner Bolt certainly wouldn't give such a project his support.'

She frowned, lost in her own thoughts. When she looked up, she saw his expression. 'Is there more, Ian?'

'Yes, there is a condition to my offer. A rather important one. If you agree to all I have just said, I would want you to marry me first. To come with me to Brighton – as my wife.'

Eva's mouth dropped open and she looked at Ian with an expression of utter and genuine disbelief.

'I . . . why? Why would you want me to marry you?'

'For the very obvious reason that I love you.'

'You *love* me?' she echoed. 'But . . . you've never said anything about it to me before today.' She was thoroughly confused.

'I'm saying it now. Will you marry me, Eva?'

'I . . . I can't answer you right away. It's come as a complete surprise. I'll need to think about it.'

'When you have, you'll realise it's the right thing to do, Eva. It's right for both of us.'

'I don't know about that, Ian. I really don't. I'll need to be convinced.'

Ian's deep disappointment showed. Standing up, he avoided her eyes as he said, 'I know it must have come as a shock . . . I'm sorry, but please think about it, I beg you.'

He had reached the door and had opened it before she called out softly, 'You'll never be able to convince me if you're somewhere out there and I remain here. I *do* need convincing, Ian – and you're the only one who can do it . . .'

When Sally came up to Eva's room, to see if she could help her in any way, she was startled to find the door open and Eva and Ian inside the room, locked in a close embrace.

When Ian kissed Eva, Sally backed away and smiled happily. Everyone in the hostel had known for a very long time how the pair felt about each other.

It seemed that, at long last, they had found out too.

She wondered how it would affect the proposed transfer of the Salvation Army's ex-captain . . . ?

90

Early the next morning, Eva received a telegram. It had been sent from the London headquartes of the Salvation Army.

The source of the telegram came as a great surprise to Eva, but even before she opened the envelope she was startled to see it was addressed to 'Captain' Eva Cassington.

The contents were equally startling. The message read, 'Have read about your highly successful foray against those who have been carrying out the Devil's work. Well done! It is in the best traditions of the Salvation Army. Come to see me in London right away.'

The name at the bottom of the telegram was 'William Booth, General'.

It was a summons that could not be delayed. It was also highly exciting. Eva had been asked to meet with one of the greatest men in the country. The immense force of his personality was felt throughout the organisation he had founded, but this would be the first time Eva had met with him.

When she did, Eva believed she could put forward a convincing argument that would allow her to adapt the principles of the Plymouth Refuge to a similar establishment in Brighton.

What was more, Brighton was close enough to London for unfortunate women from the capital to be given sanctuary, free from the influences and temptations of a big city.

There was no time to inform Ian of this exciting new development. Instead, she scribbled a brief note to him and left it for Zulu Joe to deliver. If she hurried, she could catch a train and arrive at the Salvation Army headquarters by mid-afternoon. Then, if William Booth was able to see her right away, she could make the return journey and be back in Plymouth by midnight.

She also sent a telegram to London, telling the headquarters' staff that she was on her way but had no time to await a reply.

When Eva arrived breathlessly at Plymouth station, the train was about to leave. She barely had time to settle herself in a seat before the train pulled away with a series of bone-jerking movements.

She did not begin to compose herself until the train picked up speed. Soon the famous old town was far behind and smoke from the train was drifting over green fields and woodland.

Eva slept for much of the journey, but as the train drew slowly into Paddington station the excitement of London and her mission gripped Eva.

When the engineer closed off steam to the engine, the calls of the many vendors crowding the busy station could be heard more distinctly.

The station was as crowded as a busy market place. There was food of every description and in many guises. Trinkets, too, flowers, lace, handkerchiefs . . . the variety of merchandise on offer was endless.

The vendors crowded around each arriving train, offering their wares to disembarking passengers. Eager to sell, the prices they asked fell as the passengers they were pestering drew farther away from the train.

Few of the vendors bothered the uniformed Captain Eva. Salvation Army members were known to carry very little money on their person.

She took a crowded horse-bus to the headquarters, marvelling along the way, as she always did, at the mass of people that filled the streets of the capital of England.

But Eva's excitement suffered a major setback when she walked into the Salvation Army building and announced that she was there to see General Booth, only to be told that the

Salvation Army's founder had left the building not half an hour before. He had been called to Scotland for an emergency meeting with his commanders.

It was a great disappointment to Eva. The information that William Booth had arranged for her to see one of his most senior commissioners did nothing to cheer her.

She was to see Commissioner Hubble, whose friend was the Methodist benefactor who owned the building that housed the Refuge – the same man to whom Captain Wardle had sent his telegram.

He greeted Eva warmly. 'General Booth asked me to give you his deep apologies for not being able to greet you personally. He wanted to be here, I can assure you, but the emergency in Scotland had to take precedence. However, I can tell you he is well pleased with your actions. They have brought considerable credit to the Salvation Army. He would have told you that you have struck a bold and imaginative blow against evil men. The Lord will surely be smiling upon you.' The commissioner gave her a condescending smile that made her squirm.

'I don't think the lieutenant commissioner who interviewed me when I was last here would agree with you.'

'Lieutenant Commissioner Blunt was wrong,' was the commissioner's thin-lipped reply. 'The whole of the Army applauds you.'

'Then I think you should send a telegram of explanation to the benefactor who allowed his house to be used as a refuge,' said Eva. 'He has threatened to take it back because of Lieutenant Commissioner Blunt's actions.'

'Ah yes, the generous Mr Foote. Captain Wardle has already informed me of his views on the matter. I sent him a telegram only today. I assured him that we are all proud of you and the work you are doing on our behalf.'

Eva had the distinct impression that the Plymouth benefactor's threat had done more to determine her superiors' attitude towards her than her own actions had.

Although it was a matter she would have preferred to discuss with William Booth himself, she decided to bring up the subject of opening a refuge in Brighton.

The commissioner's initial reaction was one of enthusiasm, until he asked, 'This new chief constable . . . he is a Salvation Army member?'

'No, but he sympathises with our aims.'

The commissioner's expression changed. 'Oh! I am afraid that poses a great many difficulties – for you, in particular.'

'If you're concerned about the relationship between Ian Lovat and myself, you needn't worry. He has asked me to marry him before we leave Plymouth. He wants me to be his wife when we arrive in Brighton.'

'I don't think you understand. Marriage to him is out of the question, Captain. An officer of your rank – or of any other rank, come to that – is not permitted to marry outside the Army. It is one of General Booth's basic requirements of his officers. You must have seen it in the regulations he has issued. Besides, why move when you are running the Plymouth Refuge so successfully?'

The commissioner's reaction to her proposal dismayed Eva, but she attempted to give him an reasoned reply. 'I want to move first of all because a very special man has asked me to marry him. Another reason is that opening a second refuge gives us an opportunity to build on the success of the Plymouth experiment. Finally, it is a chance for the Army to forge a link, however tenuous, with the police. That is something that's very badly needed, everywhere in the country.'

'Quite true, Captain, but you have done well with your work in Plymouth. I think it would be best if you were to remain there and consolidate your success.'

Eva left the Salvation Army headquarters as frustrated as she had been after her previous visit.

She felt Commissioner Hubble had patronised her. She was also deeply disturbed by the disclosure of General Booth's regulation about suitable marriages for Salvation Army officers.

Eva realised it was something she should have known about. However, orders and regulations flowed from the pen of General William Booth on a daily basis, filling reams of notepaper. Those dealing with marriage had never been of any great interest to her – until now.

She realised she would have to reach a decision in the very near future about the course her life was to take. She would need to discuss it with Ian upon her return to Plymouth.

She thought deeply about the matter for much of the journey, as darkness overtook the train.

It was not until the train neared Plymouth that she stared out into the night and realised the answer had already been given to her.

It was the first time in her adult life that she had not turned to someone in the Salvation Army for the solution of a matter as important as this.

91

At about the time Captain Eva was being interviewed by the Salvation Army commissioner, Ian Lovat was arresting Clara Flood at her home.

He had finally succeeded in obtaining a witness statement from the elusive Devonport Lil. The prostitute had been arrested by a uniform policeman earlier that morning, on her way home from the docks. When she was approached by the policeman, she protested that she was singing because she was happy at having made a great deal of money during her sojourn on the Russian ship. As the explanation was accompanied by a great many unacceptable adjectives, the policeman declared she was 'drunk and disorderly' and arrested her.

It was not a particularly serious offence. When Ian Lovat explained to the station sergeant that Devonport Lil was a very important witness in the case against the abortionist who had killed young Rachel Green, it was agreed that a warning about her future conduct should suffice.

The prostitute had sobered considerably by the time Ian Lovat interviewed her in the cells beneath the police station, and was at first reluctant to help the detective inspector.

However, when he assured her she would be free to go home once the interview was over, she became more co-operative and agreed with him that it was time Clara Flood was called to account for her illegal activities.

She confirmed what Robert Sanderson had already told him. Lil *had* seen Rachel leaving the house after her abortion. The girl was obviously in considerable pain; she had gone on her way doubled over and clutching her stomach.

Once the prostitute had made up her mind to tell Ian Lovat what she knew, there was no stopping her.

When Ian Lovat asked why she thought Rachel had been given an abortion by Clara Flood, Devonport Lil said it was well known among her fellow prostitutes that her landlady carried out such 'operations'. It was also accepted that she was not a particularly skilful abortionist.

When Ian Lovat said that rumour was not acceptable in a court of law, Lil retorted bitterly, 'Believe me, it's not just rumour. It's what she does.'

'You have personal experience?' Ian Lovat asked sharply. Evidence from someone who had actually been aborted would ensure that Clara Flood was convicted.

'I can't tell you that, can I? If I did, I'd be in dock alongside Clara.'

Ian Lovat shook his head. 'In most cases you would – but not with this one. It's far too serious. I'll ensure you are given immunity from prosecution in return for giving evidence against her. She's a very dangerous woman, Lil. Unless we can put her out of the way, many more young girls are going to suffer the same fate as poor Rachel.'

'Some already have,' declared the prostitute. 'I'll tell you something else she does, too. When Mother Darling is asked to provide a young girl for someone "special", she gets Clara Flood to examine her to make sure she's all she's supposed to be. Usually the girl is sent to London afterwards, although sometimes they're shipped abroad. It's happened far more often than you'd believe.'

'Are you certain of this?'

'Absolutely. She told me once. It was the anniversary of the death of her husband – the first one. She got so drunk she didn't know what she was telling me. She bragged that she had become so expert at what she did she could check whether a girl was a virgin with the girl hardly knowing what she was up to.'

Devonport Lil sniffed derisively. 'I could believe her if it was me she was talking about. Some of the men I get these days are finished before I know they've begun. But what she does ain't right – nor what Mother Darling's up to, neither.'

Looking at Ian Lovat as though she expected him to argue with her, she said bitterly, 'That Salvation Army captain did what was needed when she went down to Falmouth after them girls. I wish there'd been someone like her around when I was first put on the game. I might have had a husband, kids and a nice little home now. Instead of that, they'll find me dead in an alleyway one of these nights and no one will care any more than they would if it was some stray cat.'

Devonport Lil had become decidedly maudlin and Ian Lovat decided it was time he brought the interview to an end.

'You've been extremely helpful, Lil. Would you let me put all this in writing and then sign it for me?'

'Why not? Go on, you write it down. Mind you, I'd be a whole lot happier if you was able to put Sid Darling away before it came to court.'

'We're not even certain he's alive right now. There's a possibility he was drowned when the Belgian fishermen were arrested at Falmouth.'

'No such luck!' Lil declared vehemently. 'He's alive all right. Not only that, he's right here in Plymouth. You ask Florrie! She used to be one of his girls,' she added, as though that would explain everything.

Ian Lovat was alarmed. If Sid Darling was indeed alive and in Plymouth, then both Sally and Eva were at risk.

'Are you sure of this?' he asked.

'I saw Florrie only last night. She's got one of the finest black eyes you'll ever see – and she's left two of her teeth somewhere down on the dockside. Sid Darling found her and demanded that she give him her money. When she was a bit slow in coughing up, he laid into her. She'll need to carry out all her work in the dark for a week or two. No one's going to fancy her if they see her in the light.'

'Right, Lil. Let's get this statement down. Then I've got some urgent work to do.'

Ian Lovat knew that Sally had returned to work for Grace Philpott only that morning. He would warn her not to stray from the main thoroughfares until Sid Darling had been arrested.

Eva too would need to be on her guard. Sid Darling also had a score to settle with her. He would speak to Zulu Joe and tell him not to let her out of his sight while the hunt for Darling was on.

92

Life had taken a definite upturn for Sally. The day before Grace had sent a message to Sally at the Refuge, asking her if she would come back to work at the pie shop.

Grace made it clear that both she and Alfie missed her. She suggested she should bring Connie with her, if the young girl would come. They would find work for her in the kitchen. It would be an opportunity for her to earn some useful pocket money.

She added that if Connie proved suitable, they could no doubt offer her permanent work, with an opportunity to live in over the shop.

Sally had smiled when she read this. She felt she knew Grace very well. The shop owner would already have decided she wanted Connie to work at the shop and live on the premises.

Alfie would be aware of it too. He would no doubt accept it in the same uncomplaining way he had accepted Rachel.

Nevertheless, Sally felt it would be a very good thing from everyone's point of view. Particularly good for Connie, and she deserved any good luck that might come her way.

Sally's own life was all she could want now that Ethan had returned to her. She wished the whole world could share her happiness.

The only cloud on her horizon was the knowledge that she

would need to leave the Refuge when Captain Eva moved on from Plymouth. She was neither a fallen woman nor homeless. She would need to move back to Pin's Lane. Sally did not relish the thought of returning there just yet. There were still too many memories of Ruth – and the unresolved question of the whereabouts of Sid Darling.

Sally thought about this and about Captain Eva as she walked to work with Connie that morning. She still thought of the Salvationist as 'Captain'. The demotion seemed decidedly unfair to Sally. Captain Eva had worked exceptionally hard to make the Refuge a success. She wondered what effect the demotion and move would have upon her new-found relationship with Ian Lovat?

Sally also felt a twinge of sadness about all that was happening to the man who was her father. She could never forget the attack he had made on her, but, in time, she felt she might be able to forgive him. When he attacked her he had been drinking. In such a befuddled state he *might* have confused her with her mother, as she would have been when he knew her . . .

'Do you *really* think I'll be useful enough in the shop to earn a wage? I don't know very much about cooking. I don't know very much about *anything*, really. Although I suppose I'm quite good at cleaning – pots and pans, and things like that.' Connie's voice broke into her thoughts as they neared the shop. Sally realised the younger girl had problems too.

'I don't think you need worry about earning your money. Grace won't expect you to know all about pie making. If you're prepared to work at it, she'll teach you everything you need to know. Besides, she's already taken quite a shine to you. You'll be all right, believe me.'

'I hope so. I'd like to be able to move in with her and Alfie. I'd feel . . . I'd feel as though I *belonged* somewhere then. Not that it isn't nice at the Refuge,' she hastened to add, 'but it's a bit like the workhouse in a way . . . only better, of course.'

Sally smiled. She knew what the young girl was trying to say in her slightly confused manner. She would have felt the same had Ethan not been around.

When they reached the pie shop, Grace took one look at the

two girls standing together, then suddenly opened her arms to Sally. She managed to get out the words 'I'm sorry!' before bursting into tears.

Alfie hurried from the kitchen at the sound of her crying. Looking highly embarrassed, he tried to comfort his wife, at the same time smiling sheepishly at each of the young girls in turn.

Regaining control of herself, Grace released Sally. Shaking herself free of Alfie's comforting arm, she blew her nose noisily before resuming her usual brisk and efficient manner.

'I never was one for hiding my emotions. They're better out than in, my mother used to say. Alfie and I are pleased to have you back with us, Sally. I should never have caused you to go away in the first place – but all that's in the past now. I don't think we need ever rake it up again. We've got a whole lot of deliveries to make this morning and there's plenty of work for us in the kitchen, Connie. Come with me. Have you ever done any cooking before . . . ?'

As Grace and Connie disappeared through the doorway to the kitchen, Alfie spoke quietly to Sally. 'I knew you'd be back with us again before too long, Sally. I'd just like to echo everything Grace said. It's nice to have you back.' As though embarrassed at voicing such emotions, Alfie added, 'Now I'd better get down to some work if you're going to have any pies to deliver. I doubt if anyone else is going to do very much today.'

Sally made a number of deliveries that day. The last one in particular took longer than expected. When she returned to the shop she found Ian Lovat there, plus Ethan, who was talking to an extremely agitated Grace.

'There you are, Sally! Thank the good Lord you're safe.'

Bewildered, Sally looked from one to the other. 'Safe? Why wouldn't I be?'

'We had reason to be concerned,' explained Ian Lovat. 'I've just been given information that Sid Darling is alive – and somewhere in Plymouth.'

Sally felt her stomach contract in sudden fear. 'You think he'll come looking for me?'

'I believe a number of people are at risk,' declared the detective, avoiding a direct answer. 'Particularly you and Captain Eva. She's gone to London today, so she's out of the way for the time being. I've told Zulu Joe to keep an eye on things at the Refuge. When I learned you were back at work, I came here to warn you and I met Ethan in the shop.'

'I called to invite you to our house tonight,' said Ethan, 'but if Sid Darling is around, I'd better come with you on your final deliveries.'

'Make certain you don't let her out of your sight,' warned Ian. 'If you have to go off somewhere – fishing, perhaps – then let me know. I'll arrange for a policeman to be somewhere near her all the time. Sid Darling is a very real threat.'

'Fortunately, I won't need to go fishing for a while,' said Ethan. 'Pa and Albert have gone to look at a steam-trawler today, but we won't be buying it until agreement has been reached between the insurance company and the navy. Pa reckons that will take a couple of weeks, at least.'

Although he was very concerned for Sally, Ethan thought that being in her company from dawn to dusk would not prove to be any hardship.

'Then that's all settled,' said Ian Lovat. 'I'm greatly relieved to know Sally will have you with her, Ethan. I'm almost as worried about Captain Eva. She sent me a note saying she hopes to return to Plymouth on the last train tonight. I'll make certain I'm there to meet her.'

93

When the train from London ended its journey at Plymouth railway station, shortly before midnight, Ian Lovat was one of about a dozen people waiting to meet the arriving passengers.

The manner in which Eva's face lit up when she saw him more than compensated for his half-hour wait on the draughty station.

Tucking her arm beneath his, she gave him a tired smile, 'This is an unexpected pleasure, Ian. I never expected you to be here to meet me this late at night.'

'I would have come anyway, to see how you got on in London, but there's a more sinister reason for my presence. Word is that Sid Darling is not only alive, but here, in Plymouth.'

Eva voiced her dismay. 'That's alarming news indeed. Has someone told Sally?'

Ian thought it typical of his companion that her first concern was not for herself. 'I've spoken to her and to Ethan. He's going to accompany her whenever she leaves the Refuge. I've also warned Zulu Joe to be especially vigilant – and to make certain you don't go out alone. I've got every policeman in Plymouth alerted to the fact that Sid Darling's here somewhere. I'm confident we'll catch him, but until we do we must all be on our guard.'

'I hope he's caught very soon – for everyone's sake.'

About to cross the road outside the station, they paused to

allow a hackney carriage to pass by. When they were safely on the far pavement, Ian said, 'Now tell me all about your visit to London. Are you *Captain* or *Sergeant* Eva? Equally important, did they agree you can start up another refuge when you marry me and come to Brighton?'

'No. I was hoping to meet General Booth. I feel he would have been more understanding. I'm certain he would have appreciated the long-term advantage such a plan was likely to bring to the Salvation Army. Unfortunately, he had to go to Scotland. I saw Commissioner Hubble instead. He felt the best thing I could do was remain here and continue running the Refuge.'

'Oh! That poses a problem.' Ian experienced a sinking feeling. He knew how much the Plymouth Refuge meant to Eva. She had the chance to open a second refuge in Brighton, but he was not convinced it could take the place of the present one. 'Couldn't you appeal to General Booth?'

Captain Eva shook her head. 'He wouldn't override a decision made by such a senior officer. Besides, I believe the two men are close friends.'

She paused, but he said nothing, sensing she had more to say. She had.

'That wasn't all, Ian. Commissioner Hubble called my attention to a regulation made by General Booth some time ago. It prohibits any serving officer from marrying outside the service.'

Ian came to a halt and turned her to face him. 'Does this mean you're not going to marry me?'

When he had asked her to marry him, she had promised to give him an answer when she had given due thought to what it would mean to her career and all the things she hoped to achieve in life.

She countered his question with one of her own. 'How serious were you about helping me to set up a refuge in Brighton when you become chief constable there?'

'As serious as any man could be who is desperate enough to do anything if it will persuade the girl he loves to marry him.'

She smiled at him and he was able to see that she was very,

very tired. The strain of her day was beginning to tell on her, both mentally and physically.

'Serious enough to help me start a refuge for women and girls from London – even if it doesn't have the backing of the Salvation Army?'

Ian looked at her with increasing excitement. 'Do you think you would be able to do that? Raise the money to get it off the ground – and meet all the expenses such a scheme would incur?'

'God doesn't only listen to the prayers of those who serve in the Salvation Army, Ian. He's answered my prayers before. I believe he will again. Besides, I would call on your friend, the editor of the *Mayfair Gazette*. It's a cause in which he takes a great interest. He would help me.'

'He wouldn't dare refuse – especially when I tell him what's at stake!' Ian could hardly contain his excitement. 'The answer to your question is an emphatic "yes"! I happen to believe in what you're doing. You would have my full backing to open a refuge in Brighton.'

'Then I will not only be following the path along which I believe the Lord has directed me – but also doing what my heart tells me I want to do. Yes, Ian, I'll marry you.'

'Even though it means you will have to leave the Salvation Army?'

She nodded. 'I wish it wasn't necessary, but I have thought long and hard about this on the journey from London. I believe Commissioner Hubble is wrong, but I can't change his decision. I will leave the Refuge here in Plymouth with regret, but I believe Captain Wardle's wife will be asked to take over the running of it. She can do it every bit as well as me. So, yes, I'll marry you. Just as soon as you can arrange it.'

A group of people walking along the pavement towards them were shocked to see a uniformed Salvation Army officer being taken in the arms of a man and kissed, in full public view.

Dividing in order to pass by, the happy couple heard one of the women whisper, 'It's disgusting. They must have been drinking – and her a Salvation Army officer, too!'

Grinning happily, Ian said, 'Do you know, I *do* feel as though

I've been drinking. I feel happily intoxicated. I love you, Captain Eva. We'll be married just as soon as it can be arranged.'

'I would like that,' she said. 'Now, let's shock them some more . . . !'

94

News that the now famous Captain Eva was to leave the Salvation Army and the Refuge she had founded was widely reported in the national newspapers.

Many made much of the fact that she was being forced to leave in order to marry the man she loved.

The newspapers most opposed to the Salvation Army ridiculed William Booth's insistence that his officers could only marry within the organisation he had founded.

A telegram from the London headquarters of the Salvation Army, in response to Eva's resignation, failed to give even a grudging acknowledgement of her work at the Plymouth Refuge. It merely approved the appointment of Captain Wardle's wife, Helen, as the Refuge's new warden – with 'immediate effect'.

Fortunately, the two women had become firm friends during Eva's period of duty in the town. Helen told Eva she might remain at the Refuge until her marriage to Ian Lovat had taken place.

The wedding was planned for a little over three weeks' time, a week before Ian was due to leave Plymouth and take up his new post as Brighton's Chief Constable.

One of the first things Helen Wardle did on taking over the Refuge was to call all the residents together.

The women and girls were dismayed that Captain Eva was to leave and some wanted to leave straightaway. However, the more level-headed among them, aware that Eva would have left anyway in order to be with her husband-to-be, decided they would wait to see what life was going to be like under a new regime.

Helen informed them she planned no changes to the daily routine of the Refuge, or the manner in which it was run. The Refuge had proved itself to be an outstanding success under the management of Eva. She saw no reason to alter anything.

Her talk reassured most of the women and there was no more talk of a wholesale walk-out. Sally too was relieved. Helen Wardle had told her she should not think of moving from the Refuge until Sid Darling had been caught and put away.

Sid Darling's continued freedom remained a source of concern to Ian Lovat. In addition to his concern for those who were at risk, his failure to catch up with the elusive wanted man also dented his pride.

There was one further sighting of Darling. It occurred close to the Refuge, late one night.

When the constable detailed to keep watch on the building challenged the suspect, he ran away. The constable gave chase. He eventually caught up with the man some distance away, only to be knocked beneath the wheels of a passing carriage during the violent struggle that ensued.

The constable was fortunate to suffer no more than a broken arm and badly bruised ribs. Sid Darling, for that is who it was, made good his escape.

Ethan and Sally were discussing the incident the day after it happened, soon after she had finished work.

They were on their way to Pin's Lane. Ethan's uncle was ill once more and Ethan was taking a few items of food to him. It also gave Sally an opportunity to check that all was well with her room and to dust off the furniture. It had not been touched for some time. Afterwards, she was to spend the remainder of the evening with Ethan, at the Shields' home.

'I wonder if it really was Sid Darling?' mused Ethan. 'No one seems absolutely certain.'

'*I'm* convinced it was him.' There was no doubt in Sally's mind. 'I bet he's been watching the Refuge. After what happened at Falmouth he'll be more determined than ever to get his hands on me. He'll also want to frighten the other girls before they're called to give evidence.'

'I hope they hurry up and catch him,' Ethan sounded concerned. 'Pa's heard from the insurance company more quickly than he expected. He's going ahead with buying this steam-trawler. Before we bring it back to Plymouth, he wants us all to go off to Brixham so the present owners can teach us how to handle her. The only one not going is Joe. He said he'll look after you while I'm away, but a man with a broken arm would be no match against Sid Darling.'

'You don't need to worry about me.' Sally spoke with more confidence than she felt. The constable's encounter with the man she was convinced to be Sid Darling had unnerved her. 'We can work as we are now, with me only making deliveries that keep me to the main roads and Joe delivering to other places. Then, when I finish work I'll go straight to the Refuge and stay there.'

'Well . . . Only if you're quite sure and promise you'll take no chances.'

Ethan was deeply concerned for Sally's safety, but he was also very excited at the thought of the family owning and working a steam-trawler. It was to be a major step forward for them.

'I can assure you I'll take no chances at all where Sid Darling is concerned!' Sally said emphatically. They were turning into Pin's Lane now and she added, 'Not even here. I'll let you go upstairs and check my room, while I call in to see how Charlie is.'

Charlie gave Sally a long homily on the state of his health while Ethan was upstairs. She thought he looked no worse than when she had shared the upstairs room with Ruth, but he became indignant when she told him so.

'That's easy enough for you to say, young lady. If I was as young as you, I've no doubt I could cope with many things a whole lot easier than I do now. You just wait until you get to my age. You'll find you have more sympathy for those in ill-health then. Not that it'll make any difference what I say to you. You youngsters have no thought for anyone except yourselves.'

As she had just brought him a couple of Grace's pies and Ethan was there to deliver some items from his mother, Sally thought his comments were particularly ill-timed, but she made no comment.

When Ethan came downstairs, Sally made her excuses to Charlie and left the room. She was half-way up the stairs before Charlie came to the door of his room and called after her.

'Here, this came for you yesterday.' In his hand he held a letter. 'I was going to get someone to take it around to the Philpotts' shop for you. Your coming here has saved me the trouble.'

Sally was unused to receiving letters. She went back down the stairs and took the letter from Charlie. Holding it in her hand, she gazed at it dubiously. Who would have written to her?

Ethan had come into the passageway and she said to him, 'I've got a letter! I wonder who it could be from?'

Ethan smiled. 'There's only one way to find out. Open it and read what it says.'

Sally opened the envelope very carefully, as though she might somehow damage its contents. Then she unfolded the piece of paper it contained.

A great many conflicting expressions followed each other across her face as she read. When she eventually looked up and spoke, the reason for her uncertainty became clear.

'It's from my father. He says he's had a great deal of time to think about things while he's been in prison awaiting trial and is sorry for all the unhappiness he's caused me. He admits he *is* my father and has written down all he can remember of our relatives and feels certain they'll want to meet me. He wants to see me, to give me their details and tell me about them. He's also written a letter to Inspector Lovat that he'd like me to collect and deliver personally.'

The emotion was too much for Sally. She was very close to tears. Ethan moved towards her and hugged her to him.

Despite his happiness for her, Ethan was not entirely convinced of the authenticity of Robert Sanderson's change of heart.

He suspected it might be intended to gain sympathy with a jury when he came to trial.

In spite of such thoughts, Ethan said nothing. Happiness had been a rare commodity in Sally's life. He would not spoil this moment for her.

95

Since Eva had agreed to marry Ian, they had spent an increasing amount of time together. They discussed details of their forthcoming wedding and made plans for furnishing the home they would be setting up in Brighton.

If Eva felt any unhappiness about being forced to leave the Christian organisation to which she had devoted all her adult life, she did not allow it to show. To an onlooker, it would seem there was nothing on her mind but the forthcoming marriage.

Ian was with Eva when Sally brought the letter from her father to show to her. After reading it, Eva asked permission to pass it to Ian. When it was given, she handed it to him and said to Sally, 'What do you intend to do?'

'I shall go and see him,' Sally replied promptly.

'Are you quite sure you should? I mean, he didn't behave in a particularly fatherly fashion when you took pity on him before.'

'Things are different now. He's in prison – and won't have been drinking. Besides, I really do think he's sorry for the way he behaved and wants to make it up to me.'

When Ian Lovat had read the letter, he frowned. 'If you'll pardon me for being painfully blunt, Sally, Robert Sanderson has never impressed me as being a man who is concerned for anyone other than himself.'

When Sally made no reply, the detective apologised. 'I shouldn't have said that, Sally. I'm sorry. Robert Sanderson is your father. The fact that he's now willing to acknowledge you might mean he's at last ready to face up to his responsibilities. When are you thinking of going to Bodmin gaol to see him?'

'I can't go until Sunday . . .' It was now Wednesday. '. . . I can't ask Grace for any more time off. Business is only just returning to normal, and Ethan won't be able to take a day off before then, either.'

'Then I'll tell you what I'll do. He says he has a letter for me too. As I need to speak to him before Clara Flood goes on trial we'll go and see him together.'

Sally looked disappointed. She had been looking forward to a rare opportunity of enjoying a day out with Ethan.

Correctly guessing the reason for her lack of enthusiasm, Ian explained, 'It would be a wise thing to do. You might have difficulty in obtaining permission to see him. Some governors are reluctant to allow remand prisoners to receive visitors. My presence should ensure that you succeed.'

It was enough to convince Sally. She agreed that Ian should accompany her and Ethan to Bodmin gaol the following Sunday.

Eva was invited to come along, but she declined. Although no longer an officer of the Salvation Army, she would spend Sunday worshipping with her late colleagues.

Ian Lovat had told Sally he needed to speak to Robert Sanderson about the forthcoming trial of Clara Flood. This was true – but it was not the *whole* truth.

Inquiries had been made by his men about the chimney sweep seen with the ex-butler in the days before the fire and mysterious robbery at Lanhydrock House.

The chimney sweep's identity had now been established. When detectives went to Harry Maggs' lodgings they discovered he had not been home since a couple of days before the fire.

Searching through his belongings they found a detailed plan, which they later established was the plan of Lanhydrock House.

In the meantime, Bodmin police had questioned the house servants. They learned that a chimney sweep answering Harry Maggs' description had been sweeping chimneys at the great house only the day before the disastrous fire.

They further discovered that the story he had told, of the regular chimney sweep having retired, had been a lie. The man in question was, in fact, sweeping the chimneys of the Bodmin police headquarters while Robert Sanderson languished in the town's gaol, not very far away.

The whole thing pointed to a planned robbery rather than spur-of-the-moment opportunism. It also raised a number of grave questions about the cause of the fire and the present whereabouts of Maggs.

The Bodmin police had visited the town gaol and questioned Robert Sanderson. But that had been before Ian Lovat's detectives had located and visited Harry Maggs' room in Plymouth.

A senior policeman travelled to Plymouth from Bodmin and had a lengthy meeting with Ian. It was decided that the Plymouth inspector should try to gain as much information as he could when he visited Sanderson to tie up a few loose ends in the case against Clara Flood.

Sally was blissfully unaware of what was in Ian Lovat's mind when he suggested they should both visit the gaol together.

She knew only that at last she had a father who was ready to acknowledge her as his own. She wished Ruth might have lived to witness this day.

96

Ian Lovat was the only one of the trio travelling from Plymouth to Bodmin who did not appear to be excited. Sally, in particular, found it difficult to remain still for more than a few moments at a time.

Her mood was infectious. Ethan was caught up in it – but he had other reasons to be happy. The boat bought by his father had exceeded all the family's expectations. It would be able to travel farther and faster and use larger nets to catch more fish than their last boat. It could put to sea in weather that would keep sail-powered boats in harbour.

Once the fish were caught, it would bring them back to harbour more swiftly than the other boats, scorning the direction of the wind.

There had been a lengthy family discussion about what the future would hold for them all as a result of buying the new boat. Samuel, the Shields' third son and the most financially atuned member of the family, had costed out the estimated expenses and profits of operating a coal-burning trawler.

He estimated that each of the sons would be earning a great deal more money than they had when the family fished with the *Mermaid*.

It would be possible to put enough money aside to enable

them to purchase a second boat in another eighteen months' to two years' time.

Eventually, it might be possible for each member of the family to own his own boat, or, if they preferred, to have a family-owned fishing fleet.

With such prospects as these, Ethan decided he would ask Sally to marry him at the earliest opportunity. He knew such a marriage would have the approval of the entire Shields family.

He hoped it might be possible to ask her today, after their visit to the prison, if the opportunity arose.

Ian Lovat had already told them he would not be returning to Plymouth with them. He had arranged a meeting with some of the senior Bodmin policemen and would take a later train.

When they reached Bodmin Road railway station, the trio transferred to another train in which to complete their journey to Bodmin town and the gaol in which Robert Sanderson was being held.

Built at the lower end of the town, the prison was a dark and forbidding place. Sally shuddered as they walked through the gateway, beneath a fortress-like archway. Over it was incongruously etched the fifteen bezant shield of Cornwall, surmounted by three Prince of Wales feathers.

As this was a Sunday, the prison governor was not in the building. It was left to a senior warder to break some sensational news when Ian Lovat introduced himself and the others and stated their business.

'Robert Sanderson, you say?' said the warder. 'Well, I'm afraid you won't be able to interview him, Inspector.'

'Why not? Is he being kept in solitary or something? I can assure you, my business with him is of considerable importance – and this young lady is his daughter. He's asked her to visit him to collect some rather important information – together with a letter he has written to me.'

The senior warder appeared startled. 'His daughter, you say? We never knew anything about any daughter, or we'd have notified her right away. As far as we were aware he had no close relatives, anywhere.'

The senior warder's use of the past tense told its own story, but Ian needed to clarify the situation.

'I'm sorry . . . Notify her of _what_, exactly?'

'Of Sanderson's death. He hanged himself in his cell on Friday – the day before yesterday. Used his braces and a torn-up shirt to hang himself from the bars of his cell window. You'd have hardly believed it possible, would you . . . ?'

The senior warder's callous manner in breaking the news left Sally dismayed and in a state close to shock. Her knees felt suddenly weak. She might have collapsed had Ethan not put an arm about her in support.

They were in an office just inside the main prison entrance and Ethan lowered her to a chair, assisted by Ian.

It was the detective inspector who questioned the senior warder. 'Did the warder who discovered him find the letter in his cell that he said he had already written to me?'

'The body was discovered by his cell-mate, Ted Harris, a prisoner awaiting trial for a violent assault. Almost killed a man after he'd been drinking and a thoroughly nasty piece of work. He woke up to find Sanderson hanging and already dead. He almost shouted the place down before we were able to get there and find out what had happened. But no letter from Sanderson was found in the cell.'

'That's very strange,' Ian said, perplexed. 'He wrote to Sally to say there was a letter.'

He frowned. 'Would you mind if I had a look in his cell and spoke to his cell-mate?'

The senior warder shrugged in a gesture of indifference. 'Please yourself, but I can assure you, you'll find nothing there – and I can only allow _you_ inside the prison. I can't have a whole crowd of visitors wandering around.'

'I don't want to go to the cell,' Sally said, wretchedly.

Belatedly, the senior warder said, 'I'm sorry you had to hear the news about your father this way, miss. If I'd known he had a daughter . . .'

Looking at her more kindly, he added, 'You stay here while I take the inspector off to see Harris and the cell. Not that we'll find anything there. The remand cells may be better than those of the convicts, but there's still nowhere to hide anything.'

When the senior warder and Ian Lovat had gone, Ethan, concerned about Sally, said anxiously, 'Are you feeling all right? Is there anything I can get for you?'

She shook her head. 'I'll be all right in a while. It's my own fault, really. I should have known better than to get my hopes up in such a fashion. He didn't want to know about me in the first place. But he did say he'd made out a list of all his – *my* family. I'd have liked to have seen that.'

Feeling desperately sorry for her, Ethan took her hand and held it tightly. 'Perhaps Ian will find it. Let's hope so.'

97

By the time Ian Lovat returned to the small office inside the prison entrance, Sally had recovered much of her composure.

For her to suggest she had been heartbroken by news of the tragic death of the man who was her father would have been hypocritical. She had hardly known him. What little she had learned of him – much through unfortunate experience – had certainly not endeared him to her.

In fact, only Sid Darling had brought more unhappiness into her life. Yet, despite this, Robert Sanderson was still the man who had fathered her.

Furthermore, in his final letter he had acknowledged his paternity and promised to inform her of hitherto unknown relatives. She had been thrilled at the thought of meeting a family she had never known – and now would never know.

She found it difficult to believe he would deliberately have acted so cruelly in raising her hopes, knowing he intended to commit suicide before she arrived to speak to him.

'Did you find any letters?' Ethan put the question on behalf of Sally when Ian Lovat returned to the prison office.

The Plymouth detective inspector shook his head. 'No and his cell-mate claims that he isn't able to read, so would have no reason to steal letters, or even know who they might have been intended for, had there been any. But that doesn't mean the letters don't – or *didn't* – exist. I'm not convinced that the man who shared a cell with Sanderson is telling the truth about what happened.'

'You mean . . . he might have had something to do with the death of my father?' Sally looked at Ian with wide-eyed disbelief.

Ian shook his head. 'I'm not saying that, but there's something about this "Ted Harris" that bothers me. What's known of him?' Ian put the question to the senior warder.

'As far as I know, nothing at all. That's unusual in itself. Harris is such a violent man, even to the warders, that I would have expected him to have spent time in prison before. He claims to have no fixed address, no next-of-kin and he's not unlike Sanderson in that respect. The police at Bodmin may have more on him, but I doubt it, somehow. They usually tell us everything that's known about the men they bring to us here.'

'Could I speak to him?' Sally asked unexpectedly. 'If he does know anything about the letters he might be willing to tell me about them, where he wouldn't tell the police.'

'I'm sorry, I can't allow that,' the senior warder said firmly. 'Harris is due to appear before the court on charges involving violence – and that was against a woman.'

'I agree with all you've said,' agreed Ian Lovat, 'but it's a pity, all the same. I would like Sally to have seen Harris. There's something about him that troubles me, but I can't quite put a finger on it. Sally might just have been able to come up with something.'

'There's no reason at all why she shouldn't *see* him,' said the senior warder. 'I'll have Harris brought from his cell for exercise and take you to the governor's office. It overlooks the exercise yard.'

'Do you really think it will serve any useful purpose?' Ethan asked anxiously. Sally had largely recovered from the initial distress of learning of her father's death. He did not want her upset again.

It was Sally herself who decided the issue. 'I'd like to say I've seen him, at least,' she said. 'After all, he was the last one to see my father alive.'

Ethan shrugged. He had tried to save her further distress. He could do no more.

The prisoner had still not been brought into the exercise yard by the time the small party reached the governor's office and was gathered at the window.

There were no other prisoners in the yard and Ethan could sense the tension in Sally when she took hold of his arm.

Suddenly, there was a sound from immediately beneath the window, as the door from the prison building to the exercise yard was opened.

Moments later a warder and another man came into view. For a short while they could see only the top of the prisoner's head as he walked away from them. Then, he reached a corner of the small enclosed space and changed direction. At the same time, he looked up at the sky.

Sally let out a short scream and clutched at Ethan's arm with both hands.

'It's him! It's HIM!' she gasped, close to hysteria.

'It's who?' demanded Ian.

Ethan, grim-faced, gave him the answer. 'That's not Ted Harris, or whatever he's calling himself, and it's hardly surprising that he's in for assaulting a woman. That's Sid Darling!'

98

'This puts an entirely new light on the matter of Sanderson's death,' Ian Lovat said to the senior warder. 'Although I doubt very much whether we'll ever be able to prove to a jury that Sid Darling is responsible for Sanderson's death.'

They had all returned to the office inside the main entrance of the prison.

The Plymouth detective inspector had been detailing the crimes for which Darling was being sought by the police forces of the two counties on either side of the River Tamar.

'What would you like me to do?' asked the senior warder, eager now to help in any way he could.

'I'd like you to have him thoroughly searched before you move him. Then make a search from top to bottom of the cell he shared with Sanderson. When I spoke to him earlier, Darling claimed to be unable to read. That isn't true.' Explaining, Ian continued, 'When we arrested Mother Darling and searched her house, we found letters from him. He had made written threats against Sally – threats I believe he had every intention of carrying out. If he had seen letters addressed to Sally and questioned Sanderson about them, he might have learned he was her rightful father and that the letters were an acknowledgement of the fact. Darling would have taken a malicious delight in destroying the letters. It would have given him a good reason to want to harm Sanderson too. We believe he carried out something similar against Sally's invalid sister when he went to the room they shared and found her there alone.'

Observing Sally's show of distress, he said, 'I'm sorry, Sally but I want to see Sid Darling receive his just deserts. Hopefully, Devonport Lil will be persuaded to admit she saw him in your room on the day in question. But before she gives evidence she'll want to know there's no chance of him ever being free to take his revenge upon her.'

'I'd like to see him pay for everything he's done,' Sally said fiercely. 'For Rachel's sake, as well as for everyone else who's ever suffered at his hands.'

'I'll see that he and the cell are searched thoroughly,' declared the senior warder. 'I personally don't believe the letters exist any more, but if they do you can be certain we'll find them.'

Outside the prison gate, Sally asked, in a lacklustre voice, 'What happens now?'

'I'm going to the police station for a meeting with the police inspector,' said Ian. 'We'll have rather more to talk about than was anticipated, but it should prove very interesting indeed. We'll no doubt pool all the evidence we have to ensure Darling is convicted. I shall do my best to see the conviction is for murder. However, even if that fails, I doubt if he will ever see daylight as a free man again until he's too old to cause mischief to anyone. I'll see you two later.'

'What shall *we* do now?' asked Sally, as Ian Lovat walked briskly away in the direction of the police station. 'Our train doesn't leave for more than four hours and it's Sunday, there'll be no shops open.'

'Why don't we walk to Lanhydrock and see the damage caused by the fire?' suggested Ethan. 'We could head that way anyway, to catch the train from Bodmin Road.'

'All right,' agreed Sally. She sounded unenthusiastic, but she linked her arm through his and they made their way through the town to the road that would take them to Lanhydrock House.

Their destination was more than two miles away, but it was a fine day and they were in no hurry.

Sally had very little to say and responded in only a half-hearted way to Ethan's attempts to make conversation.

He knew she was thinking of all that had happened at the prison. He believed she had suffered great disappointment and unhappiness at the loss of her father and the opportunity to discover the identity of her relatives. He felt sorry for her. At the same time, he admired the brave front she was trying to put upon the events of the day.

Sally maintained her composure until the moment she saw the fire-stained shell that had once been the magnificent Lanhydrock House. Then, much to the surprise of Ethan and a number of other sightseers, she suddenly burst into tears.

Hurriedly, Ethan led her away, making for a nearby grassy bank. Here, an abundance of flowering plants escaped from a low-walled shrubbery and cascaded down the slope.

When Sally was seated on the grass, Ethan kneeled down beside her and held her until she ceased crying.

'I'm sorry, Ethan,' her voice was muffled as she spoke into the shoulder of his coat. 'It's just . . . just seeing the house like this. It was so beautiful . . . and Lady Robartes loved it so much.'

Sally's views on Lady Robartes, who had been so kind to her, had been echoed around the county. Most of those who knew her were convinced she had died of a broken heart over the loss of her home.

'It was beautiful,' agreed Ethan, 'and it will be again – look, they've got scaffolding up and have started rebuilding already. They're leaving the disaster where it belongs. In the past.'

Pulling away from him, Sally looked up into his face. 'Is that what you think I should do, Ethan? Is that what you're trying to tell me?'

'Yes, I am.'

Sally was silent for some minutes, then she said, 'You're right. I know you are, but it's easier for them. The family who lived here. When they're done they'll have a magnificent house again. They'll move back in and the lives of the whole family will revolve around the house once more, as it has done for hundreds of years. I don't have anything like that. First I lost Ruth; then the man who finally admitted he was my father and who was going to give me a new family; I'm losing Captain Eva too, because she's going off with Ian – and I've nothing to take their place.' Sally was trying to be brave, but she could not prevent her lower lip from trembling.

'You have me,' Ethan said quietly.

Managing a weak smile, Sally looked at him for a few moments before suddenly hugging him. 'Yes, you're right, Ethan. I have you – although for a while I was convinced I'd lost you too. I think that was the worst time of all.'

'Well, you haven't lost me – and you won't, unless you choose to, so why don't we put the past where it belongs. Behind us. Let's start building a new and wonderful future – just as they're doing with the house over there?'

Pulling back from him once more, Sally looked at Ethan uncertainly, wondering whether his words meant what she thought they did. What she *hoped* he was saying.

'What do you mean, Ethan?'

'I think you know what I mean, Sally. I'm asking you to marry me. To put all the unhappiness you've known behind you. Begin a new life, with me. With the new boat and all the plans we have for her, it should be a very good life. But only if you're part of it too. Will you marry me, Sally?'

Sally's emotions would not allow her to give him a spoken reply. Instead, she flung her arms about him and kissed him with all the passion she felt inside her.

As she clung to Ethan, all the unhappiness she had known in the past fell away.

When they eventually released their hold upon each other, they became aware of the bubbling song of a skylark, high above them.

Rising and falling on the still air, it filled the sky to overflowing. To the young couple, it seemed to proclaim to the world the joy they both felt in each other.

Author's Note

This novel is a work of fiction, conceived in the mind of the author, although many of the background incidents and the general picture of the times in which it is set are as accurate as research can make them.

The scandal of child prostitution and the procurement of young girls destined for the brothels of Europe continued until 1885, when a London newspaper editor decided on a course of action that shook the nation.

Acting in collaboration with the Salvation Army, he arranged to 'buy' a thirteen-year-old girl, have her certified a virgin, and taken to France in order to prove how easy it was.

Each stage of the proceedings was carefully supervised and reported in his newspaper. But the Victorian public was outraged by the disclosures, and the editor and those who had helped him were prosecuted and charged with a number of offences arising out of the staged incident.

Given the prudish morality of the day, the outcome was never in doubt. The editor was found guilty and served six months imprisonment in Holloway gaol.

Nevertheless, by his sacrifice, he achieved much of what he and the Salvation Army had intended. The age of consent for girls was raised from thirteen to sixteen and laws passed to severely curtail the trade in providing young girls for the brothels of Europe.

The stature of the Salvation Army grew rapidly after this. It was, and is, respected throughout the world for its tireless efforts among the poor and needy, wherever they are to be found.

Much of the beautiful house of Lanhydrock, in Cornwall, *was* destroyed in a fierce fire in 1881. The fire originated in a kitchen chimney and was fanned by gale-force winds. It is true, too, that Lady Robartes died only days afterwards, broken-hearted at the loss of her magnificent home.

Lanhydrock House was faithfully rebuilt immediately after the fire and is now one of the loveliest gems in the crown of the National Trust.